THE LEGEND OF LILITH
ELYSIUM

HILLARY OLIVER

PHOENIX
RISING

For updates on new releases, join the online newsletter at hillaryeoliver.com

Cover art illustration by Salome Totladze

Edited by Iveta Cvrkal

Map of Augusta by Hillary Oliver

Elysium / The Legend of Lilith Book II / Hillary Oliver

First Edition: October 2020

For my parents,
Don and Joanne.

Without you enduring each "bark" with silent grace, I would not have the confidence to speak my mind.

I am eternally grateful that you've allowed me to express myself in all forms.

Without you this work would not exist.

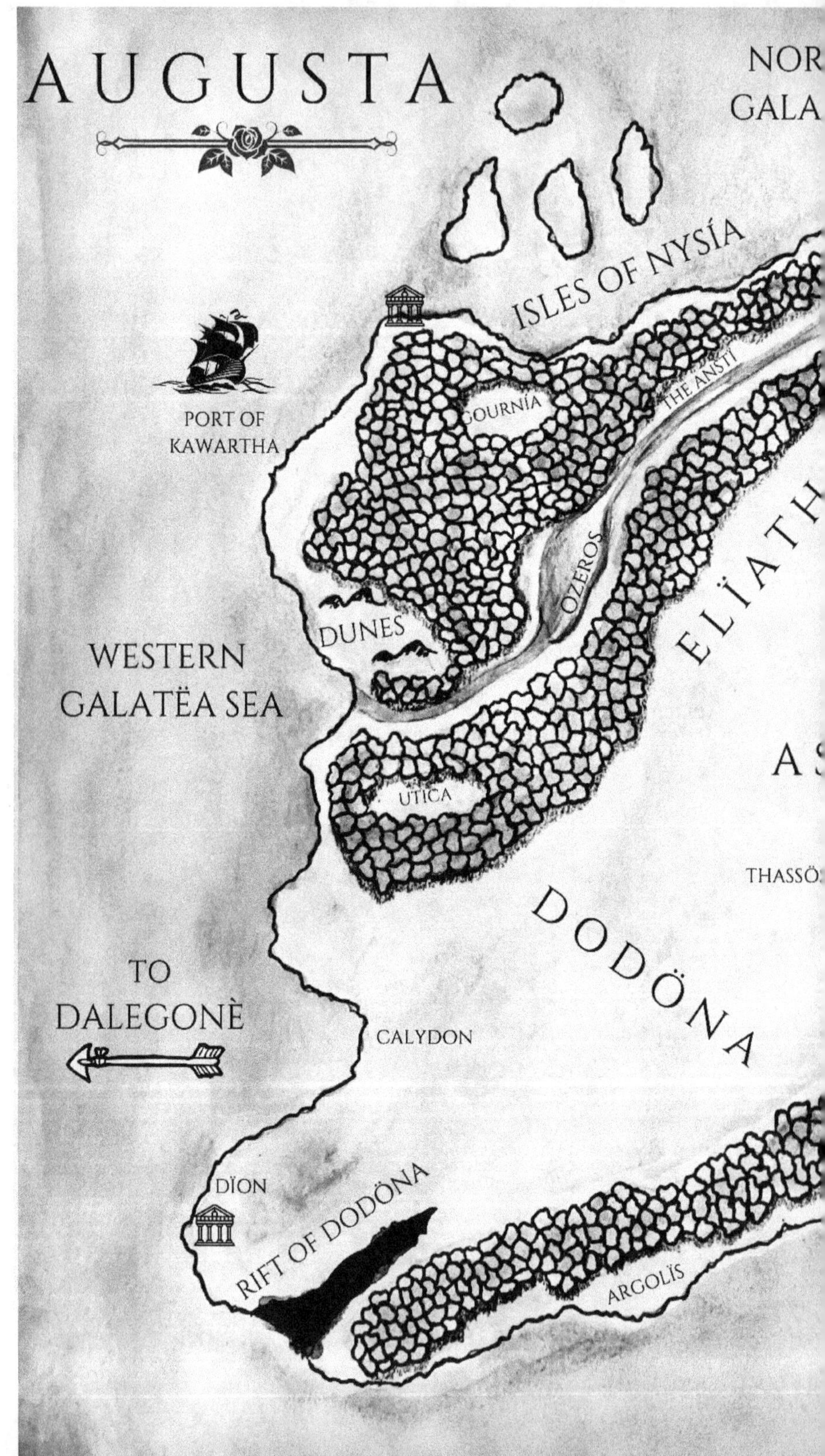
AUGUSTA
NOR
GALA
ISLES OF NYSÍA
PORT OF
KAWARTHA
GOURNÍA
THE ANSTÌ
OZEROS
ELÏATH
WESTERN
GALATËA SEA
DUNES
A S
UTICA
THASSÖ
DODÖNA
TO
DALEGONÈ
CALYDON
DÏON
RIFT OF DODÖNA
ARGOLÏS

KYNÖS
FROURÍO
THE MEGÁLOS
FOREST
SONÖS
OBSYDÍAN
MARSH
KENORA
OS
THE AOÖS
CHÏOS.
TANTALOS
HÉLORUS
THE GÁEA VALLEY
PETRAS
N
NW
NE
W
E
SW
SE
S
O

THE LEGEND OF LILITH

ELYSIUM

The full moon hung low in the sky, bathing the narrow streets of Kenora in an umber glow. The Thirteen of the Ilíos coven fancied themselves a night out on the town, seeking the presence of a virile man. *Or three*, Tatiana thought.

The city was thriving with activity. Vendors were extra vivacious, men and women took to dancing in the streets to the songs of the minstrels, and there was nowhere one could look without ingesting the utterly idyllic scenery.

Spring Solstice was upon them, the air balmy and inviting. With the warmer climate, the Thirteen coveted a trip to the capital to celebrate the changing of the seasons. After sloughing their comrades, Tatiana, Phoebe, and Hera wended their way through the throng in search of a suitable tavern to ingratiate, and thus, inebriate themselves.

The bland stone buildings of the entertainment district were less inviting than the soldiers' barracks, but the Enchantresses meandered about in search of the liveliest tavern to infiltrate. There was no sole purpose of this little escapade; besides indulging in sensual pleasures, Tatiana sought to glean recent movements within the Empire.

The Amalthea was shining extra bright, soaking into their immortal skin and lending them Her celestial beauty. Rest assured, they would not struggle to pick up a few comely fellows.

Tatiana didn't bother to conceal her smile.

Phoebe selected the first tavern. A tiny bell above the door chimed their arrival, but no one turned to acknowledge them as they entered the *Dragon's Nest*. Despite how smug her Third was being with the selection, Tatiana couldn't deny that it was the perfect location for their perusal.

"If Eudora would croak already, we'd be able to indulge in these affairs more often," Phoebe said, tossing her long mane of dark blonde hair over her shoulder.

Tatiana chortled. "Easier said than done. That woman will make it to double millennium before the Amalthea decides to take her." She got her sentence out just in time before the cacophony of the tavern drowned out any possibility of holding a conversation.

Bawdy soldiers clapped their hands, calling to courtesans passing by. Waiters walked with trays topped with chalices and tankards. The odd couple danced in the center of the room, hands roving over each other's skin as if they were in a private chamber.

Hera eyed a booth in the far back corner, veiled by shadows, crooning its loneliness, beckoning the Enchantresses to rest their travel-worn bones for a while. Tatiana nodded agreeably and followed her Fourth whilst Phoebe ran off to fetch some wine.

Hera hung her shawl on a hook above the booth, the garment acting like a curtain. "Yikes... this place is *alive* tonight!"

"What's that?" Tatiana could barely make out what her sister was saying.

Hera pointed to her ears, waving an exasperated, dismissive hand. There would be no talking without the use of magic to hear each other over the din, but casting such a spell in such close quarters was dangerous. The act would be akin to joining the minstrels on stage and announcing their immortal nature.

The music picked up as more soldiers filed in. Hera turned to inspect them, but Tatiana was more interested in the whereabouts of the nights libations.

What is taking Phoebe so long?

It was far too soon for socializing. Phoebe always insisted they get three deep before seeking out companions, but Hera was lonely, and therefore, eager.

Phoebe appeared around the corner, a convoy of soldiers in her wake. Tatiana's eyes narrowed in shrewd suspicion. Soldiers were trained to identify her kind. Would they peg them for charlatans?

Tatiana met Hera's gaze and discreetly inclined her head in the direction of their fast-approaching company. Even with their heightened preternatural senses, they had to resort to inane, expressive communications.

Phoebe halted before the booth and removed her cape, her eyes sparkling with lust and something else, something… mischievous. She shot a wry smile at Tatiana as she claimed her seat. The air surrounding their booth hardened at the Enchantress's silent command, drowning out the tumult. As she claimed her seat, Hera swatted her sister, flashing her a reproachful glare. It wasn't enough magic to alert the soldiers, especially when they were under the influence of alcohol, but Hera feared the mortal lands more than most.

"Oh, it's much easier to talk and get to know each other over here," remarked one of the soldiers, undeniably clueless as to the magical means of which such clarity was achieved. He seated himself beside Hera, immediately turning a charming smile on her.

The soldiers' navy uniforms hugged their physiques, showcasing the treasury of muscle underneath. Hera fought to conceal her blushing cheeks, and Phoebe's eyes narrowed with want. But Tatiana remained calculative. For those who were bred and forged within the Obsydían Marsh, trust did not come easily.

The three soldiers seated themselves among the Enchantresses, their fingers wrapped around silver pints of ale. They offered chalices to the women, and the Enchantresses drank it down. It was not krasì wine, but it would suffice.

The soldier seated across from Tatiana set his dark eyes upon her, his sensuous lips parting in a slight smile. Of all the lavish embellishments decorating his person, Tatiana's eyes were drawn to the simplest of rings: a band of polished gold set around his middle finger. Intricate carvings lent the ring an ethereal appeal, though there were no sparkling gems. And despite its humble appearance, the ring ignited a hunger inside Tatiana that she would have once been ashamed to reveal. Once, a long time ago.

He leaned across the table, blond curls falling over his broad shoulders. "Odéllo," he said, extending his hand, palm upward.

Crown Prince Odéllo, Tatiana realized. Phoebe hadn't wasted any time.

It had been a while since Tatiana last visited the capital. Stars, Odéllo must have been just a child then. The blithesome prince had grown into a man, and a feckless one at that, if rumors were to be believed. He'd chosen debauchery over court. Women over duty.

"Tanya," she replied with a coy smile. If only he knew just

how many years she had spent prowling the lands that would be his, one impending dawn.

He sipped his ale, his dark eyes lingering on her, just visible over the rim of his tankard. "You are not from here?" he asked, sliding a beringed hand across the smooth wood separating them.

Tatiana gave a coy shake of her head, red curls bouncing around her shoulders.

The prince's eyes sparked with desire, but his voice was smooth when he spoke. "Where are you from?"

"We are from Chïos." A lie, but if Odéllo proved himself the possessor of a brain more cunning than her own, there was always the option to bewitch him. An Enchantress got what she was due, what she wanted. Always.

"Kenora is a large city, but I've never beheld women as beautiful as you and your companions." His cheeks flushed, a stark contrast to his olive-toned skin. A beautiful man he was.

Tatiana fluttered her lashes. "There are many beautiful women in Chïos."

His eyes sparkled onyx. "None as beautiful as you."

It was Tatiana's turn to blush.

"What brings you to Kenora, fair kyría?"

The Enchantress gave a noncommittal shrug. The strap of her dress fell to reveal her shoulder. Odéllo's eyes were drawn to her bare skin instantly, smoldering with strident want.

"My sisters and I felt the pull of adventure," Tatiana said. "We wanted to travel, to explore, and as alluring as the Orösía Mountains are, we feared what lay between the peaks. Naturally, we opted for a trip to the capital." She flashed him a warm smile. "Who would have anticipated we would meet the Crown Prince himself?"

Odéllo's chest swelled at her fawning, his hand still stretched out toward her. Tatiana took it in hers, her cool touch sliding along his warm skin, her thumb gliding across each jewelled ring until it rested on the simplest of them all.

"Of all the jewels on my fingers, it is ironic you point to that one." Odéllo chuckled dryly, mouth half full of ale.

"Why is that?" she asked, mustering a guileless façade.

"It is a priceless piece, Tanya."

Tatiana cocked her head in question, batting elongated lashes, feigning ignorance of how he seemed to savor each syllable of her name.

"It is not a Stavros heirloom," Odéllo said, "but a gift from the Gods." She piqued up, leaning in closer, making certain her interest was obvious. The prince cast a furtive glance over his shoulder, obsequiously checking for eavesdroppers. "It is much too loud down here to converse, and I'd like to get to know you better, dear Tanya." He rose from his seat and lent her his palm. "What do you say we take this upstairs?" The excuse was poor, given that Phoebe had made conversation much easier with magic, a simple spell, a cantrip.

Tatiana couldn't conceal her grin. She nodded curtly, flashing Phoebe a knowing expression of excitement, and her sister loosened the air to allow for their passage.

One down.

Two to go.

Odéllo led her up the creaky wooden staircase leading up to the second floor where the bedrooms were located. Her hand was clasped in his, the calluses tickling her soft skin. His palm was sweaty, indicative of his nerves despite his collected demeanor. He was a prince after all, most of what she would see would be an illusion. Two actors about to put on a show.

The room he'd been granted was surely to have been the finest accommodations the tavern possessed. The bedchamber was still small, but quaint, furnished. The four-poster bed was large, a feather-stuffed divan called to them. The dark wood walls were decorated with paintings of foreign landscapes and frolicking deer, the Orösía peaks looming beyond.

The prince sighed. "It is not as luxurious as what I would offer at home, but the castle is quite a trek away."

"This is lovely, Prince." She stroked his hand, guiding him over to the bed.

Odéllo shut the door behind them, clicking the lock to ensure their privacy. The Enchantress seized the moment, his nervousness screaming to her.

Claim him.

Tatiana sat down on the edge of the bed, hands folded in her lap modestly. "I believe you owe me a tale, my fair prince." She gazed up at him with wide eyes brimming with curiosity.

Odéllo smiled, his nerves seemed to have abated slightly. Lowering himself beside her, he wrapped one arm around her waist, sliding her closer.

"About the ring?" he asked. "Or would my kyría fancy another tale of adventure? I have delighted in many a grand quest."

At the tender age of twenty-one? Unlikely. Tatiana resisted the urge to roll her eyes. A young buck like him wouldn't have glimpsed even the slightest fraction of what she'd seen in all her glorious centuries. "The ring, please." She trailed a hand up his torso, halting her fingers on his bare neck, at the pulse that throbbed under her touch. "Then maybe we can embark on a sort of... *exploration* together."

"Yes," he said, a decibel too loud to succeed in masking his nerves.

Yes, Tatiana! You still got it.

"Yes," she echoed, spurring him on.

The prince gulped, nodding once, the motion far too vehement to be casual. He took a moment to compose himself, removing his eyes from her and observing the room around them. "The tale has been passed down for centuries, reiterated thousands upon thousands of times." He licked his lips, those dark eyes drifting back to her. "They say this ring was created by the Gods, summoned from the Earth by Thëo. Softened by the Fire of Xander. Forged by the might of Kyril and Constantine. And cooled by the breath of Isidore."

Tatiana continued to stroke his chest, coaxing the tale out of him, each caress a promise of what awaited when he fulfilled her request. His breath hitched, and pleased with herself, she grinned.

"It was gifted to the first Divine, Elïath, as a token of trust." Odéllo cleared his throat, her hand dipping lower. "They say that the Gods have always envied our mortality, the passions that the promise of death evokes. Even for the Gods—desire, lust, longing—they are susceptible to it all."

Tatiana pressed her lips to his shoulder, her fingers slowly unbuttoning his tunic.

"Because of his envy," he said, voice faltering, "they felt compelled to create this ring, the only known weapon that can doom a God."

The Enchantress got up on her knees behind the prince and slowly pried the tunic from his limbs.

"It is called the Bow of Finality," he continued. "In the form of a ring, it is rumored to answer the call of the chosen one. It will always gravitate toward that one, toward the blessed soul who can banish a God from the mortal realm." He paused as she kissed his neck, her chest pressed against his bare back.

The prince had had enough of her taunts. He stood, his muscular chest rising and falling in rapid increments. It was not rage that coated his handsome face, but gluttonous wanting. He grasped her hand and pulled her up against him. In one swift motion, he hauled her gown over her head, his eyes darting up and down her body, still concealed beneath her undergarments.

"And how does it work?" she asked between kisses, her voice barely a wisp of breath. Of course she knew the story; the legendary tale an allegory for a weapon.

"It chooses its wielder," Odéllo said, his breath hot on her neck. "The bow only appears in that individual's time of greatest need, when a God has overstepped His bounds and entered the mortal realm."

Odéllo pressed his mouth to hers whilst his hands roamed. One trailed down her spine, the other slowly untied her corset. She sighed as it came free. It was more of a burden, truly; a crenellation guarding her womanhood. She only wore the blasted thing when they ventured into town, if only to appear more like human women. Truthfully, the Enchantress's body was svelte and curvaceous without the need for constriction. The hunger widening the prince's eyes only affirmed this as the corset fell to the floor, leaving her bare.

She wrapped her arms around herself, feigning diffidence. "And what abo—"

"Enough!" he hissed, silencing her with a plundering kiss. Then Odéllo thrust her onto the bed.

Tatiana shouldn't have been so surprised that the hedonistic Crown Prince of Augusta knew exactly what he was doing. Perhaps it was his experience—or a result of her wiles—but he gave her everything, his hands working to please her along with the rest of him. She should have known he'd be masterful, but anticipation never amounted to a culmination like... *that*. And she didn't dare pull away as his body tensed beneath hers, as guttural groans and bucking hips signaled his completion.

When he finally stilled, she lay atop him, stroking the soft hairs on his chest. He fell asleep quickly, lulled by the distant humming of other lovers down the hall, her sisters perhaps. Tatiana grinned widely, her eyes still lingering on the prince's stark jawline, the sharp stubble decorating it. Her finger traced his jaw as she whispered over him, "Câstré qu vissè un Va visarté."

Cleanse the mind of my memory.

The prince inhaled her breath, and a blissful—no, *contented*—expression crept over his features.

Tatiana leaned in and kissed those lips one last time, then she whispered, her tone bathed in majesty, "Sarst quiis, Va possé."

Rest deep, my precious.

⚇ ⚇ ⇝ ⋔ ⚆

PHOEBE STEPPED INTO THE LIGHT, BLONDE LOCKS SHINING LIKE A beacon. "Did you get it?" she asked.

Tatiana eyed her as she gathered her bearings. Both of her companions' appearances were as disheveled as her current mental state; hair in disarray, dresses on sideways. Tatiana had forgotten to don her corset, not that she wanted it. She'd retrieved what she came for. Little else mattered.

"I did." She held up her left hand, the Crown Prince's ring glistening in the moonlight. The metal was snug around her finger, still warm from Odéllo's body.

Phoebe leaned in to inspect it, then she looked up at the bedroom window of the tavern, a look of apprehension stealing over her fine features. "We best get out of here," she said to them both, extending her hand for them to grasp.

"Hyssé vaust possé, Hyssé vaust disst, Côstos fostré poiré eures, Fostré töver, essâ, eures, teq quissr." *Hide thou precious, Hide thou scent, Conceal from prying eyes, From nose, ears, eyes, and touch.*

A veil of darkness washed over them.

Tatiana nodded toward the city gates and the empty street before them, a sly grin beset her features. "Shall we, sisters?"

1

FREEDOM OR POWER

Howling winds assaulted the stones of the Divine tower. Their songs usually lulled Lilith to sleep, but since the battle at the Frourío, Isidore's lamentations only bred torturous night terrors, resulting in endless, restive nights.

When she did find sleep, it was never peaceful. There had been brief moments of repose when Julius joined her, silently wrapping her in strong arms, though those gracious reprieves were few and far between. Shadows hovered beneath her sunken eyes, her hair hung limp regardless of how she cared for it, and her limbs ached in defiance of every movement.

The others kept their distance, all but Julius and Felix who often extended invitations to spar. The inhabitants of the Frourío were unusually somber through Spring Solstice and into the scorching summer months. Not only was the climate sweltering, but the atmosphere was stifling at best, and Lilith often found her belly swarmed by wasps when she made to leave her bedchamber.

After a fitful rest, Lilith wiped the cobwebs of slumber from her eyes and let the sun lure her to the beach. As her toes sunk into the sand, she found her ill temper to be as it had been since she last saw her brother: miserable and unmitigated. She cursed the sky and the Gods that ruled it.

Glaring at the sun through squinted eyes, she willed the flaming orb to fall back beneath the earth's surface and burn the evildoers thriving in Hades. Sleep was of the utmost importance, the heaviest need, and it seemed utterly unattainable no matter how long she lay swathed in darkness.

Lilith nocked an arrow and, aiming for the sky, shot straight at the burning ball of fire. She watched with unrelenting rancor, seething inwardly as the arrow reached its summit and began its descent, painfully short of its target.

The vast blue of the Galatëa Sea boiled with her anguish, she could feel it as an extension of her being, palpable as the rush of her pulse. For as an Anointed disciple of Kyril, the sea was now a reflection of her emotions.

"You cannot shoot the sun, but it was a decent attempt," said a husky voice behind her.

Lilith paid it no heed.

Sighing audibly, she turned and strode back to the Frourío. Her shoulder brushed against Arduen's as she passed, but she avoided his gaze entirely. Keeping her eyes trained on her boots soaked in morning dew, she feigned ignorance of Arduen's eyes boring into her back.

"Will you ever forgive me?" he called after her, tone grievous.

At the sound of her Master's lament, it was as if that arrow had plummeted to the earth and pierced her chest. Lilith loved Arduen, she did, but there was no way she could alleviate his pain when he never attempted to assuage her own. "I'll consider it when you *ask* me," was all she could think to say.

Her relationship with her Master had not improved since

their quarrel after she'd killed Larkin, her brother. It had been the worst day of her life. The worst day she'd spent on this earth, and her immortal fatherly figure couldn't stand by her side and support her as he should have. He was her Divine Master, it was his responsibility to guide her through such dire situations, and yet he had acted so cowardly. A great chasm had formed between them. So great, it might have been as gaping as the Great Rift of Dodöna was rumored to be. And Lilith was reluctant to build a bridge to cross it.

The space between us is certainly as dead and soulless.

In the two months that had passed since the battle at the Frourío, Augusta had been relatively peaceful. The sun reigned longer in the sky, the leaves budded and bloomed within weeks, and the clouds drenched the soil with rain, turning the Megálos Forest floor loamy, rendering the grass an emerald fur. It was the kind of weather that could summon joy from even the most miserable of folk, but it did little to abate Lilith's dejection.

After all this time, she hadn't forgotten her promise to the Gods. She hadn't forgotten that night when she'd waded into the Galatëa's frigid waters and vowed to avenge all the lives Spiro had ripped from the earth. And she had not forgotten the promise she made to herself the morning after: she would not renege on those promises, even if it meant her own doom. Even if one of the wisest women in Augusta had warned her to never beseech the Gods for anything.

Too late.

It was Lilith's first week trying. The first week she actually felt driven to move on. Every morning she woke to sprint through the Megálos. The pines blurred into an emerald void as she sprinted at an inhuman speed. Her Divine strength was not yet fully formed—so Zurí had told her—but she was faster than she'd ever been.

Following her run, she would train with Zurí, contorting Kyril's Water as she pleased. Her control was impeccable, but the amount of Water that she could modulate lessened with every day.

It wasn't only her elemental abilities that dwindled. Discernment had grown nearly impossible. Every time Lilith lowered her mental shields and submerged her consciousness into the Galatëa, she felt nothing. This time of year, the Sea should be teeming with life, but Lilith was blind to it. Heedless of such shortcomings, she pushed herself to her physical extremities.

Lilith watched her opponent's blade as metallic obsidian flashed before her eyes, the light wrenching her from her reverie. Zurí slashed down at her with a faint grunt and Lilith parried the blow with ease. They'd been sparring for nearly two hours. Her Master did not yet display signs of fatigue, but Lilith felt the urge to spill the contents of her last meal on the ground.

Julius and Felix fought on the other side of the field, Quin and Wren bellowing orders. Quin was no longer schooling Julius, as the Crown Prince of Dalegonè was a Master Divine now. But Julius had expressed that he did not feel ready to take on the responsibility of becoming a Master, and Quin hadn't waved him out the door.

Julius aided Wren in Felix's training, and the young Divine excelled. Though Julius and Lilith were close, he'd given her space over the past two months. Since their heated moment on the beach, she had pulled away, much as she did when she lost her parents. Their relationship had devolved into trite sentiments and long nights beneath her sheets, in attempt to ease her nightmares, Julius's charming smile a slash of white splitting the dark.

A bolt of pain lanced through Lilith's right arm and her hand went numb, releasing Constance.

"Pay attention!" Zurí barked.

"I'm sorry, Master." Lilith bent to retrieve her sword. "I haven't been myself lately."

Zurí lowered her gladius. "We are done for today. Go wash up."

She jumped to her feet. "We can get another half hour at least."

"You are too distracted." Zurí waved her off. "You will go bathe and pray. We can talk after supper about whatever is on your mind."

"I'm fine," Lilith grumbled. "Really…" Forgoing what would have been a heated altercation, she reluctantly marched to the Frourío.

◎ ☺ ⇒ ℳ ◊

AMBROSE HAD QUITE ENJOYED LILITH'S HELP WHILST SHE SERVED her punishment for stepping over the protective wards during the battle at the Frourío. Now that she was free of those duties, she still preferred to assist their designated knight. After every meal, Lilith joined him at the sink to assist with the washing and drying of the dishes.

Arduen's voice drifted on the air to meet her ears and she prickled at the sound. "I wish I could say that I believe the worst is over," he said. "We have destroyed many of Spiro's beasts, but of the damage we've dealt him, he's inflicted worse upon us. We hope to have many months of peace before he considers attacking again."

The others dropped their activities in light of Arduen's pronouncement. Lilith listened intently, rubbing her aching wrist. A bruise was forming where Zurí had struck her that afternoon. These days, she didn't seem to be healing as quickly as she used to.

"Let's make use of the reprieve," Arduen continued.

"Get stronger and smarter," added Julius, Felix echoing his enthusiasm.

"If we could determine Spiro's location, we may be able to catch him off guard," Wren mused, teeth sinking into the bit of his pipe. Olga did not condone smoking inside the Frourío, but the Oracle hadn't dismissed Wren yet, the debate serving as a distraction.

Ambrose nodded toward the kitchen table. Lilith knew he wanted her to sit with the others. When she made no indication of acquiescence, the knight snatched the drying towel away from her and gently pushed her toward the table. She obliged, lowering into her usual spot, pointedly avoiding Arduen's surveillance.

"That would be horrendously stupid," Quin snapped.

Wren bristled, two jets of smoke streaming from his nostrils, but he withheld his rebuttal.

Julius added, "If Spiro caught so much as a whiff of our scent, we would be incinerated."

"It would be an advantage to know where our enemy rests their heads," Arduen said, dousing the sparks of dispute. "But we are not strong enough for ambush. Besides, we do not know how strong Spiro's army is now."

"He took a hit after the battle at the Frourío," Olga stated. "The beasts fled because Lilith prevailed over… *Spiro's noviciate.*"

"Send reconnaissance." Wren stabbed his fork into the table, ignoring Olga's reproachful glare. Still, the pipe evaded her notice.

Zurí was the first to counter their arguments, on both sides, as though she couldn't stand to agree with any of them. "Neither option is viable. We should focus on our noviciates."

Olga's glance flitted warily from face to face, her eyes beseeching Arduen to calm the brewing storm. But Arduen did not intervene, or even reprimand, as the argument heated. He simply stared into the distance, his eyes bloodshot as though withdrawing from morphine. His eyes caught Lilith's and he flashed her a belated smile, betraying his uncertainty, his trepidation. Her lips twitched as she fought the instinct to return his smile, her own fear rising, fear that things would never return to normal.

If there was anyone who truly understood her, she would have always said it was her father. But she was Divine now, and with that, she had transformed into a whole new person. Regardless of his betrayal, it was truly Arduen who understood the ebb and flow of her emotions, her unique idiosyncrasies, try as she might to keep them concealed from him.

Then there was Zurí, Lilith's second Master, the disciple of Kyril, God of Water. The woman was as elegant as she was stern, yet soft-hearted in regard to Lilith. Balanced atop her long neck was a headful of crimson curls, the face of an angel set with scalding turquoise eyes, and a lover's-inflicted scar.

Since the battle at the Frourío, Zurí acted impartial amidst the tension between Arduen and Lilith. How she was able to recognize when enough was enough for her noviciate, Lilith hadn't the faintest idea.

Around the table, the argument escalated. It made little sense why they wasted energy arguing. They had very little choice on the matter. They did not know where Spiro's base was, and half of their force was young and untested. It was a futile prospect to consider approaching the Great Divine, but one she hoped they would overcome despite the odds.

"Lilith…" It was Julius, sinking into the vacant seat beside her. "Would you like to accompany me for a walk along the beach?"

She would, but she knew it would only lead to complications.

"I'm sorry," she said slowly, "but I have not been sleeping well and would prefer to rest tonight."

There hadn't been time to sort through her feelings for Julius. She cared so deeply for him, in a way she had never before, but good sense told her not to entertain such affection. Julius would leave her eventually. He was to become King of Dalegonè, and she lacked the countenance befit of a queen.

The prince frowned. "Are you all right?"

Lilith offered him the slightest of nods, accentuated by a meek smile. It was a foolhardy attempt to assuage his worries, but he relented, silently returning his attention to the debate.

With anxiety eddying in her gut, Lilith marched up the stairs to her bedchamber.

"Wren!" Olga's voice could be heard from below. "Outside with that Gods forsaken pipe!"

Lilith chuckled.

⟡ ⟡ ⟡

LILITH'S TOES CURLED IN FRUSTRATION, HER BODY CONTORTING under the pain of the scalpel. He was slicing her, carving her, so he had said. "I must perfect you for your new Master. Your only Master."

"Please, Larkin…" she whimpered.

"Shush." Her brother soothed her with a tutting noise, his fingers stroking her cheekbone. It was a tender brush of his skin against her own, and it could have been placative, if not for the bloody scalpel clasped in his hand. "This won't take so long if you lay still. Enjoy the process, Sister."

Lilith nearly vomited as he brought the blade down to her skin yet again. "Arduen…" she moaned, a plea for her Master. "Please. I didn't mean what I said. I forgive you!"

"You do not favor him anymore," Larkin said. "Don't you remember? He gave you over to me." His voice slithered from his lips, a sibilance so unnatural, so unlike him.

"No!" Lilith cried. "Arduen wouldn't do that to me."

Larkin said nothing as he continued to work on her. The pain had given way to a numbing sensation wherever he sliced and prodded, morphing her into the perfect Divine. She closed her eyes then and allowed him to work. He'd assured her that this was for the best. And he was her brother. He had always wanted what was best for her.

"Larkin…" she mumbled as he cut into the sensitive skin of her abdomen.

"Shhh!" He patted her sweat-damp hair. "Larkin is no longer with us, dear Lilith."

Her eyes flashed open.

That voice.

"You killed him, remember?"

Lilith tried to lift her head, but she couldn't muster the strength. It was all too much for her. It was only when a shadow moved over her, blocking out the light above, did she see to whom the voice belonged.

A man with hair white as snow stared down at her with soulless blue eyes. "Hello, Lilith. I am your new Master. But you may call me Spiro."

Lilith thrashed on the table, her body smacking against the stone slab, bruising her horribly. She didn't care. She had to get away from the sadist. But with one stroke of his hand on her hair, he managed to calm her.

Magic!

"Dear Lilith," he crooned, "did Arduen not instruct you well enough?"

She cried at the mention of her Master. How could she have been so angry with him? He loved her and she loved him. Why wasn't that enough?

Lilith surrendered herself as Spiro's voice caressed her ears. "You must relinquish your freedom for power, or your power for freedom."

"Lilith!"

"Wake up!"

"She's giving up…"

"Lilith Oak!" Arduen's voice boomed through the madness.

Lilith's eyes blew wide at the sound of her name. She couldn't see anyone. She lay on her bed at the Frourío. No stone slab, no Larkin, and no Spiro. But the abyss of Aether swirled around her, obscuring the others from view.

A mighty fear speared through her then, for Aether was the most unforgiving element to wield, and she could kill them all.

Before she could stem the flow of the great abyss, it melted away before her, revealing Arduen standing at the foot of her bed. He inhaled deep, fists balled at his sides, a large vein flickering on his strong neck. He'd absorbed what she had dispelled in her night terror, she realized, as he moved to the window to release it, for no one could contain such a force for long.

Olga and Zurí rushed to her side immediately. Lilith couldn't fight the guilt that assaulted her. Night terrors were not uncommon for her, not since she'd first been exposed to battle, but they were growing evermore frequent. And now, unfortunately, more dangerous. It only took one mistake to claim a life, and she couldn't lose another loved one. Not at her own hand.

Never again.

"You're all right," Olga murmured, pulling Lilith into a tight embrace. No one could provide comfort the way the Oracle could, but it was another's touch she needed.

Since the death of Larkin, since she'd drained the vitality from her brother's limbs, Lilith had felt like she was living underwater. Everything was muted, all of her senses clogged, her vision blurred. When her comrades spoke, it was as if they were miles away, not at her side.

It was no different now, with Constantine's abyss separating her from her family.

Lilith sat up, eager to brush off their coddling. The sheets were soaked. She grimaced; she'd soiled herself. Neither Olga or Zurí seemed to mind, or to even notice, as they petted her head, their *coos* soothing her anxiety.

Julius stood in the doorway, his expression drawn, his bronze skin unnaturally ashen. He stared at her with silver-lined eyes before Arduen approached and shooed him away, assuring the prince that he would handle this.

But for the first time, Lilith wasn't so sure that he could.

2

TATIANA DASYLVÀ

"We need to send for an Enchantress," Lilith heard Arduen say.

She wanted to reach for him, to assure her Master that she would be all right, but her body had been severed from her mind, the decapitation rendering her useless.

Lilith lay swaddled in fresh bedsheets, Olga and Arduen hovering over her like new parents with a sick babe. It turned out, this was not a night terror. Lilith had spent the entire night retching up her dinner, and then continued to heave bile until she was bereft of any sustenance. When the vomiting subsided, every muscle in her body seized up, and she surrendered to the incapacitating incendiary pain.

Never had she felt worse. Her eyes were so heavy, they ached to open. Her limbs were so feeble, they were numb. Arduen had spent the night in the rocking chair at her bedside, monitoring her condition as she weaved in and out of consciousness. Lilith knew this was his attempt to atone for his mistake by her, and she wanted to thank him for trying. But he'd yet to simply ask for her forgiveness. It was as if her words meant nothing to him, as if he were the only one with control in their relationship.

The Oracle tried to relieve Lilith's suffering, but to no avail. Nothing she could do would alleviate her ailments. Olga expelled a resigned sigh. "I will write to Ophelía immediately," she said.

As the Oracle's footsteps faded, Lilith peeled open her eyelids and looked into the eyes of her Master. Once his irises were blue like the morning sky, but now they were gray, misted by turbulence.

He smiled sweetly down at her. "How are you feeling?" He touched his knuckles to her forehead. She was sweating profusely. Arduen released a sigh through his nose, and then rose from the chair at her bedside.

"Please don't leave," Lilith croaked. This was the first time they had been pleasant in each other's presence, and she didn't want the moment to end.

Arduen turned to her, relief evident upon his face. He grasped her hand and sat back down beside her. He began to tell her stories of old. Stories of false and true. Stories of great Divine long since passed.

◎ ʊ ⇁ ⋔ ◊

"How did she arrive without a horse?" Zurí said, more to herself than to Lilith.

Ophelía consented to send a healer for Lilith, if only because of her deep affection for Arduen, and the woman arrived two weeks later. Lilith wanted to greet the Enchantress upon her arrival but could not stand without falling prey to vertigo. Nausea tore through her body and she regularly heaved into the bucket at her bedside.

"Two weeks is all it took?" Zurí practically spat. "No horse."

She scoffed. "I need to take up magic."

The light thuds of footsteps, gradually growing louder, closer, signaled the Enchantress's arrival.

"Lilith." Olga stepped into Lilith's bedchamber with a mahogany-haired woman in her wake. "This is Tatiana DaSylvà. She will be attending you for the time being." Olga stepped aside, allowing the Enchantress to approach.

"Hello, Lilith," Tatiana greeted in a sing-song voice.

Lilith thought she had welcomed her healer affably, but knew it was not so when the two women exchanged bemused glances. The sickness left much to be construed.

"Have you seen a condition like this?" Zurí pressed.

"Once before."

The Enchantress did not elaborate, sparking Zurí's frustration. "Surely you must have some theories as to why she is suffering."

"I do."

Olga quickly interceded before Zurí lost all sense of hospitality. "We have had Arduen and Quintus research the many tombs in our study, but we are limited here. We know nothing of such ailments lest the victim has been born with such a condition. Lilith has never before experienced these episodes."

Tatiana never took her eyes off of Lilith, her lips pursed pensively. "Did she hit her head?"

Olga hesitated. "Well, I don't know—"

"Lilith," Zurí raised her voice as if her noviciate had gone deaf, "did you fall? Do you remember a head wound?"

Olga hissed, "I don't think she would forget obtaining a head contusion, Zurí."

"You'd be surprised the injuries we dismiss," Tatiana said.

Zurí straightened, hackles rising. Clearly her intelligence had been offended.

The Oracle took her colleague by the arm. "Right, well, we

will leave you two to get acquainted." Shooting a censorious glance at Zurí, she added, "We trust your expertise, Enchantress." The two Divine women left and Lilith let her leaden head fall back onto the pillow, the muscles of her neck aching. When had her head grown so heavy?

Tatiana moved about the room, eyeing the stained-crystalline windowpanes and the view of the Sea beyond. Lilith paid her little attention as she forced herself to relax. It seemed that if she willed lucidity, it would only cause her more pain and discomfort.

Dubiously, Lilith observed the Enchantress through half-shut lids. She envied the way her hips swayed with each step, the way her hair shimmered in the sunlight. The dress she wore was dark as the midnight sky, the lustrous fabric unlike any she'd seen before, like liquid molded to her skin.

"So, Lilith," Tatiana said, "please explain to me how you've been feeling since your symptoms began."

If she were honest, Lilith hadn't much thought about when she began to feel ill. "I guess it started a few weeks ago. I felt weak, and because of this, I pushed myself that much harder."

"Mm-hmm…"

"I'd spent longer than usual in bed following the last battle," Lilith continued. "I thought that I may have recessed slightly in my training due to idleness."

"It is possible… but unlikely," Tatiana said. "You have a fever, and you cannot retain any sustenance. Without nutrients, without digesting food adequately, your body will not be competent enough to retain muscle. You will grow weaker in time, and eventually, you will fade away. Emaciated." Tatiana lowered herself to the edge of the bed.

"What can be done?" Lilith dared to ask.

"Well, there are several remedies and spells that will help you to eat and keep your meals down. This is where we will start." Tatiana's golden irises panned Lilith's frame. "Within a week or two, you should be up and about."

Lilith sat upright at that. She hadn't realized her recovery would be this attainable with an Enchantress's aid.

"However," Tatiana intoned, "I request that you do not continue to train physically. At least not for some time. It is easy to believe you are better before you have truly recovered. I want to avoid this, for the consequences are dire."

"Dire?"

"It could cost your life, my dear."

Frowning, Lilith dropped her gaze, picking at a loose thread of her quilt. "I will do whatever you tell me," she said at last.

"Well then." Tatiana stood. "I am leaving to prepare the concoction. Try to take a bath if you can. I will send the Oracle back to you. When I return, we will proceed."

For the first time in weeks, Lilith felt truly hopeful.

Tatiana marched toward the door, but before she took her leave, she twisted to face Lilith again. Her expression was stern, dampening Lilith's hope. "This won't be easy," she warned. "This can be painful."

Lilith digested the Enchantress's words without a care. She needed to get better, however she would suffer along the way.

FOLLOWING THE MIDDAY MEAL, LILITH WENT FOR A WALK THROUGH the towering pines of the Megálos. Tatiana joined her. A week had passed since the Enchantress had arrived to oversee Lilith's care, but it felt more like a month. Lilith was restless, eager to be outside.

"How long will you be staying with us?" Lilith inquired.

"Until you are better."

"I'm feeling well," Lilith said. The remedy Tatiana had

concocted was drudgery to get down, but the relief was nearly instant. "When will I be able to continue with my physical training?"

The Enchantress considered the question for a time. "When you ingest my remedy and you no longer feel as if a veil has been lifted. It takes time. It varies from patient to patient, but it could take up to six weeks."

Lilith staggered, mouth agape. "Six weeks?"

Tatiana nodded curtly. "Your body will feel better before you truly are better. You must recognize this temporary relief as illusory. You must give your body time to redevelop all that it has lost."

Lilith doubted she could wait that long. She was more than restless now, and the idleness was maddening.

As they neared the sparring field, Lilith paused at the edge of the trees and watched as Julius and Felix exchanged an impressive array of blows. The young Divine was coming along well, even giving the prince a run for his drachmae.

"What is magic like?" Lilith inquired. "Are all Enchantresses of your coven gifted equally in the healing realm?"

A flicker of a smile tugged at the edge of Tatiana's full lips. "Yes, we are all equally blessed by Amalthea in regard to healing, but we receive a Blessing from Her that She has created for us alone. Unique gifts to aid our coven."

"Amalthea…" Lilith mused. "The Southern Guiding Star."

"Yes."

"My mother used to swear upon that Star," Lilith said on a sigh.

"Oh." The Enchantress perked up at that, her gaze falling heavy on her patient. "Does your mother write you often?"

"No," Lilith answered. "My mother entered Elysium years ago."

Tatiana's shoulders fell, but Lilith dismissed it. Pity was

abhorrent, and it got her nowhere. The only people she could talk to about her mother's suicide were Arduen and Olga, and she did not want to foist her issues on another. "It was many years ago," she assured the Enchantress.

"Time does not erase the pain," Tatiana said. "Nor does it diminish the lack of presence. You will always notice her absence."

However she was right, Lilith did not expound on the topic. "Tell me about your Blessing," she said to change the subject. "What has Amalthea gifted you?"

"I believe She has gifted me doubly. I was Blessed with a war gift, but also the Sight."

"The Sight," Lilith repeated with a wistful note. "You can see things? The future?"

"It is similar to the Oracle's gifts," Tatiana said, "though mine are not always messages. They are notions and visions, and I can retrieve them at my will."

"How does it work?" Lilith nearly whispered.

Tatiana grinned. "For nature, I only need to touch it—a tree, perhaps—and I can see it as a seedling, a sapling, a full-blown entity. I see it when it has withered, and when the last of its particles die. I see the weary travelers who rest in its trunk. I see the children who pluck its leaves and climb its boughs."

"What of people?" Lilith asked. "When you touch me, can you see me before I was born, in my mother's womb?" Then she licked at her lips, uncertain whether she truly wanted to know. "Can you see my death?"

Instantly, creases etched into Tatiana's brow. "People are much more difficult to read. We are much more complex entities than trees are. Humans are in a state of constant change, and a change of character will affect one's fate. Therefore, futures are muddy and clouded."

"What can you see?"

Tatiana's eyes settled back onto the field. "I can feel emotions and visions."

"Can you try with me?"

Without voicing consent, Tatiana turned to face Lilith and grasped her shoulders. Leveling her gaze, she bore her golden eyes into Lilith's. Tatiana bit the insides of her cheeks, her eyebrows knitting together. "I see only darkness." When Lilith's expression morphed into despair, she added, "But the dark isn't always bad. It does not always equate ill fortune."

Lilith wavered, uncertain to press. "What do you think it means for me?"

"I do not know," Tatiana said. "I see the dark, but it does not seem foreboding. It does not emit that treacherous feeling so often associated with shadows." She looked out toward the field again. "For you, it feels welcoming."

"Welcoming?"

"Yes, like you take comfort in the shadows. In the coverage that they offer."

"But there must be reasons why I seek such shelter," Lilith mused.

"Yes, we cannot have the good without being exposed to the bad," Tatiana elaborated. "We all get our due share of it. Protected by the Gods, or the Stars, or the Divine."

A FORTNIGHT PASSED, AND THEN ANOTHER. LILITH HADN'T suffered another episode since before Tatiana's arrival. Four weeks free of pain left her antsy to return to her regular schedule. Every other day she was permitted to train with Arduen and Zurí, and Tatiana in hand to oversee progress and monitor Lilith's condition. Lilith felt good as new, hale as rain. Yet Tatiana always met her hopeful exuberance with one warning:

It always seems that way until you push yourself over the brink. Overconfidence can kill.

The Enchantress left for Kynös earlier that day to retrieve more supplies, and Olga had offered her company, which Tatiana had gladly accepted. The two were kindred old souls, and Lilith found she'd grown quite fond of Tatiana.

The Frourío was alight with excitement as she entered the kitchen. Lilith watched as Zurí rushed about, and Ambrose cooked in a frenzy, flour dusting his hair and skin like ash. She spotted the others seated at the table, just sinking into dinner, and joined them. "What's going on?" she asked, gesturing to Zurí.

"Earlier this morning, Olga received a premonition," Quin answered excitedly.

"Oh?" Lilith's eyebrows peaked.

Arduen smiled warmly. "We will be receiving a new noviciate."

Lilith blanched. So the Gods *were* punishing her, and now They have Anointed her replacement. "Who Anointed the noviciate?"

Gods above, please don't say Constantine!

"Kyril," Quin answered hesitantly.

Lilith sighed through her nose, composing herself. "That's wonderful," she said, slightly too enthusiastically for her character. She ignored Arduen's questioning look.

"Zurí will be leaving us at first light," Wren said. "The trip will take her a few weeks, but it's the perfect time of year for travel."

"She's going alone?" Lilith asked, and all of the men nodded.

Excusing herself, she made her way to the stairs, but a firm grip on her arm stalled her. She turned to see Arduen, lips pursed. "You cannot go with her, Lilith."

"But she can't go alone!"

"She can, and she will." He led her back to the table, gently forcing her into her respective seat. And that was the end of that argument.

Seated between Arduen and Quin, she could listen to their conversation as well as Julius and Felix's banter. Lilith couldn't help but notice how close they'd become. Surprised by the sudden spark of jealously, she was reminded that she only had herself to blame for the distance between her and her colleagues.

Arduen addressed the table, "There is a beast mating camp not far from here. I think it's time Felix participated in his first raid."

Wren nodded, clapping his noviciate on the back.

Lilith bristled slightly. She knew she'd be welcome on the raid had she not fallen ill. There was no way Arduen would let her join them. Though she was feeling better than adequate, it was too soon to partake in a real battle.

Zurí seated herself across from Lilith, digging into her own plate. The food neglected for so long it was probably cold.

"Will you join us, Lilith?" Felix asked. "You've been looking well lately."

"I can't imagine a little adrenaline doing you harm," Zurí added, offering an encouraging nod to Arduen.

Lilith frowned at them, picking at her plate. It seemed mildly disrespectful to condone such action without Tatiana's input. Yet she wouldn't put it past Zurí to assert her dominance as Divine Master. She'd been on edge of dispute with the Enchantress, always questioning her practice and watching over her shoulder.

"If Arduen will allow it." Lilith peered over at her Master. She'd been hale for a month now, there was little reasoning as why she should remain at home with which he could contend.

Arduen crossed his arms, raising a brow. "There will be enough of us that if you should tire, you and Ambrose can retreat. That is, if your healer agrees you are ready to participate in battle."

Tatiana would not return from Kynös until late that evening, later than they would set out. Once Lilith was armed and out the door, there would be little Tatiana could do to intervene.

Sitting up with confidence, Lilith pushed her nearly empty plate away from her, insisting, "Tatiana said I'd be fit to return to training in a week. I've been doing well so far, taking it slow. The next two weeks of Tatiana's stay were just meant as a… precaution."

"Well, that settles it," Quin said.

Arduen sighed, pulling a pensive frown. "I don't think participating in battle can be considered *taking it slow*."

"Oh, come now, Arduen!" Zurí chided. "I think the witch is only allowing our girl to atrophy."

Lilith shot her second Master a withering glare. Zurí answered with a wink.

"Between Arduen and I, Lilith will be cared for," Julius cut in. "It's not a full-scale battle. She doesn't need to enter camp, she can survey the boundary with you, Arduen."

"Great idea, lad!" Quin clapped his former noviciate on the back.

"Arduen, please," Lilith pleaded. "I'll stay with you."

I'll stay with you. The words seemed to jar him. Arduen's gaze met hers, heavy with grief and regret. She was giving him a chance to atone for his mistakes by her, and he would be remiss to pass it up.

He seemed to recognize the opportunity, the challenge.

"Fine," he said, his approval inciting a cheer from Julius and Felix. "But you stay with me."

3

YOU ARE AN ENCHANTRESS

The soldier howled as Rhéa administered to him. The bone in his arm split through skin, the result of taking on an adversary twice his size. The infirmary had been nearly deserted because of this one man, his wails deafening. How such a sensitive man had managed to survive a single match in the rings was beyond her.

"Hold still!" she ordered, but the young man continued to thrash. She sighed through flared nostrils, the only outward indication of her frustration. She grasped the man's arm, right where it was broken, and ignored the resulting cry of agony. "This will be over soon." She tried to soothe him with the calmest voice she could muster, but to no avail.

The man continued to slew invectives, struggling against her ministrations. "You Gods forsaken bi—" He was cut off as his arm dropped to the table, healed. "What in the…"

"You have this *bitch* to thank for that," Rhéa said, sauntering off before the man could assault her further—or grant her some hollow apology. She was done with him, and more injured ingrates would be seeking her aid soon. Could she administer to the needs of these beasts, considering the destruction they would inevitably loose upon the people she loved? There was a simple answer: yes, because under Spiro's thrall, there was no other option.

Rhéa marched across the infirmary, peeking over the shoulder of her apprentice. "How goes it?"

Irís turned to her, eyes sunken and shadowed, but otherwise, she'd filled out since she'd arrived. She stood in the open archway, spectating the rings. "He's winning."

Rhéa stood shoulder to shoulder with Irís and gazed up at the nearest ring—the Champion's Ring. The only ring in Spiro's Stars forsaken keep that always resulted in death.

Xavier stood at one end of the ring whilst his opponent gathered his senses, readying himself for another attack. He was larger than Xavier—most men were—but he was visibly unstable whilst Xavier stood tall and poised. He was still bloody, but he appeared as though he were invincible, as if he felt no pain at all.

The young noviciate had recovered quickly from his ailments acquired at Spiro's hand. Rhéa tended to Xavier as much as she could, though there wasn't much she could do, save clean the gashes and scabs. If Spiro were to find out that she'd been treating his star noviciate, she would've found herself suffering a worse punishment than a scourging.

The dormant crowd roared as Xavier mounted the back of his opponent. The man couldn't hold his weight and toppled to the ground in a tangle of bloodied limbs. Irís winced as Xavier pounded both of his fists into the man's face. As blood splattered, she screamed.

Rhéa grabbed Irís and pulled her into her arms, shielding the girl from the gruesome sight. Xavier was their friend, they needed each other, she did not want the brutality of the matches driving a wedge between them.

"It's all right," Rhéa cooed in Irís's ear, the same ear that hid the girl's Mark. The Enchantress glanced around the great cavern, her eyes pausing on the balcony where Spiro now stood, evaluating his Divine creation.

Xavier raised clenched fists in the air and the crowd erupted with praise. A menacing smirk lit up Spiro's face, but his eyes remained blank as they came to settle on her. A jolt of electricity shot through her body then, but Rhéa held tightly to her apprentice, face buried in her chest. She brought her attention back to Xavier as he brandished his weapon overhead. He put on a show, if only because it pleased his Master.

The beasts' caterwauling was near deafening. Pulling Irís in her wake, Rhéa entered the infirmary and cleared a table for Xavier.

"What are you doing?" Irís asked.

"You are going to fix up Xavier."

"I am?" The girl's eyes blew wide.

Rhéa chuckled. "Yes, you are. I think you can do it." It was the only way to ease the girl into knowing what she was, all whilst burgeoning the healing vocation. It only seemed right to Rhéa that the girl should be familiarized with the calling of the Ilíos.

Irís inspected the rolls of gauze and the many salves and tonics. "I don't think I am ready," she demurred.

The Enchantress rolled her eyes with dramatic flair. "You can do it. He only needs his scabs cleaned, and it's mostly scar tissue now." Rhéa forced a wan smile. "I believe in you, Irís."

When Xavier entered, he was shirtless, covered in sweat and gore. He smiled at both women in greeting before taking a seat at one of the stations, eyeing Irís as if she were honey-drizzled pasteli.

"On the table," Rhéa ordered. When he did not react, she raised her voice, "Lie down, Xavier!"

His brow furrowed at the command. "A little presumptuous, aren't we?"

Rhéa gasped and pushed him down forcefully.

"My Gods, okay!" He laid himself down willingly, lying flat on his stomach. "Just be gentle. I know you two like it rough."

Irís giggled, and Rhéa couldn't help but grin. Together, they washed Xavier's body with sponges, and he told them of his day so far, launching a salvo of questions about theirs.

Just when they were nearly finished, a young girl entered the chamber, her eyes vacant, skin pale. "Enchantress," she called.

Rhéa's head shot up at once, her senses piqued.

The servant fiddled with her fingers. "You have been summoned to Master's chambers."

The Enchantress sagged in defeat, then quickly composed herself. "Xavier, Irís will tend to you, then I want you to guide her back to her chambers. Stay with her until I get back."

Xavier nodded.

Irís bristled. "I don't need to be babysat!"

Reaching toward her, Xavier wrapped his hand around hers. "It's not about that. You are still ignorant of the atrocities that occur in this fortress. We are only protecting you."

At his gentle touch, Irís relaxed slightly. Rhéa noticed a faint smile tugging at the corner of Irís's lips, and for whatever reason, she worried for them both. Irís was only a few years younger than Xavier, perhaps nineteen, twenty at most. Xavier would live forever, or as long as Spiro lived.

"I won't be long," Rhéa said, shaking the dismal thoughts from her mind. "Then we will have that discussion later tonight."

Upon her return, they would reveal to Irís what she really was, and it was up to the girl whether she would embrace it or turn away from it.

⊚ ⊛ ⤙ ⋔ ⟁

RHÉA MEANDERED THROUGH THE HALLWAY, HER MIND WORKING diligently to erase the memory of Spiro's crude touch. Her magic was receding, her well running dry, as the fàrmako worked on her, traveling through her veins, nullifying the celestial magic. Spiro spread the drug out in her food, in her water, in the wine that he practically poured down her throat. It was stronger in the alcohol, as most drugs were, but it was obvious why Spiro forced her to down a goblet of claret before ever letting her near him.

Tonight, Rhéa hadn't the strength remaining to transform her now-crimson locks back to her usual mahogany. The sight of the red curls made her gag. "Insufferable brute," she muttered under her breath. "Vile, crude bastard!"

The hallways were empty, as they so often were at this hour. Spiro didn't request Rhéa to remain in his bed any longer. It was almost as if he suspected her plotting his death. He wouldn't be wrong, nor daft. But Rhéa wasn't so dim-witted. The moment her hand wrapped around any form of weapon, the stones beneath her feet would rise up and swallow her whole.

And Rhéa could not afford to die. There was still so much that needed to be done. First, there was Irís. Second, her shattered family. And if they ever discovered how she was fraternizing with the very man who had destroyed them, well… she would never be forgiven.

As the Enchantress entered the dim corridor leading to her chamber, she passed her own door and entered the one beside it, quickly glancing over her shoulder to ensure that no one was watching. Laughter met her ears as she entered the candlelit chamber.

"Rhéa!" Irís exclaimed, rising from her seat so close to

Xavier's. "Play with us?" She gestured to the cards scattered across the floor. They'd been sitting on cushions on the rug before the hearth, cards and wine at their feet. Rhéa remembered playing such games with her children, with her husband, Miles, but she certainly wasn't in the right state of mind to focus.

"Are you all right?" Xavier asked. He knew all too well what Spiro did with her behind closed doors, but she was fighting to keep the details concealed from Irís. The less the girl had to fear, the better.

"Yes," she said, a little too breathlessly. "I've just had a little too much wine."

Irís beamed. "Master favors you," she teased. "It must be your ability to change hair color so frequently."

The Enchantress took her seat on the rug, folding her legs beneath her. Some days it shocked her just how naïve Irís was. If Ophelía ever knew about her, Irís would become the High Enchantress's favorite tool.

"Let's finish our game then?" Irís looked to Xavier, their knees touching, the flush to her cheeks matching his. Rhéa could warn them all she wanted, but they would only do what their hearts desired.

On a brighter note, she survived yet another day beneath the earth's surface. She was almost certain that no Enchantress had ever achieved such a feat. At least she held some sort of impressive accomplishment, even if none of the Enchantresses of the Obsydían Marsh would ever know of it.

Rhéa's eyes came to rest on her friend. Irís was a born Enchantress. Whether or not she warranted it, magic coursed through her veins, fueling her heart. The girl reveled in the satisfaction and fulfillment healing others brought her, even if she was hesitant and insecure in her ability. She would make a fine Enchantress.

"Irís, darling," Rhéa said. "Come here."

The girl was pulled from her trance, gazing longingly at Xavier while he counted cards. "You win!" he said to her, placing a stack at her feet.

"Again?" Irís guffawed. "You need to step up your game, mister *Divine*." She poked his bicep teasingly. It was almost too much to bear without becoming queasy.

"Irís…" Rhéa intoned, her voice brooking no argument.

The girl remained put but transferred her attention to the Enchantress. "Yes?"

"We must have a discussion. One that may be difficult for you, but it is necessary." Rhéa pierced Xavier with her gaze, forcing him to shut his mouth before he interfered.

"What is it?"

Sighing, Rhéa tucked her flaming mane behind her ear and said, "You bear the Mark of magic. The same Mark that adorns my body, behind my left ear."

Irís did not move. She did not waver or make to speak, she simply stared back into Rhéa's eyes with equal intensity.

"You are an Enchantress."

4

—————

INDOMITABLE

The Divine barreled through the trees, their war cries renting the night. Beasts swarmed from their hiding places, racing toward them on two legs, three legs…

five legs?

The beasts had anticipated their attack. The watchman sounded the alarum and shortly following, battle ensued.

Julius remained close to Lilith, one eye locked on her whilst he swung his sword, Orphëus, overhead. Maintaining pace with him, Lilith was well aware of Arduen close behind her. Both men had taken to cosseting her since she'd fallen ill, but she was better now. Tonight, she need only prove it.

Pushing thoughts of the men from her mind, she charged after several smaller beasts. Their olive hides supplied their camouflage, but Divine senses were capable of distinguishing them from the surrounding brush.

"Lilith!" Arduen cried from behind her.

At the sound of her Master's call, she twisted and impaled a beast with Constance. As she withdrew her blade from the

40

beast's gut, she flashed a grin in her Master's direction. "Thank you."

Arduen, short of breath, drew near and, reaching toward her, wiped under her nose. When he pulled his hand away, his fingers were stained crimson. "You're bleeding."

Lilith sniffed and squeezed down on the bridge of her nose. "I must have been hit," she said. "I'll be okay."

Arduen crossed his arms, impaling her with a look that portrayed he was yet to be convinced.

"I will be fine," she assured him, voice nasally.

He shook his head in defeat. "I won't argue with you."

"Good," was her smug reply as she fell into an easy trot. She didn't enjoy jilting him, but she couldn't allow this coddling to go on. She was Divine. Injured as she may be, she was eager to prove her state no longer necessitated a guardian. What she needed was a shield-mate, a Philías. A partner in battle who looked out for her but would not stifle her.

Lilith slid to a stop as three beasts converged, their teeth clicking, the chittering a conversation only they could interpret. Casting a furtive glance over her shoulder, she could see that Arduen had been targeted as well, the sliver of moonlight flashing against his blade as it arced through the air.

The beasts prowled, hostile, yet they did not seem overly eager to attack her. Still, she did not drop Constance, and her free hand was raised if she had need of Aether.

"This is the one…" came a hiss.

Lilith stiffened, and she knew from the silence in the clearing that Arduen had heard this, too.

Then she attacked.

She spun, stabbing the beast behind her with a swift jab. As she withdrew her blade, she twisted it, if only to ensure the beast would fall from such a wound. Sometimes they surprised her, walking without limbs or their entrails hanging free. Careless. Inhuman.

The beast toppled with a pained gurgle and Lilith, sensing another beast's proximity with Discernment, hopped to the side to avoid its grasp.

They weren't slicing at her with their noxious talons, they were trying to grab hold of her.

Spiro wanted her alive.

Lilith fought back panic as she faced the two beasts. Arduen had disappeared, likely lured away by his most recent adversary. Receding, she took several slow steps back, her eyes seeded on her enemies, her ears prickling at their incessant chittering.

Then, for the first time in weeks, she flared Aether.

Constantine's element torpedoed through her veins, bursting from her fingertips. Lilith cried out, not from pain, but from the exhilaration of the release.

Gods, she missed this.

The blast of Aether was small, but enough to take out a single beast. She wouldn't risk pushing herself too far, so she raised Constance and spun on the last of her enemies.

"WOAH!" Arduen deflected her blade, sending Constance soaring. He turned a scalding glare on her. "Are you even thinking?"

Lilith straightened, stunned. Arduen rarely raised his voice. Her Master expelled a suffering sigh, then marched away to retrieve her blade. As he proffered her the sword hilt first, he said, "You must watch your surroundings with more than your eyes. Use Discernment. I know it's been some time since you've felt that deep connection, but you must try. You should have been able—given the close proximity of that beast and your Philías—to detect my presence separate from that of your enemy."

Properly chastised, Lilith's shoulders sunk. What could she say? She had made a huge mistake. But she had used Discernment, she just wasn't capable of sensing the nature of each entity. She could have killed him. "I am sorry, Arduen."

He seemed to soften at her apology. "Quest out with your consciousness, got it?"

"Yes, Master."

Lilith's eyes dropped to the Forest floor, her mind expanding with Discernment. Her senses were dim, not as vast as they once had been. Perhaps it was a result, or a side effect of the remedy Tatiana had made. Perhaps the celestial magic of it dulled her mental clarity a fraction.

The chaos seemed to have pushed the others ahead, leaving them to fend for themselves. Lilith was not callow enough to believe this was a mistake of theirs. The beasts were intelligent, remarkably so, and they'd herded them apart like sheep. But when she looked to her Master for strength, she saw only a lion.

The trees were dark, shadows creeping between their boughs, crouching in their trunks. Menacing. Minatory. The Forest was infiltrated with vermin, the pines inundated by Spiro's beasts.

Arduen pressed up against Lilith, shielding her with his body. "Do not provoke them," he said over his shoulder.

"Where are the others?" Lilith squinted, struggling to make out the shadows in the trees.

Arduen leaned back into her, likely for assurance that she was still standing, still breathing. "They're in the camp. This is as far as we were to go."

Holding Constance outstretched toward the beasts, she waited for them to close in. They would have to use Aether, and given her previous attack, she wasn't certain how much she had left. There was always the option of Kyril's element, but drawing sustenance from the trees could destroy the Megálos. Lilith opted to save Water as a last resort.

Anxiety gnawed at her chest, limbs throbbing with adrenaline, with the anticipation of battle.

Amorphous figures cavorted in the shadows between the trees, too obscure to glean their proximity. But Lilith knew their intent.

"Don't move," Arduen warned. "Steady..."

The beasts encroached, licking their lips in anticipation of the feast Lilith and Arduen would certainly become. Lucent, yellow eyes flashed in the darkness. The sight was enough to make her explode, but she pressed against Arduen's back, awaiting his order. Droplets dripped from her nose again, and she fought the urge to wipe them away.

"This one's *bleeeeding*," a monster hissed.

Arduen went rigid, his hand grasping hers and squeezing tight enough to hurt. Any tighter and he'd crack bones.

Where were the others? Lilith's eyes flicked between the trees' masts, but the shadows were too dense, too many monsters impeding her vision.

All brazenness eroded.

"Arduen," she moaned, eager for his wisdom, his guidance. The most terrifying part was that her Master seemed just as nervous, he was never this laconic. "Arduen..." He did not respond, and Lilith whimpered as a beast drew near enough to slash her with its talons.

Arduen bellowed, "Now!"

Violet light exploded through the clearing, melding with fiery ribbons.

Julius! Quin!

Their comrades surrounded the swarm of beasts from the outside whilst she and Arduen fought from within.

Screeches rent the night as they blasted their elements, Lilith finally lending her own to Arduen's. For a moment, she met his gaze, one that was soaked with emotion. Was that pride? Joy?

A wide grin stole over her face, and Lilith blasted Aether into the assemblage of beasts. The moment was pure ecstasy, but it wouldn't last long. Her strength began to wane, and she struggled to maintain steady breaths. She stemmed the flow of Aether and unsheathed Constance.

Lilith swung her sword. The blade oscillated between her and her enemies, taunting, boasting of her dexterity and the promise of death should they deign to draw nearer.

She was Divine. Inviolable. Indomitable.

Assuming the offensive, she slashed out with Constance. Leaving one foe gutted in the loam, she beheaded another. Beastly ichor peppered her skin, burning like acid. Ignorant of the pain, Lilith surged onward, her muscles barking in exertion. In moments, she would need to halt and catch her breath.

Wren and Felix stormed past, waving their weapons, their free hands outstretched, the Earth responding to their beckons. Lilith smiled. They were knocking the beasts off balance and felling them with ease.

A beast's talon caught her shoulder. She winced at the bright spark of a sting but would not allow herself to lose focus again. Hefting Constance into the air, she made to impale the beast, but a hole appeared in its brow and its yellow eyes rolled back into its head. Lilith watched, slightly awed, as the beast's limp body toppled, and a bloody rock rolled to a stop a few feet away. Felix's laughter sailed off into the distance as he pursued their scattering enemies.

How you've grown! she thought with a beaming grin.

Lilith turned back to Arduen. He was surrounded by beasts, Aether a torrent around them. Xander's Fire swirled within the violet haze, sending sparks shooting from the abyss. It was always a pleasure to see Arduen and Quin fight together.

Her Master would likely reprimand her again for venturing off on her own, heedless of his whereabouts. But she was out of practice, perhaps that excuse would afford her some of his leniency.

What remained of the battle became a blur around her, most of their enemies nothing more than ashen husks underfoot. Lilith trudged back to her Master, her movements maladroit and labored, her limbs leaden, eager for respite. But when her legs began to tremble, to grow numb, she panicked.

"Arduen!" she cried as her muscles gave way to spasms, and the Forest floor exchanged places with the trees and the starlit sky.

"Lilith!" Julius was at her side in a flash of fire, warding away any beasts that dared attack. He dropped to his knees beside her with a thud, taking her face in his hands.

"Arduen…" Lilith moaned. If she were to die, she wanted her Master with her.

A second later, her head was propped in someone's lap, and their face moved into her line of sight. A familiar face, with a familiar, worried brow.

Arduen.

"It's okay, sweetheart," he said, though it was evident in his tone that he was unconvinced of his own claim. Still, Lilith took comfort in his voice.

She tried to speak, but words failed her. Glancing down at her limp body, she watched as her limbs shook violently.

Gods, the pain.

Her vision flickered.

Black. White. Red. Blue.

Fighting for air, her breath hitched, her lungs burned. "Arduen!" she gasped, her hands digging into the earth beneath her, grappling for purchase. She was desperate to stay on the ground, but the stars were swallowing her whole. They lifted her from the ground, her body floating toward the firma-ment. She wasn't ready to go. She wasn't ready to become one of them.

"No! Please, no!"

She tried desperately to keep her hands fisted in the dirt, a tether to the mortal realm, but her strength was feeble, barely existent.

"Arduen, please!"

"I'm right here, Lilith." His voice resounded through her head, but she couldn't see him.

"Arduen, don't let me go. Please, don't let me go!"

Lips pressed to her forehead, stubble prickling her skin. "I'm right here." He said it over and over, even as she was lifted up. A strong hand pressed firm strokes down her spine, coaxing the convulsions from her muscles.

"Arduen," Lilith grit out. "I'm so sorry!"

"It's all right, my fledgling," he answered. "I am with you."

That was all she needed to know before the Gods shut her heavy eyes.

5

THE CAPITAL

The journey to the capital was nothing short of eye-opening for Hestîa. Marlowë, the Walabeän Chief—the Igítís of the Isles of Nysía—bargained for an extra month at home, in preparation for battle. A quarter of their force remained at the Isles, a specialized defensive unit to ensure the safety of the Colony. The Igítís's utmost concern was the Walabeäns. Augusta came second to the Isles.

Hestîa followed their escort through the marble halls. Igítís Marlowë and his most accomplished warriors—herself and Agónas—had been invited to dine with the Emperor. After so many weeks spent on the road, the last thing Hestîa wished to do was dress up to impress a spoiled monarch. The only reason she'd dressed in such finery was for the sake of Agónas's observant eye.

Being surrounded by stone was disconcerting, and within the first hour of arriving at the capital, Hestîa was suffocating. Only through sheer determination did she endure.

Marching beside Agónas, Hestîa matched her cadence to his in an attempt to mask her consternation.

"You clean up well," he said.

Blushing to her hairline, Hestîa eyed him up and down with a coy smirk. "You as well... for a Walabeän brute!" They laughed until the Igítís shushed them.

Marlowë had been granted chambers in the castle, whilst the Walabeän warriors were to take residence in the barracks with the Emperor's guard, the *Fruits* or *Frumpa* or some inane title of the sort. Hestîa had never been so exposed to the male species, and she questioned the Emperor's morality for allowing coed bunking.

"Do you feel as I do?" Agónas asked through gritted teeth as they were led into the Great Hall.

"Like there's a lack of oxygen in the air?"

Agónas chuckled, the sound deep and rolling like thunder, sending ripples of pleasure through her body. "Exactly."

Hestîa forced a close-lipped smile as they entered the Great Hall. None of the courtiers stood to greet them as the servants rushed forth to pull out their seats. So it was that dinner commenced and Hestîa felt as though her Chief was not regarded with the respect he so rightly deserved. Though Marlowë received their hollow platitudes with grace and dignity, her blood boiled with rage. Hestîa beseeched the Gods to grant her the patience They'd blessed Agónas with.

They ate in near silence. The sounds of chewing, slurping, and screeching cutlery permeating the hall. If only she could stand and bellow her ire, but Marlowë would never condone such asinine behavior. Tonight, she was to represent him, and she would remain silent until spoken to, like the duteous warrior she was.

Hestîa was hyperaware of Agónas to her right, Marlowë across from her. Warmth seeped through her as her comrade's knee bent to touch her own. During their travels, her relationship with Agónas had finally advanced in the direction she'd been longing for. It wouldn't be long until she had him swearing oaths to her and her alone. If there was anything to take comfort in, it was that.

The Emperor rose from his seat in earnest. He swept his hand over the table, a façade of a smile twisting his flushed features. "Welcome to my home. Marlowë, you and your lovely wife have been granted chambers in the finest quarters of the castle."

"My wife did not join me," Marlowë interjected. "She is with child, and war is no place for an expecting woman, no matter how fierce she may be." The Igítís kept his gaze fastened on the Emperor.

Obadïa dipped his head. "Of course. Well, the chambers are yours regardless."

The silence that followed was insufferable, and Hestîa found herself longing of home, of Noala's furry embrace. The harpies had been stationed in the imperial stables, an insult to their majesty. They deserved space and freedom, not stalls and hay bales.

The remainder of the meal trickled on in much the same unendurable manner. When they finished, Marlowë was led to his chambers, and Hestîa and Agónas were escorted to the soldiers' barracks far beneath the castle.

Long faded were the plush carpets and lavish portraits as they descended the stairs toward what might as well be Hades. Hestîa scoffed. Some respect they had for the men and women who risked their lives for the safety of Augusta and its miser of an Emperor.

The barracks were austere, if there was any possible way to describe them. Plain wooden bunk beds lined an enormous hall, and it appeared as though the bathing chamber was communal. If the simplest tasks like bathing and relieving oneself became worrisome—daunting—Hestîa wondered just how long she would last in the capital.

The women were granted the western side of the barracks, whilst the men occupied the east. The Walabeän men camped between the women and their Augustan counterparts, something Hestîa knew the Augustans would interpret as territorial, but what her fellow warriors saw as necessary and appropriate. No women fought on behalf of the Empire until their own introduction. Marlowë simply wished to avoid any chance of misconduct. Despite the cold welcome and the women's ostracism, Hestîa hadn't failed to notice Captain Vaughn—Emperor Obadïa's Right Hand—ignore her and the other women, addressing only Agónas and the other—male—Walabeän warriors.

Despicable.

Hestîa eyed her cot from afar. She slept on the bottom bunk, and her friend, Athena, claimed the top.

"Hestîa!" Athena called from the corner. All of the Walabeän females crowded around their bunks.

Something had happened.

"What's going on?" Hestîa asked as she bisected the crowd and wedged herself between two bodies seated on her bed.

"The men," said Athena, "we're to share a bathing chamber with them."

Giggles erupted from the group, and Hestîa rolled her eyes. "The men are arguing about who has better ale and you're excited to see some cocks?"

Suddenly, her comrades' features grew impassive.

"Check yourselves," Hestîa chided. "We are here for war. Represent the Isles with pride, will you? These men do not respect you. Do you see any Augustan women here?" She spread her arms wide, awaiting a response. Nothing. "Exactly. They aren't seen as capable enough to bear arms."

With that, she grabbed her nightgown and marched to the bathing chamber. If they were going to survive this adventure, then she needed all the girls to be saddle-ready. Every warrior needed to hold herself esteemed. They needed to prove to these men that they were fearsome and capable, and could kill every last one of them if they so desired.

Ambling toward the forsaken bathing chamber, Hestîa settled herself down in the corner of the bathing pool, choosing the darkest spot in the room. Slowly, she lowered herself into the water, frowning at the tepid temperature. Had she been freed from dinner sooner, she might have been soaking in steaming waters.

Scrubbing herself, Hestîa lathered her skin and hair in milky suds before dipping beneath the surface. When she rose, she leaned herself against the edge of the bath, facing the barren wall.

She was clean, but the thought of returning to the group of hormonal, male-deprived girls did not appeal to her. The quiet was luring, it was calming despite the madness that perfused the barracks.

A familiar cadence thumped, louder and louder until it was silenced. The water rippled and splashed, but Hestîa didn't bother to turn around. No. She wanted to give Agónas the element of surprise.

A smug smile lit up her face as he wrapped his hands around her waist, one sliding down between her legs whilst the other stroked up and down her side, sending shivers racing up her spine.

Tilting her head back, she moaned despite herself, despite the lack of privacy. They'd taken things to this level during their travels. Any chance of privacy they found, they'd seized. In the capital, it would be no different.

Hestîa gripped the edge of the pool to steady herself as

Agónas prepared to take her. He pushed his weight against her, pressing her body to the edge of the tub. He wasn't usually this eager. "Agónas," she chimed. "What's gotten into you?"

He said nothing, but his hands continued to play, to torment her as she awaited their coupling. Her body thrummed in anticipation of pleasure, and she ground her hips against him, beseeching for more. He gave a hollow chuckle, and his free hand roved up to cup her breast.

Hestîa glanced down to watch as he pleasured her... and froze.

Tanned.

The hand that held her breast was... *tanned*.

Hestîa screeched and pushed back off the wall, sending the Augustan soldier tumbling back into the water. "How dare you?!" she howled.

Clatter sounded from the bunks as soldiers and warriors alike scrambled to the site of the commotion. Hestîa, outraged, struggled to control the force that was her rage. Balling her hands into fists, she walloped the soldier before her.

"Hestîa!" Agónas raced to her side, hoisting her from the pool by her shoulders.

"Let me have him!" she shrieked.

Agónas said nothing as he pulled her body into his, shielding her from the sight of the other men. Her female comrades stood huddled together with blatant expressions of shock.

"What's going on here?" It was the captain. "What is the meaning of this?" His stare was scalding as he gazed from the soldier in the pool to Agónas.

But Hestîa was the one to speak. "Your soldier thought it wise to stick his fingers inside me!" Gasps emanated from the assemblage. "I do not know what games you play here, but I will not tolerate it."

Captain Vaughn glared down at the soldier. "Well, Macario, what do you have to say for yourself?"

The soldier's tanned skin paled under scrutiny. "I thought she was one of ours. We have a servant whose hair is nearly white, like your own." He indicated Hestîa's unkempt braids. "I wasn't forceful, Captain. She seemed to be enjoying it."

Agónas's body tensed beside her, and Hestîa tightened her grip on him.

"Is this true?" the captain asked.

"Yes." Hestîa bowed her head in shame. "I thought he was Agónas, but when I saw his tanned skin, I realized he was not." Agónas relaxed again, his hand stroking her back comfortingly.

"Very well." The captain turned to face the rest of the soldiers. "When you enter into physical relations with another in the barracks, remember to look at who you are seducing." He turned back to Hestîa. "We are done here."

Done? There would be no punishment?

Seething, Hestîa glared at the back of the captain's head as he made his exit.

It certainly didn't feel over. The dread that churned in her gut told her it was not.

6

IMPENDING DEPARTURE

In the forest, Lilith hadn't felt much more than her own restless fear, as if it were a living breathing daemon taking residence inside her mind. But now, as she thrashed in her bed, fear had deserted her, and she prayed fervently for release. For peace. Just when she'd thought she had reached the culmination of her episode, her pain ascended to new levels. The peak was higher, though her threshold was not.

Pain sliced through Lilith's back like a blade, her hands gripping the mattress for support. Warm hands stroked her face, her hair, easing her back onto pillows, but her body resisted despite her willingness to obey.

"Stop!" she cried. "Stop!"

"Lilith…" *Julius*. "It's all right." He stroked her cheek as she panted through the waves of anguish coursing through her limbs.

Tatiana soothed her, placing a damp cloth against her forehead. Lilith groaned as the cold abated her discomfort, if only slightly. The Enchantress glanced down at her with maternal concern, her eyes wide with worry. She exchanged a few words with Arduen, but Lilith couldn't make them out, her ears clogged. She was underwater again. An undine, unable to comprehend the words spoken above the surface. Lilith tried to use her eyes to read their lips, but Tatiana's long mahogany hair hid her face from sight.

Gods, I wish for my mother.

Golden eyes flashed in her vision.

"What was that?" Tatiana asked.

Lilith gaped. Had she spoken aloud?

Arduen entered her line of sight then, his eyes shadowed and wet. Had he been crying?

"Arduen…" She reached out a shaky hand to touch his cheek, and he took hold of it, engulfing her hand with his own.

"Try to sleep." His words were clear, and they echoed inside her head. She wanted to obey, but the darkness claimed her first.

◎ ◘ ⟿ ⋔ ◊

WARM GOLDEN RAYS BATHED THE BEDCHAMBER. WITH A GRUNT, Lilith eased herself into a sitting position, propping the pillows up to cushion her back against the wall.

Arduen was asleep, his tear-stained face frozen in a frown, his brow creased, aging him a decade. She wanted to reach out to him, but he was too far away. Slowly, she lifted herself up and swung her legs over the side of the bed. Arduen jumped to his feet, startling her.

"No, no, no!" he said, gently guiding her legs back under the quilt.

"But I have to relieve myself!" Her cheeks flushed. She was hoping to sneak away to the bathing chamber quietly, unnoticed.

Arduen released a huff of a laugh, a slight smile trailing behind it. Warmth blossomed inside her chest at the sight of it. "Of course, little one." He tousled her hair affectionately. "I will get Tatiana, and she will assist you. Don't move."

Lilith leaned back against the pillows with the intention to wait patiently, but the room faded away, and she was engulfed by unremitting shadows.

◎ ☵ ⟋ ⋔ ◊

JULIUS KICKED OPEN HIS BEDCHAMBER DOOR AND ENTERED A ROOM so similar to Lilith's, he hoped she wouldn't notice the difference. Alas, the Dalegonian tapestries his mother had sent with him six years ago betrayed him.

"Julius?" Lilith croaked, coming awake in his arms.

"You've made a mess of your bed," he said. "Olga and Tatiana are going to clean it while you stay in my bedchamber."

She cringed, her face searing.

"There was nothing you could do about it, Lil. Don't be embarrassed." He deposited her onto the mattress as gently as he could.

As he pulled the quilt over her, she whispered, "I'm sorry."

"So am I," he said.

"Did… someone bathe me?" Lilith glanced up at him, her disgust obvious in her scowl.

"Yes, of course." Julius chuckled. "Olga handled that with the help of your healer. They dressed you in a new nightgown as well."

"Where's Arduen?"

She would have expected her Master to carry her away, but alas, Arduen was outside with Wren and Felix. Olga had sent Julius to fetch him, but when Olga transferred the sleeping Lilith into his arms, he was loath to leave her. "He is outside with Quin. I suspect he will be up to visit you shortly."

Julius lowered himself onto the bed beside her and Lilith released a sigh of relief and relaxed, leaning into him. He welcomed her with an open arm, reaching around her shoulders to pull her closer, and she nuzzled her cheek into his chest.

They'd been so distant from one another since she'd had to kill her brother. He knew he should give her space and let her mourn, as was appropriate, but he longed to help in some way. Now this malady was pushing them further apart. He wouldn't allow it. Not with his departure looming like a specter hovering on the horizon. Another trial for their relationship to face. And to overcome, Xander willing.

Just when he thought she'd fallen asleep, Lilith's feeble voice broke the silence. "Why do you think the Gods gave us the ability to wield Their elements without also granting us immunity?"

Julius pondered her question for a moment. The theology behind the question was debatable, and every Divine had differing answers.

Glancing down at her, head nestled in the crook of his shoulder and breast, he studied her pensive expression. Lilith was not the type to ask and await an answer. She was the kind of woman to ask and parse through her brain to find it before it was provided.

"I think that gifting immunity would be allowing us too much power," he said, drawing her attention to him. "It would eliminate our service as a sacrifice. We would be nearly invincible." He shrugged, the movement lifting her own head. "It would be too much power for a mortal, wielding Their elements without repercussions. We would become gods. And thus, we would become destroyers, for that is human nature."

Lilith shifted, glancing up at him with wide, emerald eyes.

"And that is not what we are meant to be."

⊙ ⊌ ⟿ ⋔ ⌀

A FEW DAYS LATER, FELIX CAME TO VISIT LILITH, BEARING FLOWERS that he'd picked for her in the Megálos. She managed a meek smile, her voice no more than a whisper.

"Wren took me on an hour's brisk ride from the Frourío this morning," Felix said. "We trained in a field full of these blossoms. The violet overpowered the greenery there." He chuckled. "Then we made it all brown."

Lilith scrunched her face, then beamed. "But you saved some for me!"

Felix blushed. "I had to. The color reminded me of Aether."

"Thank you," she said, propping herself up on the pillows.

Felix claimed the seat by her bed, the one Arduen nearly always occupied. She wouldn't be surprised if Felix found it warm. "I realized something today," he mused.

There had been a change in the boy in recent months. It was almost as if his exposure to battle had tempered some of his frivolity, though he was still—by a landslide—the most jubilant of the Divine. Lilith gestured for him to elaborate.

"Well, you see, I was always a little envious of your relationship with Arduen."

Lilith's eyebrows arched at that. "Oh?"

Again, the boy blushed, tucking a mousy tendril of hair behind an ear. "Yes, you two were always close. Like you could just look at each other and have an entire conversation no one else could hear. Since coming here, I wanted that with Wren."

A smile crept onto her face at that. Her relationship with her Master, however currently strained, was one she would treasure until her last breath.

"Like you, I lost my father to Spiro's beasts," Felix said.

"Like you, I am missing an integral presence in my life." He licked his lips, his gaze drifting. Lilith could see his mind working behind his flickering eyes, as if debating whether he should share his sentiments. Lilith hoped that he would.

"I hope you can forgive him," he finally said, "for what happened that night…"

Lilith averted her gaze. She didn't talk of that night with anyone, for so many reasons, and struggled to keep track of them all. She had already forgiven Arduen, her current state making it exceedingly difficult to ignore what mattered most in life. Though perhaps there was a little residual tension lingering.

After a moment of silence, Lilith asked, "What was your realization?"

Felix's solemn expression transformed into a grin, his eyes lighting up with joy. "That Wren and I have achieved the same unity."

"That's wonderful, Felix." Lilith flashed him a saccharine smile.

"Yes, well I just wanted you to know that," he said, rising to his feet. "You should get some rest. I hope the floral aroma is relaxing."

Lilith sniffed the air dramatically. "Why, yes. My muscles are turning to butter as we speak." Felix laughed at that, then took his leave.

Julius entered her room just as Lilith rolled onto her side to attempt to sleep.

"I will come back later," he said, flowers clasped in his hands.

Lilith sat up with a smile, and her eyes flicked between the bouquet in Julius's hands and the one already in a vase on her bedside table.

"It seems that Felix has more charm with the ladies than I."

The prince sauntered across the room, adding his flowers to the vase.

"That he does," Lilith said.

"How are you feeling?" he asked as he took his seat.

Lilith shrugged. "The best I've felt in days, since the night of the raid. I'm tired though, and every time I sleep, my dreams are torturous."

"Tatiana should be able to do something about that. Have you asked her?"

"No." She shook her head. "She's done so much for me already, I don't want to burden her with more."

"Lilith," he gasped, exasperated, "she is here for *you*. If there is anyone here who can make requests, it is Lilith Oak."

Julius was right, as almost always, but there was a part of Lilith that resisted making such requests. There was a certain amount of control she needed to retain, and if she relied upon the Enchantress's remedies for all of her quandaries, how would she ever conquer this?

Silence stole over the room.

"You've been quiet." Lilith reached out and trailed her fingertips up his forearm. A mindless gesture, her feelings rising to the surface. She noted his hesitation at her touch. She only had herself to blame. She had erected a wall between them, more for his benefit than hers. She didn't want him to see her like this. She wanted to smile and laugh and play. But there he was, the benevolent prince, picking up the stones she'd used to build a wall and tossing them away, peeking through the hole he made… just to see if she was really okay. And the fear of him putting those stones back in place. "Something is wrong," she said, retracting her hand.

Julius cocked his head, pretending to be ignorant. He shifted in the chair and glanced out the window at the Galatëa.

"Don't turn away from me, Julius." He was caught off guard

by the command in her tone. "I can see it in your eyes every time you look at me." It was true. He had been so distant, so despondent. It was out of his character entirely. What could be assailing him? "You never asked me, so now I'm asking you: *What* is it?"

The tension between them was palpable as he twisted to face her, his brow furrowed, lips pursed. "Lilith, it is no secret how important you are to me."

Whatever she was expecting, it wasn't that.

"I've just been very concerned for your health," he continued. "I've been under immense pressure to return to Dalegonè, and I do not want to take my leave while you are not conscious to hear my farewell, while I am unsure of your health."

Lilith's stomach knotted. "You're leaving?"

"Of course not. At least not permanently. But my father knows of my graduation. He will want me to return to Xanthë, at least to show my face."

"I don't want you to go," she whispered, hating how pathetic she sounded.

Julius placed his hands over hers and squeezed gently. "I don't either, my kyría."

7

A QUEEN WHO CAN FEEL

It was a stormy evening when Zurí returned to the Frourío, a small cloaked figure in tow. A fortnight had passed since the raid, since Lilith's last episode. She'd endured an onslaught of censure from Olga and Tatiana, but nothing compared to the guilt she felt over convincing Arduen to allow her to participate in battle.

Everyone stood up from the kitchen table to greet the new noviciate, including Lilith. Her name was Aspen. The little girl hailed from a wealthy family in the capital. She was tiny but healthy, plump in all the right places. Her ash blonde hair curled rebelliously, much like Zurí's. Judging by her height, Aspen couldn't have been more than ten. Though she was obviously shy, she reached her little arm out to each of them, offering her hand in greeting.

Lilith couldn't help the smile that stole across her face as her eyes met Aspen's. Flecks of gold decorated her otherwise brown irises, and if Lilith hadn't known without a doubt Kyril had Anointed her, she would have sworn Xander had.

Zurí glanced down upon her new noviciate with fondness, a

twinkle lighting her eyes. "How am I ever going to survive instructing *two* of you?" Her laughter echoed throughout the kitchen.

Aspen's eyes settled on Lilith again, wide with wonder and recognition. "You've been blessed *twice*."

Lilith nodded. "It's not that amazing. It just means that I will be a noviciate twice as long as everyone else." Julius and Felix laughed at that.

Ambrose ushered them back to their seats and set out fresh food for Zurí and Aspen. The girl dug in as if she hadn't had a meal in weeks.

As they sat and listened to Zurí's tales of her tiresome and equally lonely journey, Lilith studied her new colleague. She recalled when Felix had been brought to them, how excited and optimistic he'd been. How he had walked along the beach with her and Julius. She wondered if he would come out and openly inquire as to how Aspen died. Lilith snorted at the thought. But if not for Felix's blunt yet morbid curiosity, she and Julius would not have grown close.

"Are you okay?" Julius asked from beside her, lowering his voice to be inconspicuous.

"Yes, I'm just reminiscing about Felix's first night at the Frourío."

Julius chuckled faintly at that. "She's prickly," he said, echoing Felix's first sentiments of Lilith.

Felix piqued up at that. "Well… you kind of *were*."

"I was," she admitted with a frivolous cackle that caught Arduen's attention.

Her Master ruffled her hair, then snatched his hand away, cradling it against his chest. "She's still prickly," he said, and howling mirth ensued. It was rare for Arduen to jest, and Lilith delighted in it, even if she was the victim of their teasing.

The Oracle couldn't take her eyes off young Aspen, a

beaming smile lit up her face. When she spoke to the young noviciate, Olga's tone became softer, her voice higher in pitch. Lilith had to stifle a snicker every time Olga spoke to Aspen. And when Olga approached the table with fresh pastries she'd made herself that afternoon, the girl squealed with excitement and reached for one immediately.

And Lilith thought, *This is how it should always be.*

◎ ♔ ⌇ ⋔ ◊

ARDUEN HAD BEEN EXCITED FOR THE ADVENT OF A NEW NOVICIATE —a sentiment mirrored by everyone else—but that excitement quickly faded into indifference. Aspen's lilting, high-pitched voice could be heard from the rooftop, even if the little girl was hundreds of feet below in the kitchen. Both Olga and Zurí doted on the girl, baking her sweet treats and reading her bedtime stories. Olga had even spent nights sleeping with her to ease Aspen's lament. Those nights were rough. Just as Aspen's happy voice rang through the fortress, so, too, did her wails of grief. She was homesick, and she missed her family.

Arduen and Lilith sat together in the study. He regarded her from across the table. Looking at her now, at the color in her cheeks, at the slight pensive crease between her brows, he would never know she had suffered at all.

"Have you memorized the Hymn of Divination?" he asked.

Lilith tensed. Of course she'd memorized the verse, she sang it over her brother's corpse, immortalizing Larkin in the sky, securing his place in Elysium. He caught his mistake too late, which, unfortunately for him, seemed to be a recurring short-coming these days.

"Yes…" she grit out.

He cleared his throat. "But do you know the verse in Elder *and* Modern Tongue?" Better. That should cover up his mistake.

"No," she admitted.

Arduen nodded, slightly pleased with himself for orchestrating such a smooth recovery. "Right, then that will be your task for today."

When his command received no immediate reaction, he expelled a sigh and put his hand upon hers, stealing her attention. Lilith abhorred the study, especially when confined to it. Arduen knew how deeply she longed to get back to her training, but that physical aspect of her arsenal would have to flounder in order for her to fully convalesce.

"It will be good to spend more time in the study," he said. "Brains can atrophy just as easily as muscles, and I believe building your wits is more difficult than the latter."

Lilith nodded, though he could tell by her lack of eye contact she didn't really heed his words. She made to stand but he raised his hand to still her. "I wanted to talk to you about something."

She lowered herself back into her seat, her eyes locked on his.

"We seem to be on speaking terms again, given your recent struggles, but I want to take this opportunity to apologize for everything. Lilith, I am truly sorry I did not stand by your side that night. It should have been I in Julius' place, and I will forever regret that I was not there."

Every word was true. He would give anything to do that night over, to get a second chance at being her Master.

I thought of you as a father. But my father never would have left me to handle that in my own.

Arduen hadn't sensed Larkin's approach that night. He'd felt a shift in atmosphere when he died. He came running, praying nothing had happened to his noviciate, just in time to see Lilith sobbing the verses of the Hymn of Divination, a trail of ashes drifting up through the canopy of leaves to settle in the night sky.

"Apology accepted," Lilith said, breaking through his trance.

"I want you to know I never meant to abandon you in that moment," he pressed on. "I left you with those who love you. Now considering what was said at the Temple of Constantine, I would think you did not need me."

Understanding dawned on her face. "I never intended for my wish to be so selfish," she admitted. "Now I see how it works two-fold."

"Your Dâs Thymó is supposed to be selfish, Lilith."

A slight smile spread across her lips and she looked him in the eye. "I did not need you for physical protection. I needed your support. I needed *you*." She removed her hand from beneath his and gripped his tight. "I will always need you."

He squeezed her hand back.

"I carried you home," he said. "I always will." He cleared his throat, releasing her hand. "You and Julius have been getting close."

He watched her expression harden with dread. And almost as if he could read her mind, he knew hers went straight to Jude. His grandson. Judeaus's boy. Lilith was betrothed to him, and as far as Arduen knew, there hadn't been correspondence between them since she had arrived, nearly a year ago. For all they knew, Jude had reconciled himself with his fiancée's untimely death.

"Yes, we have," was her curt response.

Arduen sighed through his nose. How he dreaded this conversation. But the nature of her relationship with Jude necessitated this discussion. "I've learned that loving the wrong person can split you apart."

Lilith raised her hands innocently.

"Just listen." Arduen cast her a pointed look and she ceded, shoulders slumping in defeat. "Loving the *right* person, a love like that can make you whole."

Arduen didn't intend to deter her from the prince. Julius was honorable, and absolutely smitten with Lilith. But he would leave eventually, and well, as practical as it was to take to someone who was promised a similar life span, it was not always the smartest choice.

"I am not going to tell you what to do. Matters of the heart are obscure and precarious. I may never understand what you are feeling, but Julius is an honest man, and I know he holds you highly in his heart. That man almost lost his life so that you didn't have to..." he trailed off. *Kill your brother.*

"I know Julius is good," Lilith said, "but he will become King of Dalegonè. Likely very soon, as you know, his father is not well..." She paused. "And I am not dispositioned to be his queen."

Oh, Lilith. Always so terrified of failing, of ineptitude and rejection.

"Lilith, you are good, too," he said. "You are kind and empathetic. The world could use a queen who can *feel* them, relate to them, suffer alongside her people."

She maintained his stare. "But we are immortal."

"Julius does not plan to rule forever. Has he never spoken to you of this?"

Lilith gave a meek shake of her head. "I think a part of me hoped he would abstain from politics, as you always preached. Especially after fighting Spiro."

There had been many late nights spent in the study with Quintus and Julius, talking of the boy's future as a Divine King. The first ever. Arduen could think of no better man for the position. Divine were not meant to rule, but Julius was the only Fawkes born in the next generation. Arduen and Quin trusted that when Julius had an heir, primed to succeed his father, Julius would leave his kingdom for his children.

"The reason we are not to become entangled in politics is because we are still human… immortal and human," Arduen said. "We are flawed as the rest of our kin. Our longevity defies the nature of politics, for it would be cruel to be ruled by a monarch who could never die."

"Or would have to be brutally murdered," Lilith added.

He chuckled at the morbidity of her statement. "Or would have to step down. Which is difficult for many once they have a taste of power."

"Julius is different," she said, as if she needed to convince him.

"He is the sole heir and his uncle has no children to supply for possible successors, and so the responsibility of rulership falls to Julius."

"Does he truly want it?" she asked in a near whisper. "The throne?"

"Yes," he said. "Julius loves his country dearly. I cannot imagine he would turn his back on them so quickly. He will reign until his heir is of age, and then he will abdicate."

Lilith sat back, and behind her eyes, Arduen could see her brain parsing through all he'd said. "You don't think we should be together," she ventured.

"That's not what I meant," he said. He was a fool to breach the subject, but Lilith had become like a daughter to him, and he intended to school her in all matters of life. And since their existence could very well be endless, there was a lot of raising left to do.

"What did you mean?"

That was a good question. Of all the Divine couples Arduen had known, Spiro and Zurí were the most compatible, the healthiest. And look how that turned out: Spiro sick with

Philautia, off to conquer the world, and Zurí, her face scarred, heart perpetually cloven. Not the best example. But the other relationships had been too passionate. Too volatile. Sometimes, too much of a good thing could be horrendous.

"Trust your gut," Arduen said. "Listen to the Gods' notions. If it feels right, do not give up on Julius. Not because of station or distance. You can overcome both."

When his small oration was met with an astute frown, he added, "Talk to Julius. He cares enough about you to be unvarnished."

And he left it at that.

◎ ⓣ ⤏ ⋔ ◖

Lilith twirled as slowly as she could.

"Still too fast!" Arduen chided from a distance. Her Master stood watch with Quin as she and Julius sparred in slow motion, analyzing and critiquing their movements.

"If I go any slower, I won't move at all!" she rebutted. The coddling frustrated her. And she would never reach graduation —the point of proficiency—if her training were constantly mired by seizures.

Julius barked a laugh, his hands splayed on her back, molding her form and critiquing every movement with microscopic scrutiny. "You're getting there. You haven't lost much technique over the past two months," he commended.

Lilith frowned when he pulled his hands away. "That may be, but I've lost a lot of strength."

"It will come back," Quin said, "once Tatiana says you're in the clear."

Arduen eased Lilith back into training. He'd spent too long agonizing over her welfare to disregard safety. His compromise was simple: she would spend her mornings in the study learning Elder Tongue, then she would receive one-hour instruction outdoors in the training field.

One of the stipulations of their compromise was practicing maneuvers only. They would be training for style and technique, not speed and agility. Arduen had claimed that her strength was illusory. That it would deceive her into pushing herself too hard, and there needed to be strict limitations set in place to avoid such a disaster. Arduen was terrified to provoke another episode. Lilith could see it in his eyes when he looked at her, as if she were delicate like glass, that if she broke again, she may never be pieced back together. Such fears were understandable, Lilith felt them, too. But she wouldn't let herself sit around whilst the others grew stronger. Even going through the motions would be more beneficial than sitting idle.

Their Masters waved as they took their leave, assured that Lilith was safe in Julius's care. She smiled to herself as they marched toward the beach. If they weren't watching, she would likely be spending more time under the prince's hands.

Julius paused. "What?"

Lilith shook her head clear. "What do you mean *'what'*? Help me." She giggled as he continued to shape her body. "What I wouldn't give to run right now, or truly spar."

"We can pick up the pace slightly. That is, if you're feeling up to it?" He stepped back, biting his lower lip.

Excitement mushroomed inside her. "Of course! I feel great. I've been feeling fine for nearly two whole weeks."

Judging by the expression on his face, he appeared to be convincing himself rather than heeding her statement, but he didn't object. He took up his sparring position as she settled into her own. Julius decided to wield their rightful swords rather than the wooden mock weapons. Steel was lighter and wouldn't place her muscles under too much strain. Lilith didn't argue, of course. The closer she could get to a real fight, the better. She needed to feel something. Anything other than self-pity that the perpetual boredom instilled.

The hilt of Constance warmed under her palms. It had been too long since she'd danced with her mother's sword in her hands. The leather of the hilt was comforting in a way that it probably shouldn't have been, but it was. It reminded her of her journey to the Frourío, how deeply Arduen cared for her instruction, putting up with her resentful insolence.

Pouring every last drop of energy into her attempt to appear as spry as she'd been before she fell ill, Lilith lunged at her adversary.

Their blades met with an audible clash, and immediately, she was aware of just how much Julius was holding back. If he was impressed by her speed, he didn't show it. He was likely too focused on refraining from hurting her, watching every movement with calculated scrutiny. If she moved too quick, he would reprimand her, of that she was certain.

"Easy…" he cautioned, receding.

Careless of the sweat beading her brow, Lilith dove toward him, Constance outstretched before her, cutting down at his blade.

"I'm not a horse!" she snapped as she jabbed at his exposed abdomen. She was far from exertion, she only needed to prove it.

Julius parried the blow with little effort. Was she really that weak? Had her muscles really atrophied that much? Determination fueled her resolve to spar unleashed. Lilith grunted as she danced before Julius, twisting and turning in her attempts to catch him off guard.

He hopped away from her. "All right, that's enough."

But it was too late.

A blood-curdling cry burst from her lips, her body contracting fitfully, every muscle screaming for relief. She'd lost control again. The flames tore through her body, the incursion sudden and overwhelming.

Julius faded from sight. There may have been hands upon her, holding her down so she couldn't hurt herself, but they were phantom touches. Distant, leaving her adrift. Alone.

And when her eyes closed for that brilliant respite, Arduen's worried face was indelibly branded to the backs of her eyelids.

⌀ ⌀ ⌀ ⌀ ⌀

LILITH CAME TO, HER BODY A HEAP OF KNOTS AND BRUISES, BUT otherwise at peace. Julius sat in the rocking chair at her side, a rueful expression plastered across his regal face. Zurí was screaming vitriol at Arduen down in the kitchen, and several floors above her, Aspen was bellowing her own harangue.

At the sight of her open eyes, Julius was at her side instantly, on his knees, his hands clutching her own.

"I'm so sorry," she said, bowing her head shamefully. "I should have never pushed myself so hard."

"Lilith…" He reached out to stroke her hair away from her face. "I should never have agreed. It's my fault. I know how desperately you want things to return to normal, but they can't until you are truly recovered." His tone was soothing, allaying, anything but contemptuous. Which, in her mind, was what she deserved. This was her fault. No one else deserved blame.

Squeezing his hands, Lilith pulled him into her and muttered her acquiescence. She wouldn't do it again. Not that she could. After this, she'd be lucky if anyone let her out of her room, even to relieve herself.

I will refuse a bedpan until my final breath!

"I am a Master," Julius said, "and yet I put you in this position. I failed you. The person I care about…"

Lilith pulled away slightly, looking up into his eyes. "Julius, you cannot blame yourself for this. I was utterly asinine."

He bowed his head, his brow resting against her own, his lips so close. Lilith's eyes drifted down to them, then back up to those amber eyes. This was not the time for such affection, but resistance was futile when they were this close. She shifted, pressing her mouth against his. Julius cupped her face, pulling her closer, his breath growing heavy. Ragged. Desperate.

Moments like this were rare. Moments like this were cathartic.

Lilith's hands gripped his tense body, tugging at his tunic in an attempt to feel his skin beneath her fingers.

The door opened, and Julius jolted, running his hands over his shirt, flattening it. Arduen cleared his throat audibly as he entered. He inclined his head toward the door, eyes pinned on Julius. The prince pursed his lips and took his leave without a backward glance.

Lilith flushed as Arduen's gaze fell on her, heavy with the reminder of their previous conversation. "I'm sorry," she muttered.

Arduen seated himself on the bed beside her. "A letter arrived for Julius this afternoon," he said. "Dalegonians believe that the Crown Prince has renounced his claim to the throne as he has not graced his homeland with his presence in the six years since his Anointment. He must return before the winter sets in."

Lilith covered her face with her hands, concealing her contorted features as she began to sob. She couldn't go on like this. She'd let her relationship with Julius languish as she mourned her brother, and now she was going to lose him, too.

Arduen pulled her hands away from her face. "He won't be gone forever, my fledgling." With gentle fingers, he tilted her face up, forcing her to meet his eyes. "Julius is not guilty of defection. He loves his people. He will return, as is his duty. He will refute any accusations of dereliction. Then he will return to us." He wiped her tears with his thumb, but the tender gesture only encouraged more tears.

"Until then," Arduen continued, "we must make a trip to Kenora to welcome the Walabeäns and convene with the captain and the generals. It will be a lengthy trip that could be extended. If I thought you well enough to come along, I'd take you. But as it turns out, you are not ready."

"No!" she cried. It was difficult to accept this as the new normal. Especially when her understanding of her state was rudimentary, limited to the unknown, which was simply terrifying. Having to come to terms with it all without Arduen at her side, that was unfathomable.

"Lilith, I will return to you as soon as it is possible. You will have Tatiana here, and Zurí will remain with Aspen. Do what you can to help her Master the youngling." He wiped her tears again.

"Don't go, Arduen. Please." She clung to him like a mollusk.

He stiffened. The use of his name seemed to draw his attention to her without fail.

"Don't leave me here," she pleaded. "I will wilt if you do."

Arduen bowed his head in regret. "I won't leave until you have recovered a little more. Rest and we will see just how well you are when, in a couple of weeks, the day of departure arrives. If Tatiana condones it, you may accompany us."

After this last episode, Lilith knew Tatiana would deny her request to travel. The situation was moot. No one would let her leave the Frourío for months.

She watched in solemn silence as Arduen made his way to the door. He halted at the threshold and said, "I am placing a moratorium on your training for now. And, Lilith," he turned, looking at her pointedly, "there will be no flouting this rule."

8

DEEP ENOUGH TO BE LETHAL

Rhéa sat back, the grating creak of her chair stoking her agitation. Her gaze settled on the young Enchantress before her. Irís had taken the lead, healing man after man, bearing their sordid company whilst Rhéa tended to the beasts. The day would be long for Irís, as more human patients flooded into the infirmary than beasts. But Rhéa was confident in Irís's will to persist, her proclivity for hard work.

Irís glanced over her shoulder at Rhéa, her gaze imploring. It was high time for a break.

"One more!" Rhéa called across the dank chamber.

The girl's frail shoulders slumped, and she sent her last victim on his way when the next exploded into the room, blood pouring from a gash in his head.

Irís jumped back as the beast sank into the chair before her with a forceful grunt. The wood groaned under his weight, but the brute ignored it, pointing at his torn head, the white of his skull visible.

Rhéa watched intently, studying how Irís handled herself.

"You can take this one, Irís." It would be the girl's first beast, but she had handled far worse in the soldiers' barracks back at the Emperor's castle. As expected, Irís steeled her spine at Rhéa's words and accepted her new patient with grace.

Impressed, a smug smile stole over Rhéa's features. She was proud of the progress the girl was making. Irís had been thrilled to discover that she was an Enchantress. Rhéa understood that feeling all too well. Though she was born in the Obsydían Marsh, she could understand the overwhelming sense of purpose one gained when they discovered their true nature. That's how she'd felt when she'd been Blessed by Amalthea.

Many years would elapse before Irís would swear herself to the Obsydían Marsh, and many years yet until she experienced the Blessing. It would be her decision which coven she swore herself to. Rhéa only prayed it would be the Ilíos—her own coven—devoted to the Southern Guiding Star, Amalthea.

Irís fumbled with the vials nervously, the harsh groans and grunts of displeasure from the beast shattering her confidence. Rhéa studied her through slitted eyes. These beasts were nettlesome, yes, but if Irís was going to be an Enchantress, she would need to hold her own regardless of external pressures. The girl pulled the stopper from a vial of cleansing solvent and poured the solution over the beast's gash.

The skin surrounding the wound began to bubble. The beast erupted. The chair fissured and crumpled beneath his weight as he rose to tower over the young Enchantress, pounds of muscle rippling beneath its olive hide.

Xavier stormed into the infirmary, rage distorting his features until he was almost unrecognizable. He latched on to the beast's back and pulled him to the ground before it could pummel its fist into Irís's gaping face.

The beast, fueled by an irascible, atavistic instinct to

defend, righted itself and barreled into Xavier. The Divine recoiled in feigned agony, coaxing the beast into believing it would be the victor. Desks were shattered, chairs were thrown, tables were overturned. Blood sprayed. Howls ensued. Beasts crammed in the archway leading out to the arena, eager to see the cause of commotion. They wouldn't intervene, not with Spiro's favored noviciate meting out punishment.

Once the initial shock had worn off, Rhéa shook her head clear, forcing incisive thoughts. She bounded from her seat, took hold of Irís, and pulled her toward the second exit.

"Xavier!" Irís shrieked.

Rhéa held firm. "We must leave. Now."

Irís stuttered, her body trembling vigorously, "B-but it will k-kill Xavier… and on *my* behalf. I can't have that!"

Rhéa's chest caved. "I understand, but Xavier is Divine for a reason. You, on the other hand, are small. They could kill you in the scrabble." She wrapped her hand around Irís's wrist and pulled until she relented, the girl's head whipping back to watch Xavier as they took their leave.

Rhéa couldn't be certain if their friend was winning or not, but she needed to get Irís away before the infirmary became an slaughterhouse.

⊙ ⊙ ↝ ℳ δ

"How could you just leave him?" Irís drilled Rhéa with her searing gaze. The girl paced Rhéa's bedchamber, wearing a path in the plush rug.

"Think of it this way, little dove," Rhéa said. "If Xavier went through Hades trying to save you from that cretin, and he lost his life only for you to lose yours as well, would his valor be in vain?"

Irís halted her pacing. Without admitting that Rhéa was right, she crossed her lithe arms across her chest and pouted.

Satisfied, Rhéa said, "We will wait here for him and tend to his wounds when he arrives."

"But we don't have supplies," Irís countered. "All of the vials are in the infirmary."

Rhéa grinned. *They're probably shattered.* But the Enchantress concealed her doubt and fished two vials from the inside pocket of her gown. "An Enchantress of the Ilíos is never unprepared for duty." Truthfully, it was a modicum of what they would likely need. But if they ran out, Rhéa could resort to magic for the cleansing of the wounds, and a traditional needle and thread for sutures.

Irís's steely gaze softened, and she lowered herself onto the bed beside Rhéa. "I just pray he comes soon."

Xavier and Irís had become close as of late, and Rhéa feared for them both. Spiro's lair was not a place to fall in love. It was almost as horrendous as falling in love in the Obsydían Marsh —as she and Miles had. Though Irís and Xavier weren't particularly amorous, they were obviously flirtatious. Rhéa was no foreigner to a lovesick glance, and Irís and Xavier had exchanged many.

"My dove, please keep your heart guarded," Rhéa said. "Be wise about the decisions you make down here." She placed her hand upon Irís's knee, hoping that her maternal touch would placate any anger that her warning may have birthed.

"I should know better," Irís admitted, "but I can't resist. Xavier is incredible! He can take any beast or man, and he is humble about it. Spiro has blessed him immeasurably, and he still has his wits about him."

"Remember that Xavier is sworn to Spiro…"

Irís waved her off, clearly ignorant of the implications of the Blood Oath. That would be a conversation for Xavier to have with her. "He is so sweet and respectful and kind and… I want to bask in his Divine presence until my dying day."

Rhéa remembered that feeling. Viscerally. She wanted nothing more than to spend every moment with her betrothed until he passed, when she would still be young, and he would be withered and gray.

Before Rhéa could pay the girl another warning, the door burst open and Xavier strode in. He brought with him the acrid scent of ichor. He was covered in blood, but plastered on his face, beneath all the gore, was a triumphant grin.

"Do not worry, my ladies," he said. "I've decimated the beast with brutal efficacy."

Irís squealed, prancing toward him. "My savior!" She wrapped her arms around him and kissed his face, painting her own red and black.

Xavier leaned away from her and laughed at the sight of her grimy cheeks. "Now we both need to be cleaned up!" Firmly, he shut the door behind him and approached Rhéa, his arm wrapped around Irís's slim waist, the girl glancing at him with glassy eyes.

Stars bless her!

"Irís," Rhéa turned to the girl, "please go fetch a bucket of clean water for Xavier while I tend to his wounds." The young Enchantress dipped her chin obediently.

Xavier plopped his body down onto the bed with a sigh. "Well, that was fun. Fights are so much more fulfilling when there's a cause."

Rhéa snorted. "There isn't a cause every other day?"

"Maintaining Master's favor is not difficult, especially when I control the air surrounding my opponents."

"Where are you hurting?"

Xavier glanced down at his body. "I'm mostly fine, but his

talons got me in a few places. We will have to clean those wounds first."

Rhéa nodded. She had become accustomed to the poison coating the beasts' talons, knowing the signs of resulting burns that lingered too long, eventually growing like a virus and claiming whole limbs—and the lesions that took lives within hours. It cost many men their lives when they'd first arrived. If her powers weren't strong—which they weren't under fàrmako's thrall—and she didn't get to them in time, they would surely suffer a long, arduous terminus.

Xavier pointed to all of his wounds, and Rhéa began to mutter Elder Tongue under her breath. She prayed that lovesick girl would hurry back so she could begin.

Rhéa pulled Xavier's tunic over his head, exposing his bare torso. He'd packed on an impressive sum of muscle. He'd had no choice; if he wanted to remain favored by Spiro, he needed to be strong. Xavier did not protest as she exposed his body, and he remained compliant as she checked over each wound, prodding and probing as necessary. Despite his position, Xavier was a man of exceptional decorum, and under any other circumstances, she would have given Irís her approval. But, alas, the situation was much too dire to allow for the flourishing of love.

The girl stormed into the room, two buckets hanging at her sides. She stopped dead when her eyes settled on Xavier, lying nude on the bed, and her lips parted slightly in surprise—or awe—Rhéa couldn't tell.

"Enough gaping," Rhéa snapped. "Get over here!"

Irís obliged.

"Clean that wound." Rhéa pointed to a small gash on his upper thigh. Then she regretted giving Irís a wound so close to his exposed groin. With a sigh, she placed a cloth over his manhood, which Xavier held in place, his body tense, almost rigid.

Irís began to work, and together they wiped the gore from his limbs. When he was clean, Rhéa poured the contents of the vials over his wounds.

"There!" Rhéa said. "That will kill the venom. In a minute, I will—"

Xavier stopped her short, placing a gentle touch on her forearm. "Just stitch me up. Don't expel all your energy on me. These aren't deep enough to be lethal."

Rhéa released a long sigh, debating her options. She wasn't strong under Spiro's hand, with fàrmako devouring her celestial magic, but she wasn't the only person in the room who possessed the gifts of the Stars. "The needles and thread are back in the infirmary." Rhéa lied. "We will have to use magic."

Irís's concerned glance wavered between them. "I can do it," she offered. "You can teach me."

"Fine." Rhéa stepped back to consider the girl. Beginning her training on a patient would be risky. There was much that could go awry and cause detriment to Xavier. But Rhéa was nearby, and if need be, she could shield Xavier from Irís's flow of magic easily, and hopefully counteract any damage. "All right," she ceded. "It's your time to shine, little dove."

Narrow shoulders squaring, Irís assumed position above Xavier.

"You must say 'Tristè seâte Esír pevër unt Vën.' It means: '*Stars vest Your power in Me.*'"

Irís repeated the mantra several times before she got the pronunciation right.

"Do you have that memorized?" Rhéa asked.

Irís nodded eagerly, her pretty face set in a stern pout.

"Now hold your right hand over each wound."

"Why my right hand?" Irís inquired.

"Because your Mark is behind your left ear."

"So?"

Rhéa sighed. "It means that the magic has claimed the left side of your brain, so it will flow from your right hand."

Irís stared at her palm in wonder before holding it above Xavier's thigh.

"Repeat after me," Rhéa said. "Câstré."

Irís repeated the word, and her palm lit up. The glow was faint and pale, colorless because she hadn't been sworn to a coven, to one of the Guiding Stars.

"Great!" Rhéa commended. "Now that you have fully cleansed the wound, it is time to heal it." With her gaze planted firmly upon Irís, she said, "Hyàss."

Irís repeated the word and the wound knitted together slowly. She jumped away from the bed in shock.

Xavier reached out to grasp her. "It's all right, Irís."

"I did that?" Irís turned to Rhéa with wide eyes.

The Enchantress chuckled. "That you did, but you have more work to do. Do you remember the word for cleansing?"

Irís nodded.

"Good." Rhéa smiled at her apprentice. "Proceed."

Irís repeated the word and, upon her command, the discharge from Xavier's gash went limpid.

9

THIS PIECE OF GOLD

Tatiana muttered ancient words as she performed her ministrations, massaging a liniment into Lilith's tense muscles, increasing each ingredient by one or two fluidrachms. Her deft fingers targeted specific points, releasing the pressure that ultimately resulted in Lilith's seizures.

Arduen and Olga stood at the far end of the room, keeping watch over the procession, awaiting Tatiana's verdict. If the Enchantress declared Lilith capable, then she would be free to travel to the capital with her comrades.

Lilith swallowed her whines of protest as Tatiana slowly pulled her blouse over her head and removed her breeches. It wouldn't be the first time Arduen had seen her nearly nude, but still she was shy. Fortunately, her Master pointedly took his leave.

The Enchantress clicked her tongue against the roof of her mouth, but otherwise, she remained silent, kneading Lilith's legs. When finished, she ordered Lilith to turn over and began to massage her back, pulling the quilt over Lilith's bottom to grant her *some* privacy.

The suspense was stifling.

"Well, you've been clear of seizures for a couple of weeks," the Enchantress said. "The color has returned to your skin and you can climb the stairs without panting. It seems to me that you are well on your way to recovery."

Lilith beamed at the good news.

"But I am not sure you should be traveling great distances."

Lilith's heart crumpled. Quietly, she dressed herself and, at the Oracle's behest, Arduen returned.

"I have been summoned back to the Obsydían Marsh," Tatiana said. "I will set out before you take your leave for Kenora."

"What shall we do to ensure her continued recovery?" Olga inquired, eyes wide and round with maternal concern.

"I will leave with you a list of herbs that will help her," Tatiana said. "Add them to every meal. I will also leave some vials of this liniment. I have procured it specifically for her." She turned to Lilith and said, "Place two drops beneath your nose before you sleep. This will aid in a deeper sleep. As I have mentioned before, rest will regenerate your body naturally."

Lilith nodded.

"And she will need a nightly massage like the one I've just demonstrated."

Tatiana and the Oracle continued to confer, exiting the room together. Arduen remained, lowering himself onto the edge of the bed, expression stridently remorseful. "Lilith—"

"Please, don't leave me," she interjected. "Please, Arduen."

He heaved an anguished sigh. "I don't want to leave you. But I've duties to attend to. I won't be gone longer than a month."

"Please, let me come along. I'll stay close to you, amenable to all you ask. Please." Lilith grasped his hand, her grip desperate, imploring.

"I will talk further with Tatiana," he said. "I promise that I will see what I can do. It is not too cold yet, but it will be autumn when we return. I think the Enchantress is worried about exposing you to the colder climate."

Leaning into him, her muscles relaxed, her head coming to rest on his shoulder. "Please," she whispered. "I will take my heaviest cloak and my fur-lined leathers."

"I will see, little one," he said. "Until then, rest."

◎ ☺ ⌇ ⁓ ᴍ ◊

FOLLOWING A FITFUL NAP, LILITH JOINED THE OTHERS FOR THE evening meal. The Divine of the Frourío aggregated in the kitchen, the massive chamber alight with energy. Julius and Felix sat before the hearth, playing a game of Sixth Gladius. Julius always won, but Felix was spritely and would turn to pounding upon his opponent with his fists, claiming the prince had cheated. Their laughter resounded throughout the room.

At the kitchen table, Zurí was hovering over her young noviciate, her expressions dramatic as she told the girl some grand tale. These were the only moments Aspen was actually quiet. In the presence of the young girl, Zurí completely relinquished her stoical mien, allowing for a more carefree version of herself take precedence. Lilith wondered if this was what a young Zurí looked like, brimming with joy and mirth.

Lilith couldn't deny that the presence of the girl had affected the entire Frourío, the atmosphere was jovial, and she knew that could never be a bad thing, regardless of her own ailments.

At the table, Arduen was locked in a tense conversation with Quin and Wren. Lilith lowered herself into the seat beside her Master. She didn't interrupt them, but when she tucked her chair in, they turned in her direction.

"How are you feeling?" Arduen asked as Quin's and Wren's eyes fell on her with expectation.

"I'm well."

Arduen gestured to the other men. "We were just discussing the possibility of your presence in the capital."

Lilith awaited her fate with bated breath. She so desperately wanted to escape the Frourío.

"We believe that it would be wise to bring you along," Arduen said, "though you must remain close by my side. Tatiana has given me a list of herbs and instructions so that I may tend to you in her absence. But mark my words, child, there will be no training sessions."

Elation burst inside her and she embraced her Master, crushing her cheek against his hard shoulder. "Thank you," she murmured.

"Don't thank me yet! It is a long trip, and you'll be tired. I will do my best to tend to you, though I won't be as gentle as your healer." He eyed Tatiana and Olga in the kitchen with Ambrose, conversing about Gods knew what.

None of it mattered. Lilith was going to the capital!

THE JOURNEY TO THE CAPITAL WAS AS ARDUEN HAD FOREWARNED. Lilith had to stop several times to stretch, her legs stiff from riding. She had cramps in her quads that she feared would erupt into another episode. Arduen had rushed to her side, Julius close behind him, only for the pain to subside, slowly ebbing away.

After the second day, Arduen put his foot down and tied Skydancer—Lilith's chestnut gelding—to the rear of his mare, and she was forced to ride with him. Apparently, each of her movements bespoke exhaustion. Any attempt at disabusing

Arduen's concerns as paranoia failed. With Arduen holding the reins, she was able to relax her sore muscles, basking in the reprieve.

Lilith was happy to be free of the Frourío, no longer encumbered by her ailments. She began to wonder what it would feel like to be completely unfettered by such a strange malady. Who would have thought that her bed would become an anathema?

The days flew by spent seated in the saddle before Arduen. She found that riding with him allowed for her eyes to wander more, and on several occasions, she fell asleep with the back of her head resting against his shoulder, one of his arms wrapped around her to keep her secured.

Arduen was beyond worried, that much was patent in the way he coddled her. He never took his eyes off her, and she could bet he barely slept through the night.

"Evös has flown ahead to announce our arrival to the Emperor's servants," Arduen said. "I have requested joint chambers in the castle. I want to be close by just in case, and I need to ensure that you are taking your medicine."

Lilith humphed once to confirm she'd heard him.

⊙⃛ ʊ ⤙ ℳ ᕔ

"Tristè, dasírrè Vën sadiffe qístés."

Stars, safeguard me against disarray.

Tatiana inhaled, bracing herself for the cool flush of magic in her veins.

"Tristè, succè Vën unt Esír híne."

Stars, root me in Your light.

She let her feet fall to the damp earth, the rain pounding against the hood of her cloak, the long curls of her mahogany hair hanging limp down her breasts.

"Tristè, væth ustè vhis Von punnite."

Stars, take only what I possess.

A shiver coursed through her body, her energy sparking to life, converting to fuel her magic.

"Tristè, cârre Vën taníffass soulè qu ether."

Stars, carry me southward through the Aether.

The wind surrounding her churned with celestial magic, and Tatiana was swallowed whole, stealing the breath from her lungs. The beginnings of a scream died on her lips as the spell transported her miles ahead.

It was the same every time. One minute spent being blinded by the void, the cool wind unsettling her clothing, her hands clasped firmly around the thin leather strap of her travel bag. The Enchantress gritted her teeth against the strain on her lithe frame, praying the Stars would deliver her soon.

And just as abruptly as it began, it ended.

Tatiana was spit out, plummeting to the ground, the entire world at a standstill. Vertigo and nausea wracked her, the contents of her belly threatening to spill. She stared at her hands, knuckle deep in the muck. This spell used every last ounce of her energy, but the beauty of it was the speed with which she could travel, and the fact that she could not die. A crafty spell, one she created herself and shared with only her Second and Third.

Panting, she gave her body a few minutes to recover, her fingers numb, twitching in the mud. The back of her hands were liver-spotted and she could identify every bone and tendon through the sallow, thin skin. The hands of someone who had worked and seen centuries. In an hour, the skin would thicken and the blemishes would fade, her muscles would strengthen and her bones wouldn't feel so damn weary.

"One more time, Tatiana," she muttered to herself. Her chest constricted, her heart pounding within, the beat visible between her sagging breasts. Those, too, would regain their usual volume and firmness.

Rising, Tatiana scanned the horizon. The night was slowly ebbing away in a sweet surrender to the sun. As an Enchantress of the Illíos coven, Tatiana would experience an influx of power with the sunlight.

She was ahead of schedule, having spent the past four days traveling toward the capital. Kenora was a distant hum calling out to her, a beacon of sound alerting her to the finish line. She could rest at an inn before she was to complete the purpose of her journey. And then she would return to the Marsh. And to Ophelía's wrath.

The High Enchantress consented to sending a healer from the Illíos for Lilith Oak. She did not, however, consent to that Enchantress being Tatiana, First of the Illíos. Even if Phoebe, Tatiana's Second, was more than capable of occupying her place in the temporary absence of her First.

Tatiana sighed, the muscles between her ribs stretching painfully. Travel wore her down, especially using such a taxing spell. But she had to arrive before the Divine.

Lilith needed the protection of the ring, but Tatiana couldn't just gift it to her back at the Frourío with no reason at all. Such an act would brook questions, and she did not want the elder Divine knowing Lilith possessed the most valuable object in the world.

Tatiana had spent decades protecting the ring from Ophelía's greedy fingers. She'd enchanted the metal, making it appear old and dirty, the gold tarnished from years of wear, the intricate engravings only noticeable when inspected up close. It would pass as a family heirloom, only valuable to those who had memories affixed to the ring.

Tatiana had memories, moments in time that one glance at the ring would conjure, feelings she couldn't shake once they rose up. That's why she wore it around her neck on a chain, not on her finger where she was supposed to. She would give it to Lilith, warning and all, and pray to the Stars that the girl wore it always.

The ring would tether Lilith to this realm during her seizures. The bane of her existence. The reason Tatiana was able to meet her only granddaughter for the first time. Stars, Rhéa's daughter was as beautiful as her mother, magic or no. And she was immortal. Tatiana prayed there would be many more chances to see Lilith again, perhaps at a time when revealing her relation to Lilith wouldn't be so staggering, unsettling. Rhéa had really made a mess, but Tatiana couldn't deny her daughter her twenty years of life outside the Marsh any more than she could resist stealing away to aid her granddaughter.

Dark magic clung to Lilith like a second skin. Tatiana sensed it the moment the dense pines parted and the looming tower of the Divine came into view. The stench of death and rot permeated the holy grounds, most noticeable in Lilith's bedchamber. Tatiana attempted to trace the magic back to its source but to no avail. Whoever was responsible—and there was someone indeed—they were adept at concealing their trail. But not the evidence.

Such magic was forbidden within the Obsydían Marsh. If an Enchantress was capable of such maleficence, she would have to travel far away from the Marsh to perform such a spell. An ongoing spell at that. A spell that would leach the life from enemies with every attack on the victim. If there was a trail of death in this Enchantress's wake, they were clever with their cleanliness.

The ring was the only way Tatiana could ensure Lilith would be safe. She just had to get it on her finger. Only then would she return to the Marsh.

But first, Kenora.

"Only one more time, Tatiana," the Enchantress mumbled, her tongue swollen, her saliva thick. Exhaustion was close, but the spell would not leave her bereft of sustenance. She would enter the city, and then she would find a bed and collapse into it.

"Tristè, dasírrè Vën sadiffe qístés."

Stars, safeguard me against disarray.

AS USUAL, LILITH SENSED THE ROAR OF THE CAPITAL LONG BEFORE she set her eyes upon the great city nestled in the center of a gargantuan depression in the land. Her current range with Discernment was surprisingly vast in comparison to her dissipated strength; a sign she was on the mend. The others had heard it too, she noted, as their shoulders squared, their spines straightening in anticipation.

Arduen chose to enter through the eastern gate behind the Emperor's castle. It was one of the lesser-traveled arteries in Kenora and essential if one of import wished to avoid fanfare.

The blazing sun bathed the streets with its golden rays. At first, the sight of the city inspired an excitement that Lilith had been bereft of for months, but after they passed through the gates and the people were alerted to their Divine presence, she drew her hood up over her head once again.

The stench of the Plebes' refuse was more than repellant, and she began to wonder why Arduen had decided to enter the city through the eastern, less popular gate. She crinkled her nose and discreetly studied the others for signs of discomfort. Only Felix adopted a similarly disgruntled grimace, eyeballing his Master mounted beside him. Wren artfully ignored his noviciate, his eyes scanning the street for threats.

An imperial servant approached them, indicating to

dismount. He would be escorting their steeds to the stables. Arduen allowed Lilith to ride Skydancer into the city to avoid rumors of her ill health. From only two hours of riding, her legs were sore, and she struggled to lift one over the gelding's back.

"Here," Julius said, placing his hands around her waist and lowering her to the ground. The act would seem gentlemanly to any onlookers. No one needed to know that assistance was necessary.

"Thank you," she said with a small smile, and Julius winked at her before following the others down the road to the castle. Lilith could have sworn a flush colored his golden-brown cheeks.

Inhabitants of Kenora flogged toward them, the excitement and awe overwhelming. They called their names, praises of adoration sang from their lips. Lilith ignored them all whilst she sauntered to Arduen's side. Her limbs felt spindly, but she didn't dare do anything to betray that feeling to Arduen, lest he subject her to bed rest.

Murmurs of "Kin-Slayer," ricocheted off the walls of the city. She'd ended her brother's life as a *mercy*, not a punishment. He was never truly her enemy. That place was reserved for Spiro alone.

A hunched, wizened lady approached them, and Arduen halted kindly to allow her to speak. Lilith regarded the woman with astute wariness. It was as if some alien force clouded her; a mythical, magical aura beyond her recognition. The lady was much too small and frail to be a great threat. Her olive skin hung loose around her face, framing bright golden eyes. Her gray hair was a curtain of matted waves nearly reaching the ground beneath her bare feet.

"Lilith Oak," the lady croaked.

Lilith cast a quick glance at her Master, a question in her

eyes. Should she approach the lady? Did he sense something she could not?

Arduen nodded to his noviciate, acknowledging that he deemed the lady harmless.

"I have felt a pull toward you since you first arrived," she said, stretching her hand out to Lilith. Her arm trembled, as if the action summoned all of her energy.

Lilith grasped her hand gently in greeting, the way she had when she first met Julius. As her fingers wrapped around the woman's dainty wrist, an undeniable sense of magic coursed through her like a spark of electricity. She gasped and flinched, but the lady did not seem to notice.

"I know that many of us Plebeians dote on the Gods' disciples without relent, but my gift will serve a far greater purpose in your life." She reached into her pocket, and Arduen placed a reassuring hand on Lilith's spine, communicating that he was there should the lady prove hostile. But what cretin would attack a Divine in front of the Emperor's castle? Certainly not a little old lady.

"This ring is more than just a fine piece of jewelry, my dear. The wearer will find that this piece of gold becomes so much more when they are in need of great assistance. Wear this ring on the middle finger of your left hand, and never take it off." She placed her shaking hand in Lilith's, and when she pulled away, Lilith could feel the cold metal in her palm.

"Thank you," Lilith said, turning slightly toward Arduen. Her Master took the ring, holding it close to his eyes for inspection. As Lilith waited, she found it impossible to unfasten her eyes from the lady's. The golden irises, though dotted by cataracts and glassy with age, were warm and vaguely familiar.

When Arduen grunted his approval and handed the ring back to her, Lilith said, "I will wear it always."

"Well, put it on then!" the old lady said with a chuckle.

Lilith started, her trance broken, and placed the ring on her middle finger.

"Good," the lady said. "Remember: *never* take it off. This ring could save your life." How a ring could save her life, Lilith had no idea. How the woman had come to that conjecture, that was the real mystery.

Lilith glanced down to inspect the ring. It was solid gold, with worn, intricate engravings wrapped around the entirety of the band. It was beautiful and simple. Similar to the ring she'd crafted for Tavisk and Kathleen. Curiosity sparked, Lilith lifted her attention from the ring to ask the lady for the metalsmith's name, but she was already gone.

THE SAVIOR

Several days following the incident in the bathing pool, the Emperor's Epistaís—dignitaries—visited the soldiers' barracks. Hestîa tamped down her irritation and ignored their intrusive inspection as they weaved through the bunks. Their delayed arrival only proved how little the Emperor respected women, especially those who favored leather over silk, steel over lace.

Hestîa sat alone on her bunk, the others having gone out to the field to train. There was a training courtyard designated for the soldiers, but the Walabeäns needed freedom and fresh air, not four stone walls and a patch of grass.

The end of summer was unusually sweltering, and Hestîa resisted the urge to dress more modestly. Ever since the incident with the Augustan soldier, she'd become self-conscious of every curve of her body. She bathed only when the other women did, the only time the Augustans knew when to avoid the bathing chamber. It was tedious, having her guard up at all times, but it was utterly necessary. She was to be an example for the others, and young as she was, she would not fail the women she'd been chosen to lead.

Hestîa started as Agónas claimed a seat on the cot opposite hers. When her eyes met his, those beautiful blue irises had lost their brilliance. "Agónas..."

"Hestîa, *don't*."

She went rigid at his tone.

"General Achilles has ordered all of the servant women out of the barracks," Agónas said. "There will be no further instances like the last one." He paused. So many unspoken words tainted the air between them. "Captain Vaughn argues that his men need that form of release, so the women will be brought down to serve the Augustan soldiers for one hour every evening, following dinner. I've ordered our warriors to remain at our bunks during this time. It is your responsibility to apprise the other women."

Agónas stood to leave, but Hestîa reached out, halting him. She'd be damned if she let another moment pass where their minds were not settled. He needed to know that her loyalties lay with him, that he was the only man occupying her heart, the only man whose hands should rest upon her bare skin.

"Agónas, about the incident..." She bit her lip, pulse thundering an alarum. "I thought that man was you. When I saw his tanned skin, I knew it to be a stranger. Please believe me when I say you are the only man of my heart."

His eyes slowly softened as the words escaped her lips. "I believe you. Know that it has taken all of my self-control not to beat in the head of that soldier."

Relief flooded through her. "This is about so much more than us, Agónas."

"I know," he shrugged, defeated. "That is why I keep my distance from the Augustans, lest my emotions get the better of my behavior... and I break."

Hestîa pulled him into her arms, resting her head against his chest. "You need not worry, my love. For I am yours and no one else's. My heart belongs to you and you alone. Let the spectacle be washed from our minds."

Agónas wrapped his arms around her and squeezed, relinquishing a long-suffering sigh into her hair. "Know that you are in my heart and on my mind always."

IT WAS LATE IN THE EVENING, THE HOUR ALMOST UP WHEN THE soldiers were abed with the lady servants. Hestîa lay in her bunk following her evening ablutions. Her comrades chatted around her, drowning out the moans and murmurs from the other side of the barracks. The Walabeän bunks were separated from the Augustans' by nothing more than a thin tapestry.

They could hear everything.

"They're *disgusting*," Athena groaned from the bunk above hers.

Hestîa chimed her agreement.

Wellën dropped her legs off the the top bunk adjacent to Hestîa's, letting her feet dangle restlessly. "I long to hit them."

Thóra smirked, leaning into the bedpost, her eyes dropping to Hestîa with a knowing glint. "What will our Savior do about it?"

Hestîa arched an eyebrow, her eyes flashing between her comrades. "Whatever in Xander's name are you talking about?"

"You haven't heard the rumors, my friend?" Athena dropped to the floor with a thud. Crossing her arms over her chest, she regarded Hestîa with a wide grin, one that both Thóra and Wellën mirrored. What did they know that she didn't?

"Savior?"

The women exchanged knowing glances before seating themselves on the bunk across from Hestîa.

"That's what they're calling you," Athena said.

"Why? Who?"

Wellën snorted. "The female servants, of course! Because of the incident. You're their savior because they don't have to sleep down here anymore."

"They don't have to tend to the soldiers' needs all night long," Thóra added.

Hestîa shook her head, bewildered. Did Agónas know this? Why hadn't he told her? Scoffing, she rose to her feet, pushing past the girls. She was parched, and she would take advantage of the brief window of quietude. As Hestîa rounded the corner into the hallway, she stopped short at the water trough. It was bone dry. Leave it to Emperor Obadïa to treat his soldiers like cattle. She leaned herself against the wall and waited. Someone would come fill it up anon, and she had no intentions of returning to that conversation.

The Savior. They're calling me the Savior? Well, that's one way to secure a target to my chest.

Sure enough, a stout servant entered the hallway, a large bucket propped atop her head. Two more servants followed her in a like fashion, taciturn and duty bound. Together, they poured the water into the trough, careful not to spill.

Hestîa approached. The servant girls dropped their empty buckets, staring wide-eyed as Hestîa reached for the ladle.

No. Not Hestîa. The Savior.

Then, as if Hestîa had commanded, each of the servant girls dropped to their knees before her and pressed a fervent peck to her sandaled feet. "Savior," they mumbled in unison before rising, bowing their heads once, then rushing up the stairs.

The implicit proof of her new reputation left Hestîa agitated, her skin crawling with larvae, unabated and incessant. She'd done nothing to deserve such reverence. She'd done nothing to beget such ramifications.

One servant girl remained. The woman cleared her throat to gain Hestîa's attention.

"You should join them." Hestîa eyed the exit where the other girls had disappeared. She feared that if the girl stayed during this hour, she'd be pulled into a soldier's bed.

"I can't."

Hestîa tilted her head, bemused. "What on earth do you mean?"

The girl glanced up at Hestîa, her eyes silver-lined. Her face would have been beautiful had it not been so drawn, so sallow. Her brown hair fell in waves down her frail shoulders, lacking the usual luster of a healthy human.

Frowning, Hestîa asked, "Why do you call me Savior?"

The girl smiled wistfully, joy seeping back into those forlorn eyes. "Because you *saved* us."

"Your friends are still in the soldiers' beds as we speak," Hestîa said pointedly. "How did I save you? I was only a victim, like you."

"You don't understand, my kyría." *My lady.*

Hestîa scowled. "Do not call me that!" she said through gritted teeth, her tone dripping with rancor.

"I'm so sorry, my ky—I mean, Savior." The girl cast a furtive glance over her shoulder before turning back to Hestîa. "You see," the girl pressed on, "you saved us because many of us did not get any sleep before. The soldiers would use us throughout the night, then we would be woken at dawn and forced to go about a day's full of chores."

Hestîa canted her head. "And your life is better because of *me*?"

"Yes, my Savior!" she said, bursting with enthusiasm. "You

must understand, because you made them see how wrong their ways truly are."

"I did not." They would never see the evil of their nature.

The servant's eyes were bright with excitement, fervor. "Yes, you did. Because of you and your superior will granted by the Gods, you have freed us from torture. We sleep and bathe in lavish bedchambers denied to us before your great act of justice. Because of you, we only have to endure the soldiers' touch for an hour, no more."

There was movement behind the panels dividing the barracks.

Hestîa's shoulders tensed instinctually. "Get out of here now, before you are to join the others!"

"Yes, my Savior." The servant bowed and scurried away, her sandals slapping against the tiles.

Hestîa tapped her foot in contemplation as half-naked soldiers filed into the cramped hallway, trudging toward the water trough. They nudged her out of the way, and they eagerly drank what water there was to be had.

Seething with irritation, Hestîa returned to her bunk, thirsty and disturbed.

11

GENERAL ACHILLES

Emperor Obadïa cut an intimidating figure. His gaze drilled into the Divine as they strode down the plush ruby carpet leading to the dais upon which he sat, imperious and proud. Lilith channeled her contempt for their ruler into an insouciant swagger, the length of her silken skirt splitting to reveal a muscled leg.

After an official welcome and having been accosted by several noblemen, Lilith was all too relieved to sit down for the feast. Now that she was half concealed behind Arduen, she wouldn't have to fear Obadïa's devouring stare.

Prince Orìon sauntered arrogantly into the dining hall, two courtesans giggling in harmony as they hung from his arms, a malevolent smile smeared across his lips. His dark eyes were dull and lifeless, another indicator of his current inebriation.

The Emperor pretended not to notice the state of his prodigal heir as Orìon took the vacant seat next to him. The two women extracted themselves from his arms and knelt on either side of his chair, their doting stares locked steadfast on the prince. Lilith scowled at the spectacle with strident disgust as

Orìon dropped crumbs into the courtesans' mouths like they were baby birds.

Lilith had not foreseen just how disconcerting returning to the Emperor's exquisitely hewn monolith would be. The castle always left her feeling slightly agoraphobic. Bed rest back at the Frourío didn't seem quite so abhorrent now. She ground her teeth until her gums hurt.

Seated across from her, Julius was engaged in a serious conversation with Wren, his attention entirely riveted to the elder Divine. In comparison to Prince Orìon, Julius was a very different kind of prince. One of supremely principled character. One of grace and kindness. Where Julius was concerned, there was no duplicitous charm, for the foreign prince possessed no corruption in his marrow. What made Julius Fawkes so alluring was his depth of understanding, his empathy, his kindness, and of course, his good looks. But what she loved about him most of all, was that he was oblivious to his appeal. Her prince was genuine.

Spilling tea on the skirt of her gown, Lilith grumbled to herself. The dress was made of a gorgeous deep crimson fabric that hugged her figure comfortably, though she would be conscious of filling her belly too much. The trim was of gold thread, wound and looped in vine-like patterns. Olga had picked it out for her the last time they'd visited Kenora. Being able to finally wear it was the only pleasant part of the evening.

Her malady left her feeling half the woman she had been the last time she'd dined in the Great Hall. When she stood before the floor-to-ceiling mirror, she noticed the strangeness of her face. The sunken eyes and hollowed cheeks. Her bone structure so much more… *harsh*. It wasn't the most flattering appearance, but it certainly wasn't the worst she'd ever seen herself. Besides, she wasn't here to grace the courtiers with her beauty, she was here because of her Divinity. As a vassal of Constantine and Kyril, and a vessel of Their might.

The whole event was utterly tedious and outright dull until Marlowë entered the Great Hall, Agónas and Hestîa at his side. Lilith perked up in her seat as her Walabeän friend strode in, taking her seat a ways down the table. Lilith beamed, and Hestîa mirrored her enthusiasm. She looked forward to catching up with the warrior following the feast.

Last winter, Lilith had accompanied Arduen, Quin, and Julius to the Isles of Nysía to propose an alliance with the Emperor. The Walabeän Colony accepted, under the condition that Lilith and Julius defeat their best warriors in combat. The Divine succeeded, though both bouts were close, and the Walabeäns spent their summer traveling across Augusta. Lilith wondered if Hestîa was enjoying her stay at the capital, but after considering the land she hailed from, she knew the warrior would suffocate in a place like this.

"Glad you could join us, Marlowë." Obadïa nodded in their direction.

The Igítís took his seat, ignoring how painfully the Emperor mispronounced his name. Lilith scowled in contempt. After the Walabeäns had come to the aid of Augusta, he still deigned to treat them with impudence.

The Emperor and his noblemen had held court earlier that afternoon, so there was little politicking this night. This usually would have pleased Lilith, but it also meant the Divine guests were the topic of discussion, and she did not want the spotlight on her.

"Spiro wants unmitigated control over your throne," one of the elder lords said to Obadïa, as if this were news of some sort. "He wants that crown on his head."

The Emperor sat back in his throne, puffed out his chest.

"We have support from the Isles now, there is little reason to fear. Spiro and his imps don't stand a chance."

Lilith picked at whatever remained on her plate. Dinner had been delicious as expected, compared to the bread and cheese they'd been eating for the last week. The wine was rich and bursting with flavor, the bread fresh, butter melting into it. The fruit was drizzled in honey, the platter dotted by the occasional slice of pasteli. The meat was salted but fresh, a stark contrast to the dried meats they'd been forced to gnaw on during their travels.

"I saw not one beast on my trip from Chïos," said a lord with a dark complexion and a long, braided beard. "It seems like their numbers have been depleted." The lord glanced around the room with a positive grin.

"We believe," Arduen began, "this is due to Spiro rounding up his army. He may be training them at his base in preparation for another attack."

A chorus of dissonant murmurs erupted throughout the Great Hall, and Lilith had to suppress the urge to slouch in her chair.

"Yes, that is a fair statement," the lord said, his grin calcified into a snarl.

The Emperor's nefarious heir stood suddenly and took his leave, the two women dangling from his arm. He did not bother to make excuses, he only finished his meal and sauntered away without a backward glance.

Lilith's eyes roved over her companions and rested on Hestîa. Her friend's gaze was locked on Orìon as he exited the hall, her expression one of loathing.

Concurrent sounds of cutlery on porcelain rang in her ears. It was time for dessert. Nothing softened contention like pastries and honeyed fruits.

The Emperor's affluence was constantly portrayed, but he

seemed to care very little for impressing his gilded dignitaries. They were granted a slight reprieve from attention when one of the younger lord's began a speech of braggadocio. The other nobles rolled their eyes demurely or cast their attentions elsewhere.

"General Achilles," the Emperor droned suddenly, cutting off the arrogant young lord. "So gracious of you to finally join us."

Curious, Lilith piqued up at the mention of the General of the Agemas—the Empire's most skilled warriors. She'd heard much about him but had only ever been in the company of Captain Vaughn. If he were anything like his colleague, she would rather he kept his distance.

But when General Achilles stepped into the light, a part of her fractured. For the general wore the familiar face of—

"Papa?"

12

THE KING OF BEASTS

"Rhéa! Irís! You've got to come see this!"

The Enchantress fumbled her vials, cracking one against the table. Xavier had sprinted into the infirmary with a beatific grin, crying out their names.

"Come on!" he chided. "No one's in need of your expertise right now." He tugged at their arms. Irís was easier to persuade. Xavier could convince her to do just about anything. Except, perhaps, jumping into the Great Rift of Dodöna.

"Fine," Rhéa relented.

Xavier grabbed hold of Irís's hand, subtly tucking it into the folds of her gown, to conceal their affection. A dagger struck Rhéa's heart. How was her husband faring in the capital? Had he been punished for helping free Irís? How she wished she could scry him, just to glimpse his face, but Spiro had somehow warded his lair against magical communications.

With a weighted heart, Rhéa followed Xavier and Irís. A bone-chilling roar met their ears as they entered into the great cavernous arena, where men and beast alike fought for rank.

The two smaller rings were empty, which was unusual. She looked at Xavier askance, and he nodded for her to follow.

The roar sounded again, reverberating off the walls. Rhéa glanced up at the stalagmites hanging from the ceiling. Would they fall? Wary, she stepped closer to the wall, continuing on Xavier's tail.

"Xavier, I must speak with you," she whispered behind him while Irís's fascinated gaze remained on the Champion's Ring.

He glanced over his shoulder at Rhéa, eyebrows raised. "Go on…"

"*Alone*," she intoned, her eyes flicking to the young Enchantress at his side.

Xavier leaned into Irís, and the girl beamed at him before taking off into the throng of beasts. When she was out of earshot, he looked at Rhéa expectantly.

"I understand that you and Irís have found a connection," she started, unsure how to breach the subject without offending him. "If Spiro discovers eith—"

"Rhéa, don't worry." Xavier placed a pacifying hand on her shoulder. The muscles in his arms were outlined, sinewy. He was growing stronger every day. "I won't let anything happen to Irís. I *care* about her."

"I understand, Xavier. It's just that you're sworn to Spiro. You may not be able to make decisions in her best interests if he discovers your relationship. I'm trying to keep Irís as far away from his clutches as possible. Imagine Spiro doing to her what he does—"

"All right! I get it." Xavier flashed the balcony an aggrieved glare before returning his attention to Rhéa. "I will do everything in my power to ensure she is safe. *Everything*. She means the world to me."

Rhéa gave a curt nod. "In the interim, I will continue to train her in private. I want her to be able to defend herself should the situation here go awry."

He nodded agreeably.

"Just do your part to appear obsequious, and I'll do mine," she said. "Spiro won't notice the girl so long as we remain useful. But if he discovers her true nature, there won't be much of anything we can do to help her. She will be as vulnerable as we are."

"Rhéa, there's something you should know…" Xavier chomped down on what he was about to say as Irís pranced toward them, mug clasped in her hands. She offered it to Xavier, dimples sinking deep into her cheeks as her eyes settled on him. This time, he wasn't particularly eager to display his affection, but the evidence of it still smoldered in his eyes.

"I don't need to be out here watching these sycophants," Rhéa muttered.

Xavier flashed her a hurtful glance.

"Not you," she said. "I meant the brutes." She flashed several olive-skinned beasts a wary glance.

"But you need to see this," Xavier said. "He's the newest addition to the army. They're calling him Typhon the King." He tipped his mug back, gulping down its contents.

Rhéa turned to her friend, her eyebrows knitting together in skepticism. "The King?"

"Yes, the King of the Beasts."

"That's what he calls himself, or…?"

Xavier shook his head. "He doesn't appear to think much of himself. These matches are just a game to him. An outlet to quell the boredom as we await battle. But the beasts have proclaimed him their leader. Unofficially, of course. I think Spiro would smite Typhon down if he caught wind of his title."

Rhéa couldn't disagree with that. There was only room for one king in Spiro's fortress, and it wasn't a lowly monster. "But

Spiro is their king…" Rhéa glanced up at the balcony, afraid the Great Divine may have heard the blasphemy.

"Yes, and Typhon is like our general, so to speak," Xavier corrected.

"Commander of Beasts," Irís chimed in with a grin. Inching closer to Xavier, she said, "You should be the commander." It was going to prove difficult to keep their relationship concealed. Irís was ignorant of the danger Spiro posed. And Rhéa and Xavier were reluctant to tear the blindfold from her eyes, because, well… ignorance was bliss.

A shadow appeared upon the balcony, pulling Rhéa's attention from the lovers. She clicked her tongue at Xavier, and he tore away from Irís. The young Enchantress flashed him a look of offense.

Spiro glared down upon them. Xavier maintained an nonchalant mien, sipping his ale. Rhéa met Spiro's stare full force as a salacious smirk spread across his lips. Her skin prickled. She would likely have to *tend* to him tonight. Only when he turned his attention to the rings did she release the breath she'd been holding.

"Are you all right?" Irís asked her.

"Yes." She cleared her throat, ignoring the icy gaze falling on her like a blanket of fresh snow. "Let's watch the match."

Xavier nodded animatedly and turned to the Champion's Ring. The largest ring was surrounded by raging beasts and men alike, howling praises for the new victor. With his astounding size, Typhon was difficult to miss. He towered over even the largest beasts in the fortress. Power rippled off of him in waves, but his yellow gaze blazed with something else… something *more*. This beast was passionate, and there was nothing more terrifying than burning desire. A lethal intent.

Rhéa turned on her heels and pushed through the crowd back toward the infirmary. There would likely be competitors waiting for her touch. But when she arrived, she found the chamber was mostly empty, save for a few disgruntled soldiers. Some of the human healers assisted them whilst Rhéa seated herself at the desk in the far corner, digesting everything she'd just seen.

This beast—Typhon—had been born just a week ago, and he was already the size of a stallion, double the strength. How it was possible, she did not know, but she had to find out.

The atmosphere in the room grew suddenly frigid. All of the inhabitants took their leave or became suddenly *very* interested in their work. Rhéa tensed, awaiting Spiro's touch, but he stopped in the doorway, eyes piercing into her.

"Join me in my chambers when you are finished healing my newest warrior."

"Warriors carry swords," she said, her confidence eroding beneath his glare. "This beast does not require a weapon. He is one."

Spiro grinned, his cheekbones sharp as marble. "Yes, he is a savage brute," he proclaimed ardently. "I believe he will secure my crown."

Rhéa did not want to know what would happen to her when Spiro stole the throne. One thing was certain: she would rather die than become his consort—or worse, his *empress*.

Without another word, Spiro exited through the archway leading out into the arena, his beasts parting for him, dropping to their knees in his wake. Rhéa scowled as her eyes followed his wiry figure. Spiro was powerful, of that she was certain, but no man was capable of *creating* an entire race. She needed to discover the means of his power, the root of the beasts' existence.

Typhon entered through the archway, his large figure consuming the space entirely, wrenching Rhéa from her thoughts. The remaining healers scrambled from the infirmary and into the adjacent hallway, the only other exit.

They're more afraid of this beast than Spiro.

The Enchantress rose from her seat, her eyes assessing the creature before her. His skin was olive in tone, an intrinsic quality of Spiro's beasts. He matched his brethren in color, though he was at least two feet taller, a foot wider. Muscles rippled beneath his hide, and long dark hair fell to his cinched waist. She'd watched him fight, each blow perfunctory, effortless. The King of Beasts, indeed.

Typhon was forced to crouch inside the infirmary, two rams' horns curling from his brow. Due to his weight, he had no other choice but to lower himself to the floor to be tended to.

Rhéa knelt beside him, placing her tray of salves and vials on the floor. Typhon studied her as she worked. He didn't flinch or display any signs of discomfort, but black blood oozed from the gashes in his hide, indicating his obvious pain. Rhéa went about her ministrations, her inquisitive eyes inspecting the beast's hands—paws—whatever they were. Typhon would be capable of killing her just by wrapping his hand around her throat.

By the Stars, Rhéa! Don't think of such things in their presence.

Typhon brought his hand toward her and Rhéa jolted, losing concentration, her needle falling to the floor. She'd have to sterilize that before she could continue. The beast rested his hand on her forearm gently, lightly. Rhéa gaped down at Typhon's hand. He possessed hands like a human, though obnoxiously large and pulsing with veins. His nails were more like talons, though they didn't appear to be poisonous. But what caught her most off guard, was his gentle touch, still callous and rough, but light and… kind. As if a monster of his caliber was capable of such tenderness. When she looked up into his eyes, she was pleasantly surprised to note they were more golden than yellow.

Typhon grunted in what she assumed was approval as she continued to stitch up his gash.

How Spiro was creating such creatures, she did not know. But magic had to be involved, for a Divine was not a God. No Enchantress could create beings. They could repurpose life, recycle it, rejuvenate. But once something or someone was dead, they were gone. There was no taking life back from Elysium or Hades.

Rhéa resolved to discover exactly how Spiro was managing this godly feat, and how he was maintaining subjugation over them all. Did they not possess brains to rise up and usurp him? Or were they so pliant that reverent worship of him was ingrained in their minds upon conception?

Rhéa bent her head and prayed to Amalthea to grant her clairvoyance. It may be the only way her life could be conducive to a better, brighter Augusta.

13

LITTLE SPARK

Awraith? No. He couldn't be. His presence was far too palpable, his guilt far too potent, to be conjured by her own mind. This was not another one of grief's cruel tricks. She'd been done with those for a while now. This was real. This was her father in the flesh. Breathing. Seeing.

Alive.

Lilith's mind had become a gale of bitter words, with a stark contrast of elation. Her chest a hailstorm of emotions. She rose to her feet abruptly, her chair clattering to the floor. Every courtier turned to regard her with censure. How dare she be so rude in the Emperor's presence? Sometimes their ignorance—coupled with their arrogance—ran so deep as to prohibit them from realizing that others breathed the same air as they, that others lived lives of equal measure.

Her father was a mere ghost, a vision of the man she'd spent countless days preserving in her mind. Now that she knew he was truly alive, loss held a whole new meaning to her. Rather than the dull ache sucking the marrow from her bones, it transformed into a burning desire to protect. Warmth seeped into her muscles, her chest imploding with emotion she couldn't begin to delineate. Aether swirled in her gut, the frenetic humming of its power vibrating her entire body. As a result, Lilith swayed on her feet slightly.

Arduen, standing vigilant at her side, placed a warm hand on her arm, and whispered, "Are you all right? Are you going to have an episode?" He nodded to Julius to stand as well.

Lilith couldn't respond. Her eyes locked on her father's, the same emerald hue as her own. But he didn't look at her with such surprise. His expression was rueful.

How is this possible?

London Oak perished in the Battle of Elïath six years ago! *But I never saw his body…* He'd deserted them. How could he have done this? Did he even understand what his children had gone through in his absence?

Tears welled in her eyes, threatening to fall. Fingernails bit into her palms as her hands closed into fists. She fought for equanimity, oblivious to her audience, careless of their reproof.

"Lilith." Her father stepped toward her.

She shattered.

Arduen pulled her from the Great Hall and out into the corridor where she hoped to find some privacy. Her Master supported most of her weight, Julius clamoring in their wake. Lilith didn't know if her father was in tow, if he even cared enough to give her an explanation. Her surroundings were a blur, and she was fortified by a hard wall of warmth. *Arduen*.

"Lilith…" But the voice did not belong to her Master, to the man who had filled the gaping chasm her father had left behind.

The voice belonged to London Oak.

That wall of warmth stepped away from her only to be replaced by another. The familiar scent of smoke and iron washed over her, strengthening her sobs.

"Lilith, please listen to me," London implored.

"How could you?" she bellowed, driving her fists into his leather cuirass. "Do you know what you did to us? If you had been there, Larkin wouldn't be dead. But he is gone forever, all because you deserted us!"

London stepped back as if she'd struck him, his face clouded by her tears. Lilith pressed her back into the wall and slowly dropped to the floor, no longer capable of standing.

Julius came to her side, his arm snaking around her shoulders. He whispered words of comfort in her ear, but she couldn't discern what he said over the rush of her pulse.

London Oak knelt before her, his own eyes glassy, sorrowful. He pressed a ghostly hand to the skin of her cheek, and she leaned into his large callused palm, breathing in the familiar scent of the man who had raised her.

Her father hadn't changed much at all. His dark hair was shorter than usual, but he still looked so much like Larkin. At the realization, Lilith's features contorted as more sobs broke free of her throat, and she pressed her face into her hands to conceal her anguish. A second later she was pulled into an embrace, and she knew who it was the moment he touched her.

"My girl..." London said, his voice thick with rue. "It was never my intention to hurt you."

Lilith buried her face against his shoulder, ignoring the memories that his familiar scent conjured.

"Shush, my spark." London petted her head, his hand nearly the size of it. "You must relax. Breathe. I will tell you everything. I promise that you won't see me as some evil defector. I love you, Lilith. I loved your mother and your brother, too."

She pulled away slightly, craning her neck to look up at him. "You know what I did?" *Kin-Slayer.* He nodded, and she pressed her face into his chest again. "I'm so sorry, Papa!"

He shushed her. "There is nothing to forgive. Larkin was a victim, and you saved him from a far worse fate. You were brave, Lily. I am so proud of you."

"Tell me everything," Lilith demanded, though not harshly. Her need to understand was exigent, an insistent pulse in her core. "I need to understand."

"I was gravely injured in battle," her father began. "I thought I would die, but Captain Vaughn got me to the healers' tent, and I began my recovery. I couldn't walk or ride, therefore I could not abscond to Utica. The Emperor remembered who I was from my service twenty years prior, and he did not forget my dereliction. I had no other option. It was to the gallows or receive treatment and serve for the rest of my days."

"Why didn't you write us? Why didn't you let us know you were alive?"

London gave a regretful shake of his head, his short beard tickling her brow. "I'd considered this for many months. The worst part of it all was resisting the urge to write you. But I couldn't. I could not risk the chance that you or your brother would come to the capital—worse, that you would not make it."

Lilith dropped her gaze, letting it rest on the ornate golden clasp that fastened his imperial himation to his boiled leather cuirass.

"Your mother—"

"Don't." Lilith held up a hand to silence him. "I can't talk about her right now."

London's expression was one born of confusion. "You know?"

She nodded, releasing a pent breath.

Her father relinquished a long-suffering sigh. "There is so much I wish to tell you. But now is not the time. Visit me during your stay. Ask any servant to bring you to my chambers. Now that you are here, I want as much time with my girl as she will allow." He gripped her chin, his touch reverent and tender.

"I will." Lilith nodded, unable to stall the smile that erupted at being close to her father again. Something she'd only ever been able to experience in her dreams.

"Good," London said, squeezing her against him.

Lilith's smile faltered, devolving into a frown. "But I don't fully understand..." She leaned away, her eyes inspecting him closely, scrutinizing every pore, every hair, every freckle, sussing for the answers she so desperately sought, to questions she could not form with words. "Why didn't you send for us? We could have been escorted here safely. We could have lived here with you. There are chambers in this castle big enough for several families to live comfortably."

London stroked her hair, his fingers lingering within the coils, like he had dreamed of touching them after so long. She did possess the same dark mahogany hair as her mother. How had her father handled her death? London likely never shed the guilt that weighed him down. He never would.

"Lilith," he sighed her name, "this castle is not as peaceful as it seems. It is no place for a young lady to grow into a woman."

Still, she could not shake the feeling that his actions had been impetuous, a hasty result of fear. Toying with the golden clasp of his himation, Lilith muttered, "Why do they call you General *Achilles*?"

He chuckled. "Because that is my real surname. My real name is Miles Achilles. Your mother and I decided to change our names when she discovered she was pregnant with Larkin, to protect our family from our past discretions."

"So... my real name is Lilith *Achilles*?"

London nodded. "But I love Lilith Oak. I named you Lilith

Oak, so that is your name, if you want it." A warm smile spread across his face, crinkling the skin around his eyes.

"I've missed you," she said. "I kept the forge hot in your absence." *So hot, I burned the place down*—she kept that thought to herself.

Her father beamed down at her. "That's my little spark."

⊙ ⋒ ⤳ ⋔ ◊

Hestîa excused herself from the Great Hall. Lilith had taken off suddenly. Her friend's display of utter shock and devastation left Hestîa in a state of undeniable bafflement—a true feat, she must admit—and she was desperate to know if her friend was all right.

As she meandered through the hallway in the direction of the barracks, a figure tore free of the shadows. Hestîa stalled, waiting for the person to enter the light. The shadow lingered for a moment, as if hesitant to cross paths with her. She couldn't blame them. She was an intimidating figure.

When they finally emerged, all vestige of confidence dripped from her with the sweat beading her brow. With a malevolent smirk, Prince Orìon approached her on near-silent feet.

Hestîa didn't deign to greet him, she instead focused a calculated glare on him as he neared. He didn't stop until he was a hair's breadth away, his hot, whiskey breath brushing her cheek as if he'd done it with his hand.

Orìon grinned, baring cuspids. He could have been handsome, in another world, if she hadn't heard so many stories of his debauchery and lust for torment.

Racking her mind for a logical plan to excuse herself, she came up short, like her breath. Hestîa tried to imbue her voice with some semblance of esteem, but ultimately failed under

Orìon's insidious gaze. "Your Highness," she said, forcing her voice low and bereft of interest. Dull, like the wastrel before her.

"Hessa."

"It's *Hezz-tee-uh*," she amended with a half-smile.

He snorted, his sneer repulsive. "So it seems that you are the sole reason I've lost my fucking evening entertainment." Amusement laced his Augustan lilt.

Feigning ignorance, Hestîa said, "Whatever do you mean, *milord*?"

Orìon scowled. "You know exactly what I mean, *Savior*."

She gulped but remained still otherwise, the last thing she wanted to do was vex the Crown Prince. Unimaginable were the ways in which he could punish her.

"Tell me," Orìon drawled, "how *whore-ish* does one need to become to be fondled by a random man?" He cocked an eyebrow. "Hmm?"

Hestîa guffawed, her voice elusive.

The prince pushed his body up against hers, pinning her to the wall. He gripped her wrists and he held her under his weight.

Did punishment for indiscretion exist for a crown prince? Not in Augusta.

"I'll have you know, since you're new here, that I control these halls. I can have any woman I want." His hand trailed up her leg slowly, leaving behind a burning sensation. She cursed herself for selecting such a sheer gown, exposing so much of her figure. The scanty dress was only to please Agónas, not to draw the wrathful eyes of the prince.

"I make the rules," Orìon said. "If you don't like them, you can take your leave, *Savior*." His tone was noxious, spittle flying from his mouth like acid rain.

Hestîa pushed herself against the stones behind her,

desperate to get as much space between her and the prince as possible. She took his diatribe with grace, even as spit sprang from his lips and landed on her skin, burning where it settled.

She would not quake for him.

The moment dragged on uncomfortably, but she waited until he took his leave before she slumped to the ground, his incensed glare burning indelibly behind her eyelids.

And as her veins burned a permanent, glaring latticework behind her eyes, Hestîa vowed to never let that man make another woman feel as she did then.

14

IT WAS YOU ALONE

"Each corrupt asshole only raises the next, inheriting all his father's horseshit and regurgitating it to the Plebes." Spiro glowered at the servants passing them by; the open, white marble corridor near-blinding in the noonday sun.

Arduen grunted his agreement. His friend wasn't wrong, though he needed to entertain caution when slurring such disparaging speech about Emperor Odéllo. This conversation was not casual, and they both knew the Emperor had ears and eyes seeded nearly everywhere.

"We are young still," Arduen replied. "Give it another hundred years. Times will change. The people will have the power they deserve."

Spiro halted his marching, the walls of the castle open here to the elements. It was a balmy summer day, the breeze barely enough to dry the sweat beading their brows.

"People don't live as long as we do," Spiro said. He heaved an exasperated sigh, leaning on the balustrade.

Arduen joined him. He understood what Spiro meant. The life spans of the Plebes barely exceeded fifty years. Most children didn't make it past the age of sixteen. They would live their lives under the shroud of a selfish man who would always turn a blind eye to the suffering if it favored the Elite, securing his family's name upon the throne for another century.

"You think the people should hold power?" Spiro's brows shot to the sky. "You think they don't require governing?" His pale eyes were heavy, stormy as the Southern Galatëa.

Arduen shook his head. "I don't know what they need," he conceded. "I only know that I wasn't Anointed to rule." He eyed his friend warily. "We weren't Anointed to rule."

Spiro licked his lips, hands clasped before him. Veins bulged under pale skin. Tense.

"I was blessed by Constantine to defend," Arduen continued, "to mediate on His behalf—on Their behalf."

"The Divine should rule," Spiro said softly. "We are the ones with centuries worth of knowledge and wisdom in our heads. We should lead the people."

"We weren't created for that, Brother." Arduen clapped his friend on the shoulder. "You know this." It pained him that he had to say it. Spiro was older than he, and though they had been noviciates together, it was only because Spiro was learning to master four elements. It should be Spiro telling him right from wrong.

But his friend wasn't entirely wrong, was he?

"Sure, but I know what I believe," Spiro said. "We have been taught by cowards. Men and women who have been gifted the power of Elysium but deny the responsibility that comes with it."

He was stretching this too far. Since Emperor Odéllo inherited the throne from his late father, Kenora was in disarray. The young Emperor refused to attend court for almost a year. Formally, mourning lasted a month in Augusta, and whatever duties one possessed would need to be carried out once that time was up.

The Emperor had failed to do that. He'd failed on many accounts. Now the Plebeians were banging their fists upon his doors, and he was claiming ignorance. It was apparent Odéllo hadn't inherited his *father's acumen, but he had shown the same inclination to act arbitrarily. He sauntered about, flaunting a cavalier disposition, as if ruling the Empire was secondary to a greater purpose: pandering. As if the people should beg him to rule over them. Looked like Augusta was in for another forty years of plundering and pilfering, of crawling and griping, begging and walloping.*

The truth of the matter was, Odéllo had an object of great value stolen from him—a ring, in fact—and he deemed it so valuable, that when his father finally passed, the first official order he'd made was to send a cohort to the Obsydían Marsh to retrieve it. Odéllo was convinced that the perpetrator was an Enchantress. "How else could she have taken a ring from my finger?" *he'd said.* "Magic." *The legionnaires returned from the Marsh with catatonia and were still being treated for it. All at the expense of the Plebes' taxes; their indignation abiding as a result.*

Arduen smirked at the mention of the High Enchantress's retribution. It was just like Ophelía to send a message, but she never used literary tactics.

And this hapless situation was the sole reason for Arduen and Spiro's summoning.

"Odéllo has the protection of Isidore," Arduen said. "No one will oppose him. None of the lords, retinues, assemblies, apostates. None." He sighed through his nose, using Master Judeaus's breathing techniques to quell his frustration.

Spiro scowled. "They expect, because he is chosen by a God, that he will be altruistic and paternal in regard to his subjects. It's utterly asinine."

"That's why, as the Anointed individuals, we must impart wisdom upon him."

"Master Euclid said the same thing." Spiro grinned.

Arduen mirrored his friend's expression. He hated to see him like this, bent out of shape over a man with an expiration date. "The sharpest blades cut true," Arduen said.

"Aye, but dull blades hurt more."

Odéllo was a dull, rusted gladius. As callow and cantankerous as he was, the man held the throne and couldn't be deposed, even if his actions were profligate, wasteful and selfish.

Spiro leaned over the balustrade, eyes surveying a quartet of ladies strolling amid the blooms. "Shall we make our acquaintance?" He gestured to the women. "Ameliorate this trip with a consensual scuffle between the sheets, aye?"

The ladies had eyed them several times from below. Interest piqued, Arduen said no more as he ambled for the stairs descending to the garden below. He could use some release, in addition to a full chalice of claret. The day was sweltering, and he would seize any chance to remove his breeches. Arduen would leave it to his accomplice to beguile the women, seduce them. Spiro was the master of persuasion, whereas Arduen seemed to be the master of placation.

The brothers always balanced each other out.

◎ � ⌁ ⋔ ◊

"You're quiet," Arduen mused from across the breakfast table, the morning sunlight brightening Lilith's emerald eyes. His noviciate was unusually bereft of vim this morning. "Are you feeling well?" Without waiting for her response, he leaned across the table and pressed the back of his hand to her forehead.

"I'm fine, Arduen." She set those luminous eyes on him, the corners of her lips turning up.

Arduen cleared his throat. She'd become lax as of late in the use of his proper title. Lilith had many years ahead under his tutelage, she needed to practice proper conduct.

"Master," she corrected herself.

"Don't be afraid to speak up if you're not at your best," Arduen said. "I wouldn't argue with you for wanting to rest."

Lilith's eyes narrowed on him shrewdly. She always saw through to his intentions. "You don't want me to go today…"

"Maybe the event today isn't suited to your taste. I remember how you felt when Prince Orìon punished his squire."

Even Arduen had trouble forgetting that moment. If he thought about it, his mind would vividly conjure up the boy's pale face, the smacking sound of the blades against his skin, his wails for clemency piercing the air.

"I'll be there," she said. "I don't want my absence to arouse suspicion. Besides, I have a vulgar title to shake off."

Arduen nodded. "Yes, that you do." He had warned her that Augustans would take to calling her Kin-Slayer. That was inevitable. Plebeians constituted the bulk of the population of Augusta, and they rarely received elaborate education, if any at all. They wouldn't know what the Blood Oath was. They wouldn't know that she had killed Larkin to free him. To them, she was a heartless killer who had been Anointed by the Gods and turned against her family. It wouldn't be difficult for Spiro to sway the Plebes to support his cause. A connection Arduen hoped the Great Divine had not made himself.

And now, the father of those kids had just resurrected…

He placed a tentative hand on her shoulder. "Do you want to talk? About your father—"

"No," she said curtly. "There's no possibility of turning how I feel into words."

"Hmm." He averted his eyes. The last thing he needed was jealousy to divide them. Of course he was happy for her, Constantine knew just how much she had suffered, and yet he had worked so hard with her, to get her to open up to him and confide in him. "I just want you to know you can always talk to me."

A knock sounded at the door. Lilith jumped in her seat, dropping a red grape from between her fingers.

"I will get it," he said, a void churning in the pit of his stomach as he strode to the door. Arduen prayed it was not a summons to be in Obadïa's company.

He opened the door to see a young Walabeän woman standing on the threshold, her hair secured in a single braid. The pale plait hung over one spauldered shoulder.

"Hello, Arduen," Hestîa chimed. "I was informed Lilith is staying here."

"Lilith!" Arduen called. "The door is for you." He left Hestîa at the door and returned to his breakfast. He assessed Lilith's every motion as she pushed her half-eaten breakfast away, evidently thankful to have a reason to leave it behind.

"Who is it?"

Arduen merely smirked in response as he sunk into his chair across from her. He'd left the door ajar, but not wide enough to reveal who was on the other side.

Lilith looked to the door, hesitating.

"It is not your father," Arduen said. His noviciate frowned at that, but her shoulders relaxed in stark relief. Arduen sympathized with her. Though her father's situation was understandable, after all the suffering Lilith had endured in his absence, she would have a difficult time forgiving him. Not to mention catching up with him.

As Lilith traipsed toward the door, Arduen inspected each of her steps. Her gait was even, there was no favoring of a limb. Her spine was straight and erect, no telltale signs of seizure-inducing tension. He'd spent the previous evening kneading out those knots whilst she buried her face in the pillows, squeezing the fabric until her knuckles were white. Still, Arduen did not believe the pain of the massage outweighed that of an episode.

The trills of jovial chatter could be heard. Some time spent in the company of a like-minded friend would be good for her. Yes, she had Julius and Felix, but they were boys. And whilst Arduen believed friendship knew no bounds, there was nothing like the ease you felt with a friend of the same sex.

"You have to ask?" he heard Hestîa say. He chuckled into his mug at the incredulity in her tone.

Lilith muttered something in response.

"Interesting," Hestîa said. "Well, you can tell me all about it down there."

Arduen set down his mug, his eyes drawn to the gardens below. Perhaps the girls would take a walk, chat about their journeys over the past several months.

"Arduen…" Lilith entered the bedchamber. He looked up at her askance. "Hestîa wants to spar with me on the training grounds. Julius and Felix are already down there, so I won't be alone. Is this all right with you?"

Of course, he should have assumed. Hestîa was a warrior, not a noblewoman admiring blossoms.

"Yes, I don't see anything wrong with that. But you must come back here before the flogging. It would be wise to rest before such an event." He lowered his brow. "Am I clear?"

She gave a faint smile, her chin dipping in accordance. Her dark hair fell over her brow, the waves adopting a reddish hue in the sunlight. "Yes, Master."

Arduen stood to see her off. "Don't push yourself too far. I will be close by, watching." He placed a hand on her shoulder. "If you're feeling faint or tense, stop immediately."

"Yes, Arduen. I promise. I won't push myself." She grabbed her sword, strapping the scabbard to her belt. He had oiled the inside before they'd set out for the capital. Constance was as ready as ever.

A flash of a memory raced through his mind. His deft

fingers wrapping that metal hilt in leather. A strange girl seated across the fire from him, watching him through long, tangled locks. He never once imagined they would come this far.

Lilith turned back to him, lips parted as if to say something.

"What is it?" he asked, brows raised.

In one long stride, she crossed the space between them and wrapped her arms around his waist, resting her head against his chest.

"What's this?" he said with a chuckle, setting his mug of tea down on the table before he spilled its contents. Had she read his expression? Did she suspect the turbulent conflicting emotions her father's sudden survival inflicted upon him?

"Nothing." She pulled away before he could wrap his arms around her in return. "I just… appreciate you."

Arduen grinned at her, and if he wasn't mistaken, a rosy tint bloomed upon her cheeks. "I appreciate you too, Fledgling."

He watched her as she strode to the door, her steps bouncing with excitement.

"Oh, and Arduen?"

He met her eyes across the expanse of the suite.

"No one will ever replace my father, dead or alive."

Arduen swallowed, pins suddenly stinging his throat.

"My father's presence changes nothing between us," she said, a sad smile spreading across her face. "No one can ever replace you. You drew me out of my shell and showed me the world, and it was you alone who taught me how to find my place in it." She turned back to the door, and he swore he saw a little smirk play on her face. "I love you for that." Then she left.

15

ONLY STEEL BREEDS GLORY

"**Y**ou have to go *slow*?" Hestîa stood across from Lilith, her feet set wide, a fist propped on her hip.

Lilith glanced over each shoulder to see if anyone was close enough to hear. They weren't, but she whispered anyway, "I haven't been well."

Hestîa's indignant mien suddenly shifted to one of concern. "I'm so sorry, Lilith. What kind of... sick?"

"Severely painful episodes," Lilith said. "Seizures. My entire body clenches up. It feels like the Gods have reached down to squeeze me until my bones crack." Her body shuddered. She remembered every episode vividly, despite how hazy she was when they occurred.

"Well, we will go slow then." Hestîa backed up and assumed her sparring stance. "I'll be *gentle*."

Lilith smiled wide. She'd never anticipated overtures of friendship from Hestîa, but was so thankful that she had.

Heaving a sigh, Lilith braced herself for battle. The training grounds were nearly empty, save for a few Walabeän warriors.

Should her swordsmanship prove absolutely horrendous, there weren't many witnesses.

"Ustè stèle vreäqq grínndr!" Hestîa declared to the skies.

"Only steel breeds glory!" Lilith echoed in Modern Tongue.

Julius, Felix, and Agónas dueled on the far side of the field. Lilith tried her best to refrain from glancing in their direction, but she couldn't help herself. Watching Julius fight was like witnessing a stallion race or a professional dancer on stage.

"He's been looking over here just as much as you," Hestîa teased, and before Lilith could respond, her friend charged.

Lilith met her blade, expecting a jarring clang, but Hestîa's touch was featherlight. She took umbrage at her gentleness. "Really?"

The warrior pranced backward, putting several feet between them. "Yes, he is smitten with you!" she responded, feigning ignorance. Hestîa knew that Lilith was upset about how little effort she was emitting, but she chose to focus on the men again.

As usual.

Lilith advanced before her thoughts trailed somewhere inappropriate. Their grunts echoed through the training grounds. The courtyard was larger than the training field at the Frourío, surrounded on all four sides by stone walls that seemed to be a hundred feet high. Frourà legionnaires marched along the battlements, bows in their arms, surveying the countryside.

"The Fruits are watching you," Hestîa said.

Lilith canted her head. "The *Fruits*? You mean, the Frourà."

Hestîa waved her off. "Does it matter what I call them? They're a travesty! Standing around all day, their muscles must be as soft as overripe fruit."

"Hence the name," Lilith said on a laugh. "What about Agónas?" she asked, wishing to move on to lighter topics. Her heavy breathing seemed to worry Hestîa, so the warrior slowed her movements.

"We have become *one*." Hestîa giggled.

Lilith straightened, dropping Constance to her side. "Really?"

Hestîa gave a cavalier shrug. "It was bound to happen, being on the road together and all. One thing led to another, and then we were sneaking off into the trees for some privacy." She stared off into the sky, a wistful smile gracing her pretty face. "I've waited for him all my life, so I had nothing to hold back when he finally chose me."

Lilith wasn't sure what she meant, but she nodded as if she did. "What was it like?"

Her friend bit into her bottom lip. "It was painful at first, but Agónas, despite his fierce deportment, was very gentle with me. Very romantic. And he didn't stop until I was *fulfilled*."

Lilith gaped but quickly composed herself.

"Don't laugh. You'll give in to Julius someday," Hestîa said, and winked.

"We had a moment together on the beach. I thought it might go further, but we were interrupted. We haven't made much progress beyond that." Lilith twirled Constance in her hand.

"Why is that, love?" Hestîa played with the end of one of her many long pale-blonde braids.

"I got sick. It just wasn't appropriate."

Hestîa narrowed her eyes and studied Lilith with scrutiny. "I think the Gods are punishing you."

Lilith stepped back, stricken.

"Well, it makes sense," Hestîa argued. "You sang the Hymn of Divination over a traitor—no offence. That warranted some form of punishment, no?"

Hestîa wasn't being rude, she was simply speculating. And she could be right, Lilith thought. But this was dangerous thinking, and even blasphemous thoughts warranted punishment.

If They were punishing her, it would only be for singing the Hymn over Larkin's traitorous corpse. And if transient discomfort was the penalty she had to serve in order to secure her brother a place in Elysium at their mother's side, then it was worth it.

"Well, what about you?" Lilith asked, changing the subject. "How have you gotten along in the capital?"

Hestîa shook her head and jerked her chin at the wall. Together, they walked over and took their seats in the plush grass, resting their backs against the cool stone.

"It hasn't been good here." Hestîa's eyes wandered over the grounds, lingering momentarily on Agónas.

Julius had stopped dueling to inspect Lilith from afar. Even from a distance, she could make out his anxious expression.

"There was an incident in the barracks," Hestîa said. "One of the Augustan soldiers mistook me for a servant girl... the ones that satisfy particular *needs*." She sucked in a shaky breath. "And I attacked him. Fended him off."

"Oh, Hestîa..."

"I thought he was Agónas. He even touched me like Agónas. I even said his name, and the man didn't stop." Her eyes grew distant, unfocused.

"And how did you find out it wasn't...?"

Hestîa closed her eyes, leaning her head back against the stone. "I wanted to watch his hand. I wanted to watch as he pleased me, but his skin was tan. Agónas is a very pale man, no matter how much sun he is exposed to." She chuckled dryly. "For being in a large pool, I dried up *very* quickly."

"I'm sorry," Lilith offered. "But now all those servant girls have been freed from... *service*." She was trying to make light of the situation, but by the expression that stole over her friend's features, she knew she'd failed.

"They call me the Savior."

Lilith cackled. "The *Savior*?"

"Yes, and now I've made a personal enemy of the Crown Prince."

Ugh, not Orìon… the bratty, petulant prince.

"How do you know that?" Lilith asked. "He can have any one of those servant girls escorted to his private chambers. Why would he care what happens in the barracks?" Her brow hurt from all the tension; it must have been permanently knitted together since they'd sat down.

"I don't know why he cares so much, but he does." Hestîa's voice turned somber. "I know this because he told me after the feast. He made it very clear that he owns everything in this castle, and he isn't happy with a foreigner's meddling."

"How clear?" Lilith asked, her voice hushed.

"Palpably."

"Blast the bloody Empire!" Lilith cursed. "If he touches you again, I'll eviscerate him; make a necklace of his entrails."

The Walabeän couldn't help her grin. "It seems I've rubbed off on you. That would be a sight, indeed."

⊙ � ⤳ ℳ ◊

As the Divine approached the spectacle, several soldiers had lined up beside the stage, their armor stripped as a symbol of their disobedience. They were prepped for the whip with only harem pants made of cheap cloth, their expressions contrite as they shuffled to the platform with reluctant effi-ciency. Obedient soldiers who had made mistakes in the face of fear.

Throughout the square were stationed a formidable number

of the Emperor's legionnaires; the guarantors of peace and order, but mostly obedience to Obadïa. The Divine stood along the side of the stage with both Captain Vaughn and General Achilles. Periodically, Lilith's father would cast her faint smiles of reassurance. Did he know her well enough to glean how much this disturbed her?

Lilith's muscles were like sodden bread after the massage Arduen gave her following her training session with Hestîa. The Enchantress had schooled him on the procedure before leaving to return to the Marsh. His touch was more callous than hers, though that could have been due to his Divine strength. It was obvious that he was trying to be gentle, but Lilith didn't mind the firmer touch, it seemed to draw out more of the tension that resulted in her episodes.

Lilith watched as the whip cracked down upon a soldier's back. The soldier craned his neck, unleashing an agonizing cry. The tiny hairs on her body rose up simultaneously. The sight was unnerving, and her blood began to boil as chunks of skin soared through the air, splatters of claret painting the wooden platform. Yet she watched idly as the whip came crashing down again and again, eventually forming a latticework of bloody lines that would forever mar the man's skin.

The Emperor sat upon his balcony, set high into the edifice, overlooking the assemblage. Orìon sat by his side, silver goblets of the most decadent wine clasped in their fists. A smirk distorted Obadïa's florid face as the lashes sounded, mixed with the echoing cries of excitement from the crowd. How could people enjoy this? These soldiers risked their lives for the safety of all Augustans, and they took pleasure in their pain. Lilith tensed, nails biting into clammy palms, eyes scanning the crowd. The denizens of Kenora watched in mute fascination. No sympathy. No empathy. Just morbid intrigue.

The next soldier approached the platform, climbing the

steps with visibly trembling limbs. He dropped to his knees as the general announced his transgressions.

"Servan Geronas of the Imperial Milítia," said the general, "is guilty of being in possession of a blade that exceeds the lawful length limit in Kenora by an inch and three quarters. Do you protest the charge?"

The soldier's shoulders shook as he lifted his head to face the crowd. "It wasn't sharpened. It was my grandfather's blade. It was only ornamental!"

The general cracked the whip, and the soldier cried out in expectation, but he did not touch the soldier's skin. "Admit to your crimes or face trial!"

The soldier gasped. The consequence of going to trial once you have already been accused was bleak. The soldier seemed to be aware of this, for the mention of a trial made him quail worse than the whip. "I am guilty," he conceded.

The crowd jeered, hopping on their feet.

Anxiety gnawed at Lilith's chest. It was difficult to force the brunt of their emotions out of her mind. She knew Julius was more experienced with the discipline, for he didn't seem to be as perturbed as she was. *Close off your consciousness!*

After a brief moment of consideration, Julius began to silently usher Lilith away from the spectacle.

As Julius turned her shoulders, his eyes searching the crowd for the best path back into the castle, there was a stirring amongst the assembly. Lilith tried to distinguish from where it originated, but it moved so fast, a soldier, pale skin, leather armor, pale-blond braids, broke free of the bodies, panting.

"Soldier," London Oak's voice greeted the man.

"General Achilles, there's been a death in the barracks," he said through gasps. "A murder."

A hush stole over the crowd, and Lilith strained her eyes

against the sun to see the expression upon the Emperor's face. Except he was gone.

A chorus of murmurs began, cresting as the shock ceased and panic swept in.

"Time to go," Arduen said, grasping onto Lilith's arm.

She allowed her Master to lead her away, worry for her father forcing a clumsy gait.

"He will be all right," Julius said as if reading her mind.

Without looking back, they left the courtyard behind.

⌾ ⛥ ⌇ ⋔ ⚬

THE DIVINE RETURNED TO THEIR SUITES. ARDUEN STOOD AT THE large window overlooking the garden, holding a mug of tea that he did not sip from. Lilith had seated herself beside him at the breakfast table, she hadn't deigned to talk. Quin and Julius went to investigate the claimed murder, whilst Wren and Felix occupied the front living quarters as they waited.

Arduen gripped his mug too tight, his knuckles, even the joints of his fingers, were white. His anxiety yawned, awakening from its slumber, and Lilith was the poor soul who had stepped on its tail first.

"Emperor Obadïa displays his cruelty, and it sows fear in his people," she said, her voice steady. "It breeds bloodlust. Augusta will never know peace, even if we succeed in thwarting Spiro."

Breathe in. Breathe out. Arduen didn't want this discussion right now. "Sometimes a small amount of fear is needed to rule efficiently. And need I remind you that it is not our place to interfere with—"

"Yes, but fear will spawn disloyalty," she interjected. "Enough of it to break up Augusta. For those who can think critically for themselves will retaliate."

"What are you trying to say?" His tone was brusque, but he would consider her arguments. Or, minimally, he would feign consideration and mull over how he'd break the news to her.

Lilith lifted her chin in defiance. "Spiro will see this. He has eyes and ears in the capital, you said so yourself. He will take advantage of the situation the moment it arrives. I have no doubt that Spiro will plant the seed of his vision in the Plebeians. Even take his chances with the Elite, if he hasn't already. He could organize a coup, a revolution, instead of taking the capital by force. He could rip it from underneath Obadïa's ass like a rug, a magic trick fit for a usurper."

Arduen ran a hand through his hair, defeated, his anger dispelling in tangible waves that he uselessly tried to contain. "There isn't much we can do about that. We cannot control the Emperor." Not that he hasn't tried. Manipulating the most arrogant of men was an art form he'd yet to master, if he ever would. Spiro was better at that.

"Obadïa respects *you* most of all," Lilith pointed out, her voice brimming with hope. "Maybe it would be wise to grant him some Divine wisdom, with the addition of the Oracle's word, of course. I know you cannot go above her, and she is not present to voice her wisdom, but your counsel may convince him not to act so rash, to show caution where hard punishment is concerned. Maybe simply suggest he host discipline privately, not in the form of public entertainment. Or at all."

Arduen shook his head, exasperated. "Lilith…"

"Please, Master." She stood, placing a warm hand on his forearm. "Is our existence not exemplifying the love the Gods possess for Their creation? Their people? Am I not extending that love to them today by stopping this treachery?"

He sighed through his nose, a mere gust, a sign of his resignation. They'd reached a stalemate. "I understand that Obadïa's actions are—however unknowingly—inimical to his Empire, but we cannot impede upon his reign."

Lilith offered a faint smile, and it shed light on what remained of his incense, melting it away like the sun does the shadows.

"I will speak with Olga," Arduen said.

She took the mug from his hands and set it down on the table. "Are you okay?" she asked. "You are anxious."

Arduen wrapped an arm around her shoulders, and she returned the embrace by slinging her arm around his waist. "I worry, Fledgling."

"About the murder?"

"Amongst many other things," he admitted. Even after three weeks of Lilith being healthier than he'd seen her in months, he still lost sleep over her condition. He hadn't found any answers about her seizures, and without answers, how would he ever help her? "Lilith, I want—"

"Arduen!" Quin called from the entryway.

Both he and Lilith spun on their heels as Quin and Julius entered the room, Wren and Felix in tow.

"Well?" Arduen asked.

Julius was the first to respond, his eyes settling on Lilith as he spoke. "A Walabeän warrior was found dead this afternoon. Her friends reported she was not feeling well after their lunch and had gone down for a midday rest." His eyes flicked up to meet Arduen's. "It is believed she was poisoned."

"Poison…" Lilith breathed. "Do you know who it was?"

Arduen grimaced, praying it wasn't Hestîa. Lilith didn't need to suffer through more grief.

"There has been much tension between the Walabeän women and the Augustan men," Quin said. "This does not strike me as a natural death. They are investigating further, but the Igítís is rooted in the theory that she was targeted."

"It was not Hestîa, Lil," Julius said. "Though the victim was a close friend of hers."

"Oh…" Lilith held a hand against her chest, her eyes trained to the floor. Just by the set of her shoulders, Arduen knew she was fighting tears. Or rage. Or both.

"I will notify Olga," Quin said, taking his leave.

Julius drew up beside Lilith and dropped into one of the chairs. He patted the cushion of the seat beside him, signaling that he wanted her to join him.

Arduen debated giving them some privacy, but the gnawing ache in the pit of his stomach delayed him. "Lilith," he said, "I want you to return to the Frourío."

"What?" About to sit, she stood up straight, shock and dismay writ on her face. "Will you come with me?"

He clenched his jaw in resignation. "I am needed here."

"But—"

"I will take you home," Julius cut in, and Arduen was very grateful for him—if slightly concerned about the two of them traveling alone.

"Why?" she asked, eyes rounded with hurt.

"Because I do not believe it is safe for you here," Arduen said.

She gaped, searching for an argument. "Will Felix come with me?"

"Felix will stay. He is training and will need to be with Wren, and Quin and I need Wren at our sides." He looked to the prince. "Julius will return once he has seen you home."

That threw Lilith.

Felix cut in before she could lash out. "I will accompany them," he said swiftly, glancing from his Master to Julius. "That way Julius doesn't have to make the return trip alone."

Wren shrugged nonchalantly. "Seems a good enough idea."

"But why do I have to go?" Her attention drifted between

them all. "I am not the only noviciate." She was nearly in tears, and it pained Arduen to send her away like this.

"You are not at your best, Lilith," Arduen said. "That is the only reason I want you to go home. I cannot always be at your side here, and if murders are occurring under our noses, I need you to be able to defend yourself. The Walabeäns are clearly not welcome guests, and we brought them here. *You* won the fight that secured this alliance."

"I sparred with Hestîa today," she protested. "I did fine. I felt great, actually. I can handle myself and any assassins."

"You sat against the wall chatting most of the session," Julius said sheepishly, earning himself a wilting glare from her.

Arduen relinquished a sigh, rubbing his temple, a weak attempt to abate his brewing headache. "I cannot fight my own battles whilst constantly looking over my shoulder to ensure you can handle your own."

Understanding dawned, he could see it on her face. Arduen placed a pacifying hand on her shoulder, noting her caprice. He didn't want her to leave wracked by guilt. He didn't mean to say she was a burden.

"Go home, little one. I will see you in a few weeks." Though it may be longer than that. "You can leave tomorrow morning. Tonight, dine with me and I will help you prepare for the journey."

At that, the others gave their farewell and took off to their own chambers. Once they were alone, Lilith rose to join him at the window.

"You always said I was a vassal to the Gods," she said quietly, as if she could reserve this conversation for their ears only.

But the Gods heard everything.

"I'd feel more at ease if I were a vessel," she said. "A tool. A puppet."

"Why would you ever want to be a puppet?"

She gulped. "Because then I'd know what I'm doing. Or at least my misgivings would be vindicated. They wouldn't wholly be my own."

In the relief that she wasn't going to leave angry with him, Arduen let his shoulders relax. "Why do you think the Gods allow us the use of our tongues?"

She grappled for an answer—and he allowed her a moment —but she found no justification.

"As Divine, we are both vassals to the Gods and vessels of Their power," he answered. "They want us to use our voice. They want us to impart wisdom upon this world. Wisdom that only infinite years of experience can bestow upon a mortal. Years that They have given only to us." When she remained silent, he said, "We are vessels of Their power, and vassals of Their will."

He took her by the shoulders, spinning her to face him head on. "They've given you freedom to choose your actions, but that comes with the responsibility of knowing when to stand down and when to obey."

A knowing smirk played across her features.

"What?" he said, his eyes cutting to slits on instinct.

"You just explained to me exactly why you should advise the Emperor." Her smile deepened. "It seems to me the Gods have given you a tongue for a reason."

Oh, he was in trouble. "Clever."

"So…" She averted her gaze and glanced out the window. "Is it time to stand down, or is it time to stand up?"

Arduen released an exasperated sigh. "What am I going to do with you?"

Lilith shrugged at the rhetorical question.

"I promise," he said hesitantly, "that once you are safely

away from this place, I will have a discussion with the Emperor."

She cracked a grin and leaned into him. "I appreciate you," she whispered.

Arduen chuckled. What an odd way to say you loved someone. Wrapping an arm around her shoulders, he pulled her closer.

"You have no idea how much I appreciate *you*, Fledgling."

YOU BELONG TO ME

Late one evening, when the shrouded hallways of Spiro's subterranean fortress were quiet at last, Rhéa was summoned to the Great Divine's conference chamber—*not* his bedchamber. She was only ever escorted to the conference chamber when Spiro wished to mete out punishment. The Enchantress sent up a prayer for Xavier as she pushed open the imposing iron doors. They groaned as she entered, drawing attention to her arrival.

Spiro stood by the buffet, his back to her, his long pale-blond hair braided down his back like a whip.

So he didn't care much for her presence. Good.

Surreptitiously, Rhéa slumped into her designated chair when her eyes latched on to Xavier's wan face, then wavered to the slight figure in the seat beside him: *Irís.*

Rhéa blanched, the implications of Spiro's discovery dawning. *Feign ignorance. Get out of the room alive.*

"Please stand, Rhéa dear," Spiro's voice sliced through the air.

Rising to attention, she exchanged a wary glance with

Xavier, her body already beginning to tremble. There was nothing she could do to stop it.

"You've been harboring information." Spiro finally turned to face her. His usually pale face was flushed, his eyes intense, smoldering. *Stars, he is mad!* "Information that would benefit my cause greatly."

How he'd discovered the truth of Irís's identity, Rhéa would probably never know. There was absolutely no way that Xavier would have exposed her. He cared for her. She could see it in the way his eyes were fastened to the young Enchantress's fidgeting hands.

"Now, I thought you were loyal to me," Spiro said. "I thought you and I had a certain *connection*." He moved toward her, each long stride painfully slow. Taunting. Menacing. A predator stalking its prey. She forced her eyes to meet his, dreading the goblet he held in his hands, clasped between his long, spidery fingers.

Of course, he would drug her first.

Rhéa accepted the goblet, downing the contents in one gulp, paying no heed to the crimson liquid that dripped down her chin. She had little care for her appearance now.

Lowering the goblet to the table, Rhéa ignored her shaking hands. "I didn't go behind your back. You've ensured to diminish my arsenal. How could I dare move against you? I have no idea what you are talking about." This was not the appropriate occasion to be flippant, yet her mouth betrayed her better judgment.

"You've hidden this knowledge all along." His snarl vibrated her ear. Feral. "You knew from the moment you met dear Irís that she was one of your kind."

"How?" Rhéa breathed.

Spiro pulled away, a ghost of a smile on his face. Always

smug, despite his shortcomings. "Xavier," he called to his vassal. "Remove your tunic."

"Please…" Rhéa shuddered. "Don't punish Xavier. I am the one who deserves your wrath!"

Spiro chuckled, a rumble deep and rich. "Oh, Rhéa. You will receive my wrath. I simply mean to show you exactly how the young Enchantress gave herself away." The Great Divine waved her attention to Xavier's exposed back, his flesh unmarred by the familiar latticework of lash scars.

Rhéa gasped. *Oh, Irís.* The girl had given herself away. Spiro must have noted their blossoming romance, and he would have known Rhéa was not foolish enough to erase proof of Xavier's punishment for his dereliction of duty. That had been a strict order, and yet Irís did not know of that stipulation. But why didn't Xavier tell her? *Idiot!*

"The girl did not do this," Rhéa said. "I did." A resurgence of defiance clouded her nous. The Great Divine regarded her with a peaked brow. "I figured enough time had elapsed," she explained, "and since his suffering was no more, I could remove the scars."

Spiro took her by the arm, his grip penetrating to her bones. "You, my dear Rhéa, should have my best interests in mind at all times. There should be no room inside your dense skull for anyone else." Though his voice was calm, his tone even soft, she could practically smell the incense pulsing off of him in potent waves.

"Please, Spiro!" Rhéa was humiliated by her supplications alone, but she had seen enough of his discipline that the pleas escaped her mouth without volition. It was all in vain, of course. He would never grant her impunity, not when he needed to set an example.

Obadïa ruled by fear. Spiro ruled by a hard hand. Inexorable was her punishment, however long he made her tremble in anticipation.

"I hate liars," Spiro murmured, releasing her to pace the chamber, a peaceful lethality falling over him like a shroud.

"I tell no lies," Rhéa choked out, her refute delivered so weak as to betray her confidence, or lack thereof.

Spiro turned on her. "You lie, my dear. I know this is true because I traced the magic back to her hands"—he jabbed a finger at Irís—"not yours!"

How? She wanted to inquire but did not dare question the extent of his abilities. It was impossible for a Divine to trace magic. Only the most powerful Enchantresses could do that.

Unless he had formed an alliance…

Rhéa flinched as Spiro placed his cold hand on her cheek, his touch gentle enough, but his gaze was hard. Scalding. Promising recompense for her infraction. His hand draped through her hair as it so often did when she serviced him, and he gripped the back of her skull, pulling her down.

And he slammed her face into the desk.

Rhéa screamed as her cheek collided with the wood. Spiro maintained his tenacious grip on her skull, pushing her face into the wood with formidable force. Her vision flashed white, and she could have sworn the Stars' light penetrated the cavern. They were here to save her. Always. However long she remained under Spiro's thrall.

Brutally, Spiro wrapped a long arm around her svelte waist and hoisted her up so her back was pressed against his chest, his hand now wrapped around her throat.

"You belong to me, Rhéa," he breathed against her ear. "May all of your concerns revolve around me. Your Master. Your king." Her face throbbed, but he held her secure, squeezing her tight for emphasis. Was she supposed to say something?

Rhéa relented with a gasp. "Yes, Master."

Spiro released her then, though he kept a proprietary hand on her lower back. "You will go and clean yourself up, then you will join me in my chambers."

Without a backward glance, Rhéa gathered her skirt in her hands and floundered to the door. Spiro's glower was palpable, even after she entered the hallway.

Even after she returned to her own chambers.

17

LET THEM TAKE YOU

Before dawn, Lilith, Julius, and Felix set off without a backward glance. The commingling of eagerness to leave the city behind and dread to leave Arduen, evolved into a cloying ache deep in her core. A longing to escape her reality, if only for a moment. But there was nowhere to go. No place to forget who or what she was. No. Divine did not get to indulge in moments of respite.

It seemed, in her Master's absence, fear and doubt abounded.

"Are you all right?" Julius asked, shooting a glance over his shoulder, the city walls a mere shadow in the distance.

"I will be," she said, deigning not to bemoan her troubles. Worriment for her Master, her father, working so closely to that ghoul of a ruler. Graciously, Julius did not press her to divulge her consternation.

By noon, a trembling began in her quads. She'd breached the limit of her strength for the day. But as much as she longed to be close to Julius, she did not want to give in and ride with him. That would be defeat. Her greatest need was to get stronger, and she could only achieve that through persistence.

The first day crept by at a slow pace. They made camp out in the open, not yet close enough to the pines of the Megálos. As Lilith prepared Skydancer for sleep, she removed the ring the old lady had gifted her, tucking it into the small pocket of her pack where she knew it would be safe. The metal had bitten into her fingers along the journey; she must have been gripping the reins too tight.

"We will take turns sleeping," Julius said as he prepared their evening meal using quick bursts of Xander's Fire to heat the meat.

"I will take first watch," Lilith offered, spreading out her bedroll beside his.

"No, you've pushed yourself today," Felix said. "I can tell by the way you carry yourself. You're too stiff. I will take first watch, and I will wake you when it's your turn." He nodded to Julius, then lowered himself onto his own bedroll, crossing his long legs beneath him.

Lilith didn't lie down straight away. She began to knead her legs as Tatiana and Arduen had for her. The probing hurt, but it was a good feeling, massaging away the cramps that would surely amass to another episode if she wasn't careful.

"Let me do that." Julius gripped her shoulder, guiding her down onto her back. "Arduen showed me what to do last night." He opened his palm, and Lilith handed him the vial of Tatiana's liniment.

Removing her breeches, a flush suffused her cheeks. Julius didn't seem bothered by her impending nudity, though he was modest himself. He knew this was practical, necessary. Felix, thankfully, turned his back to them and began the first watch.

Slowly, she exposed her legs to the balmy night air, the hem of her blouse bunched in her lap. Ever so gently, Julius rubbed the liniment between his palms, warming it before setting his hands to her skin. A soft, involuntary moan escaped her lips.

Julius chuckled aridly. "Am I doing a good job?"

Her face searing with heat, she murmured, "I really needed this."

"Tomorrow you will ride with me. I'm not taking any chances."

Lilith capitulated, delighting in the relief it evidently brought him. She studied his face as he continued to work, edging higher and higher up her thighs, catalyzing her heartbeat. When Tatiana and Arduen massaged her, she did not worry where their fingers tread. Tatiana was a healer, and a woman; and Arduen was like her father, he wouldn't ever do anything to make her uncomfortable. But Julius had never ventured far beneath her clothes before. They'd long since overstepped the boundaries of friendship, but that borderline remained uncrossed.

Another groan escaped her lips as his firm fingers crossed the hem of her blouse. Julius didn't react this time; his expression strictly pensive, his bottom lip pinched between his teeth. If she weren't so self-conscious, she'd think he was trying not to touch her inappropriately. Her cheeks burned in spite of herself and she sat up abruptly, startling him.

"Did I hurt you?" Julius asked.

She shook her head, her breathing heavy, betraying her nerves. "No, I'm just… good for now. Thank you."

Julius regarded her with glassy eyes, the gold of his irises lost beneath thick lashes. "Lilith, I…" His voice trailed off and he flashed a furtive glance at Felix's back, then he pressed his forehead against hers.

Brazen from lust, Lilith cupped his cheek, his jaw pressing against her palm. As his stormy eyes met hers, he lost control, his lips brushed against hers, feverish and fast.

Lilith met him with equal intensity, all but pulling him into her lap. Gods, she'd wanted this for so long. He prompted her to lie down again, but she pulled away. Placing two fingers against his swollen lips, she sank back down onto her bedroll. "Enjoy the chase, Prince," she whispered against his skin. "It may well be your last."

He lowered his gaze, a bashful flush tinging his cheeks. "I can only hope that it is," he said, removing his hands from her with a featherlight caress.

She didn't move, paralyzed by his touch. How far would they have taken it had they been alone? As thankful as she was that Julius wouldn't have to travel alone on the return trip, she resented Felix for his kindness now.

Felix's voice broke the silence, "What happens when you have an episode?"

Wrapping her blanket around her torso, she said, "What do you mean?"

He swallowed, his eyes settled on the distant horizon. "You're awake, writhing, spasming, but you're beyond our reach. Then you're gone." He looked over at her. "What happens?"

Drawing the blanket tighter around her frame, Lilith considered his question for a moment, reliving the last episode she'd had. When she answered, it was to Julius she spoke. "It's all darkness. Weightlessness. Like I'm driftwood on the Galatëa." She licked at her lips, unable to meet his eyes. She could feel the weight of their gazes combined. "Then the current pulls me under and I can't tell up from down. It's a relief. I know that the pain will end soon, and I will wake. I can hear muffled voices. Gentle hands molding me, though I remain resistant. Like I'm not pliable."

"Lil…" Julius practically choked on her name.

Her mind wandered back to what Hestîa had said. This

malady could very well be a punishment of the Gods, retribution for granting Larkin the highest honor. "I suspect this is the Gods trying to shape me into who They thought I was, but maybe I am not worthy of Their power. I am not worthy to be Their vassal."

"Don't say that," Julius snapped.

"I am not passing Their vetting," she said softly. When he did not say anything, she added, "You think it's stupid, my introspection."

He shook his head, expression dark despite the glow of the fire. "I think you are experiencing something none of us have. And if it is holy, then embrace it. Let Them take you, however much it hurts me to wait for your return."

THE SECOND DAY OF TRAVEL DAWNED, AND LILITH AWOKE TO Julius's gentle prods. "It's time, Lil."

She got up, changed, and washed her face quickly. "You didn't wake me to take my watch."

Julius gave her a noncommittal shrug. "You were snoring so loud, how could I possibly wake you?"

Lilith muttered a genial curse at the jest. He flashed a cocky grin her way before tying Skydancer to his stallion. She had forgotten that she was to ride with him today. Being so close to him was proving to be difficult. Though their trip hadn't been overly amorous, she couldn't help indulging in lascivious thoughts. Thankfully, Felix's presence kept her from acting on them.

Julius mounted Stormbringer first and reached down for her.

"Behind or in front?"

"Front," he said. "I want to ensure you don't fall, in case of an... *episode*." He said the word like it would cause her to seize up on the spot.

Ignoring this, Lilith placed her foot in the stirrup, her hand in his, and he lifted her up to sit before him. Julius wrapped his arms around her and grasped the reins, spurring his steed into a trot.

They rode through the day, stopping only to let the horses drink and to relieve themselves. Both Julius and Felix had asked her how she was fairing on multiple occasions. If she possessed the candor, she would have told Julius that his breath on the nape of her neck drove her crazy, the heat between her legs a dull ache begging to be tended to. But she said instead, "I'm fine, like the last one hundred times you asked."

"But maybe, on the one hundredth and tenth time you won't be fine," Felix said with a playful wink.

It had been two days and still they had not reached the Megálos pines. They were forced to make camp beside a knoll in the open, and Felix used Thëo's Earth to raise the hill for increased coverage. Julius constructed a campfire, which only took a matter of seconds for someone blessed by Xander.

"You'll let me take watch tonight?" she asked.

Julius poked at the meager fire with a stick. "I'd rather you sleep."

"I can sleep in the saddle. You need to sleep. You've got bags under your eyes the size of Lake Ozeros."

"Thanks, Lil." He chuffed in amusement. "But between Felix and I, we get enough shut eye."

She snorted. "Shut eye isn't always sleep."

The prince massaged her, though he kept a greater distance from her upper thighs than the previous evening, she noted. He spoke to her throughout, telling her all about Xanthë and his father's extravagant palace—*his* palace one day soon. As interested as she was in learning of his homeland, she was reminded of his eventual departure.

Julius hushed her when it was time to sleep, and he even wrapped her in her own blanket tightly, sitting vigil by her side until it was Felix's turn to take watch.

◌ ◌ ◌ ◌ ◌

"GET UP, LILITH."

Lilith groaned and sat up. "Massage time?" she mumbled as her eyes adjusted to the darkness.

Julius's hand rose up and smacked on top of her mouth, his other hand bracing her back. She could make out his features enough to glimpse alarm in his hazel eyes. "Don't speak," he hushed. "We have company."

Her limbs calcified at his words, her eyes searching their surroundings for Felix. She could make out nothing in the dark.

Julius dropped his hands, gripping the hilt of his sword, Orphëus. He remained crouched, alert for any sounds of life beyond their camp. Silently, Lilith retrieved Constance from beside her pack and joined him, keeping her back to him to see the entire camp. Questing out with Discernment, dread pooled in her gut. They had visitors. They were human. And they were not kind. She struggled to control the frenetic thump of her heart as those entities encroached, their emotions betraying ill intent.

It was clear that Julius had gleaned as much as she had, his body tensing behind hers. The prince was usually imperturbable, even during battle. There was a shuffle to her left, and Lilith's eyes followed the sound, finding Felix's outline against the dark blue sky.

Could Spiro have sent soldiers after them? He had faithful

men seeded in Kenora. Word could have reached him of their departure.

There was the snapping sound of a twig and their enemies attacked with a roar. Julius and Felix met their assault with no trepidation. Lilith was slower, but she managed to rise just as one of the men descended upon her.

They were outnumbered, six to three. Their enemies must have known of her state, else they would have sent a larger force. These soldiers were smart, catching them off guard, their camp untenable.

Desperate to distance herself from Julius, Lilith hopped away from the campsite, lest they cause injury to each other fighting in such close proximity. A frisson of excitement took control of her limbs, fueling her through the fight. This was no beast, but a man, and she would have to kill him or be killed.

He darted at her with a succession of fierce stabs. Only a fool wouldn't realize that he was aiming for her heart. This wasn't a bout. This was a death dance. Thus eliminating her earlier suspicions that these men were Spiro's. The Great Divine didn't want her dead, he wanted her alive.

Regardless of the eventual outcome, Lilith met every cut with a substantial riposte, her muscles beseeching her for relief already. She panted, teeth bared, practically snarling at the man. It was too dark to make out his clothing, but if the Emperor did send these men, he wasn't about to send them clad in imperial regalia.

Lilith feinted left, and then right, then attacked his exposed side, her speed thankfully unhindered by her lack of training. Trickery was unsavory, but they were not equally matched. She needed to dupe him if she wanted to win.

If she wanted to live.

Finally, she caught him somewhere in his side, under his arm, perhaps. Slashing vigorously, Lilith seized the upper hand, but her breathing labored, and her knees weakened. A few more minutes and she'd be depleted, at risk of another episode. At least when her body seized up with searing spasms this time, she wouldn't feel her enemy's blade in her chest.

The urge to access Aether was almost unbearable. But Lilith had not trained with her elements in so long, she doubted it would be of any use. If she could summon even a draft of Aether, she may not be able to control the abyss, and she'd risk harming Julius or Felix. This rankled her, for the instinct to release Constantine's abyss was adamant. Unyielding.

Lilith moved maladroitly, lacking the finesse she'd worked so hard to obtain over the past year. Yet the drive for survival surged, a primal reaction, setting every part of her to awareness. Crying out, she swiped her blade across his and, instead of retreating, she barreled forward, her elbow grazing his jaw, taking him by surprise. The soldier fumbled backward and fell on his ass.

A deep howl sounded from across the camp, and Lilith's head snapped in the direction. "Julius!" she screamed. It was too dark to see him, but she needed to know he was all right.

Light flared, near-blinding. Julius was destroying his enemies with Xander's Fire.

A solid wall crashed into her. Lilith smacked her face on the ground, her body hitting the earth with a thud, the man's weight pinning her, immobilizing, pushing her down into the dirt. Vomit rose in her throat as he clutched Constance and ripped it from her hand, sending it soaring into the air. Out of reach. Out of sight.

She was defenseless.

"Sweet dreams, Lilith Achilles," the soldier growled.

Lilith cried out for help as the soldier lowered his blade to her exposed neck.

This was it. This was what it felt like to be defeated. This was a man, and he had conquered a Divine single-handedly.

A burning sensation shot through each limb, pervasive and insistent, the temperature reaching a new height.

Oh, Gods! She was going to explode.

As her eyes began to roll into the back of her head, the soldier called, "Hey, Saff! This one's about to have an org—"

Then, instinct persevered.

Aether flashed.

The release was cathartic, but it was not the torrent of power she'd grown accustomed to. It was paltry. Meager. A small fragment. Frayed and distorted. A dying ember of what was once a blazing conflagration. Limbs searing, melting into the earth. Metal bit into her neck, then her enemy's weight was lifted off of her. The soldier vanished, seeming to evanesce on the wind. Constantine's abyss winked out, once again dousing the camp in darkness.

Lilith lay still, using every last ounce of energy to ward off the inevitable. Then Julius entered her vision. He lowered himself onto her, pinning her legs to the ground with his knees, her arms with his hands.

"You're going to be okay," he said to her, but his face did not comply with his words.

The familiar burn crept up on her, reaching its culmination, filching the breath from her lungs. Lilith screamed, her body contorting in pain.

Julius panted above her, the veins in his neck bulging, his tensile strength waning, his eyes brimming with tears. He barked orders at Felix, his words muffled by the ringing in her ears. Still, in his panic, Julius secured her to the ground effectively, Felix, she realized, holding her head to keep her from hurting herself. Lilith could feel nothing beyond the searing of her spasming muscles. She kept her eyes intent on Julius's, committing each fleck of gold to memory, lest this be her last. She would subsist, if only to prolong the vision.

Her back stretched into a painful arch. Julius's tear-stained face disappeared from view, leaving her to succumb to the darkness that was all too eager to engulf her.

18

I ALWAYS WAKE

An awful tinnitus was the first sign of lucidity. Consciousness tugged Lilith back from the depths of Hades, foggy eyes slowly parting to reveal a blue sky.

A dark figure shifted beside her.

Julius.

He massaged her limbs frantically, seeming unaware of her nakedness.

"Julius…"

The prince pushed his arm out to hold her down. "Don't sit up yet. You've got knots throughout your legs. I'm afraid you'll have another episode. I'm trying to recall everything Tatiana did whilst you were having multiple fits, but it was all such a haze." He was flustered, his black curls a mop surrounding his face, eyes wide and bloodshot.

"Julius, don't." She tried—and failed—to rise. "You need to rest. Look at you!"

He ignored her and continued to knead her legs, his touch hasty and firm. Almost too firm.

"Stop!" she sat up and pushed him away with as much force as she could muster, which at that moment, was very little. His expression was one of hurt and shock, as if she'd slapped him. Lilith staggered to her feet and he rose with her, placing both hands on her shoulders to steady her.

"Lie down, *now!*" His tone was borderline brusque, his face irate. Taken aback by his sudden ire, Lilith obeyed, slowly lowering herself to the ground, allowing him to ease her down.

Julius took a moment to calm himself. Lilith peaked around the camp for her pants, but the sight wasn't what she expected.

Six bodies lay crumpled in the dirt, no more than charcoal themselves. She recalled the flash of light that illuminated the camp before she fell prey to another onslaught of torture.

She used Aether.

Recollection forced her hand to her throat. There was a small incision crusted over with dried blood. Only a fraction of a second had separated her from death.

"Lie on your stomach," Julius ordered, dropping to his knees beside her.

Lilith obeyed, wary of his unusual gravitas. He held the blanket up, shielding her bare bottom from his sight. She'd never seen him anything other than pacific, gentle. To see him so upset quieted her entirely.

Julius lifted her tunic and poured liniment over her bare back.

"Where is Felix?" she ventured. Anything to take the attention off her dire situation.

His touch was firm, squeezing the ache from her muscles. "He is walking the horses. They were a bit spooked by the fight."

Normally, a massage helped the tension ebb away, but Julius was working her muscles with a firm hand. Too firm. She bit down on her bottom lip, trying with all her might not to make noise, but the agony from her seizure still lingered in her muscles.

"Julius, please." She lifted her head to look at him, but he pushed her back down. "You're hurting me!"

The pressure of his touch lightened, though he continued to prod at her muscles with his thumb.

"I can't do this anymore," she sobbed, her body still shaking from the attack. Julius remained silent. "There has to be a way…" she thought aloud as he worked over her. "I bet the High Enchantress knows what to do."

Her statement met silence.

"I want to go to the Marsh."

Julius lifted his hands from her skin abruptly. "We will do no such thing!" His voice was flat, tone harsh, like a king delegating orders.

"I can't continue on like this," she argued.

Standing, he began to pace the camp. Lilith sat up, pulling her tunic down. Her breeches lay on the ground a few feet away. Julius must have removed them when her flailing eased. She retrieved them, pulled them on clumsily in her haste to clothe herself.

Finally, he burst, "This is crass! We need to return to the Frourío as ordered. I will make a trip to Kynös to inquire about more ingredients for the liniment, but we are not going to the Obsydían Marsh."

"I want to ask Ophelía about the possibility of a healing spell." She strode toward him, however floundering, her gaze imploring him to acquiesce. He gripped her shoulder to steady her. She couldn't remove her eyes from him. She couldn't bring herself to look at the bodies.

"We can't use magic, Lilith!"

"No, *we* can't, but they can. It won't be an affront to the Gods if the High Enchantress uses a spell on me."

"You'll need some form of payment, and they don't accept traditional coin," he warned.

"It's worth a shot to see if they can offer me any recourse."

"The Obsydían Marsh is a week away," Julius said. "Another fortnight back to the Frourío, following. My expected return to the capital will be delayed. Who knows what can happen in that time? I don't know if you've noticed, but our attackers were not beast, they were human. The Emperor could have sent them after us. They could have been Spiro's spies!" He paused to expel an exasperated sigh. "What if you have another attack?"

"Then hold me if I crumble," she countered. "Talk me through the pain like you always do. Your voice has always pulled me from the darkness. The pain will subside as long as you are with me."

He shook his head.

"Hey, you're up!" Felix's jovial voice sailed to them on the breeze. Julius couldn't conceal his scowl at the interruption. Clearly there was more he wanted to say.

"It's just pain," she said. "I always wake."

Julius ran stiff fingers through his hair, pulling it taut at the roots.

Lowering her voice, she said, "I am going to the Marsh, whether I go with or without you." She glanced toward Felix, looking for her steed, but the gelding wasn't anywhere in sight. "Where is Skydancer?"

Felix cast a sheepish glance at Julius, and the prince groaned as he wiped his face, pulling on his cheeks. His eyes guiltily flicked to a large heap of black ash.

Lilith followed his gaze. "No!" She nearly dropped to her knees.

"I'm so sorry," he said, holding her to him.

She wasn't sure what hurt more, being culpable for their current situation or Skydancer's death.

"Well," she started with a whimper, "I guess I'm walking to the Marsh."

"Lil…" Julius rose to his feet, stopping her with a firm hand on her arm. "I'll agree to go with you, but you will let me do the talking, all right?"

Lilith couldn't look at him. She couldn't tear her eyes from Skydancer's remains. Was it her blast of Aether or Julius's release of Fire?

Placing a gentle finger under her chin, Julius tilted her head up. She met his gaze, subdued and mournful, and managed to offer him a quivering smile in response.

"It's settled," he said. "We are going to the Marsh."

19

THE STARS' GUIDANCE

When they were finally a day out from the Obsydían Marsh, they met pines, the foothills of the Orösía Mountains visible above their pointed tips. Lilith rode with Julius as Felix trailed behind them, seemingly lost in his own thoughts. Perhaps the battle hadn't done him good. The boy had only ever killed beasts and had yet to participate in anything more than a raid. She made a mental note to ask him how he was over dinner.

Lilith sat forward in the saddle, ruminating over how to clear the air between her and Julius. They had been forged from the same ore, pulled from the same depths of the earth. But now she was beginning to understand just how considerably the sea divided them.

Julius shifted uncomfortably, and she leaned forward to appease him, neither making a point to speak. Constance wasn't sharp enough to cut the tension between them.

But his new beard was.

Lilith froze under his touch as he pressed against her,

burying his face in the crook of her shoulder. His breath tickled her neck, sending shivers down her spine.

"Please forgive me," he said. "I've been stressed about your condition. Our situation is more precarious than you think and—"

"No," she interjected. "I understand perfectly well just how precarious this situation is—*my* situation is. That is why I am resorting to the Enchantresses. I need to exhaust every possibility before I can accept this as the new normal."

Julius kissed the top of her head. "Then that is what we will do. We'll search high and low for a cure." With one hand on the reins, he kept the other wrapped around her rib cage, his thumb massaging her with lazy strokes. She leaned back against him, a smile on her lips.

When she looked up to inspect his face, his sour moue was still visible. "That's not all that's bothering you," she observed dryly.

He pressed his chin against her crown, forcing her to look ahead. "No…"

She half-turned to him in the saddle. "Skydancer… It wasn't your fault, you were—"

"Protecting us," he cut her off. "I know."

Frowning, she watched his jaw clench, a muscle flickering beneath his short beard, his pulse strong under the soft skin of his neck.

"Our gifts," he said with a rush of breath, "are meant to help people, to protect them. I killed them. I used Xander's Fire to *kill* them."

She knew she should feel a hint of sympathy for Julius, empathy even, but what she felt was utter disappointment. She hadn't even released Aether and the energy it required had pushed her over the edge, into one of the worst seizures she'd ever experienced.

"There are human soldiers in Spiro's army," she countered. "We kill them when we fight him."

"I try not to," Julius grit out, "and if I must, I don't use elemental power to do it. Still, it sickens me. I know down in my core that it is so very wrong."

Lilith faced forward again, dropping her hands to lay atop his. "It is not your fault, Jules." She let the nickname—a name she hadn't yet dared use—drift on the air. Julius didn't protest. "Spiro is the one with the bloody hands. He is the one who has turned the Gods' creations against each other." She stroked the back of his hands, her fingertips falling into the ripples of tendons and bones. "Never you."

He groaned, his chin digging into the top of her head.

"You did it to save me." She craned her neck to look up at him. "You did it to save someone you care about."

"Oh, Lil," he said on a sigh. "Only you would fail to recognize that as a selfish reason."

⊚ ⤶ ⟿ ᙢ ჱ

IT WAS DUSK WHEN THEY REACHED THE OBSYDÍAN MARSH, Discernment guiding their path. The Marsh was underwhelming compared to Lilith's preconceived vision. There were clear walkways of raised land, whilst distinct swampy areas spotted the dwelling. Small cottages rose up several feet above the moist land. What braced the structures, she couldn't be certain, but it definitely was not wood.

On the edge of the living trees, Julius instructed Felix to remain with the horses. Lilith expected him to protest, but the boy obeyed with a nod. He definitely wasn't okay. But now was not the time to pry.

The farther they penetrated into the Enchantresses' domain, the more sinister the foliage became. The Marsh was a graveyard of skeletal pines, their masts bordered the walkways, redolent of a balustrade. Flames of varying colors decorated the trunks; gold, violet, silver, and blue. If Lilith hadn't been warned about the Enchantresses' conniving reputation, she might have thought the place more beautiful than eerie.

Their constant Divine senses made them aware of the luminous eyes leering from the shadows. Ignoring their watchful gazes, Lilith strode toward the largest structure with as much confidence as she could muster. After sucking in a sharp, deep breath, she ascended the marble steps toward the palace of bones, her hand clasped in Julius's.

The prince had assumed a stoical mien ever since the ground had become wetter, ever since they'd been forced to secure Stormbringer to a tree and continue on foot. Gone were the sandals they wore in the capital; now their boots were sodden, their clothes sticking to their skin in the mild temperature.

They entered the largest structure through two large doors, left agape as if welcoming visitation. Lilith entered, hesitant but nobly, her chin held high. Making their way down the column-lined hall, she noted that the pillars were made of bone—not stone. She shivered at the thought, of both the size of the originating beast, and the magnitude of power it must have taken to overtake it.

"Lilith Oak," said an ethereal voice, echoing through the massive chamber.

The Divine reached the base of the stairs leading up to the dais. The woman atop it was striking. Her dark gown and long midnight hair blended her into the onyx curtains behind her. A camouflage of sorts. Ophelía, the High Enchantress—for this was who the woman must be—dipped her chin in recognition of the young Divines.

Lilith observed the High Enchantress through slit eyes. Her

pale skin was flawless, illuminated from within, even inside such dim interiors. Her slanted violet eyes were distinguishable even at a distance. Her berry lips were full and elegant. She was the epitome of cold and hard, yet somehow delicate, like frozen ice laced with fine cracks. Though it was clear that Ophelía was unbreakable. Beauty incarnate.

Anxiety flurried in Lilith's stomach, and she ignored the tiny bumps spreading across her skin. Courage was a virtue she would not yield in the presence of the High Enchantress, regardless of Ophelía's obvious attempts to cow them. When Lilith mustered the gall to meet that violet stare, it was as if a dormant beast from within opened its eyes to greet an old friend.

"Have you come to learn magic?" Ophelía flashed them a majestic smile.

"We are here to inquire about aid in healing," Julius spoke up, his deep voice resounding throughout the hall. He sounded every bit like a king. "Lilith has been suffering for months. You were so gracious to send us an Enchantress to assist her, but her torment continues."

The High Enchantress's gaze shifted between them. "And what do you presume I can do about it?"

A pity. And Lilith had thought that maybe, since Ophelía had already sent aid, the High Enchantress might have felt some inclination to help. Compassion was not something Lilith should have expected from a woman the Divine lauded for her wiles. *Fool.*

Lilith piqued up. "I was just hop—" Julius squeezed her hand to silence her.

"We traveled here from the capital in the hopes that you could heal her," he said. "We surmised that there may be a cure that only the High Enchantress is capable of attaining."

Perfect. Persuasion through means of flattery. Lilith withheld her grin. She would have to commend Julius's cunning later.

Julius continued, "Perhaps a gift to be bestowed upon a disciple of the Gods?"

Ophelia cackled, high and ringing. "Enchantresses do not worship Gods."

Julius hesitated. This was the first time Lilith had seen him so uncertain in the presence of another.

"You worship the Stars," Lilith said, "but the Stars were created by the Gods. Do Them both an honor by restoring me to my former health. I cannot continue to train if I am so ill. I cannot access my gifts."

Violet irises settled on her. "Yes, we cannot deny power where it so clearly exists. Have you considered that the Gods have renounced Their gifts?"

Lilith blanched, her body instantly rigid. She hadn't thought of that. When Hestîa had mentioned that the Gods might be punishing her, that seemed to resonate within. But to renounce her Anointment?

"The Gods would smite her down before They would go through the trouble of making her suffer," Julius said, tone firm in challenge, impervious to Ophelia's majesty. "Our Gods do not delight in the pain of others."

Silence permeated the hall. Would Julius be angry if the Enchantresses turned her away? They'd deviated so far from course, perhaps for nothing at all.

The High Enchantress eyed Lilith with interest. "You've been blessed twice, correct?"

Lilith met Ophelía's gaze, unflinching. "Yes."

"And you managed to slaughter your traitorous brother?"

Of course, the High Enchantress would bring that up. "Yes."

"Very promising," Ophelía crooned. "Very promising, indeed."

Lilith squeezed Julius's hand tighter, his palm warm and damp. Or was that her own?

"And you granted Larkin an Athánatos Star?" Ophelía arched a delicate eyebrow.

"I did."

The Enchantress heaved a melodramatic sigh. "Well, it seems that the Gods may just be punishing you. I'd suffer it out. Serve your time."

Lilith bristled. She refused to leave empty-handed, dejected. "I need to continue my training. I will never be able to help the others defeat Spiro if I'm constantly crippled."

The High Enchantress blinked slowly, entirely unfazed. The quandaries of the Divine were not her own.

Curiosity gnawed at the edge of Lilith's mind. She wouldn't likely visit with the Enchantresses again for a long time, she might as well take advantage of the opportunity to ask questions. "If you can use magic to see what occurs in the world, why can't you see how Spiro is creating his beasts?"

"Spiro's base is guarded by an impenetrable ward," Ophelía said. "Even I cannot break through it."

"But you are the High Enchantress. If you can't, then who can? A Sorcerer?"

Ophelía's face flushed, her eyes seeming to darken. Lilith immediately regretted her choice of words, anxiety worming through her. Then Ophelía's eyes flicked down to their entwined hands. She grinned wryly. "Interesting…"

Would she exploit their budding romance?

"What is interesting?" Julius asked.

Ophelía pointed. "May I see that ring?"

Lilith glanced down at her left hand, at the intricately carved golden ring wrapped around her middle finger. She'd put it back on when they'd decided to head to the Marsh, since she no longer had a mount of her own. She pulled it off and proffered it to the High Enchantress.

Ophelía held the ring up into the meager light. The moonlight penetrating the stained-crystalline windows created an eerily beautiful pattern of refractions on the marble floor. Lilith focused on them, to cope with the tension pervading the hall.

"I do not give aid freely," Ophelía said. "To anyone."

Lilith's heart sank.

"But I will agree to a liaison," the Enchantress added. "I will offer a bargain, Creature of the Light. I will reveal to you a way to sway the Gods'… displeasure toward you. Furthermore, I will send you on your way with fresh clothing and fill your empty vials with my praised healing oils. All paid for by this ring. Should you accept this offer, I can guarantee you will be recovered by next Solstice."

Lilith flashed a wary glance at Julius, but his eyes were fastened to the High Enchantress. He stood frozen, calculating, as if he knew that letting Ophelía out of his sight for even a second would beget their demise.

"We both want a safer, flourishing Augusta," Ophelía continued. "And this is the way."

The ring? It was the answer? And would it be any more influential in the High Enchantress's hands? Lilith felt as though she was on the precipice of a grave mistake, but she didn't have time to consider the unknown implications. They needed to get out of here.

"Why do you want it?" Lilith asked. "What is it beyond metal and ornament?"

Ophelía cracked a smile, both beautiful and clever. "Metal can be used as *storage*, one could say, for sacred spells and enchantments. It can be useful when one travels, the spell at the ready without sapping the Enchantress's strength." Her smile deepened. "I can never have too many stored spells."

Lilith looked to Julius for his counsel, but he did not seem disconcerted by Ophelía's want for the ring. He gave her a slight nod, his eyes never leaving the High Enchantress.

"Deal," Lilith said.

Ophelía grinned beatifically, flashing straight white teeth. She snapped her fingers and a tall Enchantress emerged from the shadows behind the throne. She was a mirror image of Ophelía.

Ophelía addressed the Enchantress, "Evanöra, please retrieve a gown for young Lilith, and one of our finest tunics for Prince Julius." The Enchantress flashed a hungry gaze in his direction before exiting the manor. Lilith shot her a cutting glare.

"Now, I will take your vials and fill them myself." Ophelía extended her palm, and Julius stepped forth to pass her the vials.

When Ophelía left them, Julius turned to Lilith. "I hope this works, Lil," he said, his broad shoulders relaxing slightly.

Lilith gave his hand a squeeze. "I do, too."

◎ ☸ ➴ ᗰ ◊

Once Ophelía returned with the vials, she'd pulled Lilith aside—much to Julius's agitation—to speak in private. The High Enchantress gave Lilith vague instructions, then handed her the vials, told her the words to speak over the liniment as she massaged it into her aching muscles, and wished her the Stars' guidance.

"Please give my best to Arduen." Ophelía shot them a saccharine smile.

"Of course," was Lilith's benign response. *Of course not! Arduen will never know I came here.*

Julius bade farewell, and Lilith nodded her thanks before

exiting the manor. A young Enchantress with bright silver eyes held the reins of Stormbringer on the edge of the Marsh. She seemed to be involved in amicable conversation with Felix, and their companion's eyes were glazed, his cheeks red.

The Enchantress didn't utter a word as she handed the reins back to Felix, her fingertips brushing his in what looked more like a caress than an accidental touch. She flashed Julius a warm smile and ambled back toward the skeletal trees, swaying to a melody they couldn't hear.

Lilith didn't ask Felix questions about the interaction, for the Enchantress seemed to have chased away the horrors of battle.

They'd achieved what they had come for, and now it was time to ride through the night. It was time to go home.

2 0

A CONVOLUTED SITUATION

It was late in the evening when they finally arrived at the Frourío. They dismounted as they approached the clearing where she'd faced Larkin. Where she'd killed him.

"Don't look." Julius pulled her away, as if his touch could ward off the memories assaulting her mind.

A piece of her was still kneeling there beside her brother's corpse, frozen, forever hunched and despairing. Regardless of time, that fragment of herself would never return. Time did not care about the heart or the frail mind. It would trickle on like an ancient stream, heedless of those who struggle to keep up with its pace. And it would go on until those poor souls lost stamina. For humans were not meant to exist forever; such was the curse of the Divine.

"I'm all right," she assured him, clasping her hands before her.

Though her palms were now clean, the blood remained. A stain forever marking her Kin-Slayer.

Together, they ambled toward the front door of the Frourío,

eager to get inside. Lilith's jaw ached from the concerted effort to keep her teeth from chattering, and her shoulders were so tense, it hurt just to reach up and wrap her hand around the door handle.

Entering the kitchen, she cursed herself for being so unprepared to meet Zurí's wrath. Her Master greeted her sternly, arms akimbo. Who knew what words would have roared from her mouth if Aspen hadn't been present? Lilith traipsed toward her Master as Julius and Felix stabled the horses.

Ambrose glanced out the window, his brow furrowed in question. "Where's Skydancer?"

Lilith glanced between Zurí and Ambrose warily. "He didn't make it." Julius could relay the story when he came in, he was less likely to slip up and reveal their clandestine trip to the Obsydían Marsh. When her companions finally deigned to come inside, Zurí was on Julius like a hound.

"You took over two weeks to get here!" Zurí snapped. "Need I point out, that is twice as long as it should have taken. And what happened to Lilith's horse?"

Oh, she was angry! If Lilith hadn't been the subject of her ire, she'd be sniggering.

The prince jumped into a fastidious account of their travels, omitting their journey to the Marsh, leaving Zurí no reason to impugn. "There was an incident," he said, calm and efficient. "We were attacked by men on our second night out of the capital. Men… *not* beasts." He shot Zurí a pointed look, and Lilith was shocked to see her Master's face pale.

"Were they Augustan?" Ambrose cut in, his ebony skin powdered with flour.

"They attacked us while we were sleeping," Julius said. "Thankfully, I was standing guard. We met their blades when they charged, but it was dark, and I couldn't make much of them. Not enough to distinguish who'd ordered the attack."

Zurí shook her head. "What do you mean? Why not look at their bodies in the morning?"

Julius hesitated, shifting his stance uncomfortably. "Well, that's the thing. They outnumbered us two to one, so I unleashed Fire on them. It was the only way."

"If he hadn't, I'd be dead," Lilith added in his defense. It was true, and they would know this when she removed her cloak to reveal the scar on her neck.

"Explain." Zurí crossed her arms. It was best to obey, rather than antagonize her further.

Julius assumed the lead. "Lilith shouldn't be pushing herself. She wasn't up to her full potential, and the man over-powered her. He had his blade to her throat when I killed them, and then she had an episode. Felix and I spent the night treating her to the best of our knowledge."

"Oh, Lilith." Zurí's expression of stone melted into one of sympathy.

"That's why we were delayed," Julius said. "We had no means of contacting you or Arduen." He hung up his cloak and extended his hand to Lilith, and she removed her cloak reluc-tantly, handing it over.

"Damn." Ambrose stepped closer, angling his head to better inspect her neck. "You are very lucky, my kyría."

Lilith could only nod. She was travel-worn and in need of a soft mattress.

"What's this I hear?" Olga entered the kitchen. "You were attacked?"

Everyone nodded confirmation.

"Do you think they were sent by the Emperor?" Zurí asked.

There was so much they didn't know. "They had to be," Lilith nearly whispered.

"Why?" Julius questioned.

A vision of her attacker blossomed in her mind. "Because he knew my name."

Zurí furrowed her brow. "No offence, my girl, but everyone in Augusta knows your name."

Lilith gave a vehement shake of her head. "No, Lilith Oak is not my name." The room stilled, awaiting her explanation. "My real name is Lilith Achilles, and my attacker knew it. The only other person who knows my real name is my father, General Achilles of the Emperor's Agemas. And now that it has been revealed that I am his daughter, Obadïa knows my real name, and his entire court."

"And now comes the next series of lessons: guarding your back," Zurí deadpanned.

"I just wish I knew why," Lilith muttered.

"The others should have returned with you!" Olga was pulling at her hair now. This was the most frantic Lilith had ever seen her. "Felix, you are not to return!"

The boy's shoulders fell, but he did not offer up argument. Lilith felt a regretful surge of relief. She wouldn't mind having Felix's company when Julius left.

"This is not good," Olga muttered, more to herself than the others.

Julius chimed in, "To make matters worse, the political situation in Kenora is far more convoluted than we originally assumed."

Each Divine glanced at him askance. He didn't elaborate to Lilith just *why* the situation in the capital was so dire, and she hadn't asked him. She'd been excluded from most of their courtly meetings, thankfully. It was the only positive aspect of her illness.

"Some of the lords are allying with Spiro," Julius divulged. "Supplying their men to him in exchange for greater power when he usurps Obadïa. They believe that a siege is inevitable, that the Milítia, combined with the Walabeäns, is insignificant." His tone had been diminished of its usual depth. He needed rest, and fast.

"How do you know for certain?" Olga asked.

"We kept our minds open for the entirety of each meeting. Their emotions conveyed exactly what I just said."

This explained Julius's despondency during their travels. Maybe he hadn't been that angry with her decision to go to the Marsh, his mind was just occupied with the situation in Kenora. What a foolish woman she was to assume that it was all about her.

Julius rubbed the back of his neck and yawned. "I must go lie down. I've got a long journey ahead of me tomorrow."

Lilith sighed. She didn't relish the idea of parting ways with him so soon. She was put off by his recent revelation. If there was so much political unrest in the capital, she feared that even a fortress like the castle couldn't protect her family.

That perhaps their most fearsome enemies dwelled within its walls.

Felix followed Julius up the winding staircase, leaving her in the kitchen with Zurí and Olga.

"Go rest, Lilith," the Oracle said. "Wash up beforehand, though. The lot of you smell."

Aspen cackled at Olga's levity, startling Lilith. She had almost forgotten about the girl.

"Your bark is my command, Master Olga." Lilith bowed deeply, a comical smirk besetting her features as Zurí scoffed.

⊙ ⓑ ⤳ ⋔ ⟜

ZURÍ MASSAGED THE LINIMENT INTO LILITH'S MUSCLES. THE concoction burned, but she fought back the urge to hiss, concealing her discomfort. The task proved easier when she turned onto her stomach and Zurí dug her fingers into the knots in her back.

Julius and Felix had taken their leave early that morning. The prince woke Lilith to say goodbye before his departure. As she'd clung to him, he'd requested she write often, and that she not be so maudlin in his absence. He wanted to know if their trip to the Marsh would actually prove worthwhile. And so did she.

"All done," Zurí proclaimed. "How are you feeling?"

Lilith turned over, accepting her nightgown from Zurí's outstretched hand. "I'm feeling better. Honestly."

"Hmm… the seizure you experienced during your travels was quite delayed, so don't go pushing yourself just yet."

"I won't," Lilith assured, "but that was different though."

"How so?"

"I was being attacked, adrenaline fueling my body, pushing me past my extremities." She'd even stretched her luck and attempted to summon Aether. "Everyday training shouldn't be so hard on me."

"Just don't go assuming that it's all over," Zurí warned.

Lilith watched as Zurí left. She needed the Frourío to be utterly still before she would risk her midnight vigil. It was pointless to forget the High Enchantress's suggestions—the advice she'd given Lilith in secret—and she was not about to reveal that she'd colluded with Ophelía. She believed her actions were just. Ophelía was one of the oldest and wisest beings in Augusta, it would be foolish to ignore her counsel. And Lilith couldn't sit idle whilst all she'd worked for in her new life languished.

Once she was certain that the inhabitants of the Frourío were steady in their slumber, she crept from her bed and descended the stairs on silent feet.

As she padded across the kitchen, a low grumble sounded

from the hearth. Lilith stilled, assessing. Ambrose had curled himself up in one of the armchairs before the fire, the smoldering embers the only light in the room. Under other circumstances, she might have thrown a blanket over him, but she needed to escape undetected.

Shutting the door as silently as she could, Lilith trudged toward the beach. The grass was soft beneath her feet, and slightly dewy. The Stars shone bright, Larkin smiling down upon her. These days were so hectic, the excitement rarely afforded her the opportunity to grieve. She didn't miss Larkin any less, but most of her emotional reserve was spent fretting over the lives of those she loved who still lived in this perilous world.

Lilith halted before the lapping waves, the sea a massive expanse of ink before her beneath the night sky. Her legs throbbed, beseeching her to rest.

"You sang the Hymn of Divination over a traitor—no offense. That warranted some form of punishment, no?"

This infirmity wasn't a quick punishment. It was a slow, painful strangulation, where the offender released their hold just before death's maw devours. Taunting. Feeding on constant dread.

Or were the Gods grinding her against stone, honing her for a truly altruistic life?

Or was this another preparation of sorts? Something darker. Something that required her to be capable of bearing pain of the highest caliber.

Stepping into the tepid waters, ignoring the chill that lanced up her spine, Lilith waded deeper. Her mind focused on what the High Enchantress suggested, and as Lilith allowed the madness of the sea to unfurl around her, she steeled her resolve, reciting Ophelía's words.

"Constantine. Kyril. Xander. Thëo. Isidore."

She repeated the Gods' names several times before she was confident enough to resume.

"I have been suffering under Your hands, but I cannot resume my training, I cannot better myself as a Divine." Lilith gulped, clinging to her faith in what she was about to do, in what she was about to say. "I swear to You all, and I swear to the Guiding Stars, that I will take my life on the seventh day from this moment. I will remove myself from this world if You fail to return me to my former health."

This was it. An ultimatum to the Gods.

Almost as if in response, the sea grumbled like the belly of a dragon, threatening to engulf her. Sodden and surly, Lilith turned an indignant shoulder to the star-flecked firmament and returned to the warmth of her bed.

SWORDPLAY

Every day it seemed as though Kenora's bland stone walls were pressing in on her further, suffocating and staunching any life within. Hestîa wanted nothing more than to soar through the sky on Noala's back, where no heinous princes could hunt her down.

That's when she decided to go for a ride, apt as she was to disobey. During the men's bathing hour, she'd managed to sneak away to the stables. Horses neighed and nickered as she passed with her harpy's reins in her hand. None of the servants were present, and the equerry was missing, so Hestîa was successful in leading her winged wolf out into the open.

But where would she take off?

Judging by Noala's erratic footsteps, the servants were duplicitous with their claims to care for the harpies appropriately. They were not creatures meant to be stabled. They needed constant open air. The stables weren't only too small and secluded, the herringbone cobbles that made up the floor—though great for horses' hooves—were harmful to a harpies paws. Noala's claws were bloodied from catching in the cracks between the stones, no wonder she was so eager to get into the sky and give her feet a break.

Swallowing her angst, Hestîa pulled herself up into Noala's saddle and secured her legs. Several of the Emperor's Frourà sprinted in her direction, accosting her with orders to remain on the ground. She paid their diatribes little heed and encouraged Noala to take to the sky with a yip. The harpy spread her feathered wings and took off in one powerful leap, leaving the servants toppling to the ground in her wake.

The imperial grounds disappeared beneath her, and the whooshing beat of Noala's wings lulled her into a familiar trance. No longer was she fettered to the castle, where that reprobate of a prince ruled over his father's subjects, no reprobates for comrades. No, she was free to become one with the sky, to return to her second home.

The wind tugged at her braids and her heart leapt into her throat at Noala's sudden lunge higher. Hestîa released a soundless laugh, carried off by the wind as soon as it left her lips. Her worries far beneath her, Hestîa raised her arms to the sky, letting the straps of her saddle be her only safeguard against the downfall.

Returning to those insufferable barracks was inexorable, but she could delay it for a while. Noala seemed to have a similar idea as the harpy angled away from Kenora, the fur around her neck ruffling like waves of the Galatëa Sea.

She could spend eternity in the sky.

Hestîa's mind flitted back to Agónas. How they'd shared Noala during their travels whilst the young harpy he was training flew alongside them, playfully banking only to return a moment later. He'd fly circles around them.

During their flight to Kenora, Hestîa had insisted on flying with her female comrades, and Agónas flew with his. Noala had nuzzled into Athena's harpy, Drystan, flirting in a way only a winged wolf could understand. Athena had loved to watch them, amused by the blend of animalistic instincts and human hearts unlike most wild species.

"Harpies mate for life," Athena had once told her, before they'd ever mounted a harpy of their own. "I want that too."

And now Athena would never know such a love.

Noala twisted, turning Hestîa upside down, only to right herself a moment later. Gods, she loved the feeling of blood rushing to her head. The simple act of defying gravity. The pull to Hades kept all creatures tethered to the ground, all except small birds and impenetrable harpies.

Reluctantly, Hestîa prodded Noala, guiding the winged wolverine down toward the stables.

Hestîa led Noala into the grand structure and returned her to her designated stall. The harpy whimpered and pawed at the wood of the door as it banged shut, locking her in for who knows how long.

Guilt tore at Hestîa's heart. "I'm sorry," she whispered. "I will come back tomorrow. They can't stop us from exercising our steeds."

Noala stared back at her, releasing a puff of air, her jowls vibrating.

Laughing, she stroked the harpy's pointed ears, the tufts of silken fur at the tips. "I'll be back. I promise," she said, then she set off without a backward glance.

Hestîa kept her gaze locked on the cobblestone path in an attempt to avoid conversing with any passing Augustans. They were lewd creatures, so different from the Walabeäns. Sure, the people of the Isles loved debauchery just as much, but there were lines drawn. Everyone had freedom to consent and do what they wished with their own bodies, but in the Emperor's city there were very few limits to what soldiers could get away with in regard to bodies that did not belong to them.

The door to the barracks groaned as she tugged it open, the motion drawing attention to her shoulders, sore from sparring with Wellën earlier that morning. They'd been tough on each other, pushing themselves harder than they usually did. Wellën had wanted nothing more than to intimidate the Augustan soldiers since Athena's murder. Her armor was constructed of intimidation and pretense.

Kenora was unusual, so utterly opposite to the Isles. Instead of rising above, reaching toward Elysium, they were sunk into the earth, below ground level. How they ever hoped to defend themselves against a siege was beyond her imagination. Hestîa presumed there must be some kind of symbolism to the location, for why else would an Emperor wish for his people to be so exposed? Though the city's walls were high, they couldn't keep out a swarm of winged beasts.

The barracks were unusually quiet.

Since Athena's murder, the barracks had become a sorrowful place for the Walabeäns. A hostile environment permeated the Augustan side of the barracks. Every soldier and warrior had been put on edge, making it nearly impossible to determine who was responsible.

Hestîa had clipped her tongue, petrified to let her ire get the best of her. The putrid prince was the obvious suspect. She would bet her left leg that he'd done it. He hated her for becoming the Savior and he'd blatantly warned her to watch her back.

The act was abominable. And having to watch noble ladies fawn over the Crown Prince turned her insides to stone. Their undying adulation was repulsive. If only they knew how utterly impudent he was. He'd blasted her heart to fissures, and she needed to find a way to return the sentiment.

But why was he so angry about the change in access to the servant women? He was the prince, he could have any of the servant girls brought to his private chambers…

Hestîa told no one of her suspicions. It wouldn't help her cause. If any one of the soldiers caught wind of her detestation for Prince Orìon, she would be hanged for treason, or somehow framed for Athena's death.

Without knowledge of the full extent of her lament, Agónas sought her out day and night in an attempt to assuage her sorrow. Though she would never turn him away, she wished for the coddling to end.

"Let's go," Agónas said to her one afternoon.

Hestîa had been lying on her bed after a bath, eyes fastened to the bunk atop hers. Athena's bunk. Now unoccupied.

"Where?" she inquired flatly.

Agónas didn't respond. He just scooped her up into his arms and plopped her on her feet. "Sandals," he muttered.

With a knitted brow, Hestîa obeyed and followed his lead, her interest undeniably piqued. With her hand still clasped in his, she grabbed her sword before they weaved through the bunks toward the exit.

Agónas followed an errant path to the stables, and Hestîa's heart fluttered for the first time in weeks.

We're going to fly!

But when they rounded the corner to the stables, Agónas continued on by without paying the harpies any attention. Hestîa couldn't hide her disappointment, her bottom lip protruding slightly as she turned her head in Noala's direction. She hoped her faithful steed was comfortable and content. Continuing in silence, Agónas led her through the eastern gate out onto the plains.

Hestîa's calves burned as they climbed the slope. "Why are we out here?" She struggled to mask the irritation in her tone.

"We are going to spar like we used to," said Agónas. "And *you're* going to talk."

Hestîa growled, "Talk about what?"

"You think I don't know you well enough?"

She managed a casual shrug. "Whatever do you mean?" It proved difficult to be caustic in his presence. For the first time in days, her heart was humming.

"We are alone." Agónas spread his arms wide, twisting his torso, gesturing to the fallow land surrounding them for miles. "So tell me what's been on your mind." His blue eyes narrowed into slits, impaling her with an invisible skewer.

Hestîa met his glare with equal intensity. Defiant as always.

"If sparring fails to ease your consternation," he said with sparking hubris, "shall we defer to a different form of swordplay?"

Hestîa entertained him, mirroring his expression. "Is that supposed to be a threat?"

The warrior simply leveled her with his glare.

"Fine," she yielded. "But we spar, *then* talk." She settled into her sparring stance, emphasizing the bend of her hips. "And then we take this to Noala's stall."

Agónas laughed his agreement and drew his scim from the scabbard across his back. He assumed a defensive stance, bouncing on his knees in anticipation. Though they were lovers, they gave their bouts everything they had, and they always left with marks on their skin. Bruises and scrapes they'd numb with kisses afterward.

"Ustè stèle vreäqq grínndr!" Agónas declared with emphasized theatrics.

"Only steel breeds glory," Hestîa echoed under her breath.

And lunged.

Once she got her blood flowing, her muscles blazing, then she would talk. Until then, they'd dance.

Meeting her blow for blow, Agónas grunted as he deflected her blade. For a while, the only sound was the clang of steel striking steel. Sparks flew through the air, a visual replication of the ones inside her chest. The mere image of Agónas excited her, but when he fought and his nostrils flared, she'd found the root of her weakness. Hestîa succumbed to him, short of breath, and Agónas lowered his sword, halting mere inches from her neck.

"Talk," he ordered.

Hestîa dropped her sword, careful not to breathe too deep as her lungs fought for air, lest she nick her neck on Agónas's blade. "What is it you want to know so badly?"

He didn't respond. She let him study her while her own eyes wandered the expansive landscape. But she wasn't seeing long grass undulating on the breeze. She saw cold stone walls. Disheveled, pale blond hair. Piercing blue, bloodshot eyes and a repulsive scowl.

"The prince threatened me," she finally divulged.

Agónas stiffened. His posture was enough to warrant an explanation.

"He wasn't pleased that my incident resulted in the removal of the lady servants. He was quite inebriated when he sought me out." Her own thoughts strayed back to that moment. To Orìon's whiskey-tainted breath revolving around her head like a putrid cloud. Gods, the next emperor was a vile creature. "I know that *he* is responsible for the death of Athena..." She finally met his gaze. "And I know that the poison was meant for *me*."

Agónas's irises smoldered like embers, his cheeks practically emitting heat. He dropped his blade, closing the space between them. "Leave," he barked, hands on her shoulders. "Get out of here tonight. Take Wellën with you. Go back to the Isles where you are safe."

Hestîa shook her head, heart hammering from the vehemence in his tone. "There's no point. My absence won't bring the servants back into the barracks. Besides, I am no coward, and I will not stand for such abuse!"

"If he lays a hand on you, I will kill him without remorse. I will cut off his slimy head and parade through the streets of Kenora with it dangling from my fists!"

Rarely had she witnessed Agónas so irate, so vulgar. Yes, the Walabeäns were the best warriors in all of the lands, but they were not ruthless killers. They did not lack empathy nor sensitivity.

"Fists?"

Agónas scoffed. "You think I'd leave his ugly head in one piece?"

"You will do no such thing," Hestîa intoned, "because that is what I ask of you. Remain complacent. I would never be able to live with myself knowing I was the reason for your downfall." Because he would surely be executed for such treachery.

Agónas bit his lip, gazing out over the plains to the south. "Fine. But you stay near me. And I don't care what the others say, you're sleeping with me. Gods forbid the prince acts again, because I swear to Xander, there will be so much turmoil from within the capital, Spiro won't want to siege it."

As if on cue, a horn sounded from the cluster of buildings behind them.

"They're coming!" Agónas grabbed her hand, pulling her toward the gates, sprinting as fast as their legs would allow. If the beasts were in sight from the city walls, then they could only be an hour away at most. Spiro may not choose to attack that night, but they were expected to be prepared.

The guards of the Emperor's Frourà waited for them to enter before closing the gates and fortifying them. Hestîa gasped for air as they passed the stables, angling toward the barracks.

Barks met their ears as they entered the barracks, the chambers buzzing with activity. Frantic soldiers fought to retrieve their weapons. It was amazing that they managed not to kill each other in their sloppy haste.

The general commandeered them with a calm gait. General Achilles. Lilith's father. He was a large man, tall and broad, with a fresh-shaven, chiseled jaw. His dark hair fell to his shoulders in waves so similar to Lilith's, though it lacked her mahogany luster. He seemed sound enough, but was he aware of how vile the men he served were?

"Grab your armor." Agónas gently pushed her toward her own bunk as he began to don his own.

Hestîa pushed through the throng of soldiers. Bodies thrashed, knocking her to her knees. "It's a battle, not a hurricane. Calm yourselves!" she bellowed in her angst. "If you're this petrified, you should go underground with the women and children!" She fought to get back on her feet, her kneecaps scraped bare and bloodied.

"That's where you should be!" came the response she'd been waiting for. Had the ignorant soldier been any closer, she would have knocked him out.

2 2

SHE WOULD PERSIST

A week had passed since she'd arrived back at the Frourío. The boys would be back in Kenora with the others, Olga having relented to Felix's pleas to return with Julius.

Post-training, Lilith soaked in the tub far longer than was necessary, the steam clearing her addled mind. Her thoughts returned to Julius more often than not.

Before preparing for dinner, she paused to pray. She still kept her words to herself when she knelt beside her bed. The silence seemed to be a worthy invite to the Gods, as They washed over her. She couldn't distinguish between Their entities, but she knew They listened, They watched, and They knew the desires of her spirit without her having to utter a single syllable in Modern or Elder Tongue.

As she donned her tunic, she could make out the murmurs of conversation in the kitchen below, the tone somber, if slightly on edge.

Something happened.

Forcing her heart rate to ease, Lilith descended the stairs

two at a time, her hand hovering above the railing for stability.

"How far out do you think they are?" Zurí asked.

"It's difficult to discern from the vision," Olga said. "I cannot conjecture. I have received no such notion pertaining to time or arrival. I only pray Julius and Felix have arrived safely by now. Gods forbid they get trapped behind the Spiro's army."

A sense of urgency gripped her. Lilith approached the table, her eyes locked on Olga. "Spiro is moving for the capital?"

The Oracle nodded gravely.

"Will we be going?" Lilith glanced to Zurí, whose features were masked by a veil of indifference so unlike her.

"You will not be," her Master said sternly, her hand on Aspen's shoulder, seated at the harvest table.

Chafed, Lilith said, "I am much stronger than I was. It's been almost three weeks since my last episode—"

"I don't care, Lilith!" Zurí snapped. "All of your seizures have been evenly spaced out. You are not in the clear yet. Regardless of what you believe, your convalescence is not up. You will remain here where you are safe." Her tone held an air of finality, and Lilith knew pressing would be wasted energy.

Olga placed a comforting hand on Lilith's arm. "Dear, please understand that we worry for your safety."

Lilith glanced between the two women. This was an argument she would not win, certainly not whilst they were agreeable with one another. "But the men—"

"They can handle themselves," Zurí said. "It's too late for us to travel to the capital. If we arrive behind Spiro's army, we will find ourselves at their mercy, in the center of a very hostile environment." She fixated her noviciate with her stare, as if with that look alone she could fetter Lilith to the Frourío.

"It is war. A hostile environment is *expected*," Lilith replied caustically.

Zurí crossed her arms, her voice dangerously quiet, her glare tempestuous. "I am your Master. I need not argue."

Though Olga's expression was one born of penitence, she refrained from intervening. Lilith understood why Zurí denied her, but she couldn't fight the urge to join the men. They were strongest together.

What if Spiro takes Felix? What if he kills Arduen because his best friend declined to join his cause?

No. Their presence at battle was requisite. Nonnegotiable.

Lilith rounded the table to stand before her Master. "I cannot sit idle while they are out there fighting."

Zurí's stone-cold gaze softened. She grasped Lilith's hand. "I respect your wishes. But you are not at your full dexterity, and I could not live with myself if you go into battle and do not walk out."

Relenting, Lilith nodded and took her seat across from Aspen. The little girl glanced up at her with bright eyes, not an ounce of fear. "You are strong, Lilith," she chimed. "But you are no match for the Great Divine."

◎ ॐ ⟿ ᘻ ◊

Standing on the roof of the Frourío, Lilith gazed out at the sea. She'd hoped that the Galatëa's rushing whisper would pacify her anxieties, but it only seemed to aggravate them.

Five days had passed since she'd sworn to the Gods that she would end her life if They did not restore her health—and elemental capacity—in a week's time. She'd given them just seven days. It was naïve to demand such things of the Gods. Yes, she had sworn to serve Them until her dying breath, she'd sworn to stop at nothing to destroy Spiro on Their behalf, but that meant nothing if They could not heal her in seven days.

Yet five days had passed, and the spectral presence of her malady did not feel any less potent.

Lilith refused to remain here, regardless of the wrangle it could cause between her and Zurí. She would not sit around, sullenly agonizing over the unknown. It was time to act, but she wouldn't be foolish. She would ensure herself capable. If she were to die, she might as well do it fulfilling her soul's vocation: avenging her family and felling Spiro's beasts.

Seating herself in the center of the rooftop, Lilith closed her eyes and imagined a violet sky. The sun was just rising in the east, gilding the firmament. If she could alter it to violet, then she'd know for certain that Aether was once again under her control.

Willing the sky to abide by her desires, Lilith opened her eyes. The sky hadn't changed, though it did appear darker than it had only a moment ago. She sighed. This was frustrating, and it was only made worse because Arduen had never instructed her on *how* to alter the sky to her content. He'd shown her first-hand that it could be done, but he never really told her how. He'd said that it came from within, that she need only to open the door.

The door is gaping, Constantine.

Lilith lowered herself onto the ground, lying flat on her back. She let the quietude wash over her, save for the morning trills from the birds nestled in the pines below. Again, she persisted to conceive the great vision of the sky in her mind, willing it to a reality, but to no avail.

A raindrop rolled down her neck. She sat up and wiped it away. When she studied her hand, it was painted crimson. Her nose was bleeding again. But she wasn't even edging toward depletion. She ground her teeth in frustration.

Recovering to her former glory was almost impossible

without Arduen. She needed him more than he knew, and he was so far away.

And at the mercy of Spiro.

Lilith's chest tightened at the thought of singing over Arduen's body, her tongue snagging on her teeth, the tang of iron permeating her mouth. Her trembling lips screwing up the Hymn, sending Arduen's soul anywhere but Elysium, his body anywhere but to the skies, to his Star. Where would he go if she didn't sing properly?

No. Arduen wouldn't go like that.

But the possibility plagued her, berated her, drowning her mind with crude images of the men she loved. Arduen, who'd become like a father to her; Julius, who'd stolen her heart against her better judgement; Quin, who'd welcomed her to her new home; Felix, a boy with a generous heart; Wren, a man who'd saved her life, who wouldn't hesitate to do it again. She needed them. They'd supported her through every struggle, eased her suffering in the aftermath of it all. Loyalty like that was to be cherished.

No. This was not over yet.

Lilith opened her eyes to a sky of the deepest violet, the Stars peeking out from their place of slumber. Larkin blinked at her from above, in recognition and encouragement. For him she would persist. For her brother she would prevail. And she knew then what she had to do.

◎ ⏀ ⟿ ᴍ ◌

LATE THAT EVENING, WHEN THE INHABITANTS OF THE FROURÍO were sound asleep, Lilith bounded into the forest atop Olga's stallion, Starfleck. She cared not for the darkness surrounding her, for her heart was light with hope, her limbs charged with exuberance. Prayers danced from her lips, her soul clinging to the promise she'd made the Gods only five nights ago. She'd have to remain true to her word, convincing herself, and the deities, that she would not rescind her promise.

Following dinner, when the kitchen had been emptied, Lilith had acquired what supplies she deemed necessary. There was no logic trying to be inconspicuous by taking little, for they would rise come morn and realize she'd left them, and Ambrose would know who had stolen most of the food. By the time she'd exited the Frourío, she had a pack full of food and armor.

As she passed the clearing where she'd faced Larkin, she could almost hear Julius telling her not to look. Then resignation washed over her as she gazed upon the space. A normal woman would have developed a natural aversion to such a sight, but she hadn't. There was no doubt in her mind that she'd done what was right, what was best for Larkin. And with his light shining down upon her, she rode without the weight of regret.

By dawn, she'd reached the unofficial border of Aspéndos, charging toward the capital with haste. Her situation would be precarious if she failed to reach the city's walls before the attack. Lilith would be at the mercy of Spiro and his beasts if she arrived behind their army. Urgency behooved her to ride day and night, stopping only periodically to rest Starfleck, have a bite to eat, and close her eyes for an hour or two.

On the third evening, she dug a hole with her hands and raised Kyril's Water from the earth, allowing for Starfleck to drink. She chewed on jerky and bread as she considered just how far she had left to go. She reckoned that she had three more days of travel, but she'd done this trip only twice before, she couldn't be certain.

Three more days, then an entire battle.

The following day, Lilith felt the sneaking suspicion that

someone—or something—was trailing her. Relinquishing the tension from her shoulders, she thrust the thought from her mind. She wouldn't get any sleep fretting over nothing. Her fears were irrational. When she opened her mind, she Discerned nothing beyond her mount and the insects beneath their feet. But paranoia assaulted her once again as she entered the plains and left the towering pines of the Megálos behind.

The journey was lonely, as she anticipated. Atop Starfleck, she spurred the stallion into a trot. She'd eased up on him, if only to ensure that he would be spry when she entered battle. Lilith had little experience fighting from a saddle, but if she arrived after the attack had begun, she wouldn't be able to enter the city to stable him.

Her skin prickled.

Lilith twisted in her saddle to survey the lands around her. The plains were wide open with gently rolling knolls. Though the grass was long, lush and viridescent, anyone keeping pace with her would have to be mounted as well. And if they were mounted, she would be able to see them long before they could attempt an ambush. With a sigh, she quelled her fears and forged onward.

Seven days had passed since she'd sworn to the Gods. Though she felt well enough, Lilith persisted to massage her legs with the High Enchantress's liniment, biting into her bottom lip as the searing ointment took effect. This much riding left her legs torn and cramped, but subsisting on half-stale food would do that to anyone. A week ago, she would have been writhing on the ground, her mind fading into darkness, sheltering her from the brunt of anguish. But now, besides the stiffness, she felt well.

Her time of convalescence was up.

Lilith longed to test herself. To know indeed whether she had been healed, but lighting up the plains in a conflagration of

Constantine's Aether would be like lighting a gargantuan beacon for her enemies. Stupid and boastful. And arriving to battle drained of power was tantamount to exposing her neck to Spiro himself. It was best to save it all for battle.

The balmy air made her hair stick to her neck. Stopping to rest once again, Lilith braided her long hair back. Her skin felt coated in grime. She'd sell her soul to bathe, if only it were hers to squander.

Trembling limbs indicated a need for rest. Beneath an umber sky, Lilith dismounted, and Starfleck dropped to the ground beside her with a disgruntled chuff.

"Sorry, buddy," she muttered to the steed.

Lilith leaned her back against the stallion's side, picking at dried fruit and vegetables, the meat all gone. The scent of hay was oddly soothing as she let fatigue carry her away, and once again, darkness reigned.

Lilith awoke with a start, a cold hand pressed firmly over her mouth. Instinctively, she reached for the hilt of Constance, but her sword was not there. Terror sparked, constricting her lungs until it hurt to breathe.

She was right. She had been followed, and they'd finally found her.

2 3

A DIVINE PROCLAMATION

Sweat slicked Lilith's brow as the hand pressed down harder, pushing her lips back away from her teeth.

Bite him!

Lilith tried to pry open her jaw, but his force was too much. A bead of sweat rolled down her temple and into her ear, the urge to itch it overpowering, irritating.

Why hadn't he pressed his blade to her neck yet?

Her captor spoke. "Don't think I'd let you get away." But it wasn't the deep timbre she'd expected.

Zurí.

Her Master released her grip and sat back.

"You've been following me this whole time?" Lilith contorted her mouth, loosening the muscles.

"Since I awoke and noticed your bed was empty. I used Discernment to locate you and followed your trail." Zurí lowered herself beside her. "For the sake of Kyril, do you even sleep?"

"I've been trying to reach Kenora before the battle begins." Lilith let her muscles relax. No longer was she alone.

"Sleep until morning," Zurí offered. "Then we will set out."

Lilith bristled. "I'm not going back to the Frourío with you. I am going to the capital."

"You'll do as I say," Zurí scolded. "Regardless of your claims, you are not well enough to participate in battle. It could last days. It could wage for weeks."

Lilith stood abruptly, glaring at the shadowed outline of her Master. "I will not go back. I didn't push myself this far to turn back."

"You can barely spar for longer than ten minutes, and that's at a considerably slowed pace." Zurí's tone had softened in a clear attempt to placate.

"The Gods have healed me," Lilith proclaimed.

For a woman as devout and pious as Zurí, the woman snorted.

"I'm serious!" Lilith shouted. "I have received access to my full powers. My stores are brimming with energy." She paced backward, away from her Master.

"What are you doing?" Zurí demanded. Ruffling sounds told her that she had risen.

"Stay there," Lilith barked, and silence ensued.

So, Zurí can obey orders.

"Lilith!"

I spoke too soon.

Zurí rambled on, a forceful diatribe with no physical action, but Lilith refused to allow Zurí to shrivel her resolve.

Closing her eyes, Lilith followed the thrumming sensation in her veins. The buildup was a familiar zing, expanding until it threatened to consume. Finally, the dam cracked, her elemental flow increasing. More. More. More. Just how much did the Gods heed her pleas?

A pleasant vibration began inside her core. Lilith dropped to her knees, burying her palms in the dirt. The horses neighed and bayed and pranced uneasily, the earth rumbling beneath their hooves.

Then Aether shot up from the earth, squelching Zurí's castigation. The violet essence formed a city wall around them. A fortification warding away their enemies.

Lilith shouted triumphantly. The release felt too good.

Constantine's abyss enveloped her. The element glistened as if she were inside the moon itself. The violet stream of light flickered with darkness and lightning all at once. She'd been waiting for this moment for so long, she couldn't stop the tears that flowed.

Careful not to deplete her stores, Lilith absorbed Aether, and darkness blanketed the camp once again.

"Well!" Zurí gasped. "It's safe to say, I am not surprised."

"You're not? You're… not angry?"

Zurí's tone was reproachful, but it lacked the ire that Lilith had expected. "Oh, I am angry. But I've learned that I cannot control you, and it's too late for punitive action." She released an exasperated sigh. "If you insist that you're capable of fighting, then we will fight."

Lilith grinned, though Zurí couldn't see it in the dark. "You'll be my Philías?" she asked hopefully.

"It would be my pleasure, Lilith Oak."

⑥ ⑤ ⌁ ♏ ◊

As the first of the sun's rays peeked over the horizon, the two Divine women were mounted and moving steadily south. Words were rarely exchanged as they kicked up dust. In the anticipation of battle, Lilith's mind flickered back to her first experience in the fray. How her nerves had frozen her limbs stiff. How Arduen had tackled her to the earth and sheltered her with his body. How she'd discovered Larkin was alive.

And that he'd become her enemy.

Lilith succumbed to the maelstrom of emotions flooding her. Ruminating in her saddle, she worried that this new condition of hers had tempered what brazenness she'd possessed. That if confronted with another situation such as she had with Larkin, she wouldn't act justly under the pressures of such a trial.

She still possessed the propensity to persist, to do what she believed was right, regardless of the ramifications. Malady or not, she was still herself, perhaps with an additional grain of caution. After all, she'd spent too long steeping in convalescence to be weak and brittle now. Sloughing passivity, she exulted in the thrills of transformation.

It was time to act.

Zurí ordered Lilith to reach out with Discernment as they began the last stretch of their journey. Muddy, troubled emotions assailed her mind. Hollers and aggravated voices threatened to deafen her. Lilith fought to achieve serenity within herself, if only to control her nerves.

War had commenced.

When the towering spires of the Emperor's castle finally appeared before them, Zurí commanded Lilith to display Aether on her upraised palms to the guards stationed along the battlements. They were Divine. Allies.

Once they were clear to enter the action, Lilith and Zurí charged toward the cluster of bodies. Spiro's army had chosen to attack from the southwest, much to their benefit. They wouldn't be stuck behind enemy lines.

"I will search for the others." Zurí's gaze danced across the mayhem in search of their comrades. Surely, they would be noticeable if they were wielding their elements.

The battle took place on the plains outside the capital, exactly where it had the last time, months previous. Lilith swallowed bile as they entered the disarray, men wailing cries of agony as beasts tore into them. Dread pooled in her stomach. The Augustans were vastly outnumbered.

"Over there!" Zurí pointed in the direction she'd sensed the others. As they steered their horses in that direction, a beast leapt upon them. Lilith shot it down with an arrow of Aether.

"Up there!" Zurí jerked her head toward the edge of battle. "We must convene and consider a plan of action."

Lilith didn't argue as she veered her steed in the direction Zurí indicated. Her nerves twitched at the slightest movement in her peripheries, and she fought to control her breathing as Arduen had instructed. In and out. In and out. The meditation provided her only comfort.

They steered their mounts toward the clearing, slashing down any beasts impeding their path. Lilith took a slice to the back of her calf. She was sure it was a blade that had cut her, not a poisonous talon. She'd survive.

Zurí stopped short of the clearing, her eyes blowing wide.

"What is it?" Lilith asked, drawing Starfleck alongside her Master. Gods, she missed Skydancer.

"We have company…" Zurí practically breathed the words, but Lilith could read her lips well enough.

Arduen and Julius bounded toward them. They were not mounted, as was expected.

"We sensed you moments ago," Julius said. "We started off in your direction immediately."

Panting, Arduen surveyed the battle, turning to ensure his back was not exposed to their enemies. He braced a hand on Lilith's leg as he caught his breath, and she winced. He jerked back, brow scrunching with worry.

"I'm all right," she assured him, waving off his concern. "It's just a minor slice." He dipped his head to check for himself, and when he deemed her safe, he gave his attention to Zurí.

Julius marched up to Starfleck and patted the horse's head. As he did, he glanced up at Lilith from under the brow of his helm, eyes bright. Lilith blushed, dropping her gaze, suddenly feeling foolish. Now was not the time for flirtatious exchanges.

"I'm assuming that since you're here, you are much better?" Julius asked her.

Zurí responded for Lilith. "It seems as if her blessings have returned full force. I couldn't stop her from participating."

Lilith cast a grateful glance in Zurí's direction. She didn't know what Arduen would do if he knew she'd acted out again. But she was sure to find out when the battle ended.

"Other Divines are present," Zurí told Arduen.

"We've been attempting to locate them all morning, but to no avail," Arduen said.

"They don't seem to be interested in engaging with us," Julius added.

"*They?*" Lilith's eyes widened, her gaze flicking between both her Masters.

"There's at least two," Arduen confirmed dryly.

A dreadful silence settled over them like a pall.

"We will have a better chance of locating them mounted." Arduen nodded at their horses. "I'll ride with Lilith. Julius, go with Zurí."

Lilith shifted forward in her saddle, allowing her Master room as he settled in behind her. He wrapped one arm around her, hugging her close.

Together, the four Divine reentered battle. Lilith fought to govern Starfleck but the stallion had become spooked by the beasts surrounding it. Arduen plucked the reins from her, and Lilith relinquished them subserviently. "I'll take over," he said into her ear, and as he did, Starfleck seemed to relax.

Without steering the horse as a distraction, Lilith's acute senses overwhelmed her. The clash of steel was sharp in her ears, harsh enough to make her temples throb. The aroma of iron coated the insides of her nostrils. She grimaced, wrinkling her nose in disgust. But the most disconcerting aspect was the sense of company. The atmosphere was starkly different from the last battle she'd experienced. There was an electric charge in the air.

Two figures stood behind the mass of beasts. Even from a distance, as mere flecks on the horizon, they were imposing. Contrary to their last battle, the two Divine seemed less inclined to add their arsenal to aid Spiro's army. They simply observed.

Lilith recognized the one Divine as Larkin's companion. He was still lithe and lean, though he'd been bordering on frail before. Now he stood strong, as if Spiro had worked him harder in Larkin's absence.

Good, she thought bitterly. *I hope he suffered.*

The second figure was cloaked, and Lilith noticed how her comrades' gaits altered as they approached. Something was wrong.

Arduen whispered in her ear, but she couldn't hear what he said over the din of battle.

"What was that?" she asked.

Arduen said nothing. Perhaps he hadn't heard her. Perhaps he hadn't spoken at all. Perhaps it was the wind playing cruel games with her ears.

But then she heard it, loud and clear. A hiss.

Hello.

The cloaked man turned to face them. He mouthed "Hello" and it sailed on the wind like a message, strident and straight to her ears.

Spiro.

RAGE UNVARNISHED

The Great Divine stood before them on the battlefield. His long, Walabeän-pale hair loose, billowing on the breeze, blending seamlessly with his ivory cloak, an extension of his overall carriage. His icy eyes cut into Arduen immediately, and Lilith suppressed a shiver as a curve of a smile graced Spiro's lips.

Arduen elicited no response. He didn't stiffen. He didn't gasp. His breath didn't hitch. His fists didn't tighten on the reins. He simply froze, the only sign of life his beating heart, pounding against Lilith's shoulder blades.

Lilith slit her eyes in scrutiny. This was the man who had taken Larkin from her. From her father, too. His light appearance was at odds with the harsh planes of his face. Perhaps that was his intention, to seem innocuous. But Lilith wasn't fooled. He was as she'd imagined: cut from stone, sharp as any blade, honed to kill. His entire entity rife with animosity.

Arduen halted Starfleck at a safe distance. Well, as safe as they could be. Her Master pressed his cheek to the side of her head and whispered, "I want you to take Starfleck. Find Wren. He will ensure that you and Felix get to safety." He pressed a fervent kiss to her crown, his lips lingering.

"No!" Lilith started, twisting her body in the saddle to face him. This wasn't fair. Why did Wren get to live? Why was it Arduen's responsibility to sacrifice his life? "I won't. I refuse."

"Lilith…" Arduen warned, his eyes locked on Spiro, his face placid.

"I won't leave you!" She wrapped her arms around him, seizing him in a tight embrace. "Please, I—"

Arduen cut her off, "The Emperor is running out of resources. Spiro has been fighting against the throne since before Obadïa was even conceived. He's running out of men and money. We have to take on Spiro now, and I don't want you involved."

Lilith wilted, tears stinging her eyes.

"You're a noviciate," Arduen said. "Doubly blessed. You know what that means. We know Spiro wants you. And I am necessary, for Aether is his weakness." His tone was somber, regretful, like he was resigned to this task.

As if he knew it was over.

"I'm never leaving you," she said. "I wield Aether, too." She forced her tone flat, unwavering in resolve. But when Arduen met her gaze, his eyes silver-lined, her chest crumpled. She knew what she had to do. "For you, I will go."

Arduen pulled her against him, pressing an eager kiss to her forehead.

This was farewell.

"Go," he ordered, composing himself, dismounting gracefully. He looked up at her one last time, a faint, peaceful smile spreading across his face. Then he smacked his palm against Starfleck's rump and shouted, "Ride fast!"

Lilith grappled for the reins, chary to steer the horse away from Spiro and his crony. Tears spilled down her cheeks, her body shaking without relent. Silent sobs burst from her lips, and through the tears, she could barely make out the path ahead of her. When she dared to look back, her heart plummeted.

Julius wasn't going with her.

She pulled up on the reins and turned Starfleck around. They couldn't hope to take on Spiro by themselves. What about Wren? Her eyes scanned the chaos, but there was no sign of him.

A flash of light in her periphery pulled her attention back to her Master and Julius.

The fight had begun.

Lilith's veins buzzed with adrenaline. She could not ride away whilst they faced down their greatest adversary. The reason she'd come was for *them*. How could she abandon them now? Yes, she was fleeing for Arduen. But what good would her survival be if Spiro killed the man who held the knowledge she needed?

Zurí approached Spiro first, her attack less obvious than the others'. Arduen was close behind her, Aether sparked on his fingertips. Beside him, Julius assumed a like stance, his palms redolent of a forge.

Lilith spurred Starfleck into a sprint. She crouched as low as she could, the stallion's sailing mane engulfing her face. There was no other place for her than at her family's side. Arduen was her family. Julius was her family. Zurí was her family. And she belonged with them.

Starfleck quailed as Julius's light erupted, and Lilith was forced to dismount in action. The horse had been moving too fast, and when her booted feet struck the ground, she tumbled over her head and rolled. When she finally stopped, she was at Arduen's feet. He glared down at her with an expression of pure outrage. She'd disobeyed him yet again, but she was more than accepting of punishment. He'd have to survive in order to punish her, and then she'd be so jubilant, nothing could douse her joy.

"I expected the doubly blessed to be more… skilled." Spiro's rich baritone met her ears.

And her blood ran cold.

Without entertaining a conversation, Arduen launched a steady stream of Aether at his old friend. Constantine's element was the only gift Spiro had not been blessed with. It was the only gift of the Gods that could weaken him.

Recognizing this, Lilith rose to stand at her Master's side. She grasped his free hand and lent her strength to his. Zurí raised her hand to stop Arduen's and Julius's assaults. Both men obliged. Lilith gaped at her Master. What was she thinking?

A head full of flames, Zurí stood before her past lover.

"Zurí…" Spiro crooned, wistfulness and longing thickening his voice. It was deceptive. It had to be.

Lilith couldn't see Zurí's face, but by the way she held herself, so at odds with her usual countenance, Lilith knew she was breaking. Had she forgotten how dexterous Spiro was? Standing that close to him was an act of suicide.

Zurí inched closer to Spiro, but her legs weren't moving.

Isidore's Wind.

"Arduen…" Lilith whined.

"Go." His voice was pained, and she squeezed his hand, as much to comfort him as herself.

She would not leave.

As fast as Zurí reached him, Spiro cupped her cheek,

pressing a desperate, plundering kiss to her lips. And to Lilith's surprise, Zurí returned the affection with equal passion. Spiro pulled away slightly, his eyes searching hers, his thumb tracing the scar he'd etched into her face decades before. Had they seen each other since that day?

But just as quickly as he'd kissed her, Spiro procured a dagger hidden inside his cloak and stabbed the blade into Zurí's side.

"NO!" Lilith cried, starting into a sprint.

Arduen held her back, pressing her shoulder blades against his chest. "Don't move, Lilith." She trembled in his grasp. Zurí was going to die.

Zurí dropped to her knees, her hands clutching her side, already painted crimson. Julius stepped forward, and it took all of Lilith's will not to run to him, to hold him back. The Great Divine would take her entire family.

First of her blood, then of her heart.

Spiro knelt before Zurí, his snarling face level with hers, malignant delight glistening in his eyes. They exchanged terse words. Lilith couldn't make them out. Then he retreated, blasting Zurí with Xander's Fire.

Arduen and Julius bounded forward without hesitation, the former throwing Lilith to the ground in his wake, but there was little they could do to negate the attack.

The prince stood a few paces back and began to syphon the Fire into his palms, his face set in a stern, concentrated grimace that quickly contorted with pain. His stores wouldn't compete against Spiro's.

Where was Quin?

Lilith slipped to the side, edging farther away from Arduen and closer to Zurí. Her Master was still alive, though surrounded by Xander's Fire. She was summoning Kyril's

Water from the earth to shield herself from the blast, but even she and Julius would not amount to Spiro's stamina.

Shouts from behind them pulled Lilith's attention away from Zurí.

Quin, Wren, and Felix darted toward them, barking orders to one another.

Whilst Spiro was occupied with Zurí and Julius, Arduen shot arrows of Aether at him. The Great Divine turned his attention back to his former friend.

And Lilith's knees wobbled.

No!

Spiro blasted Arduen.

Lilith might have screamed, might have shrieked. She abandoned her post to rush to her Master's side. But Arduen was fine. He'd deflected the torrent with Aether, the Fire separating around him in two streams.

Arduen remained still as Spiro approached him. Lilith called to him, begged him to retreat. There needed to be distance between them or else…

The earth grumbled, then it rose, devouring Arduen's booted feet, rising up to his knees. Arduen was seeded, and Lilith cursed herself for not foreseeing that. Spiro was blessed by four of the five Gods. Lilith had rarely seen Thëo's Earth in action, she'd always dismissed it as a lesser element, but now her mind had been swayed.

Spiro's cackle drifted through the air, menacing and cruel, a provocation as he advanced on Arduen. "I warned you." Spiro waved a long, thin finger in Arduen's face.

A strangled groan tore Lilith's attention from the men.

Zurí.

How had she forgotten her? Lilith loped toward her, dropping to her knees beside her Master, careful not to turn her back on their enemy. With Constance, she cut off part of the hem of her tunic and pressed the fabric to Zurí's wound, her eyes frequently flitting back to Arduen. Julius and Quin stood on either side of him, granting her the slightest bit of comfort.

Wren lowered himself at Zurí's other side. "We have to get her out of here, now." He grasped Zurí's arm and Lilith took the other, pulling her Master to her unstable feet. Together, they led Zurí to her steed. Wren hoisted her up into the saddle, strapping her down.

"You'll need to ride fast," he said. "The healers' tent is—"

"I'm not taking her!" Lilith cut him off, her eyes darting back to Arduen, his face inches from Spiro's. Inches from death. "I'm staying here."

"No, you're not!" Wren advanced on her, his fists clenched. He wouldn't hurt her, but he would use force if it meant getting her to safety.

"Yes, I am," Lilith pressed. "I wield two elements, and one of them is Spiro's weakness. I'm needed here!"

Wren's shoulders slumped in resignation. She'd won.

"Fine. I'll be right back." He patted her on the shoulder, his hand lingering there for a moment before he mounted the horse and set off toward the capital.

Lilith turned back to the others, suddenly so alone and in the open.

Spiro retreated, Julius and Quin pushing him back. Lilith bolted toward them, eager to lend her aid. She'd try to siphon Water from his limbs, but he would likely know it was her, and if he targeted her, she wouldn't stand a chance.

Their only hope of defeating Spiro was Aether. Only Constantine's element could annihilate the Great Divine.

Arduen's feet were still planted firmly, but Julius and Quin stood close by his side. Without waiting for approval, Lilith unleashed her might unto Spiro. She roared as Aether seared her veins, she'd given it less than ample time to amount inside her. Her palm exploded, and she grimaced as she guided the abyss's trajectory.

Spiro blocked her with a shield of what had to have been hardened Wind. Arduen shielded Julius and Quin from the recoil.

With an malicious grin, Spiro attacked.

Lilith dodged out of the way, throwing her body to the ground. As soon as she made impact with the dirt, Spiro had sent another blast of Fire her way, the Earth rumbling beneath her.

He will bury you!

"Lilith!" Arduen's strained voice pierced the air.

The only thing granting her confidence was her Dâs Thymó. *I, Lilith Oak, desire above all else that the ones whom I give my heart, and those who have a place in their heart for me, will be spared from bearing witness to my demise.*

Lilith repeated the words to herself over and over, steeling herself against Spiro. The Gods had saved her life twice now, They wouldn't allow her to die before her Masters.

Spiro approached slowly, cautiously, his arms at his sides, feigning innocence. "Lilith Oak." He simpered. "Or is it Lilith Achilles?"

She couldn't respond, every muscle itching to flee.

"Lilith!" Arduen cried again, his voice grievous, as if he were already mourning her loss. "Please, don't take her, Spiro! Please!"

"My, my… what a love you've inspired in my hard, old friend." Spiro smiled, stopping before her. "Now tell me, how would you like to serve at my side?"

Lilith trembled under his disparaging glare. The way he looked down upon her sent her blood boiling. As if she would not live up to her blessings until she was Mastered by the Great Divine.

No.

"Never," she snapped.

Spiro's chuckle rumbled like thunder. "I can assure you, Larkin was quite fond of my accommodations."

Did he really expect her to vie for a bed in his terrestrial version of Hades?

"Spiro!" Arduen called. "Don't take her! Please! Take me! I'll go with you, Brother!"

Brother. That seemed to give the Great Divine pause. Rue and remorse flickered over his features for a fraction of a second.

Now was the time to attack.

Lilith muttered a litany of foul curses. "Gods damn you!" Aether poured from her palm, Constantine urging her to strike. Spiro was thrust backward by the force of it. He tumbled until he stopped himself with a wall of solid Wind. Rising to his feet, he shot a glare at Lilith, anger flashing in his light eyes. Behind him, two figures wrestled atop a knoll.

Felix.

Spiro noted the brawl with a satisfied smirk. "Well, maybe your youngest noviciate will appreciate my offer."

"No," Lilith objected.

Arduen's voice was hoarse, but still he pleaded for Lilith's freedom, beseeching his old friend to leave her be, to take him instead. He was yielding to the one thing he'd spent his life resisting, perhaps even lost his family for. She could not let him do that. She couldn't watch Spiro take her Master away from her. Besides, she doubted the Great Divine would easily forget dissensions spanning decades. There was too much spilled blood between them, coagulated by years, clogging the channel to an alliance.

No, he would not take Arduen.

Without another word, the Great Divine took his leave, climbing atop his steed and departing, his long hair streaming behind him. A beacon of destruction.

Though Spiro was retreating, he'd made his threat clear.

Lilith's legs couldn't move fast enough. Arduen bellowed her name, a demand to come to him. But with his feet planted in the ground, he'd be of little use, and someone needed to help Felix.

From a distance, she could see how the young noviciate was languishing. He fought against Spiro's comrade with steel, his elemental stores depleted. Isidore's Wind willowed around them, indicating that their enemy was still dangerous, still lethal.

Felix feigned a jab and pranced backward, but his enemy caught him in the shoulder. The noviciate went down onto his knees, his hand clutching the wound.

"Felix!" Lilith cried. Wind blasted her back and she lost her footing. She rolled down the knoll, back toward Arduen and the others, until strong hands steadied her.

"Stay here!" An order from the prince. Lilith tried to protest, but Julius was already sprinting toward the spectacle.

Spiro's crony seemed uninterested in Lilith, as if he wasn't here for her. The Great Divine himself didn't try that hard to capture her. Though he was likely depleted, he would have been formidable against her, he could have knocked her unconscious and ferried her away.

But Arduen had pleaded. Perhaps, beneath Philautia's thrall, there was a piece of Spiro that remained.

Lilith cast a cursory glance at Arduen. Quin was still digging away at his feet, lifting his gaze often to check for attackers. She sussed through the grass, groping for the hilt of Constance, unable to tear her gaze from Felix—and Julius.

As Julius entered the battle, Felix stepped back to allow him to take control. Spiro's crony grinned. His arms were long, but they weren't bulging with muscle, he wouldn't be capable of taking both Felix and Julius at once.

Lilith approached on wobbly legs. Felix was still on his knees, blood pooling over his hand from the wound in his shoulder. She dropped down beside him.

"Can you move your arm?"

"Bloody Hades!" Felix swore. "I've never bled so much in my life!" His eyes bulged out of their sockets in pain or disbelief, Lilith didn't know.

"Can you move your arm?" she repeated.

Felix shook his head, his mousy brown hair soaked with sweat.

"Okay," she said. "Wrap your good arm around me and I'll get you back to Arduen." Lilith nudged the arm he had crossed over his chest, holding his shoulder. "Quickly, I have to get back to Julius."

Felix obeyed, wrapping his arm around her. Lilith grunted, the sound guttural, as she heaved him to his feet. They took one step in the opposite direction when Isidore's Wind assaulted them, pressing their bodies to the ground.

The air whooshed from her lungs as they hit the ground, Felix's weight pressing into her abdomen as he landed atop her. Her ears rang, the knell only intensifying with every passing second. Too much was at stake. Her mind shattered. Her vision filtered carmine. Her thoughts fragmented, limiting her to primitive emotions and instinctual urges.

Save Julius!

"Stay here," she barked at Felix, rolling away from him and rising to her feet.

Lilith inspected the duel before her. Julius was stronger than Spiro's grunt. But the prince fought with honor, he would slay any opponent fairly. She knew better than to expect the same decency from Spiro's Divine.

Julius's rage was unvarnished, his expression was all Xander's Fire. But his opponent remained composed, his features lupine. Feral. As their blades met, each man grunted audibly above the din of battle. Julius landed a blow on the man's rib cage and he cried out, then he raised Orphëus above his head, prepared for the killing blow. He was going to behead the grunt. And as he brought that blade down, Wind assaulted him, strong enough to send him flailing backward.

His body collided with Lilith's, and they both went tumbling down. The prince thrust his sword away so as not to hurt either of them. As their bodies slowed, he tugged the helm from his head, wrapped his arms around Lilith and pressed a desperate kiss to her lips. "I'm sorry," he whispered. Then he was on his feet, his palms incandescent with Fire.

"Julius, no!" Arduen shouted.

Panic seized Lilith. Her limbs seemingly unable to respond to her mind's commands, paralyzed by fear, each movement laborious.

Just as Julius released Xander's Fire, the blaze backfired. He did his best to absorb it, but it was too fast. Lilith raised a shield of Aether around them, but it was futile. Julius had been burned.

Lilith dropped to her knees beside him, cupping his face in her hands, her arms shaking from exertion. She was depleted.

Julius groaned, his face screwed in pain. The skin on his neck was already blistered, a fiery red. The damage went beneath his cuirass, the metal hot to touch.

"You're all right," Lilith said to him so softly, her voice perishing in the Wind. "It's going to be okay. Olga will heal you." He groaned again, gripping her arms and pulling her closer to him. His palms were so hot, she could feel them through her tunic.

"Well, now that we've established who the victor is," Spiro's crony drawled, "I think I'll be going home. I've had enough for one day." With a wink, he took to the sky, a flaccid figure dangling in his arms.

Felix.

2 5

FORGIVE ME, FATHER

Spiro's subterranean fortress had been quiet for nearly three weeks. Rhéa quite enjoyed the respite from the Great Divine's insufferable presence.

For the first few days, Rhéa and Irís rested well, knowing there was very little expected of them. When they'd slept themselves awake and restless, they took to perusing the hallways, opening whatever doors they fancied. The only chambers they kept their distance from were Spiro's bedchamber and his conference room. But today, Rhéa fancied herself a treat.

"Why don't we enjoy ourselves a drink, hmm?" Rhéa asked Irís as they swayed through the halls.

"What kind of drink?"

Rhéa hummed as they strolled along. "I was thinking some very expensive rum, or whiskey, or even krasì wine." She wiggled her brows at the young Enchantress, and Irís struggled to contain her cackle.

"Does it make you *craah-zee*?"

Rhéa craned her neck and barked a laugh. "Yes, if you have too much of it!"

Together, the two Enchantresses meandered through the hallways until they came upon the all-too-familiar iron doors. Even in the Great Divine's absence, they were imposing. *Like the gateway to Hades*, she thought. Rhéa fought back a swell of nerves as her palm settled on the latch, and she pushed the door inward.

The conference chamber was cloaked in darkness, the large communal table visible only by the meager light spilling in from the hallway. Rhéa could just make out the buffet where Spiro stored his impressive collection of alcoholic beverages.

"Híq duq sê Híne!" *Let there be light!*

Irís followed close behind her as the sconces lining the walls illuminated the tapestries, the lush furniture, and the polished table. Retrieving two chalices, Rhéa located the wine and filled her glass, but she filled Irís's with something far less potent.

The young Enchantress seated herself at the table, her eyes wandering around the room, taking in its extravagance. The last time the girl had been in here, she'd been interrogated by Spiro. She'd likely kept her eyes trained on her toes.

Rhéa handed Irís the chalice filled with a deep berry wine, and she lowered herself into her respective high-backed chair. Yes, Spiro's designated throne was much more comfortable, but his ass cheeks were permanently imprinted into the cushion. The thought of placing her own bottom there was abhorrent.

Since Spiro and his army set out for war, Rhéa had been free from her usual dosage of fàrmako. Gone were the throbbing migraines and tilting vertigo, the influx of celestial magic was exhilarating. If only she knew where the exit was. What she would give to bask in the Starlight. Likely her left leg, or even her right arm.

"Tell me about the Obsydían Marsh," Irís mused, snapping Rhéa out of her trance.

"What would you like to know?"

The girl propped her chin on her palm and hummed. She'd almost finished her wine, and she spun the chalice between her fingers, what was left of the wine swirling inside the glass. "Teach me about the covens."

Rhéa sat back in her seat. Folding a leg over the other, she sipped from her own chalice, the krasì burning down her throat. The taste reminded her of an old friend.

Cheers, Anastacía!

"Well, there's my coven, the Ilíos," Rhéa said. "Coven of the sun. We are devoted to the Southern Guiding Star: Amalthea." Irís prodded for her to continue. "Then there is the Asimí Fléves, the Silver Veins. Instead of golden irises like mine, theirs are silver, as their name suggests. They worship the Star of Andromeda."

Irís tipped up her wine glass and emptied it to its dregs. "Go on," she gasped, pulling a face.

Rhéa chuckled. "Then there's the Ápeiro Astéri, the Infinity Star coven. They worship the Star of Cepheus." Rhéa swirled her own goblet, her head already foggy from the krasì. She'd have to be careful. She wasn't as formidable as she once was, this wine would destroy her if she had much more. But then, what's so terrible about a few days spent under the covers dreaming of your betrothed? Nothing. Rhéa quashed the remaining wine.

"And their eyes are…?"

"Pale blue."

"Like the Walabeäns?"

Rhéa sighed. *Yes, just like Spiro's.* She nodded.

"I think blue eyes would suit me," Irís remarked with a grin. "The bright color would stand out against my dark hair."

Rhéa chuckled. "Yes, you'd be beautiful."

"And there's one more coven?" she asked.

Rhéa nodded slowly. "Nychta Skiá, the Night Shade. They worship the Dracoladen Star, so their irises are—"

"Violet!" Irís gasped. "Oh, I *so* want purple eyes!"

The Enchantress canted her head at the girl inquisitively. "Are you planning to swear yourself to the Marsh?"

Irís's face darkened immediately. "I've been thinking about it. When we get out of here, where will I go? I need a home somewhere. We won't be here forever, Rhéa." The Enchantress appreciated her conviction, but she found it difficult to be convinced.

"And what about Xavier?"

Irís waved her off. "He told me he'd follow me anywhere. He can come with me."

Rhéa shook her head. "Men are not welcome at the Marsh. Enchantresses only."

The girl gaped. "Then how do you procreate?"

"We leave. Visit a town and find a man worthy of… well, you *know*." At least, Rhéa was sure that Irís understood how a woman and a man conceived a child.

"But you don't take partners or get married? The children grow up with only a mother?"

Rhéa heaved a sigh. "Yes, I grew up with my mother only. She fulfilled all my needs."

"But what if you were a boy?" Irís's expression was solemn.

"Then he is given away. Boys—or Magí's—are taken away. Given to orphanages. Only girls bearing the Mark are permitted to stay in the Obsydían Marsh." Rhéa had witnessed the birth of a baby boy. His mother didn't even get to hold him. Once he was pushed out, he was confiscated and removed. That was how it worked in the Obsydían Marsh. Some form of *sanctuary*.

"That's awful…" Irís frowned, her brow crunching up.

"That's the way of the Marsh. You have to be one hundred percent certain that you want to live there when you swear yourself into a coven. For that's where you'll live out the rest of your immortal days. Under strict laws."

Irís shifted in her seat. "You can't leave at all? Not even to travel?"

Rhéa pursed her lips. Better to convince the girl not to go there, at least not while Ophelía presided over the Enchantresses. "You have twenty years, then you must return. Travel is only permitted by the High Enchantress."

Irís scowled. "I'd like not to live there. That sounds awful. Xavier and I were dreaming of a quaint country home anyway. Together, we will live out our immortal years free of burdens."

"Irís, there's something I haven't told—"

The iron doors swung inward with a boom and Irís jumped out of her seat, landing on the floor with a thud. Spiro stormed into the room, his usually pale face flushed, the glint in his eyes insidious.

Rhéa snapped her fingers at Irís, encouraging her to take shelter under the table. Then she uttered the spell to transform her hair to the flaming curls he desired.

"No!"

Rhéa barely had time to react before his palm collided with her cheek. Stunned, she nearly fell over onto the table.

"Not today," Spiro ground out as his hand grasped the back of her neck, pressing her cheek into the wood until she swore she heard her cheekbone crack, the pain delayed by shock. "I am so sick and tired of the same shit!" he said, his grip tightening on her neck before thrusting her away.

"What happened?" Rhéa dared to ask, finger-combing her hair and adjusting her skirts.

"They bested me," he snarled. "Those Gods damned cretins bested *me*!"

Rhéa flinched as he bared his teeth to her. Was he talking about the Divine?

"I need numbers," he said, snaking a hand through his disheveled mane. "I need more of them, more who can wield other elements!" He swung his fist, knocking her chalice to the floor, the glass shattering, exploding across the stone tiles. For a blissful moment, Rhéa was captivated by the sight. The hearth's flames caught the tiny shards as they spread; they almost looked like shooting stars. "Now, I am back where I began."

Rhéa's lips quivered. "You didn't get the girl?"

Something like sorrow passed over his face, but it was quickly veiled by fury. "No. I did not."

The Enchantress knew better than to pry for information when he was in this state, but her curiosity spurred her. "Why?"

"Because I'm a bloody fool!" he bellowed. "That's why!"

His furor was immobilizing. Rhéa pursed her lips, her hands gripping the edge of the table, her eyes rapt with Spiro's frame as he moped about the room, grumbling expletives, spouting vitriol at no one other than himself.

Spiro removed his tunic and knelt before the hearth, whip coiled around his arm like a snake. Rhéa recoiled in fear that he was going to take his anger out on her. Then he whimpered, "Forgive me, Father," as he raised the whip above his head and began lashing his own back, imparting his own punishment. He cried out as the braided leather dug into his skin, splitting flesh. Crimson leaked from the lacerations, painting jagged lines down his back. If not for his subtle flinches, his sharp intakes of air, Rhéa would not have known that he suffered at all.

But why? She'd never once witnessed Spiro harm himself. Was this penance for failing to capture Lilith? For failing to subdue the Divines who opposed him? Was he exorcising the evil within?

Spiro continued to lash until both his arms gave out. He

slumped forward on all fours, his head hanging limp, his breathing ragged. "Take Irís and leave," he ordered, voice hoarse.

The young Enchantress shook off her incredulity and scrambled to her feet, her eyes wide with terror. Rhéa took Irís's hand and fled the chamber, leaving Spiro to his brooding.

I APPRECIATE YOU

Lilith picked at her fingernails, wincing as she drew blood, though it was paltry in comparison to the sea of crimson they'd waded through only days ago. The week following the cessation of battle, she spent her days running through the halls of the castle, tending to Zurí and Julius. Though her time was equally divided between the two, it was clear that Julius had suffered a great deal more.

Julius had been confined to his bed, the imperial healer doing all she could for him. His neck had been severely burned, and some of the Fire had seeped underneath his armor, burning his chest. He broke a fever on the second night following battle, and the healer struggled to get him under control.

Every time Lilith assisted with his caretaking, a fresh deluge of tears streamed her cheeks. The woman had barked at her to compose herself, but Lilith couldn't bear to see Julius in such pain. The prince could barely speak, but in a gruff voice he'd ordered Lilith to leave, to rest. She'd only obliged because her lament was distracting to the healer, and she'd barely been capable of forming a cohesive thought. Bereft of wits, she was useless to him.

Olga had been summoned as soon as they'd returned to the castle. Now Lilith stood beside Arduen whilst Olga hovered over Julius. The prince was conscious, though he wasn't lucid.

Lilith leaned in to Arduen, and he wrapped his arm around her, stroking her spine in an attempt to quell her anxieties. She hadn't seen him much since the battle. He had been summoned into court meetings, and she had been busy helping the infirm in any way she could.

Quin stood beside the bed, Julius's hand clasped in his. Quin's expression was grave, but it was evident he had firm faith in Olga's abilities.

What if the Gods wouldn't heal Julius? What if the Gods chose to punish him for planning to ascend his father's throne? Lilith pushed the worries from her mind and fought for equanimity.

Olga approached them then, her face beaded with sweat. Arduen straightened. "He will be fine," Olga said. "But he must rest. I've induced him into a sleep. When he next rises, he should be pain-free." The Oracle offered them a meek smile before exiting the bedchamber, angling toward Zurí's.

Julius lay on his bed, the blankets rising to his naval, exposing most of his torso. His skin was pale now, fresh as a babe's.

With a sigh of relief, Lilith turned back to Arduen. "Should I go with her?"

Still holding her, Arduen pulled her into him, resting his chin on the crown of her head. The past week had been so difficult for all of them, with very little respite. They needed a moment to digest it all, to process the loss they'd endured.

"You failed to listen to me, Lilith," Arduen said. "I am your Master, and you can't even follow the simplest of my orders."

Lilith stepped away from him, her hands clasped in front of her submissively, but she held her head high. Yes, she'd disobeyed, but she did what was necessary to get them all out.

Well… all except Felix.

Arduen's gaze was one born of disappointment, not anger. The way he held himself radiated remorse, and she knew just by the set of his shoulders that he blamed himself for Felix's capture.

"I'm sorry, Arduen," Lilith said. "Felix is more novice than I, and he was engaging in a duel with Spiro's crony." It wasn't an excuse, but it was all she could offer.

"You should have come to my aid. Let Julius or Quin fend for Felix. You should have come back to me when Julius took on Spiro's Divine." Arduen was right, but the argument was too moot to bother quibbling, both of their actions were justified.

"I know, but Julius…" Lilith trailed off, her teeth sinking into her bottom lip as she glanced over her shoulder at the man she loved. When she turned back to her Master, stark understanding warmed his eyes.

"I know, Lilith. Trust me, I know."

So, he knew that she loved the prince. What did he think of her? She was still engaged to Jude, his own grandson. The thought made her stomach churn. Even if Jude didn't know whether or not she was alive, he was still her fiancé, she was still his. A promise was a promise. But she wasn't eager to discuss her love life with her Master, regardless of the familial ties.

"I'm sorry." Lilith took his hand in hers, his calluses scratching her soft skin. "But I love them. I couldn't bear… I can't…"

"I know, little one." Arduen offered a meek smile, giving her hand an affectionate squeeze before jerking his chin toward the door. They needed to give Julius peace and quiet. The Divine adjourned to the living quarters of Julius's chambers.

"Should I go with Olga?" she asked again as Arduen took his seat in the lounge.

"No, let her handle this." His tone was gruff.

Lilith hesitated. "I really should be there for her. I'm the reason she was even at the battle."

Her Master took her hand and eased her down beside him. "Let her be, my fledgling." There was a warning in his eyes.

A spark of doubt ignited in the pit of her stomach. "Olga won't be able to heal Zurí, will she?"

Arduen shook his head, a grimace forming upon his face. Lilith pressed her forehead against his shoulder, stifling a sob. What would happen if Zurí died? Surely the Gods wouldn't condemn her to Hades for loving a man. Albeit, a tyrant..

"Everything will be all right," Arduen said.

"I appreciate you," she whispered.

"I appreciate you, too, Fledgling."

They remained this way for some time, until Quin joined them. He dropped into one of the armchairs across from them with a sigh.

"Rumors spread through the barracks that Spiro pits his men and monsters against each other in rings to fight to the death," Quin said. "That's how they earn rank, and how they feed the most savage of his brutes."

Arduen went rigid. "Who told you that?"

"Agónas."

Arduen pinched the bridge of his nose. "If those rumors have reached our men, that means the Emperor's Milítia has been compromised. There is no other explanation for how they would acquire that knowledge."

Lilith blanched.

Quin stroked his beard pensively. "I will reconvene with

Agónas in private. Recruit him to investigate just where these rumors started."

"Yes, I don't think Marlowë would object to our recruiting him to perform reconnaissance on our behalf," Arduen said. "I think the sense of duty, beyond swinging his sword, would do him well."

Quin dipped his chin, his mouth twisting thoughtfully. "I'll go do that now." He took his leave just as the Oracle entered the chamber, her face drawn and pale.

Lilith rushed to her side immediately. "Well? Is Zurí going to be all right?" Her heart pounded inside her chest like a caged rodent.

Olga shook her head.

Lilith bolted, but Arduen caught her before she could leave, his grip tenacious on her wrist. She tried to pry herself free, but it was useless. "Please, Arduen," she begged.

"Listen to what Olga has to say, please."

The Oracle nodded gravely, eyes glassy, shot through with delicate veins. "Zurí was lucky. The dagger Spiro wielded was small. He pierced her lung but not enough to collapse it. She has taken in blood, though. It won't be a clean recovery, but it is possible. I've requested for an Enchantress, but I am not sure if Ophelía will be inclined to send one of her ladies to the capital. I prayed over Zurí, and for now, that is all we can do."

Arduen released his hold on Lilith. "The Gods won't allow you to heal her?"

Olga shrugged, defeated.

"Can I see her?" Lilith asked, hopeful.

Olga took Lilith by the hand and led her down the hallway to Zurí's chambers. The corridor was cast into darkness, most of the inhabitants of the castle asleep. Lilith couldn't remember the last time she'd slept soundly, without Spiro's sneer burned onto the back of her eyelids, his bared teeth flashing tauntingly, a vision of the beast his creatures emulated.

Lilith did not know what to expect as she entered Zurí's bedchamber, but it certainly wasn't what she found. Her Master sat with her face buried in a book, a chalice of red claret in her hand. Shirtless, she sat up propped against her pillows. If Zurí was in pain, she didn't show it.

This was much more palatable than the poignant atmosphere Lilith was expecting.

Ignoring her bare breasts, Lilith trained her eyes on Zurí's pinched cheeks, her sweat-beaded brow. Her Master quickly set down her wine, closed the book, and directed her attention to her noviciate. "Lilith!"

Lilith approached her Master and seated herself at her bedside. "How are you?" she asked warily, her eyes flicking to the wound in Zurí's side. It had been stitched up, and it appeared relatively clean, but the outside wasn't the cause of concern.

"Suffering contentedly." Zurí gestured to the chalice of wine. "The Gods' wills are my command." The slight slur of her speech told Lilith she'd indulged in far more wine than was wise.

"I told you no alcohol!" Olga chastised. "It thins your blood." She snatched the chalice, and ignoring Zurí's protests, downed the entire contents in one gulp. Lilith gaped at the old woman. "There. Now there's no wine to tempt you," Olga said smugly, setting the empty chalice down.

Zurí growled in frustration as Olga took her leave. Lilith watched as she left before returning her attention to Zurí.

"How is Julius?" Zurí asked.

"He will live."

"Good."

The atmosphere was awkward, and Lilith schooled her

features to neutrality. It would be no easy thing to forget Zurí's misstep.

"Now we're even," Zurí spoke hoarsely through her frown.

"Even?"

Her Master chuckled mirthlessly. "I've done something just as, if not more, foolish than you." The statement did not offend Lilith. "And now I pay the price, just as you did."

She wondered if Zurí's drinking had anything to do with her sudden mordant sense of humor. Imbibing would certainly prolong her suffering, for the glint in her eyes was undoubtedly shame. But Lilith knew firsthand the dangers of occluding one's hardship.

It was difficult to blame Zurí. What if Spiro had have taken Arduen up on his offer and stolen him away? What if he'd taken Julius? Would Lilith have tried to placate them if she stood before them in battle? Would she be able to fight them level-headed when they came for her? She'd been able to do it for Larkin, but he was possessed by the Blood Oath. Master Divines could not be controlled in the same way a noviciate could. Thus, it would be so much harder to kill them, knowing they were still in there, in control of their actions.

"Are you in love or something?"

Lilith straightened. "Huh?"

Zurí rolled her eyes dramatically. "You're not answering me."

"Apologies, Master." She wiped at weary eyes. "I'm just tired."

"Who's been keeping you up at night?"

Lilith gasped, taken aback by Zurí's oddly mercurial behavior. She shook off the bawdy jest by rolling her eyes, then she stood and took her leave.

"Good night," Zurí called after her. "Get some rest!"

LILITH FLIPPED ANOTHER PAGE IN HER NOVEL. THERE WAS something cathartic about the *whoosh* of the parchment, the turning of pages. About the visible indicator of progress as the pages on the left surmounted. She didn't read, she simply exulted in the momentary triumph. She needed a win. Even if it was illusory.

The days had been passing by unbearably slow. Her stay in Kenora had transformed into an overdrawn aberration. Arduen and Quin spent the days subjected to meetings with the Emperor and his retinues. Wren refused to leave his bedchamber. Only Olga had managed to gain entrance, and she wouldn't reveal to anyone how the Divine was faring, having been bereaved of his second noviciate.

Zurí remained bedridden, though she seemed to enjoy Lilith's company. Her wound had scabbed over, healing nicely, though no one was certain how repaired her insides were. Zurí still couldn't inhale to her full capacity without crumpling in pain. It would be a month at least before she would be fit to embark upon the return trip to the Frourío. Thankfully, her noviciate was too young to partake in battles for many years yet. Aspen would survive under Ambrose's care for as long as Zurí needed.

Julius had risen to join Arduen and Quin in their courtly duties. Though he held himself high, there was a glint in his eyes that betrayed his own grief. He and Felix had been close, and Julius would not enjoy having to end his life in a confrontation.

Often, her thoughts would stray to Felix. How was he faring on the dark side? Was he fighting in the rings as the soldiers claimed? She remembered his optimistic demeanor when he'd first arrived at the Frourío. He was so genial, even under such pressure. Lilith prayed he'd remain just as resilient in the face of evil.

The door to her chambers creaked open, and Julius strolled inside. He cast her a feeble smile before lowering himself onto the sofa beside her. He wore a black button-up blouse that he left open at the chest, revealing pale, fresh skin beneath. His natural complexion was a golden brown, and Lilith was sure that over time the new skin would darken to match.

"I've wanted to talk to you," he began, fidgeting with the cuffs of his long sleeves, consternation furrowing his brow.

Lilith awaited an elaboration, her breath hitching.

"During my convalescence, I received a missive from Dalegonè." He spoke so softly, she was forced to lean in to hear him clearly. "I've been summoned by my father. No longer can I shirk my responsibilities to my people." When his eyes lifted to meet hers, they were dark, distant, those golden flecks devoid of Fire.

"I understand." She truly did. Julius's countrymen were accusing him of defection. Of course he would never forsake his throne, his people. But they didn't know him personally, how could they ever ascertain the truth? He'd been absent for nearly six years. In order to avoid derision, he needed to return anon.

"Spiro is a threat to Dalegonè as much as Augusta," he said, "and I need to assure my people that my protection extends to them, as well." He inhaled deep. "I don't know how long I will be there, or what will transpire during my visit, but I want you to know…"

Lilith sat up, her heart swelling. Could he…?

"I want you to know how much I care for you." He pronounced each word with careful consideration.

"Julius, I care for you, too." She inched closer to him.

He grasped her hand and lifted her knuckles to his lips. "I

regret leaving you behind. I will miss you every moment I'm away."

She bit her lip, carefully contemplating her question. "What would happen if you were killed here?"

The prince took no umbrage at her query, but his expression was one of surprise. "Well, my uncle, my father's Right Hand, has been appointed to succeed me, if I should die before I have children of my own. Or if my heir is not yet of age to rule."

"If you did not desire to become king, could you not defer your position to him?" Hope blossomed inside her chest. On many occasions, Julius had seemed repelled—burdened—by the prospect of ruling. Maybe he wouldn't have to.

"Are you advocating for my uncle?" Julius asked, a dark eyebrow arched. Lilith would have balked had the amused sparkle in his eyes been absent.

"No." She smirked. "I was just curious."

Julius grazed the back of her hand with his thumb. "I recall a promise I made to you a while back. One that involves me taking you to Xanthë."

Interest piqued, she sat up straighter, withholding her girlish squeal. Was he really offering to take her *with* him?

"Would you like to come along?"

A squall of flurries swirled inside her stomach, the beatific emotions threatening to send her into a fit of squeals. "Julius, are you serious?"

He gave a shrug of nonchalance. "There's no point in staying here. The battle is over, and I'm sure castle will not shed this pall of dejection anytime soon. Neither of us need to be here for it. It's a long journey, and I wouldn't want to endure it all on my own. Besides, I make a scrumptious *fassolatha*." As if traveling with him required an ounce more of enticement.

Lilith fought to conceal her excitement, but it proved to be the most difficult task of late. "I so wish to join you, but I don't think Arduen will allow it. Especially after all of my rebellious antics."

"Let me deal with him," Julius said with earnest. "Arduen doesn't want you in the capital after the assassination attempt. Let me handle him. I don't see why he wouldn't allow it. He has to remain here, and by traveling with me, you would be removed from this hostile environment."

"If you're so sure." Lilith trusted his acumen. If he believed she should join him, there was no reason for Arduen to disagree.

Julius produced the consummate kingly grin. "Have faith, my kyría. I am a *Master*, after all."

REMNANTS OF THE PAST

Arduen strode through the deserted hallways of the castle, his gait springy in an attempt to project an air of confidence. Given the lack of audience, the illusion was for his own eyes and mind.

The looming shadow of war always left him drained. Mind. Body. Soul. And now, with two of his oldest comrades hurting so deeply, the rebound was a slow progression—or rather, regression—for his addled mind refused to cease conjuring visions of his last bout with Spiro, decades ago.

Arduen had spent the past week running errands for the injured Divine. Julius would be all right, for the Gods approved of Olga's wish to heal him, and so he was cured. But Zurí would have to suffer through her injury.

Lilith had triumphed over her tears, working diligently to ensure that Julius suffered little pain as they awaited Olga's arrival. Quin had never been so relieved to see the Oracle. The Master Divine had spent every second at his former noviciate's side. Gods, Quin had even snapped at Lilith on occasion, reprimanding her tears, stating if the droplets couldn't heal, don't let them fall.

It was then Arduen's responsibility to comfort Lilith. The girl was doing the best she could. Tonight, she'd fallen asleep as Olga massaged her liniments into her legs and backside. Arduen had sat at the breakfast table, conversing with the two women, and when Lilith had stopped voicing her opinions, he knew she'd succumbed to her exhaustion.

Olga was confident that Lilith's condition had improved, that her days of seizures had come to pass. But Arduen was wary, watchful of his noviciate's every motion. Was she favoring a leg? Was her skin unusually pallid? Did she wince when she lifted her sword above her head? Perhaps he was coddling her, but the thought of more pain terrified him. They'd been through enough. They needed a Gods-damned victory.

Arduen reached his destination and rapped on the door.

"Come in!" Zurí chimed from within.

He pushed the door inward and crept into the dim commons of her chambers. Zurí sat on the lounge, shirtless.

"Dear Eliath!" Arduen shielded his eyes with his forearm. "First you lose your better judgement, now you've lost your modesty! What's next?"

Zurí chuckled. "I cannot raise my arms above my head. It makes it difficult to don a proper outfit. Besides, I am not leaving my chambers."

"Cover up, please."

"My friend, you've seen plenty of breasts in your day," Zurí said. "I believe you've seen these ones before."

"Yes, well…" he trailed off. Those were instances where Spiro had deigned not to lock his bedroom door whilst tangling up with Zurí.

"You've seen Lilith's, for Kyril's sake," Zurí grumbled.

Arduen waved off her counters with his free hand. "That is different. Lilith was in desperate need during that instance. It was an emergency, and we could have lost her. I think my mind was not focused so much on her nudity as it was on ensuring she opened her eyes the next morning."

The sound of shuffling and Zurí's long, drawn-out sigh told him she'd acquiesced.

"You can look at me now, Arduen," she said.

Arduen did. Zurí was seated on the lounge, a throw wrapped around her.

"Better?" She arched a brow in challenge.

He nodded, claiming the other half of the lounge. Looking her over once, he said, "How are you feeling?"

Zurí gave the slightest of shrugs, even that bit of movement made her wince. "I've been better," she admitted. "The sutures are annoying, especially once the swelling set in. Other than that, Olga keeps me sedated, relatively pain-free."

Palaís—the only drug in Augusta that could diminish pain—was ineffectual on Divine patients. There was nothing to nullify her pain but Augusta's finest wine and an enthralling story.

Zurí launched into a dramatic recounting of just about every epic tale she'd read whilst confined to her chambers. She referenced the original five Divine and how the stories related back to them.

But there was a reason he'd come here, and idle chitchat wasn't it.

"Why did you do it?" he burst out. "Why?"

There was a long stretch of silence. The air seemed to still around them, holding everything in place. Arduen wasn't sure he could breathe past the lump in his throat.

"I wanted to be the one who killed him," Zurí said. "I was ready to attempt the impossible or die trying." She shuffled, then winced. "I was always left in the background during battle. Being a woman and Kyril's vassal, I was pushed to the back lines. Every Master always deemed my capabilities as lesser. They deemed my gifts useless on the battlefield—"

"You've done well to prove them wrong."

"Yes, well," she sighed, "not enough. Kyril's Water didn't save me from Spiro."

Arduen looked up at his friend. A single tear carved its way down her cheek, its path deviated by the deep scar over her eye. In this light, she looked so different from the Zurí he'd come to know and love like a sister.

"When I stood before him," she continued, "I swear I glimpsed remnants of the man I loved. He's still in there, Arduen. A part of him is, at least."

"Zurí..."

"Listen!" she snapped. "I know he took more from you than he ever did from me, but at your pleas for Lilith's mercy, he left her. He must have known how much you love her. And so, he turned away."

"You weren't even there," Arduen said.

"Olga told me everything. She agrees with me, Arduen. Perhaps there is a way to cure Philautia."

Arduen pinched the bridge of his nose, trying to compre-hend all that she'd said.

"I know you don't believe it," Zurí said, "but I do. He wouldn't have left her for any other reason. He could have taken her by force. She was depleted, and he has stores beyond our imagination."

Perhaps their old friend was fighting back against the illness, but he'd still committed unforgivable crimes. Spiro still made it abundantly clear that he no longer cared for them. These acts he must pay for. He'd taken too many innocent lives.

"If he ever attempts to harm Lilith," Arduen ground out, "I

will not hesitate to kill him. Even if it means my life. Spiro's transgressions cannot be overlooked."

"Arduen…"

"Enough!" He stood, breathing heavily through his nose to cage his ire. "I will not hear it, Zurí." The woman shrank back into the cushions. "If you cannot be trusted to fight with us, you will not be permitted to leave the Frourío."

Arduen didn't have the authority to arrest Zurí and confine her to the Frourío grounds, but Olga did, and he did not truly believe the Oracle would listen to such horseshit. Spiro was evil, and each of them needed to remain guarded against him.

28

MISSION COMPLETE

Rhéa kept her eyes trained on the polished surface of the table as Spiro paced the length of the conference chamber. This was not the only indication that he was growing impatient. A chalice of wine was clasped in his hands, but he did not sip from it. He simply swirled the claret, gnawing on the insides of his cheeks, his eyes flitting about the room in search of his next victim.

Upon his return, Rhéa had resumed her normal intake of fàrmako. An invisible insurgent. Her constant companion. The drug slithered through her veins, a vigilant reminder of the serpent she now served. The unsolicited substance dulled her senses, which only favored her when she was summoned to service her *Master*.

Which she had not done for some time. Spiro had been in a morose state since his return. He hadn't even requested her assistance to heal his self-inflicted lacerations. The memory played again and again in her mind since that day. She parsed through his sentiments, searching for the allegory. Who was

Father? But she did not possess an extensive knowledge of the five Gods religion, and thus, she couldn't make sense of Spiro's convictions.

Giving her own wine a swirl, Rhéa gulped it down. She had spent the night mulling over what this meeting could entail, and just as she had managed to fall asleep, a servant woke her. She'd been summoned to Spiro's side to—apparently—welcome Xavier home from battle.

Fortunately for her, she did care about Xavier, and she did want to welcome him, though her idea of a homecoming was much different from Spiro's.

Rhéa had seated herself quietly whilst Spiro poured them some wine to enjoy together. She downed her first chalice in one gulp, eager to sedate herself for the upcoming spectacle. Spiro only chuckled, the hollow timbre vibrating inside her chest, and refilled her chalice. Rhéa sipped this one delicately, aware of her Master's devouring gaze.

"Thirsty, are we?" he crooned, his eyes betraying his salacious thoughts.

Rhéa shivered.

Xavier entered the chamber then. This time he did not deign to knock, and thus, Spiro deigned not to greet his noviciate. Instead, he simply chose to stare him down balefully. Xavier did not display even an ounce of trepidation, he simply bowed his head in deference and gestured to his unbound captive.

The new young Divine entered slowly, but he held himself erect, posturing confidence. His brown hair was a halo of tangles and gore, his cheeks flushed as Spiro surveyed him from foot to head, and back down again. When the Great Divine's eyes lingered on his boots—a tactic Rhéa knew he used to make his victims quake—the new recruit stood taller, vouching for his competence.

Stars, he is so young! But Rhéa was relieved that it wasn't—

Spiro cracked a smile. "Not exactly how I wanted this mission to end, child."

Mission? Rhéa perked up, her eyes inspecting the boy with a new dose of intrigue.

"Perhaps not, Father." The boy seated himself without invitation, and Rhéa began to sense that he was no new acquaintance of Spiro.

Spiro clenched and unclenched his fists, visibly frustrated but withholding his desire to lash out. "You can enlighten me of your findings later, you've been gone long enough."

You've been gone long enough. So this boy had been here before? Father? Who had birthed Spiro's human child?

"Yes, Father. There is much to catch up on." The noviciate's voice was deep and steady, an accomplishment to say the least. His gaze flickered to Rhéa and she shrank back into her seat, much to her chagrin. Felix's bronze armor glinted in the light of the sconces. Impressive metalwork, Rhéa thought, likely a gift from a venerable lord pining after the Gods' favor.

Xavier moved to take his seat at the table, but Spiro waved a finger. "Xavier, please remain standing."

Xavier obeyed, folding his hands before him in subservience. His face remained impassive, but Rhéa knew him well enough to know when he was trembling.

"You failed."

"I brought back your son, as instructed," Xavier said. "You left the girl."

Rhéa restrained her surprise at Xavier's audacity. It was rare for him to ever point out Spiro's shortcomings.

It was the wrong argument to make.

"Felix is more than capable of finding his way," Spiro said.

"But his cover—"

"It doesn't matter now," Spiro said. "His time with them is up. Mission complete. Yours was to bring Lilith to me."

"I recall you claiming that right," Xavier ground out, a single vein bulging on his neck.

Before Spiro could lash out, servants poured into the chamber, carrying silver trays mounted with food. They set the platters down in the center of the table, kneeled before Spiro, then kissed his sandaled feet before promptly taking their leave in a flurry of tulle and silk.

Felix's stomach growled—Rhéa's preternatural senses magnifying the grumble—but the boy didn't reach for the food.

Never removing his eyes from Xavier, Spiro commanded, "Dig in, son. You've traveled long and far. I can't have you wasting away on me."

The young man bent forward, both hands grasping on to a greasy quail leg, and devoured it ardently. Xavier didn't make a move.

"I assume they have skewed my ideas over the years," Spiro prodded, waiting for Felix to elaborate. "Sending swarms of… *fiends* unto Augusta does not exactly aid my public image. But they have been beneficial in maintaining order, cutting off trade routes, supporting my claim to the throne. This country needs me to flourish. It is only a matter of time before Augusta sees it."

"They've deluded themselves on the idea that you're sick," Felix said with a scoff, pieces of meat flying from his mouth.

Spiro chuckled. "No. I care more for the future of this empire than I do myself and my own image, *clearly*. I want to destroy the imperial government. No more shall the common people submit to a man whose only claim to the throne is his diluted blood. Rulership will be granted by merit, and who is more worthy than the Divine?"

The atmosphere in the room grew stale, like the calm before a mighty gale.

"Obadïa is weak," Felix said. "I spent the past several weeks attending court every day. He is a waste of drachmae and wine. His son is even worse."

"And during those weeks, you couldn't manage to sweep the girl away? We've spent nearly two years in preparation for this mission and you've returned empty-handed." His hands flexed against the back of the chair. "She can hardly be *that* elusive."

Felix's chewing stalled as he considered his father's criticism. "Wren was on me the entire time. Rarely could I steal a moment's time to shit, let alone concoct a seamless kidnapping."

Spiro sighed. "That asshole. He hasn't changed."

"A mule like that never does," Felix said. "And this one's immortal." He took another bite and before he finished chewing, he said through a mouthful of food, "I almost had her months ago during a raid, and on our return trip to the Frourío."

"And?" Spiro leaned against the table, cocking his head as he looked down at his heir. "What excuse will you feed me now?"

Rhéa didn't notice much of a resemblance. Spiro's hair was such a pale blond, it was almost white. Felix's hair was a mousy brown, though it was difficult to discern when caked with blood and muck. Their noses bore the same gentle slope of the Walabeäns, but where Spiro's skin was alabaster, Felix's was tawny. His mother must have been darker.

Felix arced his hand through the air angrily. "The raid was all Wren's fault. And Thébés fucked up the timing of Lilith's seizure."

Thébés? Must have been a beast. But to cause seizures? There was too much missing information for Rhéa to make much of that.

"On our trip from the capital, I had six of your best spies trail us," Felix explained. "I took watch so that Julius and Lilith would be caught off guard, half asleep and drowsy. But Julius is tough, and Lilith is resilient, even encumbered by her condition. I thought it would be easy to dispatch the prince and knock her out before she could cause harm, but Julius proved more brazen than I had anticipated. He summoned Fire. Killed all my men instantly."

Spiro's expression was anything but impressed.

"I was lucky to have escaped with my life," Felix said in his defense.

Apparently, Spiro cared enough about his son's life because he averted his attention, dismissing the argument altogether. He rounded on Xavier, but before Xavier could protest, Spiro raised his hand and a blast of Isidore's Wind forced him into the wall. Xavier's body slid down the stone, his limbs slack, lifeless.

"Get up!" Spiro spat as he advanced toward his noviciate, his tone carried that contemptuous note that chilled Rhéa to her marrow. Felix continued eating, careless of the scene.

Slumped on the floor, Xavier groaned, incapable of rising.

"Now," Spiro seethed. But no matter how hard Xavier tried, he could not right himself. Then Spiro charged, both palms incandescent with Xander's Fire.

Rhéa held back her cry of protest. *He's going to kill him!*

Without hesitation, Spiro ripped Xavier's armor from his limp frame, sending the plates of metal soaring through the air. The meat clasped in Felix's hands dropped to the plate with a *squelch*, and Rhéa was forced to jump from her seat to avoid being decapitated by flying armor.

Once Xavier's torso was bare, Spiro lowered his glowing hands to his chest, penetrating him with Fire. Xavier's cries were insufferable, though he did not try to flee. Xavier was the epitome of strength and perseverance, but he was not inviolable.

Rhéa lost her nerve, screaming for Spiro to relent. If he continued, he was going to eviscerate Xavier. Rhéa clamped her mouth shut at the realization that her pleas for clemency were only exacerbating Spiro's rage.

Blood pooled around Spiro's hands as he bore his might into Xavier, his teeth bared in a snarl that sent phantom fingernails raking down Rhéa's spine. Felix kept his eyes locked on the platter of food before him, though the boy—young man—seemed to have lost his appetite.

All throughout, Xavier's spine did not wilt. When Spiro finally ceased and drew away from him, Rhéa feared her friend would never rise. But Xavier pushed himself up, his chest slick with blood.

Rhéa paled. It would be a difficult injury to treat, difficult to ward against infection. But if she had Starlight, if her blood wasn't tainted by fàrmako... Suddenly, she wished she were not so inebriated. She was useless to him tonight.

Xavier floundered to his seat, slumping himself down into the chair without a glance at the others. Above all else, Xavier exuded his imperturbable demeanor, and scooped several potatoes onto his plate.

As Spiro continued to expound details of his vision—his ire apparently mollified—Xavier finished his meal, and when Rhéa's eyes fell on him, she gasped. Xavier's chest was unmarred. His skin flawless, whole.

Spiro wasn't a God. How on earth was he capable of this? What had he done to her friend? Xavier was calm, impervious to the pain that Spiro had caused him only moments before.

And as the young men took their leave, as Spiro's looming form shadowed her, Rhéa couldn't control the frenetic beat of her heart.

Who was this man?

29

TEETH BIGGER THAN LIPS

Elation and disappointment warred within Lilith when Arduen expressed his approval—and support—for her to travel with Julius to Xanthë. Quin affirmed that her company would make it difficult for Julius's family to delay his return to Augusta, where his presence was needed most.

Since the battle, Lilith had recovered exceptionally faster than usual, despite her recent illness and less than adequate rest. Rather than consistent fatigue, she was thrumming with energy, a torrent of power writhing beneath her skin, awaiting her call to action. She'd be ready the next time she faced Spiro, she only hoped that he wouldn't attack in her absence.

Olga sent a servant into the city to procure clothing for Lilith. In Dalegonè, it was strange for women to wear tunics and pants, so Olga had ordered several light chiton gowns. Lilith doubted she'd be able to fit them all in her pack, but the dresses were of a thinner material, as Dalegonè possessed a warm climate year-round, and were thus perfect for cramming.

Lilith had donned her usual black breeches and blouse, Constance strapped to her hip. They brought cloaks to use as blankets, and also to keep their swords dry if they happened to get caught in the rain. Prepared as she was, and thrilled to be alone with the prince, Lilith was reluctant to join the others at the stables. Julius had gone down to saddle up their steeds. He would wait there with Arduen for Lilith, but she had one farewell to make before she met with them.

With her heavy pack upon her shoulders, Lilith traipsed through the hallways, ignoring the servants as they rushed past. Zurí's door was open a crack, as if she knew Lilith would be paying her a visit. It creaked as she eased it open, and Zurí called to her from within, "Come in, Lilith darling!"

Closing the door firmly behind her, Lilith entered the living chamber of Zurí's quarters. Her Master had recovered quickly, though she wasn't permitted to leave her chambers in case of infection; Olga's orders, and if Zurí would obey anyone, it was the Oracle.

"All ready, I see?" Zurí eyed Lilith's bulging pack.

"Yes, as ready as I'll ever be."

Zurí smirked, an amused gleam in her eyes. She was seated upon her lounge, a pile of books on the table before her. Sequestered to her chambers, she'd taken to reading tale after epic tale.

"I thought I'd come say goodbye," Lilith said, seating herself across from her Master.

"I'd be hurt if you didn't." Zurí eyed her from under prim brows, her expression as enigmatic as ever. "And I wanted to discuss something with you."

Lilith straightened instinctually.

"You are traveling alone with a boy—sorry—a man," Zurí began. "A young man who happens to be very handsome, and from my perspective, very fond of *you*." She narrowed her eyes on Lilith for emphasis. A blush burned her cheeks. "I just want to ensure you are educated on certain *matters* regarding the male species…"

Oh no, this was *that* kind of conversation.

"Zurí, I know how babies are made," Lilith interjected. "You really don't need to explain it." She laughed breathily, hopeful to evade the embarrassing topic.

"Good. Don't make one." Zurí's tone was serious, grave, just like it had been the morning she'd warned Lilith not to ask the Gods for anything. "But just as a precaution, take this." She gestured to the palm-sized glass vial on the table. "It's a contraceptive I had Tatiana prepare."

Oh, Gods. Lilith's cheeks burned.

"I did not tell her it was for you," Zurí clarified. "But after seeing the way Julius handled you on the battlefield, I figured it was time." She sighed heavily. "One drop after intercourse. That's all you need. Within an hour afterward, not the next morning. Got it?"

"Yes," Lilith confirmed. "We've only ever kissed," she added with an embarrassed, breathy huff.

Zurí chuckled. "Oh yes, but kissing leads to more, and more leads to babies."

Lilith waved her off with a scoff.

"I'm serious!" Zurí said. "Kissing is fine. Petting, too. Just do not join your—"

"Goodbye, Zurí!" She chose that moment to rise and amble toward the door.

"Wait!" Zurí called after her, and Lilith froze under the arch of the open doorway. "I have one more thing."

She twisted on the spot to lock eyes with her Master.

"You're treading a dangerous line, my girl."

"Zurí," Lilith groaned, "please don't speak so cryptically." Leave it to Zurí to reave the joy out of Lilith's departure, riddling her with misgivings. She'd been excited to spend time alone with the prince, why would Zurí seek to ruin that?

Her Master sighed, her expression lacking the humor it held only a short moment ago. "Beware the kiss of the lover whose teeth are bigger than their lips."

"Zurí…" Lilith waved her off. This was foolishness. Julius had a kind and gentle soul.

"I say this with love and respect, but above all else, I say this with concern." Zurí cleared her throat. "Do not become so enamored by the rose that you are oblivious to its thorns." She spoke slowly, as if she feared Lilith wouldn't understand her. Those turquoise eyes brimmed with tears, like the shallows of the sea, and Lilith wondered if her riddle had anything to do with her dangerous affection for Spiro.

INHABITANTS SWARMED THE FRONT GATES OF THE IMPERIAL grounds, screeching foul expletives at their ruler. Obadïa was likely smiling down upon them from one of the many looming turrets of his castle, as far away from the violent throng as he could get.

Of course they were angry. They were being taxed ridiculously, and in a country without trade, drachms were sparse. Their labor had been conscripted for the war effort, and they'd been granted next to nothing in exchange for their skills and crafts. They now spurted their vilifications to the Emperor and his useless heir as the Frourà pushed them back with dulled spears.

Lilith doubted that the Emperor's troves contained much gold. His treasury had to be waning over the past decade as Spiro amped up his attacks on the Empire. Though Spiro had never trounced the Emperor's Milítia in battle, his army of beasts seemed to be easily replenished, whereas human men took many years to train. It was only a matter of time before the Emperor was just as poor and destitute as the bulk of his subjects.

Arduen had mentioned that the Emperor's usual resigned demeanor was disintegrating with each courtly meeting. As it became clearer that his allies were turning away from him, his countenance had become volatile in the face of fear. In frequent raging fits, he would have to be talked down by the healer who stood vigil by his side. A pity, Lilith thought, as so many wounded soldiers were in desperate need of her aid. The Emperor's Malitia was dwindling and it wouldn't be long before Obadïa became desperate. The man was blinded by incense, unable to see reason, and Lilith dreaded the day she witnessed him succumb to fear.

No, it was safest to leave Kenora behind. But Lilith loathed to relinquish her tenacious grip on Arduen. She knew she'd miss him terribly, but her Master had argued that the road would be the safest place for her, and she had to heed his wisdom. Besides, he had Zurí here to help him, and none of the Emperor's retinues could resist that woman's wiles.

Arduen had expressed that their farewell be as succinct as possible, if only to avoid drawing attention to their departure. They didn't have time to spare for loitering citizens interested in the comings and goings of the holy Divine. Nor did they wish for rumors of their absence to meet the ears of Spiro's spies. Arduen was paranoid that they'd be followed, and they still hadn't discovered who had sent the assassins after them the last time.

The imperial stables were located near the eastern gate. Arduen and Julius stood waiting for her with another figure.

"Hestîa?" Lilith canted her head, her lips splitting into a grin.

The warrior sprinted toward her, colliding with Lilith, the woman's strength the only thing keeping Lilith on her feet. She cackled as Hestîa pulled away only to hug her again.

"When you return, you must tell me everything!" Hestîa said with bursting enthusiasm. A stark contrast to the atmosphere in Zurí's chambers. Lilith felt slightly whiplashed. She looked at the men fleetingly, worry gnawing at her core. She didn't want either man to overhear.

"It's Dalegonè," Lilith said. "It is an arid land. Plus, it's more densely populated than Kenora! Are you really that interested?" She side-eyed her friend. Another person to miss and worry over.

Hestîa giggled, averting her gaze. "Oh, you are so naïve, Lilith. It's cute."

Cute? Lilith wrinkled her nose.

"I want to know everything about... you *know*!" Hestîa chided.

Now it was Lilith's turn to giggle. "Right," she said under her breath as Hestîa waved her off, trudging toward the barracks.

Arduen's gaze was steadfast as Lilith approached. "All ready?" he asked, taking her oversized pack and fastening it to her horse. The stallion was a thoroughbred, muscles rippling under its silky black hide. Olga had braided its red mane into hundreds of elaborate plaits, so tight, Lilith doubted even the most harrowing of winds could disentangle them. His name was Feørno. They'd purchased mounts they could board once they reached port, Olga having refused to allow them to take their own steeds.

"Why, thank you, gentle Divine!" Lilith said. Her cheerful croon was a poor attempt to mitigate the dourness hanging heavy in the air.

"I am glad you are escaping this macabre metropolis,"

Arduen said, a quirk of a smile tugging at one corner of his lips. His blue eyes were bright today. A good sign. Much more affable than that storm-washed shade of blue he'd been sporting as of late. "Write me when you arrive."

"Yes, Master." Tears stung the backs of Lilith's eyes, but she ignored them.

"Julius is your Master on this journey." Arduen gestured to the prince, already positioned in his saddle, ready to abscond before the sun rose high enough to reveal their departure. "No rebellious behavior," he said. "Or I will come and retrieve you myself."

Lilith quipped, "Gods know you're too old to survive a voyage that far!"

Arduen scoffed, pulling her into a lung-crushing embrace. "You listen to Julius, aye?" he said against her ear. When he pulled away, all evidence of amusement vanished.

But Lilith's grin never faltered. "Yes, Master," she conceded with a playful smirk. "So, if I find that I miss you too much, all I have to do is act out and you will be on your way?"

Arduen grinned, the skin around his eyes crinkling. "Yes, my fledgling."

They looked into each other's eyes for a moment. Arduen's pale blues darkened, his smile crumpling, all sanguineness abandoned. Lilith hadn't given much thought to how her absence would affect him, especially so soon after battle. And this wasn't just any battle, Spiro had been present, Felix had been taken.

Lilith viscerally recalled a time when she had looked to Arduen to fill the hole of her father's absence. But now, he was more than that. If something ever happened to Arduen, he would leave behind a hole entirely of his own. There was no replacing, no replicating the bond they shared. Losing him would be akin to the death of an internal organ, an integral part to the mechanism that was the human body. Without him, she was sure to flounder, to slowly shut down, piece by corroded piece. Rusted and oxidized by tarnish. Totally and utterly inept.

"Battle is ugly, yes," Arduen said, as if reading her mind. "Yet it's the ghosts that linger long after that do the most damage. The carnage changes a warrior. It makes us harder; strangers to mercy and kindness. These ghosts make up the walls that separate us from our kin, from those who can help us heal." He assisted her up into the saddle and patted her steed's rump. "Ride fast so they do not catch you."

30

A FOREST OF IVORY TOWERS

The Dunes rolled before them like miniature foothills of the Orösía Mountains. The sight had stolen Lilith's breath from the moment they'd emerged from the oaken forest. Julius, on the other hand, was pleasantly underwhelmed. He'd been the one who had argued to take the route trespassing the notorious Dunes. Truthfully, he knew not what to expect. He had a preconceived image in his head, but, as a man who had grown up in a desert nation, there was a stark contrast in size. The Dunes of Augusta were paltry in comparison to the Dunes of the DíTakas Desert, and that was putting it nicely.

They walked beside their mounts, taking the trek through the sand at a slow pace, making their way along the edge of he oaken forest. Not before long they would reach their final destination before the voyage overseas. Both excitement and trepidation battled for the upper hand within Julius's stomach, but they seemed to be at a stalemate. He'd never imagined returning home would be so… perturbing.

"Tonight we sleep in a real bed," Julius said wistfully as he observed the rolling mounds of sand. He was sick and tired of bivouacking. They'd been traveling for two weeks and were desperate to rest their limbs. At dawn, they would board the ship to Xanthë, and with nothing else to occupy their time in their private cabin… Julius grinned beatifically.

He glared out at the mounds of sand. "This should be easy," he said with a sardonic air.

Lilith surged forward, beckoning for him to follow in her wake. "We must be careful," she cautioned.

"Why is that?"

"Because there are sand daemons here!"

Julius flinched, a sarcastic and thematic gesture. "Okay, calm down." He patted her shoulder. Even the slight, very platonic touch send shivers racing up his arm, heat pooling in his core.

A lump formed abruptly in the side of one of the dunes. Lilith squealed, casting an *I told you so* glare at him.

"Come," he said, and at her lack of acquiescence, he hefted her up from under her armpits—not unlike someone would lift a child—and threw her over his shoulder. Her fingernails dug into sinew as she attempted to turn to face whatever danger had found them, but Julius positioned himself to obstruct her view.

"Julius…"She'd made it abundantly clear that she didn't want to tread too close to the Dunes, nor was it wise to stray too far from their horses. "We travel within the trees!" she chided, but her voice held a note of fear, a small plea.

What he assumed was a sand daemon erupted from the dune, shaking its scaly hide clean in a spray of sand. Its robust form was nothing short of intimidating, its body seemingly hewn from marble. It skittered nearer, far faster than Julius thought possible for such a stout creature. Scales stood out stark, as if seashells had been welded onto it. He knew he should attack, but his curiosity betrayed him, pining for a few more seconds of inspection.

When the beast was just a few feet from contact, Julius braced himself to attack. Lilith clung to him like a mollusk, squirming and whimpering. He squinted, taking in the beast close-up. He couldn't see any eyes, but it mattered not for the beast could smell them, and its snake-like tongue was curling in the air, tasting their scent.

"Put me down, Julius!" Lilith commanded, panic seizing her. He didn't respond to her, nor did he make to move or defend them. "Please…" She buried her face in the folds of his cloak.

Too bad he loved teasing her like this.

It was a pity the creature had to die. At least it would be quick. Xander's Fire took no more than a fraction of a second to react to Julius's summons. Sparks burst from his fingertips, startling the creature. A second later, a dart of flame struck its head, taking it clean off. Red blood erupted from the severed veins, and the daemon toppled.

When Julius returned Lilith to the ground, she took a moment to adjust her disheveled hair, then she surveyed the landscape, wide eyes pausing to take in the headless carcass. It was now a heap of charcoal in the sand.

"Gods almighty," she whispered.

"Dinner fit for a princess!"

"Lucky for you, I am not a princess," she deadpanned.

⊙ ⊌ ∽ ℳ ◊

Julius shut the door to their bedchamber silently, one hand balancing their dinner tray on his flat palm. "It's just soup and a fresh loaf," he said, his voice low and husky.

Lilith sat by the fire, the flames licking at the grate. She hadn't moved since they'd arrived, since she'd set her belongings on the bed they would be sharing for the night. A very small bed that wouldn't leave much space between them.

The prince shucked off his tunic, revealing a well-muscled torso. Lilith stared at his back, her chest constricting with nerves and excitement. They'd touched and kissed and played during their travels, but they never took things too far, whether from nervousness or assumed boundaries. How was she supposed to tell him she wanted more, that she wanted it all?

"I'm starving," she rasped, reaching for the loaf before he'd even set the tray down.

Julius chuckled, low and rolling. "I bet you are. I can always go and request more later. The maid said the kitchen wouldn't shut down for another hour."

A flutter tickled her core. Lilith didn't want to be leaving this room for the next hour. She wanted to be curled up in that little bed, limbs tangled with his.

"You seem tense," he said. She hadn't noticed him studying her. His eyes darted to the bed and back and flashed her a knowing smirk. "I can sleep on the floor."

"No!" she said in a desperate rush. "I mean…" She inhaled a sharp intake of air that did little to conceal her desire. "It's been a long journey for us both."

Good cover. Lilith tore off a bite of loaf.

Julius's grin widened. "As long as you're comfortable." He shrugged, his skin growing taut at his muscular chest. "It's not like we haven't been sharing a single bedroll since we left Kenora."

Right. Her eyes narrowed, her nerves abating slightly, the tension ebbing away.

They ate in near silence save the crackle of the fire. When it was time to settle into bed, Lilith had surrendered to her desire. When she removed her attire, she didn't bother to don sleepwear. She stood by the bedside, her breathing ragged, her skin pebbled by the cool air.

When Julius finally set his eyes on her, his jaw went slack, his attention roving over her naked frame, halting momentarily on her peaked breasts, on the dark V at the apex of her thighs.

"Lilith," he said.

She could see the sharp planes of his face, the valleys and rolling hills of his torso, the increasing tempo of the rise and fall of his chest.

"Please tell me you want this," she whispered.

His gaze softened, and he reached a tentative hand out toward her. "You know I do."

"Then what are you waiting for?"

Julius closed the distance between them, scooping her up into his arms and depositing her on the bed. He settled atop her, his forearms bracketing her head. He brought his lips to hers in a whisper of a kiss, a tease. He shifted and his taut body ground against hers.

It was maddening.

"Julius, stop teasing me."

He stilled, pulling away only enough to allow for eye contact. "What do you mean?" The caress of his breath against her neck increased the torment.

"I mean…" What did she mean? That she was ready for more? They'd been skirting the line of *more* for weeks. Reason slowly crept into her mind, shrouding out the delirium of desire. Would his respect diminish if she gave herself over to him? Lilith knew little of the expectations of Dalegonian women, but Augustan women did not fall into bed with their partners until they were promised. "I want this." She gestured to their entwined limbs. "But I cannot read your mind, and I know that this is new and fragile."

Julius drew away further, his face pulling an offended

expression. "My love is not fragile." The surety with which he said it sparked a flame inside her, searing her cheeks. "I will never pressure you, but there is nothing you could show me that would tamp down what I feel." He ran a calloused finger along the line of her jaw, tilting her chin upward to meet his lips. "There is no light that could ever diminish your beauty."

She sighed deep, expelling weeks of tension. But Julius's face hardened, lines etched in his brow. As if he'd misread her relief and took it for worry, for hesitation. "You know I would never overstep my bounds with you, Lil."

That was never a thought on her mind. She loved Julius. For more than his good looks and more than his title. He'd sacrificed so much every day for the ones he holds dear. He was a man who deserved all the love and adoration the world could bestow upon him. And she wanted to give him everything.

Lilith parted her legs a little more, and her stomach fluttered as his eyes dipped down to take all of her in. "You know I want you too, Julius." And that wouldn't be enough. "Take me." But it was a start.

His jaw tensed, his eyes locked on her navel, as if afraid to drift lower. She'd never seen him so vulnerable before, that pleading look in his eyes, it was almost as if he were another person.

But he was still Julius, her Julius. This was his rawest form, clothes and shell discarded. And he was all for her.

A warm flood of satisfaction pooled in her chest, that she was the only one who knew him like this was immensely comforting, satisfying. Electrifying.

"Are you certain?" he asked, voice hoarse and grating.

She tugged at his dark curls in frustration. "Please."

His serious expression breaking into a mischievous grin, Julius surged above her, his hands making quick work of removing his pants. At the sight of him, bare and exposed and

definitely prepared, Lilith's legs spread wider of their own volition, throbbing with a desperate need for him. Opened for him,
she braced herself for a tidal wave of flesh and flame... but
Julius did not take her as she'd imagined.

Instead, the prince trailed his lips down her chest, her
breasts, her abdomen. His hands roamed her body, teasing and
toying where he seemed to know she needed it most. Gently, he
lifted her legs, molding her, and she forced her body pliant.

The meager light with which to see by lent more to the
imagination than she would have preferred, and the first shock
of his tongue between her legs sent a jolt of pleasure through
her entire body. Julius held her hips as he worked, his grip
tightening as she began to writhe, her hands twisted in the
sheets, her lips cinched between her teeth to keep from crying
out. Pleasure erupted, spreading through every crevice of her
body, every muscle clenched and shaking.

And then he was atop her, inside her, so abrupt she barely
noticed the intrusion. She expected him to continue, but he
froze, his eyes intent on her face, scrutinizing.

"Are you all right?" he asked. "Did I hurt you?"

Lilith shook her head, breathless, her chest heaving. "Don't
stop," she gasped, and reaching up to wrap her arms around
his neck, she pulled him down.

⊙ ⊛ ⤳ ∧ ◊

TWO WEEKS SPENT IN A CRAMPED CABIN, CONSTANTLY ROCKED BY
the Galatёa's waves, made Lilith queasy, her stomach in knots.
The double-masted brigantine was not luxurious but it had
charm, and their private cabin was—fortunately—intimate.
Candlelight offered a dim view of Julius's body as he worked
over her, her eyes rapt with the sight of his muscular chest,
heaving with every thrust. By the third day, their bodies ached too

much to continue. They spent that time bathing one another and gently teasing in preparation for the next bout of lovemaking.

The prince's company offered a welcome distraction. After all this time, and even being Anointed by the God of Water Himself, Lilith was not a strong swimmer. When up on deck, she kept far away from the railing, far away from the roiling sea below. Julius had proven himself masterly in quelling her anxieties, reminding her of her many lessons spent in the waves with him, learning the movements that would save her life, should she go overboard. Though she doubted that, in a state of panic, she would remember how to move her limbs.

When the Western Galatëa's waves rocked the ship to and fro, and every night invited lightning and thunder, and the ship's crews' frantic footsteps made sleep impossible, she'd turned to Julius for distraction, and he gladly took her in his arms.

Every night they basked in each other's presence, exploring the new nature of their relationship, with few boundaries. Lilith fell into a coquettish mien, her fingers teasing, her giggles suggestive. Little worried her, for what danger could find them surrounded by Kyril's domain?

The sea was responsible for separating them for their entire lives, it only made sense that they gave themselves to one another—mind, body, and soul—amidst the roiling waves, overcoming their greatest geographical obstacle to be with one another.

JULIUS SAT ON THE BED THEY SHARED, THE SHEETS A CRUMPLED heap beneath him. The sudden stomping of feet called his attention away from a half-dressed Lilith. Curiosity tugged at him, and he jumped to his feet, grasping at her hand. "We must go up top!" he said, and just as she'd pulled on her tunic, he threw both their packs over his shoulders and dragged her behind him.

"Julius!" She raised her voice. "What is it?"

He didn't respond. A visual would provide a better answer than his muddled words could at the present moment. They emerged onto the deck of the ship. The corpulent bosun barked orders, his crew sprinting past to obey the pithy commands. Julius ignored them as he weaved his way through the fray toward the other passengers lined up along the railing of the main deck. He found a space and squeezed through the throng of bodies to claim it, pulling Lilith to his side. He positioned her in front of him, and wrapping an arm around her chest, held her against him.

Across the azure expanse, petrels soaring just above the sea's surface, was Xanthë, capital of Dalegonè. The stark silhouette of a gilded Xanthë was enough to sunder him. They were close enough that he could see the oblong outline of the palace, his home. The city's many domed turrets and spires rising high, the buildings crawling up the coast.

With his free arm, he pointed. "Home!" he shouted, but his voice was drowned out by the wind and the clamor of the workers' ministrations. Still, Lilith seemed to understand him, as if the new nature of their relationship no longer necessitated words.

Lilith asked questions about the many idiosyncrasies unique to Xanthë. She pointed out that the roofs of the smaller buildings were painted bright, in a myriad of colors. Julius explained the hues signified what house that family hailed from, and the colors of the roofs of the shops identified the craft the owner mastered. Nearly every building possessed a tower with a balcony, curtains swaying on the ocean breeze, the sight utterly idyllic.

As they drew nearer and the other passengers dispersed to prepare to dock and disembark, they remained at the railing, their packs—having been prepared the night before—already slung over their shoulders. Lilith was stiff and quiet, unusually so.

"Are you all right?" Julius glanced down at her.

"Y-yes," she stuttered. "It's just a lot to take in."

Indeed, it was. Limitless multihued lights glistened throughout the coastal city, blinking out as the early morning sun perforated the clouds above. The Enchantresses' Guild worked with his father to maintain the fires, and to color them.

It was an overwhelming deluge of emotion returning home for the first time in six years. He only hoped his return pacified any unrest and facilitated his Divine image. Perhaps, seeing him for the first time since his departure, more mature and with godly power sluicing through his veins, his people would come to respect him as they did his father.

His reputation was sterling before he'd left, his mortal death ensured that, gilded it. But Dalegonè hadn't anticipated the length of his absence, especially with his father's impending death. Six years was a long time to wait for your heir to return. And when that time was spent mostly at war… well, Julius had come to sympathize with them, to the point of empathy.

There were many times I didn't expect to see Xanthë ever again.

Today was not only the first time Lilith would see his home, but it was also the first time he would celebrate her birthday. He'd meant to mention it first thing when they'd woken, but other matters of import had taken precedence in the moment. His body flushed at the memory.

"I want to give you something," he said, sifting through his pack at his side.

Lilith turned her back to the railing, Xanthë forgotten for a time. Her eyes narrowed as he retrieved a small velvet pouch. "What is it?" she asked.

Arduen had been the one who had told him of Lilith's birthday. Julius knew that Arduen was saddened he couldn't spend it with her, the sentimental brute. But Julius assured him he would make it special. He'd even gone out to purchase a little gift, something to commemorate their trip.

Julius tugged on the double drawstrings, an eager smile tugging at his lips. He tipped the pouch upside down, a mass of gold dropping into his palm. He stretched out a long dainty chain, a small golden pendant swinging from it like a pendulum. "For your birthday," he said almost nervously.

Lilith gawped. Rarely was she ever at a loss for words. That was a good sign, wasn't it?

"Turn around," he said, and she obliged. Julius brought the chain over her head and fastened it behind her neck. She glanced down to inspect the pendant. It was a small golden flower, the center of which sat an emerald. An intricate piece of jewelry, yet simple. It reminded him of her upon first glance.

She gasped. "Julius, you really shouldn't have…"

"Nonsense! It's your birthday."

Lilith gaped, spinning to face him. "How did you know?"

"Arduen told me when we were in the capital. I had to get you something."

She stepped up on her tiptoes and pressed a light kiss to his cheek. "Thank you," she whispered against his skin.

Julius's eyes flitted from hers to her lips, and back again. Reason warred with his primal desires, his carnal need for her. It would be a few nights before they could indulge in each other like that again. So he took her face in his callused palms and leaned in.

The kiss was both long and brief. Hard and soft.

When Julius pulled away, he smiled down at her, those emerald eyes of hers bright with emotion. "Just another reminder of how much I care for you," he said, planting another kiss to her brow.

THE DOCKS WERE TEEMING WITH STEVEDORES AND PASSENGERS alike, but Lilith and Julius managed to push their way through the disarray. Before Lilith could inquire as to how they were going to travel up the mountain to the palace, Julius halted. Ahead of him stood several men clad in crimson harem pants, matching sashes crossing over bare torsos, and matching bullion sandals. Each wore their dark locks pulled back into rows at the nape of their necks. *These are Julius's servants!* Lilith realized, noting that their attire was indicative of royal servitude.

"My prince, we have come to escort you to the palace," said one of the men. "The Queen has requested that we carry you and your, uh"—his eyes raked over Lilith—"your *lady-friend* inside the royal couple's palanquin." His foreign accent possessed a captivating lilt much like Julius's, though Lilith was aware that she was the one with the accent in these lands.

The escort's arm swept through the air, gesturing to the elaborately gilded carriage. Each of the accompanying servants knelt then, and Julius rested his hand upon his chest and bowed his own head, a gesture seemingly meant as a signal for his servants to rise.

Lilith caught her breath in her throat. Whenever Julius donned his royal decorum, her blood thrummed in her veins, boiling. An image of him rising over her in the moonlight flashed in her mind, and she had to close her eyes for a moment to force clear thoughts. She could not enter Julius's home corrupted by a lascivious mind.

Julius beckoned her closer, and Lilith inspected their form of transportation. The palanquin seemed to be forged of solid gold, the windows fogged to grant the passengers some privacy. "My parents have sent their personal palanquin."

"Is that unusual?" Lilith glanced around furtively as passersby stopped to gawk at their Crown Prince. Julius seemed impervious to their attention. Of course, he was used to this kind of treatment, but it set Lilith off. Wary, she gripped Constance's hilt as she took notice of several looming figures surrounding them. Guards.

"Yes, I've never been in it," Julius admitted. "I have always had my own single-seat." He handed their packs to one of his servants.

Lilith relaxed slightly. "Well, I'm glad to be joining you for your first time."

Julius flashed her a charming grin. "I as well."

Taking her hand, he helped her into her seat before climbing in behind her, then he shut the door, assuming the servant's job —who was reaching out to aid the prince. Lilith stifled a giggle. Julius had spent so long in the absence luxury, he seemed to have forgotten how to accept assistance.

Lilith sat with her hands clasped in her lap, her eyes trained on Julius's travel-worn boots. She wished fervently that the ride would be over and the people of Dalegonè would stop gawking at her, the woman who'd arrived on the arm of their long-lost prince.

Obsequiously, the servants each claimed a corner of the palanquin and they rose steadily from the ground. The ride was surprisingly smooth, despite the uphill climb. The streets were narrow, civilians scrambling to get out of their way, pausing only to catch a glimpse of their prince.

When they approached the palace, Lilith struggled to imagine the imposing structure as Julius's home. The palace was a forest of ivory towers. The whitewashed walls rose high into the sky, the spires rising up even higher. Gaping holes inside them indicated open floors, crimson-dyed curtains sailing on the winds from the openings. In awe of the city's exotic beauty, her anxiety abated.

Growing up in a small town, Lilith struggled to comprehend the mass amount of wealth Julius's family undoubtedly possessed. Her understanding of his upbringing was parochial at best, but somehow they'd found a connection to one another.

"Come, my love." Julius held his hand out to her. "It is time to meet the King and Queen of Dalegonè."

3 1

XANTHË

The Queen of Dalegonè rose from her throne to welcome her son. Though, Lilith noted, she refrained from embracing him, despite their years apart.

In the presence of the King and Queen, Lilith found herself laconic, aloof. Rendered mute from her lack of tact, not unlike when she first met Emperor Obadïa. Though this time in the presence of royalty, she found herself vying for their approval.

The royal couple's skin was deep bronze, their hair black as night. The Queen wore hers long whilst the King's was cropped short, thinning, Lilith surmised, as a result of his illness.

Lilith steeled herself as the Queen's luminous eyes fell upon her. The only comfort the Queen's shrewd gaze provided was their likeness to her son's.

The Queen's dress was cream-colored, frippery jewels glittering on the sleek tulle skirt that fell past her feet. Lilith was certain that she'd need at least a few servants to hold the train as she walked.

"My boy," the Queen crooned, though there was little affection in her tone. "How marvelous to be graced by your presence."

Lilith cast a questioning glance in Julius's direction, but he had his eyes locked on his father. The King sat regally on his throne, his eyes brimming with unshed tears. An ornate cane was clasped in his hands, and he used it to heave himself from the great seat. Julius rushed forth, climbing the stairs to the dais two at a time. The Queen released a long gust of air through her nostrils to stress her censure. Her son paid her disapproval little heed. When he reached his father, they embraced, Julius towering over the man.

The King was frail in his final decade. The Queen appeared to be in her mid-forties, which could mean that the illness had drained the vitality from his father's body. He'd spent six years suffering without his son's support.

The King spoke through sobs, pausing only to cough. Julius knelt before his father, his hands folded on the King's knee as he listened intently to his words.

A woman, tall and willowy, stood behind the throne, barely noticeable amongst the luxury despite her vibrant crimson locks. Lilith nearly gaped when she took notice of the violet irises. *An Enchantress!*

Julius rose and descended the dais, reclaiming his position at Lilith's side. He flashed her a bolstering smile, and she reached over to wipe a tear from his cheek. He chuckled as her thumb brushed over his skin, lingering slightly too long to be considered platonic.

The Queen turned her attention on Lilith, forcing a smile that was obviously artificial. "And who is your friend, dearest?"

Julius smiled up at his mother, nudging Lilith as he did. "This is Lilith Oak, fellow Divine. I needed a travel companion, and she proved herself a worthy warrior, and a loyal comrade. I'd promised to bring her to see the wonders of Xanthë."

When Lilith met the cold eyes of the Queen, the expression on the woman's face quickly melted Lilith's grin, chasing away her son's infectious joy.

The King looked upon Lilith with warmth, his cheeks flushed, his eyes crinkling around every edge. "Welcome to Xanthë, Lilith. I pray you enjoy your stay and find yourself at ease within the walls of our home. I've arranged special accommodations for you, and you will be assigned servants to care for you during your stay."

The King returned his attention to Julius. "You must stay with us no less than seven days, my son. Please grant me at least that much of your time. I may not be around the next time you come home—"

"Father, please! Do not say such things."

The King bowed his head solemnly. "It is true, my boy. And I can deny it no longer. But enough of this talk!" His frail hand arced through the air like a scythe. "Go and clean yourselves. Rest and enjoy my majestic city. Tomorrow evening, we will host a ball in your honor. The future King of Dalegonè returns!"

Lilith smiled up at Julius, a flutter in her stomach at sight of the rosy tint to his cheeks. She returned her attention to the King and Queen. The edges of Faustus's eyes crinkled as he gazed dotingly upon his heir, but the Queen's eyes were locked on Lilith.

And that's when Lilith recognized her mistake. But it was too late, for she had rolled over and exposed her vulnerable, deliciously soft underbelly to the Queen. And the grin she received in response left no doubt that the Queen noticed, she saw, and she would devour.

As Lilith and Julius were escorted out of the throne room, Lilith exhaled a pent breath. Servants were standing at the ready. Most of them flogged to Julius whilst the rest tended to her. They touched her hair and picked at her tunic. It was dirty and rumpled, but what did they expect? The journey had taken a month!

Lilith frowned. A month had passed since she'd last seen Arduen. Was it too soon to act out?

With a sly grin, Julius turned to her. "Fancy a trip to witness the brawls of Xanthë?"

Her interest piqued, she nodded enthusiastically.

"Good. Now go and get yourself cleaned up, and I'll meet you out front in an hour."

With a nod, Lilith followed her servants as they walked through the long hallways. The walls and floors were all made of polished white marble. Long corridors were decorated with flowers, vines, and tapestries depicting historical events. The left-hand-side walls were lined by tall, arched stained-crystalline windows. Lilith could barely hold her attention in one place before another caught her eye.

"Come now, Lilith," one of her servant girl's chimed, tugging at Lilith's arm. "We only have so much time to beautify you!" Lilith couldn't discourage the gentle upturn of her lips as they led her to two golden doors.

"The King has truly favored you," said the servant girl with deep skin. "At the Crown Prince's behest, of course!" They all giggled in response.

Unable to diffuse her blush, Lilith entered the chambers she'd been graciously granted, and her jaw dropped.

The large chamber was one cohesive room. Rather than separated chambers like in Emperor Obadïa's castle, this suite was wide open. A large four-poster bed occupied the far wall, shaded by long white sheets.

One of her servants rushed to the bath to begin pouring hot water. The sunken tub was made of marble, four pillars surrounding it, vines crawling up their lengths.

The servant girls wasted no time tugging off Lilith's dirty garments. Gods, they must think her slovenly! Lilith made to cover her exposed body, but the girls swatted her hands away, giggling profusely.

"Don't be embarrassed of what the Gods gave you. They made us to be pleasing to the eyes," said the servant with the deep skin.

"To the male eyes in particular," said another.

"To my eyes as well!"

"True."

The girls erupted in an uproar of mirth, and Lilith climbed the stairs and dropped into the steaming liquid. With a sigh, she leaned back as two of the girls climbed in after her. They ignored her bemused look as they began to wash her, paying little care to where their hands roamed. Lilith jumped as they ventured to places no one else's had.

Well, except their prince, but she couldn't tell them that.

Forcing herself to relax, she allowed them to scrub her clean. One servant focused on her hair and skin whilst the other buffed her fingernails and toenails.

Was Julius receiving the same attention? Was he used to this growing up here or was this treatment reserved only for guests? Her cheeks seared at the thought of female servants putting their hands on his body, and her chest contracted, her heart a heavy rock.

"Don't look so sullen, Lady Lilith," one of the servant girls said, untangling Lilith's hair and scrubbing the suds into her scalp.

Without announcement, Lilith formed horses from the Water and sent them frolicking through the air. The servants squealed and giggled, requesting she animate creatures that Lilith had never heard of before. Her brow furrowed in confusion as they chattered, their foreign accents making it difficult to interpret what they were saying. That is, until she realized they were speaking Dalegonian.

⊙ ⊖ ∽ ∧ ◊

Lilith had been pampered thoroughly by the time she emerged from her chamber. She'd selected a chiton dress Olga had gifted her, but the servants shook their heads with outright disdain and procured another from the wardrobe. The outfit they'd selected was simple: a thin fabric blouse, the hem just touching her navel. There wasn't much of a neckline, the two thin straps over her shoulders did little to conceal her breasts. A servant placed a band of silver bullion around her head to hold back her long hair. Her bottom half was clad in an ankle-length skirt of silk, a slit running down the side to reveal a single leg as she walked. Perhaps it was to please the eye. Perhaps the scorching climate demanded such revealing ensembles. Silver bullion sandals—matching the material around her head— snaked around her feet in an intricate weaving she was sure she could never replicate.

As she descended the stairs leading to the front courtyard, her eyes took in the city from above. The view of Xanthë was beautiful in the daylight. They'd arrived as the sun was just rising in the east, bathing the city gold. Now that the sun had illuminated the streets, Lilith could clearly see the colorful domed rooftops, the temples' columns rising above them, and the bustle of city life as inhabitants went about their day.

As she reached the bottom step, her attention settled on Julius. The prince waited for her with a handful of servants and three single palanquins. A man stood beside Julius, his long sable hair tied back in an intricate plait, white hairs streaking through it. His face was angular like Julius's, his cheekbones sharper, but his round eyes were warm and dark like the King's. He must be Julius's uncle, Lilith realized. Second in line for the throne. The King's Right Hand.

Julius's eyes fell on her and she could have sworn he staggered. His golden-brown skin flushed at her approach, and he dove into a deep bow as she drew near.

"You look gorgeous," Julius whispered in her ear as he embraced her. "Like a woman born of the stars. A woman who shines despite the darkness." He brushed a featherlight kiss to her cheek, dangerously close to her lips.

Lilith bowed deeply as he drew away. "Thank you, Your Highness. You look handsome as well." Indeed, he did. He'd been dressed in harem pants the color of his house—a deep sapphire—and a single, elaborate golden sash crossed his bare torso, wrapping around his waist. Muscles rippled beneath his bronze skin, a testament to his six years training as a Divine. Her throat dried out at the sight of the marbled skin on his chest, a reminder that she'd almost lost him.

Julius gestured to the man beside him. "This is my uncle, Prince Odêus. Uncle, this is Lilith Oak."

The prince grasped Lilith's hand and pressed her knuckles to his lips. "Pleasure to meet you. We are ever so grateful to you for taking such great care of our heir." He was garbed in similar attire to Julius, though the sash crossed over both of his shoulders. She made a mental note to inquire about the meaning of the different sashes when next she and Julius were alone.

Julius took her hand, guiding her to one of the palanquins. A servant opened the door and helped her inside. Many embellished cushions littered the seat, she had to push them to the other side. She realized, as the ground disappeared beneath her, that the excessive number of cushions had been serving a purpose: support.

Lilith stiffened in her seat, her hands braced on either wall of the palanquin. She was skeptical to move or adjust her position, afraid she'd throw her bearers off.

Once in the streets of Xanthë, the people cleared the route for the royals, their eyes roving over the palanquins, curious to catch a glimpse of the Crown Prince or the King's Right Hand.

Lilith slumped in her seat, attempting to conceal herself behind the solid gold frame of the palanquin, but most of it was —like the royal couple's—a foggy, stained-glass. She clutched the pendant Julius had gifted her, the warm metal offering the slightest comfort.

As they made their way, she noted the corner houses at intersections were bereft of windows, the stone walls bearing artwork. Julius had mentioned that Dalegonè praised their artists, and various paintings permeated the city, serving its denizens as navigation markers.

When at last she came to a stop, Lilith adjusted her skirt and smoothed down her hair. The door opened abruptly, and Julius's head dipped inside. He flashed her a smile, exuding excitement, extending his hand to her. The servant that was supposed to open her door stood to the side, an expression of irritation besetting his features. Lilith bowed her head to him in thanks regardless.

She noticed the bearers of her palanquin, short of breath, each of them gulping down the contents of their water skins. They had about five attached at their belts, as if they were prepared for a long day of carrying them around. Their brows glistened and sweat dripped down their bare chests. They wore no shirts, save for a single crimson sash identifying their roles, and harem pants that hugged their ankles just above their sandaled feet.

Julius led her forward, his uncle already marching up ahead. "The Grande Stadium," he announced.

Lilith craned her neck to take it all in.

The Grande Stadium of Xanthë was a round structure of ancient stone, much of which had chipped off over the years. The interior hallways of the edifice were visible from the outside, the windows absent of glass. Had anyone been thrust from them in the event of a dispute? With a grimace, Lilith banished the vile image from her mind.

Spectators cleared the path as they strode toward the gate. The people whispered to one another; their prince had returned. They dropped to their knees when they took notice of Julius, but he offered them no more than a faint smile or a subtle nod.

Lilith walked poised beside him, her skirt parting with each step. She kept her attention locked on the man beside her as the eyes of the people inspected her shrewdly, muttering to one another about the peculiar foreigner at their prince's side.

Upon their entrance, they were escorted the the royal gallery overlooking the stadium. There was no roof, exposing the spectators and combatants to the elements. Prince Odêus explained that Xanthë rarely experienced inclement weather and the open roof symbolized just how the brawls were a testament to the Gods, and in order to please Them, the brawls must be presented to Elysium.

Julius pulled out a chair for Lilith, and once she was seated, he settled into the one next to hers.

Curtains lined the gallery, billowing on the wind. They were meant to offer the royals relative seclusion from the audience, but the salty draft prevented them from enjoying much privacy. Spectators were incapable of prying their eyes away from the royal gallery. Lilith's skin itched under their scrutiny.

Lilith leaned into Julius. "What do the sashes mean?" she inquired, indicating the crimson strip of silk crossing his torso.

"Men of high status wear these." He fingered the material. "A single sash represents a single man, and a double sash represents a married man."

"Your uncle is married then," Lilith observed.

"Yes," Julius said with a wistful smile. "Unfortunately, his husband could not be here with us today."

Lilith directed her attention to Prince Odêus as he engaged in genial conversation with other noblemen seated in the galleries beside theirs.

Julius inclined his head toward her, blocking her view. His hazel eyes sparkled with mischief. "Do you remember what I told you about the brawls of my people?" His fingers trailed up her arm reverently, inciting shivers down her spine.

"That the men fight naked?" she nearly squeaked.

He laughed, his fingers continuing their seductive rhythm up and down the back of her arm. An intimate gesture. One that promised more. One that a prince should not be entertaining in the public eye.

Down on the center platform, a man strolled out from the shadows, his gait wide and cavalier, his presence summoning cheers from the gathering audience. Both Julius and his uncle stood and approached the balustrade, their presence inspiring the opposite to the man below.

Silence.

Julius turned back to face Lilith, waving her over. She obeyed, wincing as she rose, the *swish* of her skirt making the most noise in the arena. She paused beside Julius, breath bated, spine ramrod straight.

"Welcome home, Prince Julius!" the orator announced, speaking into some form of horn to project his voice. He continued to speak in Dalegonian, and despite being in a structure with thousands of other humans, Lilith suddenly felt very isolated. As the last echoes of his voice faded, the crowd roared to life in exultation of their Divine Prince.

Prince Odêus turned to Julius, and it was only because of her close proximity that Lilith overheard what he whispered. "Perhaps a demonstration," he said through gritted teeth, a devious grin bringing his placid features to life.

Julius mirrored his uncle's expression, his attention now turned on Lilith. "What do you say?" he said. "Care for a little fun?"

Wordlessly, she signaled for him to proceed.

"Julius! Julius! Julius!" the crowd chanted.

The prince beamed triumphantly as his people sang his ardent praise, awaiting his display: the sole reason he had been absent for so many years. They wanted to see that their future king had indeed left them for good reason.

Julius stepped forward. Every face turned to him in expectation. Lilith stood back, Prince Odêus following, his hands clasped before him, knuckles white as snow—though she doubted he had ever seen snow in his lifetime.

Then Julius's hands rose, stretching out before him. Tendrils of molten gold streamed from his fingertips like silk ribbons. The stadium was silenced as the thin serpents snaked outward, down toward the main platform where in only moments, the athletes would fight.

The Fire looped back, changed directions, the ribbons coiling and tangling like lovers. The streams expanded, Xander's Fire building until they were thick as columns. Julius raised his hands like a maestro to his musicians, and the serpents obeyed. They climbed invisible stairs, seven of them, equally spaced throughout the arena.

Then Julius brought them together.

Sparks exploded, raining over the people, disappearing

above their heads. The crowd gasped and cooed their awe.

The columns of Fire pooled together, forming one massive piece. Lilith's eyes trailed from the sight back to Julius. A bead of sweat rolled down his temple, the only sign of strain.

With a flick of his finger, the slightest twitch, Xander's Fire formed a single beast. It began as one of those scaled creatures Julius had described to Lilith during their travels, its legs small and short, clawed fingertips on bony hands. Its tail was indistinct from its body, its skull triangular and disproportionately large.

Then it sprouted wings.

The arena thundered with adulation as the beast swooped over them, its body undulating, slithering, orbiting high above the stands. Its wings beat lazily, sparks dripping like liquid gold. Its scales crackled like embers, moving over its oblong frame; black, gold, red, yellow, and all shades in between.

Gradually, Julius called it in. The beast surrendered, disintegrating into ribbons of golden silk once again, floating on the breeze toward the prince's awaiting fingertips.

Proof that he was more than noviciate.

Prince Julius was a Master Divine.

When the display was over, the stadium exploded with tumultuous excitement, and Julius waved to his people before retreating to his seat.

"Too bad you couldn't make it roar, eh?" his uncle said, pounding him on the back with overflowing affection.

Julius directed a lazy gaze at Lilith, exhaustion evident upon his features. "That was a dragon," he said, somewhat breathless.

"And you nearly depleted yourself for this *dragon*?" she quipped through a traitorous grin.

Julius chuckled, his mirth strained but genuine. "Any Dalegonian would." Then his attention returned to the platform, and the brawls commenced.

Two burly men emerged from opposite sides of the stadium. The gallery was fairly high up, enough to get an unobstructed view of the entire arena, but not far enough away to blur the men's exposed groins.

Lilith sat back in her seat, her face burning. Julius nearly howled at her reaction and reached over to cover her eyes. He leaned in closer to whisper in her ear, his breath hot and damp on her skin, "I cannot have my lady watching these brutes."

Giggling, she swatted his hand away, a coy grin splitting her lips. She cast a furtive glance at his uncle, but he was nearly out of his seat in suspense. He wouldn't hear a word they exchanged.

"My eyes are for you alone," Lilith purred.

Seemingly satisfied, Julius pressed a gentle kiss to her cheek, so soft and quick, she almost didn't think it happened.

A gong sounded and the stadium exploded, the din nearly deafening. Julius's attention had been torn from her, now directed at the spectacle below.

The two men were unarmored, unclothed, as they advanced on one another. Fists raised before them, they exchanged blows, each one enticing the audience to scream, cheer, or boo. It was obvious the public lionized the combatants. The crowd resembled a menagerie as the fight escalated. Lilith was more interested in the spectators, barely paying attention to the brawl until the two men dropped to the ground in a pile of dust.

Lilith winced. "How do they fight like that?" she asked Julius. "How do they fight and protect their... you *know*?" She eyed his lap pointedly.

"Unspoken rules," he replied, chuffed. "No man would ever target another man's groin. It is almost unheard of. If it does occur, it's usually an accident, and in that event, the fighter who landed the blow to the nethers would be forced to forfeit the match. Which, if you haven't realized, is disgraceful. These bouts are meant to be good natured." He winked at her. "If slightly lewd."

The combatants continued to wallop each other, kicking and sputtering. The crowd cheered at what profanities were exchanged, but the royal gallery was too elevated to discern the banter. It was clear that what few words were exchanged, they were antagonizing.

"Have you ever fought?" Lilith asked, but quickly regretted the question as she realized what it implied.

"No member of the royal family is permitted," Julius said. "We are meant to merely watch and enjoy."

"Why?"

"Because bodies of the ruling class are not for public display. Men we may be, but as rulers, our bodies are considered sacred. Only our betrothed may glimpse it." His eyes lingered on her for a moment longer, flicking from her eyes to her lips. To kiss publicly would be impetuous. She was a stranger to these people. A foreigner.

And Lilith had seen his... *everything*. Julius wouldn't have allowed that if he didn't plan to court her, to stay with her, devoted. But it was obvious the Queen did not deem Lilith an appropriate match. It was apparent her views were antiquated, and her voice was one to be heard.

Even over that of the Divine.

Even over a throbbing, lovesick heart.

THÉBÉS

The halls of Spiro's fortress were deceptively quiet, but Rhéa ignored the warnings of her inner conscience. Tonight was the perfect opportunity to scout the lair. The perfect opportunity to discover the true means by which Spiro was conceiving his beastly species.

Rhéa navigated the vacant corridors with lithe grace, her slippers silent against the rough stone floor. Flashes of light illuminated the slick walls, casting shadows through the cracks in the stone. She followed the light, her curiosity stealing her common sense. When she arrived at its source, she dropped to her knees to avoid detection.

The great stone cavern was empty save for three figures. These men were the source of light, spewing Godly Fire from their maws and their palms alike.

Spiro stood across from his opponent, a vitriolic grin stealing over his features. Xavier, across from him, held flames dancing upon his fingertips, his face set in a focused trance. Felix stood behind his father, his face mirroring Spiro's.

The beat of her heart catalyzed in her ears, and Rhéa was

forced to squint in order to protect her sensitive sight. She'd been there that night when Xavier returned from battle with Felix as his badge, and she'd thought Spiro punished him when he burnt his chest with Xander's Fire.

But Xavier had healed almost immediately.

Could Spiro have transmitted some of his power unto Xavier? Was it possible for a Divine to invoke gifts to another? Every muscle along her back flexed at the realization. If Spiro had somehow been granted the Gods' support, it was over for Augusta.

Not entirely convinced that was the case, Rhéa slowly crept across the highest level of the arena. Spiro would be busy with training tonight, he wouldn't notice her wandering through the halls.

There was a secret he was hiding, she was sure of it, and as an Enchantress, it was her responsibility to get to the bottom of it.

Rhéa swept through the archway leading to Spiro's conference chamber, but she'd never ventured far beyond it. The hallway continued to wind, the sconces blazing, illuminating her path. The tunnel narrowed until it was little more than a trench, and Rhéa was forced to crouch. Her knees ached the farther she tread, but sconces still lined the walls, indicative that this small passage possessed some sort of purpose.

So, Rhéa pressed onward.

Stairs appeared before her, descending into a pool of darkness. Rhéa perched herself on the topmost step, resting her cramped legs. If only Spiro would let her outside at night to refuel under the Starlight. She made use of the respite to survey her surroundings. The stairwell appeared to be well-used, and beyond the void, she could glean no life.

Fairly certain she was alone, she descended the stairs, and when she reached the brink of darkness, she raised her palm and uttered, "Líne Va pâte." *Light my path*. An orb of golden fire appeared suspended above her palm, its warmth soothing her muscles, spreading up her arm and down her spine. It was warm and inviting, and if she hadn't had her wits about her, she would have ingested the orb.

With a deep breath to steel herself, she continued her descent, careful to keep her steps light and silent. She prayed to Amalthea for equanimity as the stairs delved deeper into the earth, leading her farther away from the Guiding Stars. The pull toward Them wrenched her gut, her body beseeching her to retreat, to return above the earth's crust. There was no worse punishment for an Enchantress than being buried alive, and if she died down here, who would light her Blaze to send her to the Southern Star?

No one.

When Rhéa reached the last of the steps, smooth slate tiles led into a cavern. The round chamber was unfurnished, save for a desk, and there appeared to be a quarry in the center. Light flared from within, and a musky, putrid scent permeated the air, mixing with burnt flesh.

Rhéa's lips curled in disgust, her nose crinkling.

What in the Stars' names?

Curiosity daring her to draw forward—closer—Rhéa edged toward the drop into the quarry, her thundering heart coming to a standstill. Nestled in the center of the pit was an neonate beast. At the sight of her, it cried out, its screech enough to curdle stale blood.

Its wails enough to wake the dead.

But Rhéa cared not for the little one, for standing before the premature beast was a cloaked figure.

A man.

At first sight, he appeared innocuous, his long sable hair plaited down his skull, hanging like a thick rope down his spine. His limbs were lean, thin enough that Rhéa thought she'd be able to take care of him without the need of magical tactics. That was until he turned to her, until those all-white eyes melted away any remaining confidence she'd been harboring. Confidence in herself, and in Augusta's survival.

A Sorcerer.

Rhéa grappled for the wall behind her, preparing to bolt up the stairs should he prove as belligerent as Sorcerers were rumored to be. His gaze was insidious, searing her very flesh as it assessed her. It was too difficult to conceal her fear. A chill sluiced through her limbs, coating her skin in a freezing sweat that made every muscle shake visibly.

Abandoning all pretense, Rhéa bolted, desperate to escape the wrath of the Sorcerer. A wall of flame burst to life, impeding her path to the only known exit. A cry tore from her throat as hands wrapped around it, constricting mercilessly.

Since the death of Larkin, Rhéa had forgotten what it felt like to strive for survival, to cherish living, breathing. She'd forgotten the drive, the instinct to persist. It engulfed her then, the desire burning, raging, superseding all other urges, all other wants and needs. Her hands wrapped around his bony wrists, her eyeballs threatening to burst from their sockets.

"Did Spiro send you here?" His breath was a cold mist shrouding her. If he truly wanted an answer, he'd ease his grip.

Rhéa thrashed as he raised her, his brute strength at odds with the frailty of his stature. He pressed his body against her to hold her flailing limbs still, prominent hip bones digging into her thighs. If he increased the pressure, her bones would surely crack.

"Thébés." *Spiro.* "Drop my Enchantress, please."

With a reproachful grunt, the Sorcerer obeyed, and Rhéa slumped to the cold stone floor, incapable of supporting her own weight.

"Continue," Spiro ordered, though his tone was much gentler than when he commanded Xavier, even Felix.

Thébés obliged, his white eyes softening as his gaze drifted from her to Spiro. "As you wish," said the Sorcerer, and clasping his long pale hands in front of his chest, he bowed at the waist and returned to the quarry.

Rhéa had almost forgotten the insufferable cries of the grotesque infant until it resumed its keening.

"Rise," Spiro said, standing over her.

She wanted to obey, for rising would lead to leaving, which would put distance between her and the Sorcerer. But to her chagrin, Rhéa was trapped in a state of inertia. To her astonishment, Spiro bent over her and scooped her up into his arms. Without uttering a word, he exited the chamber and ascended the narrow stairs, the tenebrous void enveloping them.

In the darkness, Rhéa had ears only for her rasping breath, still struggling to draw a substantial amount of air into her lungs. Spiro leaned over her, opening his mouth to breath into her. Without warrant, her body accepted it, and leaning into him, her lungs expanded in relief.

"That was foolish of you," Spiro intoned as he drew away from her.

Rhéa flinched, resting her head in the crook of his neck, eyes cinched tight, dreaming of Miles' arms wrapped around her. Soundlessly, Spiro carried her until the hallway opened up, until the sconces were brighter. Only when they reached the conference chamber did he put her down.

From her respective seat, Rhéa tentatively observed him as he poured two goblets of wine. This time they drank from the same decanter.

Who was Spiro to sweep in and rescue her? Who was this man who wiped the tears from her cheeks and tended to her wounds?

Rhéa welcomed his touch, too exhausted and deflated to resist. If she closed her eyes, she could almost see Miles holding her close. Her husband's touch was much warmer, gentler, firmer in the way a lover's should be.

Spiro reached out and held her head in his hands. His pale-blue eyes pierced hers, unwavering, his flinty gaze somehow resolving the pain in her head. "You must understand, Rhéa darling," he began without dropping her face, "that my reign will be one of acceptance, where all races will be given an equal chance to prosper. It will be the dawn of a glorious age of redemption for those who have been oppressed by the Stavros Dynasty—including the Enchantresses."

"Including Sorcerers…" Rhéa whispered, more to herself than in response to his speech.

"*Sorceresses* as well," he added.

Of course, how hadn't she seen it before? A Sorcerer was the only guarantor of success in Spiro's plight for imperium. But also, a Sorcerer or Sorceress was the only being capable of thwarting Spiro. Thébés was no doubt stronger than his master. So why hadn't he retaliated? Why was he subservient? A very dangerous, dutiful vassal.

If only Ophelía knew that a Sorcerer had been responsible for the creation of Spiro's beasts, she'd never give him her support. The existence of a Sorcerer or Sorceress was perilous to all of Augusta. To all of the continents. Their expanse of power was unGodly, *unStarly*. The power a natural-born Sorcerer encompassed was enough to rival an entire pantheon of Divine, enough to challenge even the Gods and the Stars.

Rhéa needed to warn the High Enchantress, but there was no way to communicate from within Spiro's fortress; it was warded against scrying from within and without.

"I saved Thébés many years ago," Spiro said. "He had been reviled by his fellow orphans. I couldn't simply let him rot in desolation his entire life. He was destined to serve a purpose, and I gave him one." He cracked a smug smile as he took his seat beside hers.

Rhéa forced her gaze to meet his, swallowing every ounce of fear shuddering through her frame.

Spiro stroked her cheek, his brumal touch awakening those survival instincts she'd felt locked in Thébés's clutch. "Now, I cannot fathom what possessed you to stray so far from your designated realm, but I will dismiss your errant ways."

Rhéa sighed in evident relief. Displaying her gratitude would save her from worse punishments than a backhanded blow.

"I know you don't trust me yet, my guileless Enchantress. But someday, you will come to love me."

A DALEGONIAN FEAST

The following day, Lilith spent the morning being escorted through the palace by her lady servants whilst Julius attended court with his father and uncle. He'd promised to join her for lunch, but he had to cancel as several emissaries from the Wandering Tribes of the DíTakas Desert paid them an unforeseen visit. According to Zörra—the deep-skinned handmaiden—this was an exceptional event as there had been an abiding enmity between the Tribes and the crown. Thus, Lilith was not to resent Julius for canceling their plans as his actions were justified.

It was for the best, she knew. The circumstances distancing them helped to keep the true nature of their relationship as covert as possible.

"If you enjoy a good read, I will have to take you by the library," Zörra said, her narrow shoulders squared as always. After knowing the young woman for only a day, Lilith already arrived at the conclusion that her mind was as sharp as any blade.

It was Zörra who led the tour whilst the two other servants,

Mïa and Estêvia, trotted along beside them, constantly chittering and giggling. Lilith quite enjoyed their company, even if they were excessively frivolous.

"And this," Zörra said, waving a svelte arm at two ornate gilded doors, "is the Conception Chamber."

"There's a *Conception* Chamber?" Lilith blinked. Most married couples shared a bed and did all other functions in that bed. *But when you have an exceeding amount of drachmae at your disposal, perhaps that is not preferable.*

Zörra waved her off. "It is tradition that the King and Queen conceive every child in the Conception Chamber. That was where our prince was created. The belief is that the Gods will bless that child if it is conceived in the holy room."

In Augusta, it was common belief that any room was holy once the act of intercourse commenced. That when two people came together in such an intimate way, the Gods were present to sculpt and shape the new human. As was the belief that a woman with child was surrounded by the Gods throughout the term of her pregnancy, as They continued to mold the babe until birth.

When it came time to prepare for the ball, Zörra once again assumed the lead, selecting Lilith's outfit with care. This one was much like the last, yet the fabric was like molten gold. *Fit for a blacksmith*, Lilith thought. Her father would approve. Larkin, too.

The servants bathed her, slicking her skin with fragrance and liniment to deepen the tone and make her glow in the Dalegonian style. Her hair had been done up tonight, a bejeweled headpiece encircling her head. With her long tresses coiled up, most of her torso was exposed, her shoulders and décolletage practically bare. The sides of her dress cut down to her hips before opening up again to expose the length of both her legs. Lilith bore no other accoutrements, not even Julius's necklace, for Zörra was insistent that she need none. If Zörra had her way, Julius wouldn't be able to tear his eyes away from her tonight.

When Lilith gave Zörra her nod of approval, her three faithful servants giddily escorted her to the Grande Hall where the ball in Julius's honor was to be held. The girls pushed through the crowd, skipping the line stretching endlessly down the hallway.

"You must not wait," Zörra chided. "You are a guest of honor!"

The hall was an entire chamber of white marble congruous with the rest of the palace. Columns thicker than any tree Lilith had ever seen, stretched along the longest walls. At the far end of the hall, upon a rostrum, was an oblong, low table decorated with flowers and odd prickly plants. Chalices lined the tables stretching along the length of the hall. There were no chairs, only plush cushions, just like the dining set up in Lilith's private chamber.

But what stole Lilith's breath was what lay in the center of the hall. The center of the hall was cleared for what Lilith assumed would be dancing, and the floor, white marble streaked with gray, was painted. The paint was every color on the spectrum and, though it was too large in scope to distinguish for certain, it appeared like desert dunes and mountains, split down the middle by a column, no doubt a walkway for the royal family.

Lilith couldn't remove her eyes from the artwork, not even when Zörra stole away with a grunt. When her handmaiden returned, she visibly struggled to hide her malcontent.

"What is it?" Lilith asked.

"Your seat is here." Zörra pointed to a place at the very end of the right-side table, located on the opposite side of the hall from the high table, where Lilith knew the royal family would sit.

Zörra didn't bother to hide her scowl. "How dare she sit you all the way back here with the lowest ranked noblemen. You're a disciple of the Gods, for the Mother's sake!"

"Who did?" Lilith asked, though she need not inquire, for she knew of whom Zörra spoke. She was disappointed not to be seated near Julius, though she didn't expect to sit at the royal family's table. There was no reason to feel aggrieved, surely this had been a mistake.

"The Queen," Zörra answered, biting into her bottom lip. "I'm going to see what can be done to remedy this. Perhaps it was only a mistake, given how swiftly this was organized. Guests always sit with the royal family. I am sure this was only a mistake."

The contents of Lilith's guts spoiled. This was a subtle message if she'd ever received one. Lilith was Divine but she was not royal nor of noble birth. Would that matter if her son was happy? If he was fortunate enough to spend his life with another immortal soul? A love that was truly Pràgma—or at least felt like it could be?

Struggling to mask her unease, Lilith watched as Zörra tromped off, lost in the flood of guests as they rushed to claim their seats. The display of extravagance was immense, enough to make even her outfit feel casual. Jewels glittered like stars against bronze skin. Women laughed as they passed on the arms of their significant others, jovial and undaunted.

No one seemed to notice Lilith standing against the wall, a few feet from her seat, a few more from the exit. She could leave. She could return to her chamber and dine with Zörra. But what would her absence say to Julius? That she doesn't long to be with him? That she was reluctant to embrace his culture? No, she would not abandon him. Not tonight. For that would be giving in to the Queen's wishes. Unfamiliar as she was with this nature of warfare, she would not cede.

With her back to the wall, Lilith watched the last of the guests file in. Two men entered last, their garb quite different from that of the Dalegonian sash and printed harem pants. These men wore robes ending at their knees and crisscrossing over their torsos. They looked naked compared to even the least modest of Dalegonians. *The Tribesmen*, she realized. *These are the dignitaries from the Wandering Tribes!*

Watching them closely, she reached toward them with Discernment. Perhaps she had missed something. Perhaps their attendance was the reason for her seating position.

"…take King Faustus," said the older of the two, his long black beard peppered with grays.

"But I want to take the King!" the younger Tribesman protested.

His companion slapped his hand against his chest in chastisement. "Do not speak so loudly." The older Tribesman cast a furtive glance around the hall. Lilith dropped onto her designated cushion, escaping notice.

What do they mean by 'take'? Unease flared, a familiar sear coursing through her veins. She quested out with Discernment, but the gift did not give her the ability to read minds, only sense emotions and physical entity. She was successful in segregating the two from the rest of the guests, but their emotions were far too convoluted to distinguish intent.

"As an Elder," said the older Tribesman, "the King is mine. You will see to Prince Julius. Do you remember the movements? Did you at least remember to bless your sand?"

Sand? Lilith homed in on their conversation.

The younger Tribesman relented, and together the two dignitaries proceeded to the rostrum to take their place at the end of the high table.

A drum sounded, its echoes reverberating through the hall. The guests stood to welcome the royal family. Lilith rose with them, spitefully, suddenly self-conscious of her position.

The King and Queen entered first, arms looped through each others'. Lilith diluted the strength of her glare as the Queen pranced by her table, trilling meaningless greetings to her guests, ostensibly oblivious to Lilith's presence. But when the Crown Prince entered the hall, the Queen was the least of her concern.

Julius was resplendent in a black ensemble, the silken sash crossing from his shoulder to his hip, emphasizing his muscular physique. A golden saber hung at his side, silently vouching for the warrior he was. Whispered praises filled the hall as he walked arm in arm with another woman. A constellation of awe-washed eyes followed them down the aisle.

She was beautiful, her dark hair matching Julius's, falling heavily over her narrow shoulders, the silver diadem atop her head signifying her noble heritage. Her eyes were wide as they settled on the prince, and Julius laughed at whatever it was she'd said. He, too, seemed oblivious to Lilith's presence.

A spear of desperate longing shot through her. It was silly, she knew, for the sentiments Julius whispered to her in the dark could not be fabricated—by her mind or by his lips. No. She need not worry about this woman. Her true quarry sat next to the King, waiting to strike.

Lilith dared a glance at Julius as he lowered himself onto the large pillow beside the woman's. Whoever she was, it was clear that she held affection for the prince. Julius was seated between the lady and his mother, whom he turned on immediately. His expression transformed from one of contentment to one of ire, but his mother waved him off dismissively. Even with her son's chastisement, the Queen exuded no less than impeccable decorum. But without her royal charm, the Queen looked like an ornamental old hag.

The Queen turned her shoulder to her son and took a sip of wine, and as she tilted the chalice to her lips, her eyes met Lilith's over the rim. As the chill of the Queen's gaze settled over her, all of Lilith's bravado evaporated, pooling at her feet. It was apparent she knew what Lilith and Julius were, and it was clear that she was of the opinion that their relationship was ill-fitting, either for her son or—selfishly—for *her*.

As the food filtered in, Lilith side-eyed the high table, inspecting the Tribesmen. They'd been engaged in a genial conversation with the King since he'd taken his seat. Tears watered her dry eyes, a burning sensation soon followed. Had she really not blinked for that long? Placing a hand on her gut to hold herself together, she pressed her chin to her collarbone and watched her chest heave.

She wanted Arduen. He would assure her that everything was all right. And she'd believe him. She would march right off the edge of the world if he told her faith would give her wings.

Lilith chewed absentmindedly. Servants attended to the guests, feeding them like a mother bird would her chicks—minus the pre-chewing. She was well aware that her lack of servant attendance was a blatant affront from the Queen herself, but she didn't possess an appetite to indulge in the foreign delicacies.

"Fret not, my kyría," whispered a voice behind her. "I am here to serve you."

She didn't have to look up to know that it was Zörra. Her faithful handmaiden knelt on the marble floor, reaching for the fruit tray in front of Lilith. "I don't—"

Zörra's withering glare was enough to cut her off. "You will eat. It will help."

Lilith opened her mouth to protest but Zörra seized the

moment to place a purple grape on her tongue. Lilith chewed begrudgingly, boring her eyes into Zörra.

"Don't be mad at me," said the handmaiden. "I am the one helping you."

"I'm sorry," Lilith muttered, her shoulders slumping, her eyes flicking up to the dais, drinking in the sight of Julius and his date, the Queen, the King upon his throne, the lethal Tribesmen. Julius's eyes flicked to her, knowing and warm. Lilith slouched out of view, feeling overwhelmingly diminutive and inadequate.

"Don't dwell on it," Zörra warned.

"Who is she?"

Her handmaiden didn't need to follow Lilith's gaze to know who she was referring to.

"A friend from childhood," Zörra said. "Favored by the Queen. She's using her to taunt you." Zörra fed Lilith some cheese and a piece of a fluffy bread, sweet to taste. "Look as unperturbed as you can. That's your only path to revenge."

Gripping her butter knife beneath the table until her bones threatened to crack, Lilith grimaced, but it didn't help to alleviate her jealousy. If she had to watch the prince's date giggle vivaciously one more time, she'd send that knife sailing through the air straight at her eye.

Lilith blinked at the morbidity of her sudden daydream, compunction forcing her to place the knife back on the table where it belonged.

As the meal came to an end, the sconces dimmed and a deep, rolling melody began to play. Lilith felt Zörra's hand on her arm, helping her to stand. The guests, cooing and cawing, began to rise, migrating to the center of the hall to witness whatever spectacle was coming next.

"You won't want to miss this," Zörra whispered in her ear,

pulling Lilith after her, pushing through the assemblage to get to the front.

The guests encircled the dance floor as the King and his Crown Prince took position in the center of the hall, in the laneway bisecting the beautiful painting on the floor. Lilith's eyes were fixated on Julius as he and his father began to move to the music.

Father and son danced. They never touched, but just by watching them, Lilith felt as though, through movement, a story was being told. A tale of inheritance. Leadership, valor, justice, and love. A tale about a king who loved his people. A king who sacrificed and fell before his subjects knew suffering.

Julius mirrored his father's movements. The dance was eloquent and exotic; as the rhythm of the music swelled and escalated, so did the dancers. Their sandaled feet skewed the painting, the dunes and the mountains, the sunset-painted sea; it was all muddled.

"It is dyed sand from the DíTakas Desert," Zörra said.

What Lilith had assumed was paint was actually dyed sand, and it rose up, curling around the King and his heir in a multi-colored cloud.

Out of the shadows, the Tribesmen approached. Lilith's spine straightened instinctually, her entire body primed for action. Her heart was rioting inside her chest, competing with the beat of the dance.

When the music faded, the King and the Crown Prince lowered to the ground facing one another. They bowed deep, their hands cupped before them as if to accept water.

The Tribesmen moved forward, determination and intent writ on their features. They were going to kill Julius!

Lilith cried out and bolted.

QU SAFICESU

Lilith lunged, tackling Obscundí to the floor. His father, Oramir, dropped the handful of sand he was about to bestow upon King Faustus and moved to protect his son.

Julius lost his senses to a state of inertia birthed by perplexity. He'd never before performed *Qu Saficesu*, an event he'd anticipated since he was old enough to understand its value.

And now, the woman he loved had destroyed the long-awaited moment.

Lilith straddled the prostrate Tribesman, seizing his arms behind his back at angles that couldn't possibly be comfortable. Obscundí howled in pain as she said through gritted teeth, "You thought you'd get away with it."

"What are you talking about woman?" Elder Oramir shouted, fists clenched at his sides. Julius didn't doubt he would use them.

"What is going on, Julius?" his father gritted out, obviously reluctant to move, or admittedly, locked in a similar state of shock akin to Julius's own.

"Your plot to assassinate the King and his heir," Lilith said, her eyes alight with a fervor foreign to Julius. He'd never seen her like this. She pulled harder on Obscundí's arms and he released an agonizing scream. "I overheard your conversation upon your arrival. Not very stealth of you."

Obscundí began to take on an unhealthy pallor, and it dawned on Julius that Lilith was leaching the Water from his body. She would kill him if she took this too far. It would destroy the peace his father had worked his entire life to uphold between the crown and the Wandering Tribes.

"Lilith," Julius said. "Enough."

She didn't look at him. Those emerald eyes smoldered with a ferocity that scared even him. She drilled Elder Oramir with that glare. The Elder stood above her, looming, a weaponless threat. Julius knew, out of respect for Dalegonè, Oramir would not attack a Divine.

"What are you doing to my son?" he demanded, projecting his deep rumble for the entire hall to hear. "You're killing him!"

"I am restraining him," Lilith replied. "At least until guards come to take my place." She looked around for the guards, but they maintained the doors and calmed the crowds. They were not to interfere with Divine matters, that was strict protocol. Though they haven't yet had a situation where said protocol was necessitated, they seemed to know their place.

"Lilith," Julius repeated. "Let him go."

She heard his demand, he knew she did, and yet she did not capitulate. Obscundí groaned, his throat audibly dry.

"LILITH!" Julius bellowed.

The crowd shrank back, obviously afraid of the Divine utilizing their gifts. They wouldn't, not in such a clustered environment.

Even so, Julius did not trust Lilith's judgment right now.

He approached her slowly, every motion cautious, like one

would approach a stray animal. "Lilith," he said softly, "let Obscundí go. You will kill him if you do not stop leaching."

Gradually, the glint in her eyes dissipated. Julius held her gaze, obviously their eye contact was helping to calm her rage.

After a tense moment's consideration, Lilith released a long-suffering sigh and lifted off the Tribesman. Oramir pushed her out of the way and dropped to his son's side.

"Water!" he yelled. "Please, someone get me water for my son!"

The guests sprang into action, offering chalices of crystal liquid which he poured into his son's open mouth.

Hesitantly, Julius took Lilith by the arm and gently escorted her to the gargantuan doors and out into the hallway. He had the guards shut them to grant them privacy. He did not want to be trailed as he guided her back to her chamber, neither uttering a sound.

As they entered her chamber, Julius swung the door shut and locked it, watching as Lilith removed her sandals, swaying on her feet as if in a drunken haze.

Impossible was the task of sorting through his thoughts, his feelings.

"Julius," Lilith whispered, her eyes dark with realization. "I am so sorry." She didn't approach, she merely stood in the center of the room, wide eyes imploring him for forgiveness.

"Explain yourself," was all he could think to say.

Turning away from him, she said, "I overheard them talking about taking you and the King. It sounded…"

"Like an assassination plot," he finished for her.

Lilith nodded sheepishly, no doubt feeling foolish in hindsight. "I watched them all night, convinced of this. When they stepped toward you tonight, the look in the young Tribesman's eyes was all the confirmation I needed. I couldn't stand idle any longer. So I acted."

"My father," Julius said, gulping, "spent his entire reign working diligently to garner peace between us and the Wandering Tribes. Their attendance to this ball meant so much to him. To me. To all of our guests." He choked on the words as they fell from his lips. "Do you have any idea of the magnitude of what you've done?"

Other than a slight quiver of her lips, Lilith elicited no reaction.

"The dance is called *Qu Saficesu*," he said.

"The Sacrifice," Lilith echoed in Modern Tongue.

Julius nodded. "The image painted on the floor with dyed sand was a representation of all the geographic assets of Dalegonè. The dance was a paradigm of how the King and his heir will tread into the unknown before their people must take the risk, that the land is in our hands." He wiped at his face, the implications of her actions finally dawning on him. "And by the Tribesmen pouring the sand from their hands to ours, it meant that they were entrusting us with their welfare, their safety, their future. It was everything my father worked for."

Lilith wept, her sobs subtle as she did her best to conceal it. Watching her, with her back to him, shoulders shaking, he knew he was being too harsh. How was she supposed to know the importance of such an event? She was acting in his best interests. She didn't kill the man, she just restrained him, made him a little sick.

At the end of the day, Lilith was a foreigner. She may never come to understand Dalegonè's customs, and Julius knew there was only one person to blame for that: himself. He should have spent more time teaching her their ways rather than bedding her.

With a sigh, Julius lowered himself into one of the chairs near the door. He still hadn't moved into the room. "This was likely the last time we will ever witness *Qu Saficesu*... at least for many years." At least until he chooses an heir of his own. Kingdom and children seemed impossibly far away.

"Thank Xander you refrained from using Aether," he said with a dry chuckle, hoping some levity would turn her back to him.

It didn't.

"I understand why you did what you did, Lil." He walked over to her, placed a hand on her shoulder, spinning her to face him. Her eyes were closed, tears leaking from their corners. Her lip was cinched between her teeth, clearly fighting for composure. He knew she would beat herself up for this. "It was a mistake, Lilith. A grand mistake that we will laugh about in years to come."

Lilith sniffed, opening her eyes for a brief moment before locking them away again. The sight of him seemed to only exacerbate her distress. He knew she did not want him to see her like this, but her rue was palpable, and he would not leave her alone in this state.

"Talk to me, Lil." He reached out to touch her cheek, and she allowed it. Taking her by the hand, he led her to the bed, and they sat side by side. He stroked her spine, and she leaned into his touch, but she still did not speak.

"My mother can be cruel at times," Julius began softly. "She has become ever more obstinate since I left for Augusta. I gave her Hades when I found my seat and yours wasn't beside it. Once the dinner begins, I cannot do anything. I assumed it was best to let it go, that you wouldn't want so many eyes on you all night." Pulling her against him, he kissed her temple and said, "I couldn't take mine off you."

With a whimper she wiped at her eyes, and breathing deep, she looked up at him. "I'm so sorry, Julius."

"You were acting as a Divine should," he said. And she had, however mistaken she was. "But I am afraid you will have to remain in your chamber tomorrow. At least until I can clear this up, ensure that everyone involved is mollified."

She nodded, leaning her head against his shoulder. "Will you stay with me tonight?"

Julius smiled and pulled her down onto the bed.

CUT FROM THE SAME STONE

"Kafés!" Zörra lilted, giving her porcelain mug a peck. "The Mother's nectar!"

"The Mother?" Lilith inquired. "I thought Dalegonians worshipped the five Gods?"

It was the morning after the ball, and though Julius had told Lilith to remain inside her chamber, nothing else had changed since her little mishap. Even Zörra didn't draw any allusions to the debacle, and Lilith wasn't willing to bring it up, especially since Zörra was a Tribeswoman herself.

"The traditional Dalegonian does, of course," Zörra said. "But I hail from the Wandering Tribes. We worship the Mother. Our Savior and Sister; Mother."

Taking a hesitant sip, Lilith tried to resist the urge to scrunch her face at the bitter liquid. "What is this?"

Zörra chortled, taking a smaller set of mugs off the tray. "It is recycled crops, steeped to perfection." She lifted the goblet to her lips and her eyes rolled back into her head dramatically.

"Why doesn't that sound appealing?" she deadpanned.

Zörra waved off her caustic response. "Sure, it doesn't

sound great, but it's amazing. Add some milk and honey!" She pushed the smaller mug across the table, then continued to eagerly sip from her own. "Mmm."

When Lilith copied Zörra's formula, she couldn't deny how indulgent the drink became.

"It really helps to mitigate the pain of a rough night." Zörra breathed in the steam rising from the hot liquid.

"I'm surprised such a warm drink is favored in your climate."

"Everything is hot here," Zörra said. "The food, the water, the *princes*..." She batted her long eyelashes.

Lilith gaped.

"Come on, tell me everything!"

"There isn't much to tell, really."

Zörra scoffed. "The Crown Prince was in your bed."

Lilith smirked, on the verge of divulging all the details to her new friend. But she resisted Zörra's cajoling.

"I came back here last night to check on you," Zörra informed her. "Then I heard... you *know*. I let you two be." She spoke as if Lilith owed her an explanation.

"Oh, I *know*." Lilith wiggled her eyebrows, mocking the handmaiden's tone with consummate sarcasm.

"You know, Julius is special, even for a Divine man," Zörra said. "If there was ever a human deserving of the Gods' blessings, it is him." She chewed her lip, then quickly sipped her kafés. "Has he ever mentioned how it happened?"

At the wary note in Zörra's tone, Lilith merely shook her head. She knew what she meant, but Julius had never divulged that part of his life to her. He'd shared so much with her. Many of their conversations had been deep and unvarnished, philosophical, even. But he'd never once mentioned how his mortal life had come to an end, and she never pressed.

Zörra's voice dipped low. "It happened one evening in his

father's study." Zörra fidgeted with the handle of her golden chalice, the milky brown liquid of the kafés rippling with every motion. "The alarum sounded. Poison had been discovered in the kitchens. Guards assumed that whoever the assassin was would have hid it if they were going to wait, but the vial was left out in the open.

"The guards rushed to the King's parlor but found it vacant. They stormed in on the Queen in their shared bedchamber, but the King wasn't there. The only other place was the study, and when they arrived, it was too late. Three bodies lay in that room, and only two rose again."

"Julius and the King," Lilith finished somberly.

"Yes." Zörra nodded. "The King is suffering a long, slow death, thanks to that fateful night. He'd had most of the toxins purged but there was permanent damage. No Enchantress could heal him. They surmised that the poison was cursed, resistant to magic. The healers estimated he'd only live a few months, but it's been over six years, and he's still with us."

"And Julius?"

"He arrived too late," Zörra said. "He engaged in combat with the assassin and managed to subdue him, but Julius had taken a wound to the gut and bled out. Slowly. Internally. The worst way to die. The Queen held him in her arms as the Gods carried him to Elysium."

"And how did he wake?"

The handmaiden smiled wryly. "He awoke on his way to the funeral procession, disoriented. The healers checked him over, his body in impeccable condition. Then sparks erupted from his fingertips, and they knew right away."

"He'd been Anointed."

"Yes."

Lilith blanched. "That didn't set the entire palace on Fire?"

"No, we keep Enchantresses nearby at all times. They were able to put out the flames."

"I couldn't help but notice the woman standing vigil behind the King's throne," Lilith said. "Is she an Enchantress?"

"That's one word for her," Zörra said, but her tone held no disdain, only indifference. "She serves the King faithfully, reading the emotions of those who visit him. In a way, she's saved his life on multiple occasions, sensing hostile subjects before they lash out."

"If only Augusta could be so accepting," Lilith mused.

"Yes, Augusta could learn much from our way of life," Zörra said smugly. "But Julius is the best man. He seems to love you very much. He even made your night special despite the Queen's petty machinations."

Despite my own.

"He is besotted with you!"

Lilith blushed, unable to hide her grin. At least until the image of the noble lady on Julius's arm flashed behind her eyelids. "Zörra, if I ask you a question, will you be honest with me?"

The handmaiden nodded agreeably, placing her goblet down gently with a delicate *clink*. "Of course, Lady Lilith."

She didn't hesitate. "Who was the young woman who attended Julius last night?"

"She is a fine noblewoman." Zörra swallowed audibly. "I am not familiar with her personally, but she has made it well-known that she loves this country very much. I've been selected to serve her every time she stays here."

Lilith grimaced. "But *who* is she?"

"Her name is Annika. She is a… *friend* of Julius."

Every muscle in Lilith's body clenched. "*Friend?*"

Zörra stood, a pained expression writ on her face. "The

prince should be the one to tell you. I cannot answer your questions."

Without a further explanation, Zörra took off, leaving Lilith alone with her consternation.

⊙ ⑤ ᗆ ᛉ ◊

IT WAS DINNERTIME WHEN JULIUS FINALLY ARRIVED. A SERVANT followed him into her chamber, pushing a cart with two covered dishes on it. He greeted Lilith with a charming smile.

"Apologies for missing lunch," he said. "I expect Zörra kept you company. I've brought the finest dinner to make up for my shortcomings." He approached her and leaned in to brush a tender kiss to her lips. "I hope you can forgive me?"

"Of course," she said, moving out of the way as the servant rolled in the cart and began to set up their table.

As Lilith lowered herself onto the cushions, Julius escorted the servant out before joining her. He shrugged out of his sash, leaving his pants as his only garment. Despite her current misgivings, Lilith loved how candid and unguarded Julius had become in her presence.

In a thespian display, the prince revealed their dinner: fish bathed in a spicy sauce on a bed of steamed vegetables, most of which Lilith had never seen before.

"Tell me," she said, "why does Dalegonè worship the same gods we do?"

Julius surrendered a quirk of a smile as he chewed a bite of whatever sprout it was. "Because the Stavros Dynasty branches from the Fawkes Dynasty."

She tilted her head in surprise. "Really?"

"Really." He nodded once.

She prodded him to elaborate.

"All right." Julius pulled a face. "Many moons ago, within

this very palace, King Arcaro summoned his three sons to the throne room." He paused to clear his throat, allowing the anticipation to build. "The princes had been waiting for this day since they were five, when their father sat each of them down in turn to apprise them of their futures, that only one would be king, the most-worthy."

"And the others?"

The prince flashed an amused grin her way, one that told her she needed to be patient. "The second most worthy would become seneschal to the king. The third would have to settle for the role of prince and serve the country in another way, bowing to his brothers."

Lilith leaned in closer as Julius lowered his voice.

"Dïon, the eldest, had been a natural born leader," he continued. "He was certain the crown would be his. And when the King announced the parameters and stipulations of the tournament for their generation, Dïon knew exactly how he would secure his future as king.

"But the middle son, Thassös, who had been content with serving Dïon for the rest of his days, found a surprising spark of competitive spirit. Driven as he'd been to serve his brother, he now discovered that vocation leaned more toward his people than his familia. Thassös reasoned that he would be a great king, the most kind and soft-hearted of the three brothers. And so he vowed to set down his own path and give all he had to the tournament, letting the best prince win."

Lilith quirked an eyebrow. "And the third prince? What of him?"

"Ah, *him…*" Julius smiled, truly smiled, wide and white in all its glory. "Aspéndos—"

"The first Divine of Isidore?" she interjected, perking up with the realization.

"The youngest and most timid of the three Dalegonian

princes," Julius confirmed. "He'd been invited to the meeting out of courtesy and he knew it. It was his birthright to participate, though he was well aware that his brothers, and even his father, had already considered him the loser. But he had the support of their youngest sibling, Princess Augusta."

She gasped.

"She is another story of her own," Julius said, a knowing chuckle rumbling through him.

"I'd love to hear it."

"Someday, when I can do the tale justice, I will tell it to you in all of its grandeur. The story I tell you now is finely threaded with hers."

"And what were the parameters of the tournament?"

"Conquest."

A small word for such a complicated goal, Lilith thought.

"The princes set sail. They were granted six months. Whichever prince returned with the greatest conquest would claim the Dalegonian throne."

"And who won?"

"That is a very complicated question," Julius answered on a gust of an exhale. "It is a convoluted story, complicated in ways that have probably grown more entangled over the centuries of recitation. There is, however, a book that I find quite detailed in its recounting of the story. I will search for it so you can quell your curiosity."

"Well," Lilith said on a sigh, "I can only assume one of the princes claimed Augusta for himself, and he was obviously quite fond of his sister."

Julius's eyes twinkled with wisdom untold. "Something like that," he said.

Looking away from him, Lilith turned her attention to her dinner plate. She'd barely eaten, lost in conversation and that swirling pool of anxiety in her gut. She knew she should ask him about the woman from the ball. It was her right to know, after all. But the doubt that hovered above her like a pall only dissuaded her from prying. She didn't want to be a burden, to cling to him as if he were the only thing she lived for. Then Julius reached forward, pulling her from her revery.

"We are cut from the same stone, Lil." His hand came to rest on her knee, warmth blossoming from the contact. "And if we have the same roots, who is to say we cannot grow together?"

Her fingers reached out to stroke his jawline, his short beard tickling her skin. She studied him for a moment, and the prince closed his eyes and sighed through his nostrils, his long lashes casting deep shadows beneath his eyes. In the pale moonlight, he appeared carved from stone. Both elegant and masculine.

"How in the world are you related to Prince Orìon?"

Julius's eyes snapped open with such immediacy, she nearly fell backward. "You've been thinking of that knave?"

"Difficult to forget such a thorn."

His smile flattened into a thin line and his eyes dropped to her untouched food. He'd done most of the talking tonight, her plate should be nearly empty by now. "You've barely touched your meal," he said. "Is it the fish? I know it's not for everyone."

Silence reigned.

"You're distant tonight," he said, a tacit invitation to divulge her worries. He reached across the table to place his hand over hers. "Please don't feel guilty for what happened. It was a mistake, a misunderstanding. I took care of it today. All is well between the crown and the Tribes."

She took comfort in that. At least Julius was able to amend what she had done, though the dance he'd waited all his life for had still been ruined.

He squeezed her hand once to draw her attention. "It is a good thing for us that both our countries worship the same gods," he said, "for there will be little objection when I make you my queen."

Lilith pulled away. She needed answers. She needed to know the intent behind his words. That the affection they shared was no travesty, but a reality. Because it felt real to her. Too real to ignore the doubt gnawing at her insides. Rising, she moved to the window, her eyes panning the rows of flowers, unseeing in their surveillance.

Julius followed her.

The night sky painted the room in a golden glow. It would have been the perfect romantic evening, if not for…

Lilith rounded on him, her fury coming to a culmination. "Who is Annika?"

He paled, his mouth hanging open. "There's something I've been meaning to tell you."

"What is it?"

The prince ran a trembling hand through his curls, brushing them away from his face. "From birth, I was sworn to marry a nobleman's daughter, and we grew up together, close enough to become friends."

"*Friends*?" Lilith's heart lurched into her throat, causing the word to come out as a pitiful, pained squeak.

Julius continued, an inconsequential air to his tone, "We are just friends. Our relationship has never been romantic. That wasn't necessary when we agreed—"

"You've been betrothed this entire time?" Tears pricked the backs of her eyes, but her anger helped her stave off the downpour.

"Our betrothal is history, Lilith." Julius took her face in his hands, pressing his forehead to hers and forcing her eyes to meet his. "My father knows of my wish to marry you."

"And…"

"He approves," he said with a wry smile. "Of course he does."

Her heart melted, the tears finally falling, but for a completely different reason than when they were summoned.

Julius chuckled, wiping her tears with his thumbs, his touch gentle. "I love you, Lil." He devoured her lips with his own. She fell into him, allowing him to lift her up into his arms and she wrapped her legs around his hips, feeling the hardening ridge of his groin pressing against the throbbing ache between her legs.

"Bed," she gasped. "Now."

36

THE WILL TO DEFY

"Lady Lilith! You've been summoned to the King's study." Zörra marched into Lilith's bedchamber, madly scanning the room for Gods knew what.

Grousing a host of complaints, Lilith rolled over, her cheek landing on a thin piece of parchment. A note from Julius. He'd gone to court with his parents and would return for lunch in the garden. Lilith smiled to herself, tracing the swirls of his handwriting with a fingertip.

Zörra forced her to sit at the breakfast table, to nibble on bread and butter. The handmaiden offered her a mug. "Kafés," she said. "It helps with everything."

Lilith accepted the mug, downing the contents with a groan. She hadn't gotten much sleep between couplings with Julius, the only respite being several moments spent panting in post-coital delirium.

"Please, hurry, Lilith! You'll be leaving in a couple of days, and you must meet with the King to discuss what form of aid would be—"

"Aid?" Lilith shot up, the thin strap of her silk nightgown

falling off her shoulder. "What do you mean *aid*?" Aid for the damage she'd caused during the ball? Aid for Augusta? Aid for his father?

Zörra froze. "I'm sorry. Amidst all the excitement yesterday, I'd forgotten to visit."

"What is it?"

Her handmaiden shifted her feet uncomfortably, then she floundered over to the wardrobe to ostensibly procure a dress.

"Zörra…"

The handmaiden spun on Lilith, eyes alight with fear. "Prince Julius has accepted to ascend the King's throne before his father's reign is up, in exchange for an army to accompany him across the sea to defeat the Great Divine." Zörra swallowed nervously. "He has agreed to the terms that he will be crowned upon his return and married to his queen."

Julius knew that Lilith wanted to spend her life with him, her very long life. But she never once felt confident becoming queen, especially of a foreign country. Apprehension churned in her gut. Zörra, noticing immediately, made to comfort her, but Lilith waved her off.

"I'm fine," she stated firmly. "But I won't be wearing a Dalegonian dress today."

The handmaiden staggered back, stricken. "Whatever do you me—"

"I *mean*," Lilith said, "that in lieu of traditional Dalegonian garb, I will wear the customary attire of an Augustan. Because I am Augustan, and I should represent my Empire—my home—with pride. Especially today." She hoped this would make a fine statement: that she was not an ornament but a voice to be heard. Dressed as such, the Queen would definitely see her as an aspersion to Julius and his regal image. Rebellion never felt so good, despite how subtle the message. After all his mother had done, she couldn't keep Lilith and Julius apart. Lilith would wear her Augustan garb for the announcement. Their countries would unite with the impending marriage, and it was time they got used to it.

Taken aback, the handmaiden dipped her head reverently. "As it pleases you." Turning on her heels, she retreated to abide by her lady's request.

Lilith dressed herself in her finest blouse and breeches whilst Mïa and Estêvia worked on shining her boots and braiding back her long hair. She checked over her appearance in the mirror. The royal-blue blouse she'd selected to represent Augusta fit her figure well, accentuating the curve of her waist. Her breeches, hugging her form in a flattering way, bespoke her physical dexterity.

Strapping Constance at her hip, Lilith deemed herself ready.

"I will send no more than five thousand men," the King announced, reiterating the bargain he'd made with his son. His voice echoed out into the corridor.

Lilith blinked, the only portrayal of her shock. Five thousand men? There was no possibility the King had been able to prepare such a force on such short notice. No, this was an ongoing negotiation she had only just been made aware of.

A servant stood in the open doorway and announced her arrival and Lilith entered. The room was nearly three times the size of the study at the Frourío. The bookshelves rose to the ceiling, the only furnishings being the King's desk and several other ornate chairs, which were occupied by avaricious retinues and viziers. The floors were the usual polished ivory marble, reflecting the various expressions turned her way. Lilith had difficulty imagining Julius's blood staining it.

Julius stood stoic at his father's side, his eyes fastened to

Lilith as if he could hold her in place. But it wasn't the prince's gaze that held her spine erect, but rather the Queen's glare denigrating, impaling Lilith from across the room.

As she had presumed, the Queen balked at the sight of her attire, at her outright display of temerity. As for the dignitaries, her appearance only seemed to whet their disdain.

All eyes shifted to Lilith as she stood in the center of the chamber. The pariah of the gathering had arrived. Steeling her spine, her eyes were for the King only.

"Welcome, Lilith Oak," King Faustus greeted, inclining his head. A warm smile spread across his face, almost sympathetic. Lilith returned his sympathy when the King erupted into a fit of violent coughs, so guttural, he spewed into his handkerchief.

Julius stepped closer to his father, placing his hand on the King's shoulder, but his eyes were still rapt with Lilith. She shot him a reassuring smile that he did not mirror. Her apprehension turned to full blown alarm.

What had he done?

When the King finally composed himself, he patted his son's hand. "My son has failed to notify me that you are not only our guest but an emissary on behalf of the Augustan Empire."

The realization that Julius must have been brokering this deal with his father for months—all whilst she was in the dark—had left her leaden with resentment and bitterness. Had Arduen known? Quin? Olga? They must have been aware.

Lilith smirked. "The Crown Prince failed to notify me of my duty as well."

Julius flinched, his expression stricken at the formal title she'd used in place of his name.

"Otherwise," she continued, her focus never wavering from King Faustus, "I would have been more forthright with my *courting* you." The prince's brow furrowed, but he did not open his mouth. Lilith arched an eyebrow in challenge.

"My son has cured our people of their disaffection toward their prince." The King cast a pointed look at his son. "Therefore, you will depart in public as a hero. I'd been granted a mere six weeks to cultivate such a force; five thousand soldiers, fifty ships. That will do. Upon cessation of battle, you shall have your crown and your queen."

"Yes, Father," Julius said.

Lilith caught her breath, reining in her raging emotions, a maelstrom she couldn't comprehend. Though Julius's ulterior motive for this trip was, in her honest opinion, judicious, the fact that he had left her out of his plan stung. Sure, the state affairs of his homeland were not her direct business—not before she'd been declared queen bride—but she was still Divine. Did her station not warrant a slight degree of counsel? The blatant obfuscation of his intentions left her jilted.

"Might I interject?" One of the noblemen stood, regarding the King with a casual dip of his bearded chin. The King signaled for the man to proceed. "I must commend your generosity, Your Highness. Five thousand men is a great commitment to such a precarious cause."

Lilith glared at the man. He wore the Dalegonian nobleman's sash, crisscrossing his torso to signify his marital status as espoused, though his physique was considerably less suited to the fashion.

"It would be my honor to send along my daughter," said the man, "the future Queen of Dalegonè."

Excuse me? Did Lilith hear that correctly? Of their own volition, her eyes cut to slits.

Ignorant of her censure, the man continued. "Annika has had extensive training in the healing practice. I believe it would be a humbling experience for her before she is to ascend the throne beside Prince Julius."

Now it was Lilith's turn to feel stricken. Her eyes instinctually rose to meet Julius's, his face betraying his every emotion; regret, longing, pain. She clenched her jaw, her teeth singing a macabre lament only she could hear.

The pretension in the man's request was painfully obvious. It was such an opportune moment to ensure that it was known by all persons of import that the throne beside Julius was to be occupied by his daughter.

Not Lilith.

How foolish was she, to ever believe she could stand beside Julius in his reign? They'd always been separated by more than an ocean.

"Yes, I agree!" the King said belatedly. "I will send along ten healers as well. Annika may lead them all."

Silence ensued, and Lilith gripped the hilt of Constance for strength, feeling the weight of Julius's stare boring into her. Her body trembled, her muscles numb and cold, her skin burning. Once she stepped foot outside this room, everything would change. In a single moment, she'd lost her closest companion.

Think of Arduen! You will see him soon.

King Faustus looked to his heir. "I know I had asked you to stay for the week, but this sudden change of events has left me with an overwhelming sense of urgency. The sooner you depart, the sooner you will return." He coughed again, the entire study awaiting his next words. "We will spend the rest of the day in preparation. You set sail at dawn."

The noblemen raised chalices in the King's honor. "Long live the King!"

A servant approached Lilith, offering her a chalice of whatever liquor the royals fancied. She declined politely and took her leave before Julius mustered the gall to confront her.

"Annika is going *with* you?" Zörra stared wide-eyed at Lilith as she scrubbed at her hair. The handmaiden had awaited her return from the meeting, a tub full of steaming water prepared. She thought Lilith would need it. A wise woman she was.

"She will be playing the role of a healer. Julius's *personal* healer," Lilith asserted dryly.

Zörra offered a rueful shake of her head.

"I cannot help but wonder," Lilith continued, "why he told me I would be his queen, only to broker a deal with the blaring stipulation that I wouldn't be?" It hurt more than she wanted to admit, knowing what she'd lost. "I want to believe that he loved me—that he *loves* me—but now that he has formally consented to marry her, it seems to disavow everything he's ever said to me."

"I'm sorry," Zörra said. "Politics are always... convoluted. But I truly do not believe Julius would hurt you on purpose. His intentions were honorable, I couldn't fathom they were anything but. And I can say this with certitude, he never would have taken things so far with you if he did not love you."

Lilith shrugged. It didn't matter anymore. Julius did what he had to. He put the welfare of the entire world before his own desires. And truthfully, she was proud of him for exactly that. Even if it rendered her heart in fissures.

Yet, when she truly considered the predicament, she was no better than Julius. He'd had a fiancée just as much as she did, and neither one revealed that information to the other. Who was she to judge him so harshly? Who was she to be angry with him? She'd also been promised to another, and she'd just as quickly fallen in love with him, even fallen into bed with him.

"Do not question his love!" Zörra chastised. "That man is true of heart, I know it. I'd swear my life on it."

"I know Annika is only joining us because she knows of our relationship." Lilith dunked, letting the water caress her scalp.

"Who cares about Annika." Zörra scoffed as she rose from the bath. "I don't think Prince Julius has ever loved her!"

"They seemed fairly smitten with each other at the ball," Lilith countered.

"They are friends," Zörra said. "But did the prince dance with her? No. He deserted his own ball for you, to protect you. And it was to your bed he retired." She snickered, nudging Lilith's shoulder.

When she remained unresponsive, Zörra donned a more serious expression. "A powerful marriage, the weight of a crown, and godly Fire searing in his veins… despite all of that, it is not enough to keep a man like Julius Fawkes warm at night." She leveled Lilith with her kohl-lined stare. "He needs you. He wants you. And, if the great Western Galatëa failed to keep you apart, I don't think Annika is strong enough to accomplish such a feat, either."

Lilith let her head fall back against the stone rim of the tub. "Annika will win," she said. "Royal blood always triumphs."

"Only in stories," Zörra countered.

Lilith snorted. "This is definitely no story."

"For once, my friend, we are not in consonance." Zörra scooted closer, the steam curling around her like phantom, god-like fingers. "At every turn, I was met with disdain and contempt. You see, Dalegonians have respect for the DíTakas, but they do not respect those who choose to dwell in it, to make the monstrous dunes their home. Truly, their contempt is a result of my peoples' separation from the King's thrall.

"But I've learned to bask in it. What bolsters more than the will to defy? The will to prove your greatest cynics wrong."

Lilith met her gaze. She hadn't realized there was such contention within Dalegonè. Julius had always implied how righteous his country was in comparison to Augusta. But it appeared there were races that faced scrutiny for their differences, just like the Walabeäns and the Vunosoï.

Would Dalegonians welcome a foreign queen?

"It has been made abundantly clear that I am not welcome here, Zörra."

"Don't stop loving Julius because everyone wants you to. Love him because what you have is strong enough to overcome the great Galatëa. Strong enough to overcome death."

Lilith frowned. She wanted to love Julius. She wanted him to love her. But for fear of Annika being chosen over her, she couldn't do it.

"Come on, cheer up!" Zörra groused. "It's our last night together."

When Lilith opened her eyes, she was face-to-face with a pouting handmaiden, Zörra's bottom lip stained with wine.

"I'm sorry!" Lilith said. "Come with me. I'll sneak you away, and you can live out your days with the Divine." She raised her eyebrows dramatically, splashing her friend with suds.

"Ugh... why can't you be my queen?" Zörra said. "I could be the Queen's handmaiden!"

"Couldn't you be the Queen's handmaiden now?"

Zörra scowled. "You know most of all why that position is unsavory, at least for the time being."

Lilith offered nothing more than a knowing smirk.

"The Queen's exterior embellishments make her seem like a dignified lady, but she possesses more authority in politics than what a first glance would have you believe."

"You don't say," Lilith deadpanned.

"But," Zörra ignored her caustic jest, "if there was ever a man to put her in her respective seat, it is the one she birthed. And I don't think Julius is willing to give up on you so easily.

With or without Annika present to witness." Zörra splashed her to attention. "So, did that convince you to stay, or do you need another of my magnificent orations?"

Waving her off, Lilith dunked again, hiding all evidence of her amusement. When she broke the water's surface, Zörra's voice echoed, "Stay and be my queen!"

Unable to contain her mirth, Lilith cackled, the sound far more jovial than she felt. "If I stay here any longer, I will become a glutton!"

"Well, for one, I do not mind being a gourmand."

"Your slender frame would suggest otherwise," Lilith stated.

"Blame my desert roots."

Lilith smiled at the thought of making this palace her home. She'd never imagined herself having a personal handmaiden. She regarded Zörra as a friend rather than a servant. A special kind of confidante, like Kathleen had been in her youth.

"Please tell me of your homeland!" Zörra said. "What is Augusta like? What is the capital like?"

"It's not as… clean." That was the nicest way to put it. Of what Lilith had seen of Xanthë, the buildings, the lawns, the streets, all was kept manicured. So unlike Kenora, where the people lived and bred in their own refuse. "Trust me, servants are shy there, for horrid reasons. Your rulers care for you here. The grass is greener in Dalegonè."

"Grass?" Zörra wrinkled her nose. "The only grass here is at the hilt of a man's member!"

With a voracious giggle, Lilith tugged Zörra by the arm, pulling her into the tub. The two women splashed and drank late into the night.

At dawn, Lilith set sail for Augusta.

37

TO CEASE ITS WRATH

Julius barked stringent orders at his soldiers, so incongruous with his benign composition. This new authoritative demeanor inspired a flurry of butterflies in Lilith's stomach, which quickly devolved into wasps. Every day, he was inching deeper into the skin of a king, and she would never be his queen.

Tearing her attention away from the prince, Lilith swung Constance through the air, dragging the blade through her imaginary opponent. The ship rocked on the waves, the Western Galatëa surrounding them on all sides, Xanthë lost in their wake. The horizon was a forest of ships' masts, the sheer size of the legion a fulsome indicator of the King's wealth.

Lilith gasped as she spun, jabbing out at the railing of the poop deck and the ravenous waves beyond. They'd been at sea for a week. They had another seven days before they would reach the shores of Augusta. Having been granted a private—however austere—sleeping cabin, Lilith had finally gotten some rest. Unlike their trip to Xanthë, she did not have Julius to assure her that her seasickness was an ailment of her imagination, and so she'd had to resort to the fetal position and vigilant prayer.

Julius had been insistent that he and his uncle travel aboard the same ship as Lilith... along with Annika sleeping a few doors down. Lilith almost wanted to trade places with a soldier. A cramped berth in the company of sweaty men was preferable.

For the duration of their voyage, she'd kept her mind closed off, shielded against Julius. They could, if both their minds were left unguarded, communicate through emotions and notions alone. It would only be more difficult allowing him to take part in her suffering, and Gods forbid he doesn't feel as she does. The last thing she ever wanted from him was pity.

The sky was dark in the distance, threatening to rock the ship and capsize them. It would be a wet evening, even without the threat of disembarkation. Only when the gale drew near would Lilith be able to move it. She still hadn't mastered that particular skill of Aether, but she'd try to protect this army. And, with Constantine's blessing, the palace in Xanthë would be flooded to the ankles by dawn—save for Zörra's quarters, of course.

Her energy suddenly combusting, Lilith gritted her teeth and slashed at the air—and stopped abruptly. Shoulder jarred, she glared at the sword that just parried her blow, her foe no longer imaginary. Unimpressed, she backed off.

"Care to spar?" Julius asked, that charming smile daring her lips to quiver.

"I'm finished for the day," she replied with an indignant shrug and sheathed Constance at her hip.

Julius stood back as if she'd taken a swipe at him. "Maybe tomorrow?"

Grunting in response, Lilith let silence speak for her.

"I won't have this, Lilith!"

She froze at his sudden outburst. Such caprices were not characteristic of Julius.

"You have been abnormally quiet since we last spoke. I won't have it," he repeated.

"Spoken like a consummate king," she quipped, her fingers reaching for the pendant at her collarbone, the one he'd gifted her for her birthday. It felt wrong to wear it now.

With a brusque tug, the clasp tore free. Without hesitation, without looking him in the eyes, she held the necklace out to him.

Julius's lips parted, confusion and pain flashing across his features. "That's yours," he said, his voice rising with indignation.

"Don't be stubborn," she retorted. "I cannot wear it."

He looked as though he was going to argue, to put up a fight. The last thing she wanted was a scene.

"Take it, please." She cleared her throat, willing her voice steady. "I don't want it."

Julius said no more, wrapping his deft fingers around the dainty chain, his skin brushing hers for the briefest moment. An electric current shot up her arm at the contact, and she flinched.

This animosity hovering between them had thrown her entire world off-kilter, there was never a passing moment that he wasn't on her mind, that Julius and his impending bride were not on her mind.

Turning her back to him, Lilith made her way down the stairs to the main deck where the soldiers had taken turns training. They danced in pairs, swirling around one another, their movements balletic, unlike Augustan or Walabeän styles. Now she knew where Julius received such graceful form. Though obviously skilled, these men had never been exposed to the likes of carnage she had. They'd never tasted blood on their tongues, felt the sting of poison in their gashes, grit in their teeth, the scent of offal and decay in the air as they fought for their lives.

Lilith debated selecting one of the most handsome warriors to spar—a petty attempt to inspire jealousy in Julius—but decided better of it. She would not lash out in such petty ways.

"Julius!" Prince Odêus called, waving both Julius and Lilith over to him. Eager for a distraction, she gripped Constance's hilt and approached the prince.

"What is it?" Julius asked from behind her.

Odêus grimaced, the subtle wrinkles of his brow deepening. "The men I have selected to watch the waters have notified me of their worries. They have seen unusual movement beneath the sea's surface They suspect incursion—"

A lean, blue-skinned figure leapt up from the waves. She perched on the rail of the ship and wrapped her arms around Prince Odêus, pulling him overboard. All color leached from the prince's face as he fell away from them, out of reach.

Alarmed, Julius shouted, lurching forward in a futile attempt to save his uncle.

Lilith tugged him back. "Don't, Julius!"

Composing himself, Julius shouted mandates to every soldier in sight. "Get away from the railings!" He twisted on the spot until his eyes locked on Annika, her dark hair tousled about her head as she ran to him.

"Julius!"

Lilith stepped back to accommodate Annika as she fell into her betrothed's arms.

The sound of the crashing waves was drowned out by the hiss of hundreds of sabers being drawn from their sheaths. Lilith stepped away from Julius and Annika as he ordered soldiers to take Annika to shelter belowdecks.

Soldiers were nonplussed, encumbered by inertia. They

raced up the stairs from below, tripping over each other to assume formation. Julius muttered curses at their impotence.

For the first time in days, Lilith opened her mind to her surroundings. In the middle of the sea, the swarm of entities was overwhelming, but she'd expected the familiar din. She'd fallen asleep to it on the loneliest of nights. It was a simple task to sort through what was normal and what wasn't. There was no mistaking the number of astute minds surrounding them for miles.

The Ophïon.

Lilith twisted to bark a warning to Julius, but the ship turned to chaos. The entire sea did. An army of sirens rose up from the depths of the waters, climbing up the ships, slaying the soldiers with nothing but their claws. Their skin was of varying color: blue, green, gray, and all the in-betweens. Shining scales decorated their bodies, shielding their most intimate areas as if they'd been bred for battle.

Bolts of Fire shot over Lilith's shoulder, and a greenish body slumped to the deck behind her, yellow liquid pooling around it.

"Lilith!" Julius's voice rose over the tumult. "Use your gifts!"

Could she stop the attack? Was she strong enough to control the sea?

"Lilith!"

Julius's bellow forced her into action. She sprinted to the poop deck to get a better view of the assault. The surface of the sea was littered with bobbing heads of silver and gold hair. The Ophïon shot seashells at the soldiers with slingshots, their aim impeccable, the range almost magical.

A pale-gray siren flipped onto the deck beside her, rolling onto its feet with preternatural stealth.

Lilith was ready.

The siren pounced, the muscles beneath its skin rippling like serpents thrashing to break free of their prison. It dodged her blade, and wrapping its long arms around her middle, it threw her to the deck.

Lilith's head smacked the wooden planks with a *crack* that echoed through the chamber of her skull. Stars danced before her eyes, impeding her vision, her assailant blurred. The siren hissed, releasing putrid breath that seemed to leave Lilith's skin coated in grime. It burned.

Thrashing to throw the siren off her, Lilith pried her eyes open. The siren bared its gapped teeth, the white pearls pointed like daggers, its once beautiful face rendered spectral.

Her blood was a torrent in her ears. Her breath quickened. Her chest heaved. Emotions threatened to undo her. Explosions of pain. Anger.

Fire seared inside her, roiling in her gut, overwhelming her with the primal need to defend. Visceral sensations urging her to fight, to survive.

The siren lunged for her throat.

Without a moment's hesitation, Lilith embedded the tip of Constance into its neck. The siren gurgled, its solid white eyes slowly losing luminosity. And when she removed her sword from its jugular, yellow fluid erupted from the hole, bathing her blouse in its icy blood. Her enemy's body went slack, its weight holding her down.

Lilith pushed the creature off and stood to survey the attack. The sirens climbed the sides of the ships, their hands and feet sticking to the wood, the webs between their fingers sparkling in the remnants of the setting sun. Flaming arrows tore through the air, knocking the sirens back into the sea. Their screams pierced the air, and everyone fell to their knees, their hands clamped over their ears to ward off their abominable screeches.

Julius materialized at her side, seemingly unperturbed by

the insufferable noise. "The sea, Lilith!" His eyes were wide, conveying his message.

Lilith nodded, dizziness disorienting her. The prince looped a strong arm around her waist and pulled her up. She swayed, unwilling to lean on him for support.

"The sea…" Julius repeated, coaxing her addled mind to lucidity, and her eyes shot to the scene before her.

Through the wooden spindles of the railing, the once green waters had turned a muddy hue. Blood. With a groan, she pushed off from Julius and inelegantly approached the rail. Quick footsteps sounded behind her, and Julius's hands were on her shoulders, ensuring she would not fall over the edge.

"I'll be right here," he said. "Focus." He pressed a kiss to the back of her skull. An act of affection that would once have turned her insides to liquid, now boiled her blood.

But Lilith obeyed, closing her eyes and extending her mind out toward the sea's brawl. She could sense every siren floating around her, their pain, their anguish—but mostly, their fear. She could sense life akin to her own, wavering and winking out of existence, departing on the voyage to Elysium.

Sympathy and ire warred within her. This had all been but a mistake. The Ophïon attacked because they'd felt provoked. Good men had fallen today because of a misinterpretation, and lack of communication.

Julius's hand stroked down her spine in encouragement, his face still buried in her hair, his breath hot on her neck. Any sirens that dared to approach, he blasted with Xander's Fire. His body tensed against her with every explosion.

Lilith willed the sea to obey her command, to cease its wrath. To still the undulating swells threatening to rock the ships into oblivion.

Just at that moment, thunder cracked above them. The ship rocked tauntingly.

Fast. Faster. Now.

Drawing forth every ounce of energy remaining, Lilith commanded the sea to harden like ice. Screams rent the night as the Galatëa obliged, and cracking sounds fractured the air like whips. The Ophïon froze in place, the attack at a stalemate.

For now.

The Ophïon spoke, their trilling voices too high in pitch to carry effectively. Lilith couldn't make sense of their calls, if they even spoke Modern Tongue. Why hadn't she asked Arduen more about them?

Her limbs trembled under the exertion, but she held firm, long enough for the general to convey their intentions. The Ophïon wouldn't care about a war inland.

Losing grip of the railing, she whimpered as she lost control. A dam broke within her, the flow of it leaching every last measure of her strength. She slid down, and Julius guided her to the deck with gentle hands.

"Lilith…" He was trying to keep the worry from seeping into his voice, but he was unconvincing.

She shouldn't feel like this.

Something was terribly wrong.

"Help!" Julius called to the others. "Get one of the healers now!" he wailed, his voice cracking in panic.

She glanced up at her prince and managed only to croak his name.

"Annika is coming," he said. "You're going to be all right." She tried not to flinch at the name. He cupped her cheek, his thumb stroking her skin reverently.

When Annika appeared beside Julius, her face was pale. Whether from exposure to her first battle, or the sight of the hand of her betrothed on another woman's body, Lilith didn't care.

Gods damn the woman.

Gods damn Xanthë.

Gods damn the Ophïon.

Lilith's vision flickered, the flashing clouds dissipating from her vision.

Annika gasped. "She's dying, Jules."

Julius.

38

A GREAT CHASM

The discovery of the Sorcerer weighed heavily upon Rhéa's conscience. Spiro had tripled her dose of fàrmako, if only to keep her powers too dull to act out, too dull to act irrationally. Any resistance would be futile now. Spiro had a Sorcerer under his command, Xavier, and now Felix, the consummate vassalage. Together, they would disarm her before she so much as lined up a shot at the Great Divine. She would be as good as buried alive. Spiro already possessed her replacement: Irís.

But if Spiro had even an inkling of intelligence and self-preservation, Thébés would be buried far beneath the earth's surface, rotting. And that's exactly where Rhéa wanted him, desperately. For the bastard had played a hand in Lilith's suffering.

Every night, the image of the mutated baby flashed behind Rhéa's eyelids. Was that how he created the beasts? Human babies? She shook her head, tossing and turning. Every night, she'd awaken slick with cold sweat, her heart racing without a reason, without recollection of a night terror. She needed to do something, but unless her skin could bathe in Starlight, she was powerless.

Amalthea was what she needed.

Rhéa sprinted for her bedchamber door. She didn't stop to put on more than her shift. Her bare feet slapped against the stone floor as she sprinted through the shadows lining the hallways. She knew what to do, but not exactly how to accomplish it.

But she knew who did.

When she reached her destination, she pounded her fist against the wooden door. She waited, listening for movement inside.

Nothing.

She pounded again, harder. "Xavier!" she called. "Open up!"

The door swung inward, and Xavier stood before her, his hair disheveled, torso bare. "What is it?" he demanded through clenched teeth.

"I need you to take me outside."

His eyes widened incredulously.

"Now," she urged.

"Thëo's balls, Rhéa!" he spat. "Have you lost your mind? Do you even begin to understand the consequences if we are caught?" He ran his fingers through his hair as if convincing himself this was a dream. "Spiro will sense us."

"But you can shield me, as well as your own mind, no?"

Xavier nodded, reluctantly giving in. "There is a way. But I swear to Isidore, if we get caught—"

"We won't!" Rhéa clasped her hands, nudging his chest. "Please, Xavier." Her need was great, far exceeding any other urge she'd experienced before.

"All right." He sighed, reaching behind him to close the door.

"Wait," she said. "I need a mirror."

Xavier looked confused. "A mirror?"

Rhéa nodded. Time was of the essence and she wanted to spend as much of it as she could preening under Amalthea's subtle rays.

Xavier disappeared, and when he emerged from his room, he carried a small handheld mirror and a cloak draped over his arm. "For you." He held it out to her.

Accepting the cloak, Rhéa grasped the mirror like it was her last chance for salvation.

Because it very well could be.

Following Xavier through the halls, she donned the cloak, clutching the mirror to her chest, the metal biting cold against her skin. Her eyes were trained on Xavier's heels, her body going through the motions, leading her toward freedom with every step.

They walked until the air became lighter, until breathing no longer seemed like a menial chore. Her celestial being thrummed with excitement, in expectation of revitalization. Arriving at the base of a narrow stairwell, Xavier placed one foot on the first step and twisted to face her. With a meek smile, he extended his hand to her. Taking a deep breath, she let him lead her upward.

The stairwell ended abruptly, and it led nowhere. There was no door at the top of the stairs, just a wall of dirt and dangling tree roots.

"Xavier…"

He put a finger to his lips, signaling her to quietude. She obliged, dancing on her toes in anticipation. He closed his eyes, lips pursing in a concentrated moue. Just when Rhéa was about to voice her concerns again, the wall of earth grumbled and parted, revealing darkness in an open doorway behind Xavier. Fresh air permeated the stairwell, and Rhéa whimpered, rushing forward past him.

"No!" Xavier whisper-shouted, wrapping a strong arm around her waist and holding her against him.

The Enchantress pushed him. "Let me go!"

"No, Rhéa," he said, breathless from her blows. "It's not what you think."

She restrained her excitement enough to let him speak, but the cool night breeze caressing her neck, rushing down her spine, was a tantalizing promise of freedom. One that she would not be able to resist for much longer.

"You would have fallen to your death," Xavier said. "This is the Rift of Dodöna."

After a moment of shock, Rhéa stepped toward the edge and, at what she saw, muttered a string of obscenities.

The Rift. The great chasm Spiro created that fateful day when he lashed out against his own kind, nearly laying to waste all Divine. Many remain at the bottom of the Rift, denied their Stars, unable to ascend to Elysium where they belonged.

"How do we get to land?" she asked, taking in the sheer drop, the lengthy cliff separating them from the land above. The doorway was set in the side of the cliff face, about a hundred feet from the top. When Spiro's army departed for war, they must rely on those bred with wings, and the Divine blessed by Isidore.

A ghost of a smile tugged at the corners of Xavier's lips and he spread his arms. "Hold on."

With a steadying breath, Rhéa curled herself into his embrace. He folded her in his arms and stood upon the edge. The night was so dark, she wondered if she would see any stars at all.

"Don't scream," he said, then stepped off the ledge.

Rhéa swallowed her scream, her neck craned to take in the strange sight. The Rift's walls were less like broken dirt and more like slate. Moonlight shone off the sleek sides of the trench, moonbeams penetrating into the void. The Enchantress smiled as they flew through the spears of luminosity, her heart singing with anticipation.

Xavier rose above the edge. Flat, fallow land spread out for miles in every direction. When he landed, Rhéa pushed away from him, her eyes locked on the night sky. Her breath caught in her throat, and she thrust the mirror into Xavier's chest. Stifling a sob, she spun on her bare heels, looking to each Guiding Star. The violet, silver, azure, and golden jewels blinked at her in recognition of Their daughter, welcoming her home.

Andromeda, Dracoladen, Cepheus, and…

Amalthea!

Rhéa sobbed now, she couldn't contain the pure relief emanating from her lips. Her gaze settled on the golden Amalthea, and the Enchantress's knees buckled. She dropped to the earth, crawling toward the star, her hands and knees scraping against the rough ground, drawing blood.

Desperate to get closer, to soak her skin in the light of the Southern Star, Rhéa ripped free of the cloak.

"Rhéa…" Xavier cautioned.

She ignored him, pulling the straps of her gown over her shoulders. The silk drifted down her body, and she shuffled out of it. Nothing could confine her any longer.

Naked beneath the Stars, Rhéa's skin sang with solace.

Her blood heated once again.

Celestial power coiled within her.

A presence at her side pulled her attention from the Amalthea, and Rhéa cast the creature a glower.

"Relax, it's just me." Xavier placed a soothing grip on her shoulder. He kept his eyes locked on hers, his restraint noticeable. "Do what you must but be mindful that we do not have long."

He was right. There was a greater matter to be dealt with. Her reunion would have to wait.

"The mirror," she said to him, her voice arid and ragged, scraping past the dry skin along her throat.

Xavier passed her the mirror. "Do what you have to."

Rhéa nodded, not fully attuned to her heightened senses just yet. Her body was still adjusting to the Starlight, awakening from a slumber that could kill even the strongest Enchantress.

Placing the mirror in the silt beneath her, she blew the dust away from its surface. Clearing her throat, she began the spell, "Se qu pevër seâte unt Vën, ahírr va setenté vuthé qu ontè va vuíll tèles." *By the power vested in me, align my vision with the one my soul seeks.*

The High Enchantress's angular face appeared in the mirror. Her violet eyes focused on Rhéa, growing wide in disbelief.

"Rhéa DaSylvà," Ophelía intoned. "My little miscreant. Would you like to tell me just how you've been evading my search?"

Rhéa nearly caved at the familiar sound of the High Enchantress. She used to imagine how she'd eviscerate Ophelía, but after all she'd been through since she'd left the Obsydían Marsh, all she wanted now was to run into her arms.

"Well, what is it?" Ophelía snapped, her tone reprehensible.

"I've been captured by Spiro," Rhéa sputtered. "That's why you can't contact me."

The High Enchantress gaped, but quickly regained her reticent demeanor. Of course she would conceal her shock, for under Ophelía's pedantic rule, it was an embarrassment that such an abomination had ever escaped her notice.

"I've discovered the means by which he has created his army of beasts." Rhéa nearly choked on the words as they left her lips, disbelief clouding her mind, daring to wipe her memory.

"How?" the High Enchantress pressed.

"A Sorcerer."

For the first time in her life, Rhéa witnessed the High Enchantress pale as she divulged all she had learned. The means to Spiro's army of beasts. The location of his lair. Rhéa knew this would be her only chance, and so she occluded no detail.

"Rhéa," Xavier said, cutting through her concentration.

Rhéa watched in dismay as the mirror's surface clouded, then returned to normal. Ophelía was gone, and Rhéa hadn't the strength to bring her back.

"We must go," he urged. "Please, Rhéa."

The Enchantress stood on wobbly knees. She only just realized her discarded dress was nowhere in sight.

"Here," Xavier said, handing her the crumpled garment.

Almost in a daze, Rhéa slipped the diaphanous nightgown over her head. It was a shame she couldn't stay out under the Starlight longer. Her skin was smarting after just a brief moment of exposure.

"We must go back." Xavier placed a firm grip on her arm, as if he suspected she might flee.

The thought hadn't occurred to her to use this opportunity to escape. If she ran, Xavier would be Spiro's first suspect. He was one of the few who knew the enchantment to open the doorway out. Spiro would know that Rhéa couldn't fly, and he would know that with fàrmako in her veins, she could not summon the power to fuel a flight spell.

No, I will not abandon Xavier and Irís.

Together, they walked back to the Rift—though her gait was more of a shamble. They both were silent and mournful, and when they reached the brink, Xavier cradled Rhéa in his arms and kicked off from the ledge without a word.

39

FOUR ANCIENT SOULS

The torrent ripped at her skin, shards of ice abrading her limbs.

Lilith cried out for release, for mercy, but there was no one to answer her pleas. She thrashed with whatever ounce of strength she had left.

She wouldn't give in.

This wasn't over.

Voices sounded in her head, echoing through a great chasm that opened up, and her weightless body descended.

Vàst vû fíng vuthé salídr stèle.

Descending.

Down.

Deep.

May we fight with valiant steel.

Was this Hades? Were the Gods finally sending her to her afterlife of agony?

Was Larkin's Star worth eternal affliction?

Forgée courcí teq víne.

Forged courage and might.

Lilith wailed, her body engulfed by flames, Xander's Fire burning to her very core.

Vàst qu Tsat wadnn unè pâte, teq duínn unè vledreè teq tísse.

The fever subsided, edging toward neutrality, then tipping over the edge of the chasm, deeper into the frozen depths of the rift.

May the Gods watch our paths, and quell our bleeding and strife.

Ice shot through her again, waves of sensation piercing every crevice. If she could cry, she would have, but this body she was in now, it wasn't her own. It wasn't the terrestrial shelter she'd been sauntering through Augusta in.

This wasn't Augusta anymore.

This wasn't the mortal realm.

Tepid waves melted the ice away. The calm easing the pain, and easing her muddled brain.

Constantine, save me.

Kyril, forgive me.

Eight smooth hands scaled her ethereal body, bestowing her with the will to draw breath, the strength to move the lands.

Vhedn säl uit qínn, teq vû sví vestinn unè pevër…

The sensation was an aberration, unwelcome, abhorrent even. Lilith grappled with invisible hands for anything to brace herself.

When all is done, and we are beyond our power…

Four ancient souls lilted their estranged melodies as their hands roamed, caressing, healing. Ancient whisperings resounded through her entire being, calling Lilith to attention as their hands molded her, creating her anew.

She groaned under their otherworldly touch.

Gasping for air, desperate to draw it into her lungs, she braced herself as she rose.

Escalating.

Up.

High.

The light blossomed until it was near-blinding. The hands released her. Fingertips trailed along her body, sending bone-chilling sensations coursing through every limb.

Limbs.

She had limbs! Her invisible body cavorted, excitement swelling within her.

The voice of her home called to her. Sang to her.

Vàst Quy cârre zî unsà Elysium funewër.

To rise.

To live.

To breathe.

To shine.

May They carry us into Elysium forever.

"THE HYMN…"

"Sing, my prince!"

"…Divination…"

"Julius."

The worldly voices cut through the symphonious whispers. Lilith gasped, her body lurching. Steady hands grasped her by her shoulders, replacing the mighty hands that had held her only seconds before.

Had the Gods taken her? Had They decided that she wasn't ready for Elysium? Was she deemed unworthy? Inferior?

The hands shook her to lucidity. Her eyelids fluttered open, her vision less than substantial.

"Lilith!" *Julius.*

The prince entered her line of sight, removing his hands

from her shoulders and taking her head between his palms, his grip like iron. He pressed vicious kisses to her lips, her nose, her forehead. Then his embrace engulfed her, sheltering her as what remained of her soul transported back into her body.

"Julius…" Her voice was hoarse, barely audible amidst the chaos surrounding them.

"Lilith, you're all right!" He didn't let her go.

How much had transpired since her transcendence? How many would not complete their first voyage?

"The Ophïon…"

Julius pulled away enough to look at her. Fear swam like mighty sharks in his eyes. "They're gone. My uncle spoke with them," he said with certainty.

"Your uncle…?" She'd thought Odêus had been slain.

He gave a solemn nod. "He climbed back up the side. He's a little shaken, but otherwise fine."

A cruel reality settled over her like a pall. "How many did we lose?"

"The count is sitting at just under four hundred." His tone was somber. They'd lost so many before they'd even reached Augusta's shores.

Julius's thumbs stroked her cheeks as she mentally digested their situation. Lilith closed her eyes and leaned into him, resting her forehead against his, breathing in his scent. He knelt before her, edging closer. Every other crew member, every soldier and healer, might as well have gone overboard.

But this could not happen. Not with his future wife bearing witness. There were delicate matters of much greater import requiring their attention.

"Lilith, I—"

"Don't." Wrapping her fingers around his wrists, she pulled his hands free of her. "We can't."

Something like pain flashed across his features. "Please, my love—"

"I am not your *love*, Prince Julius."

With a grunt, she forced herself to stand, to put distance between them again. "I must bathe," she announced, glancing down at her Dalegonian blouse. The yellowish fluid staining the lavish fabric stuck to her abdomen, outlining her figure.

"I'll heat the water for you," Julius offered, rising to his feet and Lilith acquiesced, if only because she needed the warm water to relax her muscles.

Once she'd entered her cabin, Julius lighting the sconces with Xander's Fire, she removed her gore-stained blouse. He halted at her wash basin and turned to stare. She ignored him, removing her clothing, eager to be free of the siren's blood. The creature didn't need to die, yet it had given her no other choice.

"It's hot, so be wary," Julius said. "I'll go and retrieve a clean cloth for you." He made to exit, jaw set firm, eyes locked on the door, not daring to stray to her bare flesh again.

When he returned, he passed her the cloth without so much as a glance at her, leaving her alone in her cabin. Why did she undress in his presence? She couldn't fully comprehend her intentions. She loved Julius, she always would. But what he felt for her, was it only fleeting lust?

Perhaps she was just being foolish. Julius had chosen his people over her. How could she resent him for that? Is that not what a good ruler should do?

With a sigh, Lilith began to clean herself, the siren's dried blood turning the beige cloth a greenish color. She studied it, curiosity igniting within her. They'd met the Ophïon. She was eager to learn what Julius's uncle's interaction had been like. Did they speak Modern Tongue? Elder Tongue? Dalegonian? Had Julius assumed the lead for the interaction, or was he loath to leave her side? Her chest constricted. She had died—or she thought she had. And the Gods hadn't even wanted her.

Booming footsteps thundered on the deck above and dust sprinkled over her unmade bed. She continued to clean, changing cloths when one became too dirty to be of any use. Holding her bar of soap firm, she lathered the suds onto her skin and hair, scrubbing the grime from her face. Scrubbing away the remnants of the phantom touch—holy or not.

What advice would Arduen have given her then? She missed him fiercely. There was a faint tug at her soul, pulling her to the east. Somehow, her Master could make any situation better, and she longed for his wisdom now.

The meager light of the sconces flickered, the Fire losing its power. Julius losing his power, she realized. He was likely close to depletion. They all were, but the duties of the Crown Prince far exceeded her own. He'd have to handle the bodies, decide what to do with them.

She swallowed, her throat so dry that even her own saliva seemed abrasive. This was going to be a long night.

⊙ ⊚ ⟿ ᚗ ◊

"Only their general spoke Elder Tongue," Julius explained to Lilith, catching her up on what had transpired after she'd fallen unconscious. He spoke quietly over his shoulder as they made their way to the study. "Prince Odêus is well versed. His vocabulary exceeds my own. He will reiterate the conversation in the study."

They took their seats at the long table inside the small cabin, one of the servants pouring each of them a generous glass of whiskey. Though it was messy, there were a few books, scrolls, and shelves of odd trinkets. Most of the mess was a result of the empty liquor bottles.

Julius pulled out a chair for Lilith and she sat down, her gaze inspecting the other men at the table. All generals with skillful arsenals in the art of warfare. But did they possess the necessary compassion to spur their army on? To allay their fears and the horrors that lingered long after battle's cessation? No. Lilith doubted they did.

The prince lowered himself into the seat at the head of the table, eyeing each of his men with appreciation. His black blouse was unbuttoned casually, exposing his sinewy chest and the remains of his injury at Spiro's hands.

Lilith's eyes locked on him expectantly. Reluctantly. Just the way he held himself erect despite such a shoddy chair implied his regality. A leader, unflappable amidst chaos.

Julius began, "Prince Odêus, please give us a quick summary of the conversation that transpired between you and the Ophïon general."

"Well, the siren explained that they had seen the ships from below. King Aègaeon dispatched his army to investigate. He'd ordered them to attack if they felt threatened. So they did." He cleared his throat, tentatively glancing at the others, the red outline of a siren bite stark against his tanned skin, sutures carefully holding the riven flesh together. "The general said that they had felt threatened and were only protecting their domain."

An older general with a graying beard interjected. "With this behind us, we must discuss what to do with the bodies. And the supplies we have will only last a month. What if we are to stay longer? We will need provisions for our return voyage as well."

"I will rest tonight," Julius said. "I must allow my stores of power to replenish. Tomorrow, I will take care of the bodies myself. They must be burned, the ashes cast overboard. Unless we can somehow locate canteens to store them, that is the only option. I will write letters of condolences to their families. Gurlan—" a younger, plump man sat up at his future king's call, "—can you finalize the list of the deceased?"

The man nodded eagerly.

"As for provisions, I was going to ask you, Lil—ith." Julius flinched, as if saying her nickname pierced his skin. "Do you mind returning to Utica to talk to the lord there? I will send you with an official missive requesting aid. I hope that our joining their Emperor's cause will be enough of compensation."

Each of the generals turned their heads in mute disdain. Needless to say, they seemed convinced her words lacked credibility. After falling unconscious mid-battle, in their eyes she was a pathetic example of a Divine. Yet she'd stalled the water, hardened the sea making movement nearly impossible. She was the reason they hadn't lost more men. Perhaps it was best she did not become their queen. It seemed she would never gain the respect she deserved.

The door creaked as it swung inward, and Annika entered the room, gliding on effortlessly graceful feet to stand at the end of the table.

"Lady Annika," Prince Odêus announced. "We are forever grateful for your skills this afternoon. You have proven yourself quite the promising young queen-to-be." Odêus's eyes shone with pride and admiration for the young woman. *Maybe he should be king. Maybe he should marry Annika. Have a husband and a wife.*

"I thank you, my prince." She bowed her head slightly.

Julius addressed her, "And what do we owe the pleasure?"

Annika fiddled her fingers nervously, her eyes visibly reluctant to meet her betrothed's. "I was hoping to steal you away, my prince. For just a moment."

Julius's jaw clenched. Likely no one had noticed, but Lilith did. She could read him like a book. Without so much as a glance in her direction, Julius rose and lent Annika his arm as they exited the cabin.

"I hope she is well. The first battle is always the worst." Odêus frowned after them, his curious stare frozen on the closed door, his glass of whiskey seemingly melded to his lips.

Lilith lifted her own glass and gulped the bitter liquor down. Questing out with Discernment, she cut out the conversation that resumed within the study and focused in on Julius and his future bride. She prayed he wouldn't sense her eavesdropping, but she couldn't help herself. Muddled were her thoughts regarding their situation, and she hoped Julius could clear it up for her. Maybe listening could help her understand him.

"We have a duty to our country, Julius." Annika's voice had regained its confidence. "We have a purpose to fulfill for the Gods. It is what They have always desired of us. I've been devoted to you over the years, even in your absence—"

"I have sworn to do right by you," Julius cut in, tone harsh, "and I will uphold my word. But you must accept that I will live on after you ascend to Elysium. You cannot be so petty as to deny me happiness in the future."

Annika gasped. "Julius, my love, I would never deny you your right to happiness. All the Gods know you deserve it. You are the hero prince, after all. I only aspire to please you."

Julius sighed. "Do you really want that, Annika? Why would you want to go your entire life without experiencing what I have with Lilith?"

What he has? Lilith snorted.

"Are you all right?" Prince Odêus asked from across the table, tugging Lilith back into the study with the other nobles and generals.

"Oh, I'm just fine." She waved him off, her face burning. He'd just assume it was the whiskey.

The conversation in the study continued. "So I stood there like the Darllen trunk I am and let him have it out. By the Gods, you've never seen a man so irate until…"

Lilith drew her mind away from the men around her and back out toward Julius and Annika.

"I want you, Julius," Annika said on a sultry note. "At the end of the day, we are friends. We have always been friends. I don't care about romance and love. I care about you, and I want to fulfill my rightful place at your side." She sounded genuine enough, but was that all she wanted? Power? Queendom?

"But you do not want me in the way that you should," Julius countered. "You want to be queen."

"Of course I do! I love our people," she defended, her conciliatory tone enough to make Lilith cringe. This woman knew how to get what she wanted. "This is the position for me. I've been working toward this my entire life."

Silence.

"What if you kept her?" she continued.

Kept her. Like Lilith was something to own. Some kind of belonging.

Julius did not entertain a response.

"In time," Annika said, "you will see that there is no choice. You must decide between this affair and your crown, your people. For you cannot have both." Her tone softened. "I don't mind you having a mistress, as long as the royal children are of my womb."

Lilith's insides churned. She would not *share* Julius. Not like that. Just the image of him—

"No. I will be devoted to my queen," Julius said. "That is nonnegotiable."

Lilith flinched. He was done with her. She flexed her jaw so hard, the roots of her teeth hurt, all just to resist the urge to run from the stifling cabin and wallop Julius in the hall.

What had he been thinking? That after six years Annika and her sycophant of a father would forget a marriage arrangement to a crown prince?

Annika heaved a dramatic sigh. "Then I suggest you keep your distance from her, love. It won't be easy, but it's the only way to bank such passion."

Again, silence.

Sounding exasperated, Annika exclaimed, "What were you thinking, my prince?"

"I don't know what to tell you," Julius admitted. "I was away for nearly six years. I thought my life was planned. Set. That I would rule, and my army would destroy Spiro. Then Lilith arrived and… I was caught off guard. I tried to fight it, but I failed. And now I want no one else." He heaved a troubled sigh. "But I am bound by duty and honor and, unless you release me, I cannot be with the woman I love."

Lilith's bottom lip quivered, but she bit down on it, the taste of iron suffusing her mouth. She was only listening with Discernment, for if she had allowed herself to *feel* them too, she would be in shambles.

She would also have been discovered by Julius.

"I don't know how to explain this to you," Julius continued. "I never meant for this to happen. I thought you'd move on in my absence. I thought a Divine woman would be enough to satisfy my parents. I thought Lilith could be my queen."

Waiting for Annika's response, every muscle in Lilith's body tensed with anticipation.

"I will be your queen," Annika said firmly. "Have your *Divine* woman once I am ashes and dust."

Lilith gulped down the last of her whiskey, letting the burn be an excuse for the tears that fell from the corners of her eyes.

The men around her laughed, slapping her on the back and filling her glass with more of the molten gold. She accepted it, and she tipped her glass back again and again to drown out the thoughts of the prince.

Whatever she had with Julius, despite how strong they both felt, it was gone now.

40

NOT FOR THE WEAK OF HEART

Blood pooled in runnels in the dirt, liquid ruby spilled from the throats of his comrades. Arduen sat at his fallen elder's side. Master Korhen had been eviscerated by Spiro's blade. The Great Divine had fled on the Winds of Isidore, both their Master's in hot pursuit.

Arduen muttered several quick prayers under his breath, followed by a litany of curses. With shaking hands he pulled Korhen's eyelids down forever. In a moment, the Divine would be a diamond in the void above.

Pull yourself together.

Arduen fought off the tears as he sang:

"Vàst vû fíng vuthé salídr stèle,

Forgée courcí teq víne.

Vàst qu Tsat wadnn unè pâte,

Teq duínn unè vledreè teq tísse."

He paused, breath hitched. More figures appeared on the horizon, but from his location, he couldn't glean whether they were beast or human. By the end of battle, how many of his family members would lay cold in the muck and gore?

"Vhedn säl uit qínn,

Teq vû svï vestinn unè pevër,

Vàst Quy cârre zî unsà Elysium funewër."

"Arduen..." Olga appeared behind him. She sheathed her gladius, dropping to her knees beside him as Master Korhen's body disintegrated into fragments, each of which floated up into the air toward Elysium.

He glanced over at her mournfully. "We must help Master Judeaus and Master Euclid," he said.

"We should retreat." Her voice trembled with trepidation, true fear.

"We cannot abandon them."

"We are not abandoning them," Olga said, a defensive note in her tone.

All the clues aligned. "Judeaus requested that you watch over me."

Olga gave a guilty grimace. "He asked me to get you out if this confrontation turned to folly."

Folly was putting this lightly. There were casualties, and there could be more. What was meant to be a civil conversation had resulted in elemental battle. It had resulted in carnage. Sure and true, a message had been delivered, but it wasn't the one they'd intended.

"I cannot leave him," Arduen said. "You must understand."

Sympathy and dread shone in her eyes, but she wouldn't yield, she'd drag him back to the Frourío herself. "We must leave," she insisted. "It is over." She expelled a beleaguered sigh and stood, glaring at the flashing light in the distance.

The fighting had begun.

"I'll go with you," Arduen ceded, "if that's truly what Judeaus wants." He rose to stand beside Olga. He looked down at her, noting the tremors that ran through her lithe frame. Guilt speared through him. "Go sing over Master Alisse," he said. "I'll sing for Master Mihal."

"All right."

Arduen watched as Olga traipsed toward Alisse's corpse. Once she lowered herself beside the prostrate woman, hand placed upon her still body, he released Aether. The dark haze shot from his palms, two streams twisting with one another, dancing as the fallen Divine coalesced, transcending into Stars. Olga cried out in response, but she must have known Arduen did not intend to hurt her. He guided the torrent's trajectory, and once it had reached its destination, he spread it, shaping the abyss into a dome. Protection.

"Stay," he said to her. "He can't hurt you in there."

Olga gaped at him incredulously, a mixture of pride and anger stealing over her features.

Without wasting another moment, Arduen set off toward his Master… and his brother. His feet couldn't carry him fast enough. As nerves took flight inside his gut, his legs tingled, muscles twitching, his movements erratic.

Ah, the merciful gift of adrenaline. Stymieing fear and silencing alarm.

It wasn't until he reached the battle that his heart sank to his intestines. Master Judeaus was locked in a ring of Fire, and Spiro's own Master was nothing more than a clump of charred limbs, the hardened Wind he'd used to shield himself was paltry in comparison to Spiro's might.

"Run, Arduen!" Judeaus roared over the tumult. But Arduen's feet were planted, the Earth having consumed them. He'd failed to notice until he couldn't move. He chanced a glance downward and his heart plummeted at the sight, confirming his suspicions.

"Run!" his Master repeated. "Arduen, ru—"

Arduen looked up, blinded by the blaze before him. He slumped to his knees, the strain on his calves and tendons enough to capsize him. One arm raised before his eyes, he prayed. His palms burned from the inferno, desecrating his Master.

"Judeaus!" Arduen bellowed. He couldn't save him.

The Fire bled out, dissipating like frozen breath on a winter's eve. Tears carved paths down his cheeks as his Master slumped onto his knees, then dropped face first into the dirt, the movements ungoverned.

Dead.

Spiro cackled, the sound maniacal, sending shivers raking down Arduen's spine.

Pull yourself together!

Arduen shook as Spiro turned to him, a smirk lighting up his face. The Great Divine held a ball of Xander's Fire above his outstretched palm, the light casting eerie shadows over his face. "My friend," Spiro said.

Arduen could not reply. He was done. Spiro had carved a permanent line of demarcation between himself and the Gods. Rogue. It was now Arduen's responsibility to end him. Spiro had never been blessed by Constantine. Aether could destroy him. Arduen was his weakness.

And yet, he couldn't summon a flicker of the element.

You are not my friend *was what he wanted to say, but when he opened his mouth to speak, his voice was elusive.*

"I'm sorry, Brother," Spiro said, now standing mere feet from him. "It had to be done. He wouldn't stand down. Neither of them would." He glanced toward the remains of his own Master.

Arduen choked down a sob. He shouldn't have come. Livëana had begged him not to. She'd cried as if he'd already been killed. His wife had claimed to know the repercussions of Philautia. He hadn't listened to her. Perhaps it was her inferior age or his faith that Spiro could never turn against them, not like this. But he'd left her behind, along with his boys. And now they would grow up without a father to guide them.

Arduen prepared to meet his end, blood thrumming through every crevice of his body, demanding awareness, alert.

His thoughts were reeling. Maddeningly so. Memories of him and Spiro flooded his mind. Fond moments of their brotherhood. Times of struggle when they'd refused to leave each other's side, stubborn and insistent. He'd always heard Philautia was abominable. It had the power to erase everything a person was, molding them into something other. A beast. Unlike other mental illnesses, it seemed impossible to cure. And so far, it had proven to be. Spiro was the prime example of the irredeemable.

"What have you done?" Arduen croaked.

Spiro stepped closer, his lips pursed in thought. Perhaps thoughts of compunction. Regret. Maybe even pity.

"This life is not for the weak of heart, my brother." Spiro splayed his arms, breathing deep, his eyes darting over the remnants of the massacre. For that's what this truly was. "I did what one must do when others stand in the way of their purpose." He dropped onto his haunches, cocked his head as his pale eyes assessed his friend. His brother. "Come with me, Arduen."

Arduen shook his head, eyes cinched shut. "I can't," he breathed. "Livë. My boys..."

"They can come with us," Spiro pressed. "They will live comfortably as we work for a better Empire." He inched closer, warmth creeping into his features once again. "If Livëana joins us, Zurí may change her mind." He sounded genuinely hopeful, like somehow despite his sickness, he was still in love.

"I cannot." I will not.

Voices sounded behind them, screams and cries from Arduen's surviving comrades.

The Great Divine stood tall, aware that it was time to fight or flee. "I'll come back for you," he said. "I'll come back for you, Brother."

Arduen only shook his head, his sight blurred by unshed tears.

Pull yourself together! End this now!

But he didn't. Spiro ceased his Fire—perhaps a final act of contrition—and the world went dark once again.

"Wake up, Brother," Spiro said. "Smell the scent of victory, the

scent of change. A new season is upon us. A season where the Divine will flourish."

⊚ ⽺ ⤳ ♏ ◊

"ARDUEN! WAKE UP!"

Arduen opened groggy eyes, wiping away the visions of Spiro's wanton blood frenzy. He had remained in the same chambers he'd shared with Lilith. The main bedroom had been emptied out, and he hadn't bothered to move there. The second chamber was more secluded, which was preferable given the circumstances. Solitude was rare these days.

"Arduen!"

With an irritated grunt, he rose. Olga's slight frame was visible through the stained-glass doors.

"I'm awake," he called to her.

The Oracle danced on her feet, sliding the door open and standing in the shadows. "I know it's late," she said apologetically.

Arduen wore nothing but his short under-breeches, which did little in preserving modesty. The sight of him wouldn't faze Olga. She'd administered to him on so many occasions, there likely wasn't a part of him she hadn't seen.

"What is it?" he asked.

She hesitated for a fraction of a second. He knew her well enough to catch it. "We have a situation on our hands."

He calcified. "What is it? A vision?"

"It's Lilith."

Spurred into action, he pulled a robe from the bedpost and wrapped it around himself, tying it at the waist. He crossed the room, pulling Olga toward the breakfast table. The moon was high and full, bathing the garden with its silver glow.

"What happened?" His tone was much harsher than he

intended, but this was Lilith. If she was in trouble, it would take weeks to get to her.

"Julius and Lilith have been attacked," Olga said. "The Ophïon were provoked as they crossed the Western Galatëa with a legion of Dalegonian warriors."

"So Julius succeeded…" Arduen mused.

"Arduen!" Olga swatted his arm. "They lost over four hundred men! Lilith was hit during battle, she was unconscious for a time… at least, that's how it appeared in the vision. When she awoke, Julius tended to her, but she was different."

"Different?"

"I can't describe it." Olga paced, hands tugging at her ashy mane. It fell in ringlets down her back. "Then They sent me clarity."

Arduen waved for her to elaborate, his frustration surmounting. He didn't have patience when it came to Lilith. He never should have let her go. He'd only allowed it because Kenora seemed more dangerous than traveling to a peaceful country, with the Crown Prince as her escort. He'd allowed it because he'd hoped that her presence would ensure the prince's return.

"Either Julius or Lilith have been blessed by Thëo," Olga said.

Without waiting for Olga's approval, Arduen sprinted from the room and down the hallway barefoot. He hadn't spoken to or seen Wren since the battle, since his noviciate was taken from him. Another casualty fated to be chewed and digested by the Great Divine. Wren deserved his time to mourn and mope…

But this could not wait. Not even for that.

Arduen didn't bother to knock. His hand wrapped around the metal handle and twisted, pushed, but the door did not give. Spitting out a litany of colorful curses, he banged on the door for Wren to rise.

"Arduen," Olga said from over his shoulder, "he hasn't risen in days. He barely eats. He does not speak."

"Wake up, Wren!" Arduen pounded his fist against the wood. "I know you hear me!"

"He has only ever let me in to bring his meals," Olga said. "Let me speak to him."

Arduen stood aside reluctantly, every muscle in his body poised to fight. If something happened to Lilith because she didn't have the knowledge to control her new gifts, Arduen would wring Wren's neck.

"Wren, sweetheart," Olga's honeyed voice rang out. "Please let us in. There's been an emergency, and we are in need of your intellect."

Arduen relaxed as footsteps sounded from within the chambers. The door swung inward, and a haggard version of Wren stood before them. He didn't open the door wide enough to grant them entrance, only enough to be seen and to allow conversation.

"Lilith or Julius has been blessed by Thëo," Olga said. "They fought with the Ophïon tonight... that tells me that they are a few days away from shore."

"There is not much damage they can produce at sea," Wren grumbled, easing the door shut.

Arduen braced a hand against the door, leaning his weight against it. Judging by Wren's appearance, he would not be capable of besting Arduen in fisticuffs.

"Wren, please," Arduen said. He hated asking Wren for anything, but he would drop to his knees for Lilith. "I think we both know which Divine was blessed. Go to her, please. You can sense the earth's shifts, you will know where to find her."

"She will be with Julius," Olga said. "At least, if Thëo blessed our Julius then they will be together and can confirm who it was."

Wren grunted.

"Please, Wren," Arduen said, pushing on the door for emphasis. "They will be somewhere along the northwestern coast."

"Not as north as the port, I do not suspect," Olga said.

"No." Arduen shook his head. "We advised them to dock somewhere closer to Utica—if they succeeded in securing a legion from Dalegonè, which Olga has been informed they did."

Wren disappeared for a moment, leaving the door ajar. Neither Olga nor Arduen felt inclined to enter. They stood in the corridor, listening to Wren's incessant grumblings. When the Divine emerged once again, he was dressed for travel, a leather pack slung over his shoulder, a cloak folded over his arm.

"I'll leave now," Wren said, then looked at Olga. "I will take Mountainslide. He is the swiftest and healthiest." He pushed past them into the hall. "I will also need provisions for two weeks, enough to feed two. I will get to Lilith and bring her back immediately. Julius can remain with his legion."

Olga paused, mouth gaping. "But what if it is Julius? You cannot take him from leadership."

Wren turned back to the Oracle, face grim. "I think we can both agree that it was not Julius who has been blessed."

"No risks, Wren," Arduen warned. "You bring her right back."

"She'll be fine," Wren grumbled over his shoulder. "That girl's got a spine coated in brass."

Arduen watched him go, wishing it were possible to shirk his duties and run to Lilith's side. But wants and needs were very different things, and he was all too accustomed to forfeiting his desires.

UNTRAMMELED

When they arrived at Augusta's western coast, Julius had approximated that they were a half day's travel from Utica on foot. Lilith hadn't waited for his approval. She'd packed up her possessions and was the first to disembark.

The beach was a disarray of soldiers reuniting with friends from the other ships. Tears were spilled at the discovery that some hadn't survived the attack by the Ophïon. Lilith had left as soon as she could possibly break away, the soldiers' grief overwhelming.

Today would be tough enough without sharing in their lament.

Skirting the Dunes, Lilith jumped at every sound, at every flicker of movement in her peripheries. She'd been walking with her hand outstretched before her, prepared to spew darts of Aether at the first sign of sand daemons. Julius had demolished one—the first she'd laid eyes on—with a single flash of Fire. Without a doubt, Constantine's element would prove just as fatal.

Utica appeared through the trees. The gray stone walls seemed smaller than they did when she'd last seen them. Lilith halted at the edge of the forest, lost in the mental turmoil that returning to her hometown summoned. The last time she'd walked into town, she was returning from her evening under the tempest that had dismantled her world.

With a shuddering breath, she traipsed toward the gates. The guards shot her curious glances, but they permitted her entry. She did not recognize either sentry, but the fact that their gazes followed her even after she passed through the gate told her that they recognized her. She couldn't relate to them on that front, for she had become a stranger to her own reflection.

It rattled her, the realization that the things she once thought defined her, never really had. She was a smith, but that was not all of Lilith Oak.

Lilith Achilles.

She was also a vassal of the Gods. A vessel of Their might. She was a daughter. A sister. A noviciate. A friend.

A lover.

So many identities wrapped into one unique carrier. She would be remiss to judge another so quickly, without enough information to form such conclusions. The thought unnerved her. Sometimes it was difficult to reconcile herself with the new Lilith, the Divine Lilith.

Avoiding the narrow street leading to her home, she wended her way through town. Almost immediately, she was overwhelmed by nostalgic scents, sights, and sounds. She drowned in them, wading through a current that longed to suck her down under. A current that once would have provided immeasurable comfort, she now considered disturbing.

The sky was overcast, a storm blanketing the town in darkness, menacingly threatening to dispel its contents. She welcomed the coverage from prying eyes. Between the meager light and her hood, no one was likely notice her presence, to recognize her. Today, she wanted only one townsman to notice her.

It was nearing harvest, and Jude was in his field as she'd predicted, kneeling amongst his crops. Lilith approached on silent feet, locked in an internal argument with herself.

She should stay.

No.

She should leave.

Before she could turn on her heels and retreat, Jude lifted his golden head and his eyes met hers.

He froze.

Naked confusion stole over his features. His eyebrows knitted together, eyes narrowing on her, long eyelashes fluttering in disbelief. He blinked several times, as if she were nothing but a figment of his imagination. How many times had he looked up from his work to see her standing before him, only to watch her vanish on second take, a wraith of his fiancée?

"Lilith." He spoke her name as if he'd forgotten how to pronounce it, as if he'd forgotten the sound of the two syllables.

Gods, he looked so much like Arduen.

She nodded once, as if a single motion could confirm that she was real.

The trowel dropped from his limp hand and Jude sprinted for her. She gasped as he threw his arms around her, cradling her head against his chest. Breathing in his familiar scent, her wariness and indecision receded.

Jude drew away, lifting her face in his hands. "It's really you," he breathed.

"Yes." She gave a wan smile.

Jude quickly sobered, his face falling. "What happened, my kyría? What took you so long to come back to me?" He looked as if he would lean in to kiss her, but hesitated. Confusion transitioned into stark realization, pain and anger. All of it.

And it was all deserved.

"I am Divine, Jude," she said. "That's why I had to leave." Her voice came out more insecure than she'd intended. "Constantine Anointed me several nights before the forge burnt down."

Jude's lips parted, but he didn't appear capable of forming a coherent response.

She pressed on. "I sent a letter to Larkin, but he had already been taken to the capital for interrogation." Her eyes were wide, pleading for his understanding. "And when I was escorted to the training facility—for my safety, as well as yours —I was not permitted to return to say goodbye."

"What an honor..." He stepped away as if she were some sacred relic that would be damned if touched. Scratching at his head, he walked away from her, his steps erratic as if lost in a daze.

"Jude. Are you all right?"

When he turned back to her, his face was rife with a confused mixture of grief and resentment. He had always been unvarnished, just like Arduen. Unafraid of emotion. Undeterred by suffering.

She hated how palpable his pain was, radiating off him in waves—a pain in which she was culpable. She hated the way he looked at her now, so fractured, and yet so unlike him. The way he used to look at her, when she was not but a dissenting young woman, she much preferred it to this.

"I didn't—"

"You abandoned me!"

"I had no choice, Jude!"

"You could have stayed!"

"The Gods would have killed me if I refused Them!"

Jude shook his head, tears spilling down his stubbled cheeks, his long blond hair falling over his shoulders in a tangled mess. Maybe it was a mistake to come here, she only managed to exacerbate his suffering.

She never wrote him, she realized. He deserved that much at least.

Jude succeeded in calming himself, his chest rising and falling visibly even at a distance. Her own frenetic heartbeat began to ease as she watched him grapple for a semblance of calm.

"You're here now," he said finally. "That's all that matters."

Lilith hesitated, spitting out the words with remorse. "I can't stay. I've come with a legion from Dalegonè. I must return to them anon."

His eyes narrowed into slits, as if she weren't the woman he'd grown up with, the woman he'd loved. "An army?"

"Dalegonè has sent aid to Emperor Obadïa," she said. "We suspect the Great Divine will attack the capital again soon. We must march to Kenora immediately. I am here to request provisions from Lord Alexaus before we depart."

Jude crossed his arms over his chest, sinewy lines deepening along his forearms. He'd grown since she left. Arduen would be proud. "You've come to formally end our engagement."

Swallowing past the lump in her throat, she said, "I did."

Jude straightened as if she'd struck him. She might as well have. He probably would have preferred a physical blow to the emotional one she'd just dealt. "I see."

Lilith started toward him, but he held up his hand to stop her. She halted. "Jude—"

"Don't. I understand." His voice was weighted by sorrow, and she could sense an undertone of betrayal. A flicker of shame singed her cheeks, and she bowed her head to hide the color from him. Having been spurned herself, well, it resuscitated all those emotions. The pang of bitterness. The bite of resentment. The burn of unrequited affection.

From her periphery she watched him lower his head. He heaved a sigh through his nostrils. He always did that when he was trying to reason with himself.

Arduen did it, too.

"Do you… understand?" she ventured, lifting her eyes to meet his.

Jude nodded, that same soft expression that used to make her feel at ease. At home. "You are Divine, so you're immortal, no?"

She confirmed this with a slight dip of her chin.

The mound of his throat bobbed once. "Then it would be cruel of me to expect you to hold fast to your promise. No one should have to watch their betrothed wither and die." His lips quivered, but he secured his composure. "I dreamed of this day since that fire, but I never imagined… *this*."

"I am so sorry, Jude." She truly was, but her purpose for coming here ran deeper than a simple farewell. Jude deserved to move forward with his life, untrammeled by her ghost.

He waved her off, his face abandoning gravitas, returning to a sliver of his usual geniality. "It's not your fault. I shouldn't be angry with you. After all, you must be as amazing as I've always known you to be if the Gods have chosen you to exact Their will upon Augusta."

Lilith smiled. If only he knew half of what she'd done since she left. She was the Kin-Slayer, for Kyril's sake.

"I always loved you, Jude Alanís."

"And I will always love you, Lilith Oak."

STORM CLOUDS BREWED OVERHEAD. LILITH SPRINTED TO REACH HER

second destination before the nebulous reached Utica, before she was caught in the gale. There was always the option to mold the firmament to her liking, but she didn't have much experience or energy left. She'd abandoned the idea of forcing the storm away anyway. Let it come. Let it cleanse the land.

And maybe her soul, too.

She shook off the emotions that reuniting with Jude had inflicted. How much more could she take?

The scent of honey cakes wafted through the air, her mouth salivating in response. Her mother used to make honey cakes once a week when her father would take the morning of the Seventh Day of the Gods off to spend sitting around the hearth with his family. Larkin would play cards with her whilst her parents would sit together on the rug, commentating and commending whoever won. When tension surmounted between her and Larkin, her father would always be the buffer between them.

The ache in which she missed them intensified as she meandered through town, her head downcast so as not to be recognized. Returning had ignited a sense of loss greater than any she'd known before. It wasn't a loss of a person or loved one, but of herself. She was an entirely different person now. The Gods had taken her in Their hands, made her new, and released her into Their world.

Time was moving so fast, she had difficulty keeping up. It flashed by her like a torrent, like the vortex of Water she'd created from the Ansti River. Yet less than a year had passed, and she'd died twice. The old Lilith was dead and gone.

Keeping her head downcast, her long hair a curtain shielding her face from the sight of passersby, she received little more than a few curious glances. None were prying. None seemed to recognize the mahogany hair.

Lord Alexaus's manor was at the far west side of town. The

austere gray building was nothing more than a large, imposing square. Guards sat atop the roof, watchful for beasts beyond the walls. They jumped to attention as her feet stepped onto the pathway leading to the door. They refrained from raising their crossbows, so Lilith ignored them.

Before she'd reached the door, it swung inward on its hinges, revealing the dark interior and Lord Alexaus standing in the shadows. The old lord was far frailer than she remembered him. His long white hair fell past his once rotund waist, and his beard hung even lower. His robes draped over fragile shoulders, indicative that he was not well.

"Greetings, Lilith."

She inclined her head reverently, trying desperately to conceal her pity as the old man erupted into a fit of coughs.

Leaning heavily on his cane, he asked, "What may I do for you, my kyría?"

"I've come from Xanthë with an army of five thousand." Lord Alexaus piqued up, but she continued with caution. "Crown Prince Julius of Dalegonè has led them here to aid in Augusta's fight against the Great Divine, but we are desperate for—"

"Provisions," the lord rasped.

"Yes," she confirmed warily.

Alexaus clicked his tongue thoughtfully. She waited patiently, her toes aching to tap.

"There is not much to give," he admitted with a rueful shrug, "but I will see what I can do. I can supply them with enough food, at least, to get them to Kenora. After that, I am afraid Emperor Obadïa will be responsible for outfitting them. I am assuming that's where you're headed?" He raised an unruly eyebrow.

Lilith nodded.

"Well then, I will have some of my servants travel to you

tomorrow morning. Can you describe to me where your lot have set up camp?"

A servant rushed out, parchment and quill in hand, and wrote down the directions Lilith recited for him.

"We will be there for a few days while some of the soldiers recover," she explained.

"Recovering?" he asked, rhetorical. "Was the voyage beleaguered?"

"We were attacked by the Ophïon." Lilith was reluctant to divulge any more information than that. "We lost an exorbitant amount of good men."

The parochial opinions in Utica did not favor the Ophïon. The sirens were mythical creatures to the townspeople. Lilith didn't want to set them on edge in her brief visit.

"Hmm…" The lord's grip tightened on his cane, the wood groaning under his weight. "Alas, it is inevitable that I must send what supplies we can sacrifice. Besides, it is an ill omen to refuse." He cast her a feeble smile.

Though it was not required, Lilith bowed. It was the least she could do. This was likely the last time she would ever see the man. "We are beholden to you, Lord Alexaus."

◌ ◌ ◌ ◌ ◌

THE SKY HAD DARKENED TREMENDOUSLY, AND SHE NEEDED TO return to camp before the storm hit. Oaks surrounded her, blocking out the harsh light of the sunset, already muted by storm clouds. The emerald leaves silhouetted against the tangerine sky slowed her progress, her eyes rapt with the sight.

Lilith inhaled deep, the nostalgic scent sending shivers down her spine. Or was that her mother's touch? She'd spent so many nights outside under this same canopy of leaves by her side. If only life were as simple as it had been then. If only her biggest worry was securing enough meat for the winter.

Lost in a world of memory, Lilith opened her mind, letting Discernment guide her to the army of Dalegonians. Her eyes wandered through the forest that had shaped her, had provided safety and shelter for so many years. She'd grown into herself in these woods. She'd found herself in these tangled boughs, the woman Constantine chose as His vassal.

As if sensing her Divinity, the trees seemed to part way for her, guiding her path back to camp. Their trunks grumbled and melted as she approached, the ground crumpling at their base, their roots becoming limbs to walk.

Lilith stopped dead and shook her head, blinking in bewilderment.

By the Gods, she really was sleep-deprived.

She inhaled and sighed deeply, dispelling all tension from her muscles. The entities were closer now. It wouldn't be much longer, and she'd be able to rest her head and recover.

As she stepped forward again, the trees resumed their dance, the earth bellowed its agitation with a seismic grumble.

She felt it then. Drainage. As if she'd been wielding Aether. Her eyes blew wide as she stared down at her palms. Gravity lost control at the realization: she'd been blessed yet again.

Lilith could wield Thëo's Earth.

BETWEEN ONE AND MANY

The Crown Prince's tent was as crowded as Lilith had predicted it would be. The Dalegonian legionnaires set up camp inside the coverage of the trees, keeping close to the Anstï.

The previous evening Lilith had retired upon her arrival. One of Julius's esteemed generals escorted her to her assigned tent, nestled amongst the oaks. Julius had been far too generous. Not only was the tent larger than the other soldiers', but her bedsheets were of the finest Dalegonian spider silk, the cushion of the pallet thicker than her thigh. Normally, she'd be celebrating the luxury, especially during travel, but her return to Utica had left her with the urge to bathe in creosote. She would have much preferred sleeping on the ground, and so she did.

As the sun rose above the trees, she donned her plated leather suit, Constance at her hip. The soldiers paid her little heed as she strode through camp, Julius's pavilion peeking above the other tents. She ignored the churning of her stomach as she approached, her heart heavier now that she'd officially broken ties with Jude.

Pushing aside the flaps of the pavilion, Lilith entered. She ignored the shrewd gazes of Julius's retinues as she announced, "Servant's from Utica should be arriving at any moment with enough provisions to last until your arrival in Kenora."

"Wonderful!" Julius exclaimed, clapping his hands together and grinding his palms. The other generals seemed contented with the information as well, though they deigned not to direct their contentedness at her.

"I must warn you that Utica is a town, not a city," she continued. "There are limitations to their generosity. I am fairly certain what they donate will be mostly barley mush and dried quail, but you will need to instil rations. You cannot afford to be gluttonous, lest you spend days starving before you reach the capital." She didn't mean to scold, nor to come across as condescending, but she worried for the success of Julius's mission, despite that his success meant his betrothal to another.

Lilith leveled her gaze on the prince, feigning ignorance of the glares she was receiving from several of the dignitaries. What vitriol existed between them, she knew not. Perhaps they did not fancy Augustans. Perhaps they interpreted her relationship with Julius as a threat to his future reign. Or perhaps they were allied to Annika's father.

"Don't you mean, 'we'?" Julius tilted his head, his gemstone eyes narrowing.

Lilith bit her lip uneasily, shifting on her feet. She'd prefer to have this conversation alone, without the censorious looks directed her way. "Could we talk in private, Prince?" she asked, her tone depicting none of the angst roiling beneath her skin. Would the earth shoot up around them if she failed to control her emotions? She desperately needed to hone these new gifts before it became her demise.

"Of course." Julius signaled authoritatively to the exit of his pavilion. Each Dalegonian official bowed in respect to their future king and departed without so much as a nod in her direction.

"What is it?" Julius approached, placing a warm hand on her arm.

Shying away from his touch, she said, "I must leave you." She kept her voice low and hushed in the odd chance that one of the generals eavesdropped.

The prince's lips parted in shock.

"There are certain situations that I must deal with," she pressed.

"We will deal with everything together," he said, his strong demeanor dissolving.

"There are some things we cannot do together," she said. "Not anymore."

His brows met in a fierce, dark line. "What is that supposed to mean?"

"You failed to include me in your ulterior plan to acquire an *army*."

Julius pinched the bridge of his nose, grimacing. "I didn't want to stress you. I brought you to Xanthë to relax and enjoy yourself."

"Some getaway," she said under her breath. The caustic remark earned her an exasperated sigh in response.

"Lilith, I've been meaning to talk to you about—"

"I don't want to talk about it," she cut him off. "It's over, Julius. That much I understand."

He flinched at her tone.

"I also realize," she added softly, "it is for the love of your country, and the responsibility of rulership must supersede all other desires."

"I only want…"

Lilith watched, hopeful, as the words writhed and died on his tongue. Placing a finger over her lips, she shook her head, her heart cracking as his eyes brimmed with unshed tears. "I must go alone, Julius," she said. "I must figure this out for myself. I will remain perceptive. I will listen for unrest, and I will be at your side at the first sign of trouble. I promise." She nearly choked on the words. "But I must go." She offered him a meek smile, the slightest assurance that things would be fine.

"But why? I don't understand." He leaned back against the desk, careless of the maps and quills, the ink pots scattering across the surface.

"I've relied too heavily upon you and Arduen," she said. "I need to figure some things out for myself. I need to learn to be all right alone." *And to Master a new element.*

Julius comported himself. "I am a Master, Lil. I cannot allow you to leave on your own. You are a noviciate. Not a fully-fledged Divine. Doubly blessed or not."

Triply blessed.

"Arduen will understand," she argued. "I have survived many nights alone in these woods. I need no assistance."

Placing himself between her and the only exit, he paced, his hands tugging mercilessly at his raven locks. "You're leaving my care to wander the earth like a vagabond?"

"Julius…" she groaned. She wanted to comfort him, but the only way she knew how would cross boundaries that they'd been forced to implement. "I will not allow my training to waver in stagnation, to flag as I have so flippantly allowed."

His shoulders sagged at that. "We will designate a few hours a day to your training. I will oversee it myself. We will distance ourselves from the legion for their safety."

"But we are traveling, Julius. That will not be easy."

"No, but we will make it work," he said resolutely. "I will

hand over authority to my uncle whilst we are gone. We will meet up with them when our session is complete."

This plan would not do, she knew that, for Lilith did not wish to reveal the truth behind her sudden need for distance and solitude. One mistake and she could kill the entire legion! But she had to be honest with herself at the very least, that was not the entire reason she wanted to distance herself from camp.

"You'll be all right without me," she said in a dulcet tone. "You have Annika, and your uncle."

"You think I want Annika over you?" Julius said, his voice strained and sour, his gaze piercing. "Is that what this is about?"

"I think you chose your *country* over me," she said in an attempt to mollify. "How can I ever resent you for that? I am one, and they are many."

Julius paused, mouth agape.

"I have suffered through many losses, Julius. One more is not going to break me." He stepped forward but she held up a hand to stop him. "We each have our designated duties, and unfortunately, we've reached a fork in the road. I will be more than fine on my own. My welfare need not be a concern of yours."

"Lilith," he all but choked on her name, "I cannot—will not —allow you to leave."

She ignored him. "Perhaps in fifty, sixty years we will find each other again. Assuming we aren't entirely different people."

"I don't want to get to know you again." He held her by the shoulders now, his gaze troubled and imploring. "I may die tomorrow, and I want to go knowing you are mine." That would be selfish, for many reasons, but Lilith bit her tongue.

"Unfortunately, being selfish is below our station."

As was his way, always doing what surprised her, the prince dropped to his knees.

"Julius…"

"Lilith," he said, hands gripping the backs of her thighs, "I really messed this up. I fucked this all up."

She averted her eyes, and wiping a hand over her face, she groaned, "Julius!"

"Stay with me," he begged. "Stay with me and we will sort this out. I never meant to hurt you. I never meant—"

"You were always meant to be with her," she countered.

He gave a vehement shake of his head. Rising to stand before her, his hands moved to grip her shoulders. "But I do not feel that way for her. I accepted to marry Annika for the better of my country and the Fawkes dynasty, but I never anticipated I'd fall for anyone. Ever. Duty had always superseded any of my own desires… until I met you."

"Julius," she said again, a warning lacing her tone.

"There is no other woman I want at my side. I've always wanted one queen, and I want that queen to be you."

In his desperation to get closer, he pushed her back onto the desk, his lips claiming hers. She knew better than to engage in this manner of intimacy, but the insistence with which he touched her was too passionate to resist. She leaned back against the wood, splaying her arms to clear the desk; the maps, the quills, the scrolls, they all fell, the ink bottles painting the grass black.

His mouth crashed over hers almost hard enough to hurt, plundering and desperate. The sharp stubble of his jaw was enough to light a spark, and in response, Xander's Fire ignited in her veins. His hands moved in their frenzy, searching for her flesh, his lips painting sensations across her skin. She arched into him, desperate for more, for everything, his body stiff against hers in want. His fingers dug into her backside, but they did not wander, they did not roam like she wanted them to.

Lilith couldn't deny that she loved him. It did not matter whether he was Dalegonè's most destitute subject or the heir to the damned throne, she loved him despite status. And if she were to be denied a place at his side, she wanted one last moment to experience this nature of union.

Abandoning all reason, she bit down on his bottom lip, then she tore his tunic up over his head, baring his flesh to her. Julius tossed the garment aside, his deft hands making quick work divesting her of her own. With her suit wrapped around her ankles, she parted her legs in silent ascent and he took her.

Nothing, and somehow, everything between them.

With their chests pressed together, she could feel his heartbeat against her own. It was as if this act alone could bind two people together. Spiritually. Indefinitely. And she clung to him as if his body was the essence of all life, as if he moved to sustain her.

This was stolen time. She knew as much.

Just one last time…

Julius buried his face in the crook of her neck, his pants tickling her skin, sending shivers through her entire body. Her eyes locked on his chest, the rise and fall of his breathing, the flexing of muscles with every thrust.

"Gods, Julius." She nibbled at his earlobe, nails digging into his shoulders as he sped up.

Don't let me go…

The flaps of the pavilion's entrance swished.

Julius jumped away from her immediately. His eyes glazed, lips swollen. He half-turned to their intruder, his chest rising and falling in audible—and highly visible—increments.

Prince Odêus stood in the entryway, his flushed face downcast to offer them what little privacy he could. He looked as if he were the one caught in flagrante.

Lilith pulled up her suit, though Julius stood protectively before her, blocking his uncle's view. "I'll take my leave now," she said to him, her voice still breathless. He turned to protest but she cast him a pointed look and marched to the exit, skirting politely around Prince Odêus as she did.

The familiar pang of loss met her as she entered the fresh air. She'd lost so much already, another wasn't daunting. At least, not like this. No longer was it insurmountable, the road of grief, the mountain of sorrow. She would recover and adapt. To love was to accept the accompaniment of grief, for the two were entwined; one could not exist without the other. Lilith had spent a quarter of her life in despair, suffocating beneath the vise-like grip of grief. That loss had stifled her growth, and Arduen had helped her let go.

And so, once again, she did.

Julius would remain her friend. For he would return to Dalegonè to be crowned and espoused to Annika. And then they would have an entire sea to drown their passion, to douse the flame that kindled. But somehow Lilith didn't think it would ever be enough.

Perhaps there were no happy endings for a love forged in the crucible of carnage.

TYPHON AND THE BOOR

The torches surrounding the Champion's Ring seemed to burn brighter for Typhon as he ascended the platform, arms raised high as his fellow beasts screamed his praises. Their adulation was tumultuous, deafening; their stomps shaking loose shale from the cavernous ceiling.

Rhéa was dragged from the infirmary by Xavier. He'd claimed she needed to bear witness to Typhon's match. She obliged, if only because the joints of her fingers ached with the power of Dracoladen, the High Enchantress's Guiding Star.

The crowd around the Champion's Ring was rowdy. Typhon's eyes gleamed with bloodlust, or lack thereof since the beast rarely spilled blood. Never enough to kill, anyway.

"He has yet to lose," Rhéa observed.

Across the platform, Typhon's opponent assumed his defensive stance. The beast was nearly Typhon's size—a rarity—but he quivered in fear, the nervous vibrations of his muscles visible even at a distance. Rhéa almost pitied the beast. Typhon wouldn't kill him, would he? Every bulging muscle in Typhon's oil-slicked body advocated for his brutality, the savage beast he was created to be.

The arena was packed full of beasts. Every one of Spiro's minions abandoned their posts to observe the match, their stench cloying with the scent of stale air. Rhéa grimaced. Stars, they were putrid creatures housed in an equally squalid domain.

Typhon stood tall and mighty, even in a hunched stance. The bend of his knees was reverse that of a human's, his feet wide and withered, thin sheets of webbing connecting his toes. The beast's arms and face were his only human assets. The swells of his barrel chest were so large, they threatened to tear through his hide. His physique alone brooked no opposition, for who could dream of laying waste to a creature such as Typhon?

Apparently, many.

Combatants lined up around the Champion's Ring, dancing on angsty feet, awaiting their turn to fight the consummate beast. They couldn't possess more than feces for brains. Even if Typhon never landed a fatal blow, that didn't mean his opponents never died as a result of their bout against him. Rhéa had had many beasts go limp in her chair. A waste of her precious magic and meager resources.

Rhéa's eyes scanned the cavern, taking in the sea of bobbing cretins, their chitinous skin making a disturbing *shushing* noise. How had she never realized it before? The color of the silt, the hewn slate, the Empire's inability to locate the lair… the location made perfect sense. Yet Rhéa was not conscious when she was transported from the capital to Spiro, and when she'd awoken and discovered her new role to serve, the miniscule probability of escape doused any curiosity as to her exact location.

Typhon's opponent squared his shoulders, bellowing to the

ceiling, his horns curling above his head. When Rhéa had first glimpsed the brute, she'd thought his horns to be intimidating. But now that she'd seen him fight, as impressive as he may be, his horns had become his weakness. Many a smaller beast had hopped onto his back via the leverage the horns offered. Unless he could discover how to skewer his opponents with them, they were of little advantage.

"This is the Boor," Xavier said, and indicated Typhon's adversary. "He's usually mouthier than this, but I think he's a bit tongue-tied in the presence of the King. Unwieldy as he may be, I don't think he can conquer Typhon."

The Boor moved first, daring to make the first assault. He charged at Typhon, sprinting toward a wall of pure stone. He held a large club in one hand, and his second weapon appeared to be a lasso tied around his waist. He struck with the club, rising on his toes to smash Typhon over the skull.

The surrounding beasts' pitiless eyes blew wide as the first blow landed. The King took it well, barely flinching, he didn't surrender even an inch of ground.

Typhon grinned, the expression gentle, benign. Rhéa smirked. The King's demeanor was so at odds with the rest of his ilk.

The Boor stepped away, his grimace disintegrating into a scowl, for his first assault had barely summoned a twitch from Typhon. His club dropped to his side as he resumed his defensive stance several feet from his enemy, elongated cuspids digging into his bottom lip.

"How long have you known?" Rhéa asked.

In his attempt to remain inconspicuous, Xavier did not turn toward her. "About Thébés?"

"Yes."

Typhon charged at his adversary, only to stop short and wheel away, a chuckle heaving his broad shoulders. The crowd echoed his mirth, screaming accolades for him and thus, eulogies for the Boor.

"For a few months now," Xavier said. "I've earned a great deal of trust as of late. Spiro introduced me. I think he did it as a threat. Step out of line again and he will sic the Sorcerer on me."

A tremor ran through Rhéa's body at the mention of the title.

"Don't worry." Xavier cast a furtive glance over his shoulder. "No one in here has half the brain to repeat what we're saying. They can only fuck and fight."

Rhéa released a chest-caving breath.

Xavier nudged her, the action affectionate. "I'm scared, too."

As they should be. With a Sorcerer on his side, Spiro might as well be a God.

There will be a sixth God.

Those words had echoed in her mind since she'd first heard them twenty-five years ago.

"But what is a Sorcerer?" Xavier asked, his voice as hushed as he could manage whilst remaining discernible. "How is he any different from you?"

Rhéa didn't answer straight away. She was too aware of Spiro's eyes panning over the cavern, frequently pausing on her.

"A Sorcerer is a mage of extreme caliber," she finally said. "There isn't much he cannot do. One often holds a particular affinity in the realm of necromancy." She gestured with her hands to the creatures surrounding them. "Hence, the beasts."

"So a Sorcerer is just a strong mage?"

"No," she said. "A Sorcerer is the product of two mages' love. An Enchantress and a Magí."

Xavier's eyebrows rose but he did not speak, nor did he

display any other reaction, his eyes locked on the match before them.

The Boor barrelled toward Typhon, his roar setting the hairs of her arms on end. Typhon didn't move this time. He let his opponent throw his weight against him, and he barely flinched.

"That is why," Rhéa pressed on, "it is forbidden for an Enchantress to mate with a Magí."

In blatant frustration, the Boor bellowed and walloped against Typhon's swelled chest. The King bore no weapons, for he needn't any. His arms were longer than any of the swords, his talons sharper.

"I see…" Xavier mused. "And I wonder how Spiro has aligned with one." He said this so dryly, Rhéa had half a mind to suspect Xavier knew exactly how, but she wouldn't press him to divulge.

"And how he has earned such reverence from one as superior as a Sorcerer," she said.

He frowned, the lines on his brow deepening. Still he did not address her directly. "Thébés is dense and loyal to a fault. He would follow Spiro to the ends of the world."

Typhon puffed out his chest, sending the Boor skittering back in fright, yellow eyes wide with fear, a sight Rhéa had rarely indulged in.

The King pounded fists against his chest and howled to the ceiling. A war cry, urging the Boor into the offensive, but his opponent did not heed his King's concessions. What made Typhon so at odds with his contemporaries was his lack of bloodlust. The beast didn't take lives, he played with them.

Finally, the great beast stomped toward his opponent, his reversed knees cringeworthy. The Boor ran for his escape, but Typhon's arms were longer than he was fast. Typhon secured one giant hand around the Boor's neck, pressuring just the right nerve, and his club fumbled from his grip.

The crowd erupted. The ground beneath Rhéa's feet trembled.

Typhon lifted his prey into the air, legs dangling, dancing, desperate to make bone-crunching contact with his enemy. But the King was smarter, a beast of size *and* intelligence—the Boor's feet didn't come within an inch of Typhon's exposed flesh.

"When I discovered him," Rhéa said, her tone quiet and somber, "I saw a baby... or at least, what resembled a baby." Her breath shook. "Its screeching still keeps me up at night."

Xavier didn't respond, likely to protect them both from prying ears. Spiro wasn't entirely stupid, he'd have ears just about everywhere, regardless of the competence of the brain between them.

The King waltzed around the Champion's Ring in a grand display of victory. The Boor's legs danced in the air, his arms gripping Typhon's wrist, tugging relentlessly.

"As you mentioned, every Sorcerer's power varies," Xavier said through gritted teeth. "Thébés has excelled at necromancy. Each beast that survives a battle is expected to return with spoils; a lock of hair, a toe, a fingernail. One beast even returned with a man's—"

Rhéa held up her hand to silence him. She didn't need details.

"Right," Xavier cleared his throat, "well now you know. He only needs one piece of the deceased's body to create a whole new beast. Half the mind of a human, or less, but twice the strength and stamina."

A boom sounded throughout the arena as Typhon slammed the Boor into the bloody ground. The Champion's Ring saw the most bloodshed, the most death. The ground was always sticky with viscera, the dirt resembling crimson clay. Thankfully, the Enchantress wasn't the faithful servant responsible for cleansing the arena of detritus at the end of a long day of brawls.

"That was a human babe?" Rhéa nearly whispered, dread coiling in her gut.

"No. It was a beastly babe," Xavier amended.

Rhéa suppressed a shiver. And here she'd thought the beasts' ability to reproduce so quickly was simply natural fecundity. She had been terribly mistaken in that assumption.

Returning her attention to the Champion's Ring, she watched Typhon parade around with raised fists. Usually, the matches against Typhon ended there, with a few broken bones and gashes, no additional deluge to augment the bloodbath that became of the platform.

But the Boor was an ambitious one, and he would not go down so easily.

"I'm treading on thin ice," Rhéa muttered.

Xavier looked at her askance.

Typhon blocked another attack from the disoriented Boor. With a chuckle, he pushed his opponent away, barely flexing a muscle to do so. His entire hand consumed the Boor's face as the Boor pushed toward him, attempting to impale Typhon with his horns.

Rhéa heaved a fervent sigh. "Thébés knows what I am. He knows that I know what he is. The true nature of his being. A fool he would be to assume I don't resent his existence. His seeking me out is inexorable."

The King released his hold on the Boor, grasping his adversary by the horns, and thrust him to the ground. A cloud of dust blew up around them. The Boor didn't move, he didn't twitch, as Typhon towered over him.

"Do you have any idea who his mother is?" Xavier asked absentmindedly.

"A vague idea… yes." Ophelía monitored births amongst

the Enchantresses of the Marsh in her quest to keep Sorcerers existences strictly nominal. But there was always a chance, as with Irís, an unknowing Enchantress beds a Magí. True, it was rare, but it wasn't impossible.

"Xavier…"

He turned to her expectantly, forgetting to remain covert.

"He is the reason for the fire… not Spiro," Rhéa ventured. "Spiro is no god, he cannot bless. But he can give you magic, through Thébés."

Her friend dropped his gaze, his expression somber. "Yes. Spiro can only grant Isidore's Wind, and how he manages such a feat as that, is unclear to me. Perhaps he is truly so favored by the Gods that he is ascending to join their ranks. Other than that, whatever elemental blessings or abilities he grants originate from Thébés."

Typhon exited the Champion's Ring, an expression of idyllic triumph upon his ghoulish face, golden eyes ablaze with delight. The beasts lined up, eagerly awaiting their chance to take on the King. They bowed their heads in deference as Typhon sauntered to the exit. Several of Spiro's beastly generals flocked to engage in heated contention with the *King*.

"Another thing," she ventured, "Felix?"

"Is Spiro's natural son," he finished for her.

"Who was his mother?"

Xavier turned away, but not before she saw the flash of pain.

Rhéa knew not to press, and so she gave her friend a departing touch and made to leave.

"I wasn't going to tell you this," Xavier said, stalling her leave. "When I was with Larkin at the Frourío, Thébés requested that I return with a lock of his hair, should the battle go south."

"What?" Rhéa gasped, spinning on him. "You didn't!"

His expression was hesitant, plaintive.

"Tell me you didn't," she whined.

Xavier averted his gaze, shame falling over his features like a veil. "I did," he admitted. "Honestly, I did not know why he'd asked. He said it was for Larkin's own good. So, as his friend, I obliged."

The Enchantress scanned every beast in the cavern for any likeness of her deceased son. "You think he is one of these beasts?"

Xavier nodded gravely. "I think Typhon is Larkin Oak."

44

I SEE ONLY DARKNESS

Lilith walked in a semi-aimless torpor, stopping only to survey her surroundings, to gauge her trajectory. She needed to put enough distance between her and the camp to ensure that none of the soldiers would notice her training. And altruistically, that none of them should mysteriously disappear as a result of her naïveté.

The north was the safest bet for a secluded environment; the oaks were slightly less dense there, offering opportunities for open space, best for elemental training. The last thing she needed was to be crushed by the thick mast of her namesake.

Settling in a small clearing, Lilith seated herself in the tall grass to ponder her new ability. Waving her hand above the hairs of the earth, she commanded the strands to dance for her. They obeyed, just as Water did when she played with rain droplets on the leaves. She'd taunt Julius, halting them inches above his shining raven mane. His laugh echoed in her mind, bringing a pained smile to her face. Had their coupling been a mistake? She forced the memory from her mind.

For Xander's sake, focus!

Closing her eyes, she listened to her emotions, most of which were still muddled and sour, thanks to the prince. He was probably feeling the same, if his brief bout of passion was any indication. But Julius had a legion of soldiers to care for; love was—and should be—the last thing on his mind.

And hers as well.

Focus!

Perhaps they were on divergent paths, internal and external, and they would never collide in the way she wished they could. It was time to stop fighting and let him go. There would be no future if Spiro became Emperor, and therefore, love must be cast aside until the Great Divine's campaign was thwarted.

She would get over Julius. The sea dividing them would make it easier to repress their feelings. In time, they could just be comrades again, when the world called for the Gods' champions.

Focus!

Lilith surveyed the land, the extent of her current situation pressing down on her, a hefty weight she knew not how to bear on her own. The complexities of each gift necessitated years of formal instruction, and yet she was imprudent enough to believe she could master it on her own.

What a foolish way to meet my end, she thought bitterly, surprising herself by how little she feared the risk, the repercussions.

Unfortunately, spending so many years grieving her parents had left her with an inherent flaw: a pestering self-doubt and a foolhardy determination to do just about everything on her own.

She could return to Julius, beg him for help, admit that she'd been harboring sensitive information. He wouldn't be pleased. He was a Master, and she was under his guidance. But the option of returning held little appeal. Julius had more than enough to handle, and she would bury herself alive before endangering him.

And right now, she was dangerous.

Bloody Hades! Focus, woman!

Steeling herself, Lilith stood, shaking off fatigue's clutch. If she wanted to master Earth *Masterless*, she'd need to go at it withholding nothing. The only way to get comfortable was to jump right in. Zurí had schooled her in this manner, yet Arduen had not. The difference being that Constantine's Aether came from within, if she expelled too much, she would certainly die. Whereas with Kyril's Water, she'd have only the amount she was given. Thëo's Earth had to be similar, though there was an abundance of it surrounding her, which left the infallible parts of her unsettled.

The land surrounding her was shapeless, bland, like the Gods had grown lazy by the time They set Their sights on birthing this blotch of Augusta. The flat plain could use some creativity, some furnishing. It was the perfect canvas to set her new Divine gifts to.

With her consciousness open, stretching out to the creatures around her, she began to mold the Earth. Instead of closing her eyes as she did with Kyril's Water, Lilith set her face into a moue of concentration, muscles rigid, her entire being willing the Earth to rise.

Nothing happened.

This was stupid. She sang a litany of expletives through gritted teeth. She should have told Julius. He wouldn't have been able to train her thoroughly, but he would likely have had some information about wielding Earth. He was closer to Wren than she'd ever been. Felix, too. But it was too late to turn back to him.

It would be wisest then to start small, she thought. Test

herself and see exactly how much strength and endurance Thëo had gifted her.

Focusing on a slight patch of Earth, Lilith willed it to rise. The ground trembled slightly as it obeyed, the grass parting, brown dirt spilling from the gashes. Lilith whooped, her excitement causing the Earth to rise faster. She ceased her control—much the same way she would when wielding Water—then she stood back to examine her work.

A formidable knoll was before her, rising to her hips. She'd succeeded. No one and nothing had been harmed. But how would this be of use in battle? Sure, she could throw her enemies off-balance whilst she slashed at them with Constance or blasted them with an arrow of Aether, but could she do it fast enough to take them by surprise? Certainly not. Arduen had been fast, with preternatural strength, and Spiro had engulfed his foot with Earth faster still. There was no possibility that she would excel with that much speed. She'd have to be smarter than that.

Sucking a deep breath into her lungs, she braced herself and *willed*. The Earth grumbled in response as several knolls rose at once. Just like the first, the grass cracked, dirt rolling free, spilling like blood. Unlike Aether, she felt no different, no decline in energy.

More.

Lilith roared in triumph as several additional mounds escalated. *This is addictive!* she thought, her skin prickling with fervor. The Earth was hers to shape now.

The brief resurgence of hope was too transient to spawn a lasting effect, and Lilith was left feeling far more destitute than before. When she released her hold, fatigue finally overwhelmed her. She dropped to her knees, her chest heaving.

Wielding Earth *did* have its drawbacks. So it was, wielding all elements required a tithe.

When Spiro had commanded the dirt to trap Arduen's feet, no matter how much Wren or Felix tried to free him, Spiro's grip was stronger, even as he retreated.

At this rate, she didn't stand a chance.

Lilith allowed herself a moment to rest. She certainly wasn't drained as she had been when wielding Aether, but her ineptitude was a stab at her confidence.

She needed to gain speed.

Rising again, she stretched her muscles in preparation. Amending her past mistakes, she focused on a smaller section, willing the ground to rise faster. A knoll rose higher than its predecessor.

Blessed Thëo, she'd done it!

Unwilling to relinquish her hold on the power, Lilith continued to will the knoll to rise. Higher. Higher. If she could raise mountains, no one could stop her. But she didn't know her limits. If she worked too much, released her hold, would she drop dead when her energy was finally traded for the work she'd done?

She balked, shutting down. This gift was more unpredictable, wilder than Water. Less tameable than Aether. Cursing herself, she kicked at the ground, her legs trembling from exertion, the rounded sole of her boot making a hoofprint in the dirt.

She missed Arduen. Her Master had always been the one to pull her back from the brink. Time and time again, he would coerce her mind to see reason, to think incisively. What would become of her without him?

Lilith berated herself. Why hadn't she paid attention to Felix's lessons? She couldn't recall an instance where he'd trained with his element. Wren had always taken him far away from the Frourío to perform elemental training. And why was she so stubborn? She should have asked Felix what his training was like. He'd always shown interest in her element.

Now your self-centered nature will be the death of you.

Felix was gone. The everlasting, resilient, jovial noviciate was suffering in Spiro's clutch. He'd likely already taken the Blood Oath. He was as good as dead if he had.

Lilith was as good as dead too if she didn't get this new gift under control. *Thëo, guide me!* she beseeched the God, but the air didn't so much as stir in response.

"Why me?" she asked the sky. Her sojourn in Xanthë must have proven something to the Gods, for why else would Thëo bless her? Why now?

With Water, she could drain the world. With Earth, she could shape it. And with Aether, she could raze it. She could control the sky, the ground, the in-between. Lilith marveled at the limitless possibilities of their unification, and of the devastating results. She paled to think the Gods deemed her worthy of possessing such power.

Perhaps They know you're useless with it!

Lilith drained her waterskin in one gulp. This training had sucked all the sustenance from her limbs. If she wished to continue, she'd need more water. And food. The walk back to the Ansti would take far too long, an hour at least, and time was of the essence. Julius wouldn't keep his soldiers situated for more than a couple of days. Long enough to gather supplies and recover from the attack at sea.

Regretfully, she sauntered back to the trees, dragging her soles in the long grass. The trees contained enough Water. It had rained the night before, so she knew they would be well-nourished, they could afford to share.

Lilith sat with her back propped against the base of an oak, her waterskin open before her. She searched for Kyril's Water with her mind. The Ansti was too far away to float the Water to her from the river, but there was a considerable amount contained within the trees' trunks. She leached Water from them and it seeped from the bark like sap. Once it made contact with the air, she floated it into her waterskins, filling them completely. The task took nearly half an hour. She'd moved on several occasions, afraid to take too much from a single tree, killing the wildlife in her wake. If she left a trail of desiccation, it would be a banner revealing her location to any nearby beasts.

Returning to her training location, Lilith sat down and drank, replenishing herself. She didn't have much energy left, she'd have to take a break or retire for the evening soon. The sun was low upon the western horizon, the orange glow warming her back. The late-summer evenings had become cold, and it would be a long night under the stars, without the prince's embrace to warm her.

Perhaps this was all a futile prospect. At the end of the day, she'd still amount to little, her strength wielding these elements would remain inadequate. She'd come close once, striking Spiro with a bolt of Aether. Would she get lucky enough to do it again? Another battle could be months off, but without the proper guidance, any attempt at taking on the Great Divine would be utterly asinine.

The sun plunged over the world's edge, relinquishing power to the darkness.

The darkness has become my safe place. The only place I can find repose. The only place I can truly hide.

Lilith sighed.

Tatiana bit the insides of her cheeks, her eyebrows knitting together. "I see only darkness." When Lilith's expression morphed to despair, she added, "But the dark isn't always bad. It does not always equate ill fortune."

Lilith wavered, uncertain to press. "What do you think it means for me?"

"I do not know," Tatiana said. "I see the dark, but it does not seem foreboding. It does not emit that treacherous feeling so often associated with shadows." She looked out toward the field again. "For you, it feels welcoming."

Resigned, Lilith turned back to the trees and set up camp. She'd taken enough jerky to last her a day, after that, she'd have to hunt. A prospect that strangely enticed her.

As she began to settle in for the evening, the ground beneath her rattled. She fell forward onto her knees, her hands rising just in time to shield her face.

Was she losing control?

She glanced over her shoulder. The field was rising like a swell, redolent of the tsunami she'd summoned when Kyril had Anointed her. Lilith cried out for Arduen. For Julius. Maybe they'd sense her peril, but they'd never reach her. She bolted. If the swell of Earth followed her there, the trees would only make the assault more perilous.

"Lilith!" a deep voice boomed.

The ground stilled beneath her and she crumbled in relief, gulping down air as if it were water.

"Lilith!" the voice called again.

Hands grasped her shoulders, pulling her up. Tears spilled from her eyes as Wren's face became visible.

"Lilith," he rasped, cupping her face. "You're all right." He pulled her into an embrace, stroking her hair as her limbs shook violently.

Safe.

Wren's soft-brown eyes soothed her anxiety. In them, she could glean traces of his sorrow, and a deep affection.

"You've got a lot to learn, my girl."

45

A KING MAKES DEMANDS

Lilith still hadn't returned. Questing out with Discernment, Julius grappled for any trace of her, but he sensed nothing. She said she wouldn't tread far, but clearly that was a lie. He should have sniffed out deceit when they spoke, but his traitorous manhood blinded him.

They were bound, he and she, their souls entwined. His heart was now a prisoner in her hands, there was no way to take it back. He'd have to live without it for now, but what good was a warrior without a heart?

Seated at his desk—the very desk he'd taken her on hours before—Julius flipped through the various battle plans his generals presented him, each of them eager to earn greater favor with their future king. Or were they testing him? He found the job tedious, but it sequestered him to his tent where he wouldn't be bothered.

Sipping from his chalice of wine, he pushed the parchment away, tired of reading. They'd been generously donated supplies and provisions from Utica, and Lord Alexaus had gifted them with more wine than was necessary. From what

Lilith had told him, the old lord had seen many battles himself. Maybe there was wisdom behind this gift. The generals joked that they would need the alcohol to swallow down the horrendous sights they predicted battle would inflict, but Julius thought it would be more useful to cleanse wounds should the healers run short on supplies.

For many of his men, this would be their first experience on a battlefield, their first time quashing life. Julius hated to be the one to take them to war, but it had to be done. Spiro was a threat to Dalegonè as well as Augusta.

And now they were minus a Divine.

Julius ran his hands through his hair, his fingers snagging on tangled curls. Why did she have to leave? Did she not believe him when he'd told her of his love? They were Pràgma, of that he was certain. But how sure was she?

Whatever compelled Lilith to leave, to traverse these lands on her own, it must be a considerable force. She was well equipped, blessed by two Gods, a sure-shot, and an incredible swordsman—*swordswoman*. He chuckled at the memory. At how feisty she'd been, so determined to succeed.

And she did. She'd prevailed. She was resilient, even if she failed to recognize it.

Without his even realizing, Lilith had stolen his heart, and he'd fallen for her. He'd given her everything, surrendered all. He'd risk his life over and over to prove what she meant to him. And sure, maybe the physical act wasn't enough to convince her, but what man could deny the woman he loved the pleasure she sought from him? Only a fool. And Julius Fawkes was no halfwit.

What was so wrong with relying on him? Xander knew how he'd relied on her. Multiple times. She'd saved his life as much as he had saved hers. Where he fell short, Lilith ascended. When she fell short, he rose to the occasion for her sake.

What good was their separation? Was she distancing herself from him as a means to cope? Gods, she'd accepted his engagement to Annika so quickly…

No. That couldn't be it. She loved him, he knew.

Focus.

Julius tugged the parchment back toward him as the flaps to his tent flew open and in marched his uncle.

"My boy, I do not mean to disturb you at this time, but there is a matter that requires your attention."

Julius reluctantly lifted his gaze from the parchment. "What is it?"

Prince Odêus secured the flaps behind him and approached. His cheeks were sunken, his eyes shadowed as if he hadn't slept in days. Julius knew his uncle loved the sea, but only for its aesthetic value. Two weeks at sea had been hard on him. Being taken overboard by a siren, that was a nightmare. It was a miracle he'd even survived.

"Well, you see," his uncle began hesitantly, "as generous as the townspeople have been, we only have enough to last a few days. We lost so much during the attack."

Julius spread his arms, eyeing the desk before him, none of the wood grains visible beneath piles of parchment. "We will have to dispatch a unit to hunt. It's the time of year for it. We will make it to Kenora."

"Yes, of course."

He returned his attention to the desk again, but his uncle seemed disinclined to take his leave.

"What is it, Odêus?"

The prince stepped toward the desk, bracing his hands on the edge, and leaning into his nephew. "Boy, if you will hear me, I'd like to speak wisdom over you."

Julius stilled. Was his uncle finally going to talk about what he'd witnessed between him and Lilith? Well, it was about time for a scolding. Perhaps that was just what he needed. Resigned, Julius indicated for Odêus to speak.

"I know your heart is soft for the Divine girl, and any one of us can see that she returns your affections."

Julius stood now. Crossing his arms over his chest, he leaned a hip against the desk, giving his uncle his full attention.

"You will be king when you return to Xanthë. A king may do whatever he wishes. Including marrying *whomever* he wishes."

"I made promises, Uncle."

"Yes, and you are honorable, I understand. But think of Annika for a moment." Odêus pointed a long finger in the direction of his betrothed's tent. "She can serve her people without being queen. If she marries you, she will age and wither whilst you remain youthful. That is a prospect not even love can overcome, and the two of you don't even have that."

Julius waved him off. But maybe he was right. His uncle was his father's Right Hand for a reason, not just by blood, he'd earned his position through merit. But would Annika's father take kindly to Julius reneging on a promise to his family? Unlikely. Even if he were the king.

But if he married Annika, all three of them lost. Annika would never know love as he had. Lilith would lose him. And he would lose the love of his life.

Prince Odêus placed a hand on his nephew's shoulder. "Be with Lilith, boy. If you'll have me, I will be your Right Hand, and I will ensure that Annika is taken care of."

His uncle turned and pushed the tent flaps out of his way, but before he left Julius to his thoughts, he twisted back around to face his nephew. "A king is not told what his options are," he said. "A king makes demands. He never cedes to them."

Julius lay on his pallet, the crickets outside his tent lulling him to sleep. An off-kilter lullaby. The same rhythm he had fallen asleep to with Lilith in his arms, only a few weeks ago. That blissful era seemed so long ago now. Ages and impossible to reconvene.

He was a fool to ever let her out of his sight. Out there somewhere, she was sleeping under the night sky. Alone, in the dark, at the mercy of whatever beast stalked the land.

Soon after Odêus left him, he had marched over to Annika's tent, the spring in his step courtesy of his uncle's bolstering wisdom.

A king makes demands. He does not cede to them.

Julius sat his fiancée down and told her that he would not marry her, for both their sakes.

At first, Annika refuted him, offering up every argument he'd predicted she would. When he remained steadfast in his decision, she'd broken down. It was difficult to hurt a friend, and he'd offered her comfort, promising her titles to fulfill her lifelong dream of serving the people of Dalegonè. He'd explained that by marrying her, he would be depriving both her and Lilith of their right to be loved. It was a modicum of the comfort she truly required from him, but he had other places he needed to be. So he returned to his own tent, granting Annika space to accept what he'd done.

The necklace he'd gifted Lilith for her nineteenth birthday dangled from his fingers, swinging like a pendulum above his head. Taunting. Time was of the essence and he was wasting it.

He wouldn't have it.

Lilith had had enough time to mull over this on her own. It was time he helped her. He was going to bring her back whether she resisted or not. And if she was adamant she stay, he'd stay, too. Make love to her under the stars like it was the last time they would ever hold each other—even if it were the first of many such occasions.

His heart sped up in anticipation, catalyzed by the thought of reuniting with Lilith. He wasn't leaving his men. He'd come back for them with his future queen on his arm.

Julius dressed himself quickly, breeches and a tunic, strapping Orphëus at his hip. He needed no other embellishments—though he finger-brushed his hair, suddenly urged to consider his appearance. His heart pounded in his ears like Walabeän drums.

He was going to find Lilith.

The prince set off in the direction she'd left, deftly weaving through his soldiers' tents on silent feet. There was an oppressive languor to the air that he longed to leave far behind him. One more night under the stars with Lilith. That was all he needed to win back her affection.

The beat of his heart grew louder and louder until the tumult was overwhelming. Incendiary. Shouts sounded throughout the camp, soldiers rising and running from tent to tent.

"Don your armor, Dalegonians!" his uncle bellowed. "Spiro has arrived!"

46

THËO PROVIDES

Wren chastised Lilith for being so reckless whilst he made a campfire to warm their limbs. She didn't argue with him. He was right. She shouldn't have taken it upon herself to… train herself. What a fool she was! But if Wren was anything, he was forgiving, and Lilith had to admit his fortitude was commendable. He'd lost two noviciates and he'd still taken her under his wing. Being indentured to him would not be easy, but it would be bearable.

She owed him for this. Eternally. Yet she drowned out his harangue regardless, her nerves frayed from the day's self-training.

"…and to think I was only a minute or two away from digging up your body!"

Lilith took a deep breath, exhaling days of tension. *Why am I relieved that his caustic tongue is still intact?*

"Unlike the other elements," Wren continued more softly, pensively pulling on his growing beard, "Earth draws from your emotions, not just energy. In order to will it to obey, you must do so by honing your passions. A man—" he cleared his throat "—sorry, a woman who is in tune with her inner sentiments will prevail." He lowered his voice. "Therefore, I request that you close off your consciousness during your training. I will too, save for when I conduct surveillance for security's sake."

Lilith sat back against the trunk of an oak as her new Master instructed her. Wren had boasted the intellectual importance of her instruction. Apparently, there was much she needed to learn before she should even attempt to wield Earth. Well, she'd failed on that front. It was better to be under Wren's tutelage than roaming the land, antagonizing it until it retaliated, consuming her whole. Which she already knew it would.

One thing was clear: if she wanted to learn to wield Earth, she needed to stave off her fervor for Julius—both the ill and the bliss—lest she cause an earthquake. How the ground didn't cave beneath the desk when they'd—

"…therefore, it is imperative that you find ways to mellow yourself out," Wren finished.

"How did you know I'd been blessed?" Lilith asked. "Did Olga receive a vision that one of the noviciates had been Anointed?"

Immediately, she regretted the question. Of course Wren hadn't been sent by Olga. The Oracle would know the location of the Anointed, but there was no possibility that Wren had come for her from the capital. Kenora was nearly two week's travel away, and she'd only just been blessed by Thëo a day ago.

Wren sighed. "It's a long story—"

"Regale me," she said with a smirk that he didn't deign to return.

"Olga and Arduen—as you probably assumed—came to visit me during my…" he trailed off uncertainly. "Anyway, she told me that either you or Julius had been blessed by Thëo."

"When?" Lilith asked. "I was only blessed a day ago."

Wren shook his head slowly, his long brown hair shaking with the motion. "You were blessed *nine* days ago, and I set out immediately in this direction. I rode day and night, stopping often enough to recover Mountainslide." He patted his sleeping horse's rump. "Then we pressed on."

"I'd been blessed when I was at sea…" It wasn't a question, but Wren nodded anyway.

"Yes, and I followed that direction," he said. "I angled north when I felt the Earth alter."

"You can sense what I did?"

He chuckled, the sound hollow. "When you get to my age, you can sense every change in the terrestrial realm. Besides, my senses were heightened. Thëo was leading a Master toward His new noviciate in need of guidance."

Lilith pursed her lips, perplexed by her situation. She'd never imagined herself in liaison with Wren, alone in the wild, no less. "How is Earth going to help me against Spiro?" She glanced across the fire at her new Master. He was a contrarian, dispositioned to oppose and countermand. If she was after answers, the truth specifically, he would certainly provide on that front. But he wouldn't listen to excuses, and he certainly wouldn't provide her with the luxury of wielding any.

Wren grimaced, his eyes dark and devoid of emotion. "We do not know how Spiro has come to be so strong. I am older than he is, I should be stronger. Yet, he stands the victor."

Lilith looked away, finding his countenance to be off—likely because he was still mourning Felix, she reminded herself.

"Earth can be useful in many ways," he said.

She looked at him through the darkness, following his gaze to his free hand. A small rock lay nestled in his palm. Before she could formulate a question to quell her building curiosity—and mild frustration—the rock began to move.

Lilith crawled across the space separating them, the heat of the fire reminding her to give the flames a wide berth.

"How is a stone birthed, noviciate?"

"Attrition," she said. "Gradually worn down by the shifting of Thëo's essence."

In his palm, the rock morphed, as if its surface were skin and its substance bone, marrow, tendon, and muscle. Invisible hands shaped the stone, molding it to its new purpose. It grew and elongated until she was staring down at the most perfectly formed arrowhead she'd ever seen.

Wren held his hand out to her. "When you are weaponless, Thëo provides." Dropping the arrowhead into her waiting hand, he said, "Now you are not without."

Marveling at the stone's transformation, Lilith's sense of awe was augmented by a newfound gratitude for her third blessing.

"Get some rest," Wren said. "You'll need to be in top form for training tomorrow. We stop only to eat." He rolled over on his bedroll, his back to her.

Lilith lay on her back, her blanket pulled up to her chin, eyes locked on the fine-tipped arrowhead between her fingers. She slipped the stone into the pocket of her leather suit.

Now, she would never be helpless.

◎ ☿ ⁓ ♏ ◊

"SHALL WE BEGIN?" WREN ASKED. HE STOOD BEFORE HER, hand raised, a signal for her to remain seated. "You will spend the morning spectating, acquiring a mental grasp of what wielding Earth entails. Only then will we venture forth into the practical portion of your training on our journey."

They'd awoken before the sun's first rays. Wren had

prepared oats for breakfast, 'Kenora's finest,' he'd added. Lilith now felt them churning in her belly.

"Journey?"

"We can't hide out here," he said. "Battle will be upon Kenora. We must travel back to the capital. I can train you there. I have strict orders from Arduen himself to bring you back immediately."

Like she needed to be reminded. Now that Wren was her Master, she'd have to abide by his word. There would be no dispensation.

Wren strode away, far enough that he needed to shout to school her. Lilith sat with her ankles crossed, folded legs pressed against her chest, arms wrapped around her knees. Waiting.

He turned to her, his eyes closed tight, his wide mouth turned down at the corners, disappearing beneath his scruffy beard. "As I am sure you know," he said, voice distant, "Aether and Fire are drawn from within you. When you reach the bottom of your well of power, it ceases. If you attempt to go beyond that, you die."

Wren pierced her with his gaze as the ground beneath him rumbled. He rose into the sky, the Earth beneath him becoming a platform, a stage. The sides were steep, spotted here and there with other matter. Bones, perhaps.

"Earth is like Water, in a way," he said. "We are surrounded by it. It is gifted to us in abundance. That is why it is such a beneficial element to wield."

Lilith stood now, gaping.

"But…" Wren raised a rigid finger to the sky. "It is not as easy to wield on the battlefield. It takes time to master. Years we do not have."

Slowly dropping back onto the ground, Lilith watched as

Wren molded the Earth into a staircase leading down from his stage.

"Water, Wind, and Earth drain your energy—" the ground beneath him slowly corroded, returning to normal "—when you release it." His broad shoulders slumped as if to emphasize his fatigue. "It is easier to lose control and drain all of the sustenance from your body when you release your hold on the Earth."

"So, I can't create mountains that will last while I'm gone?"

Wren shook his head. "No permanence."

"But I thought I'd heard tales of Thëo's Divine shaping the Earth to their liking. Is that not the history of the foothills of the Orösía Mountains? Of the Great Rift?"

"All of those tales are myth," Wren said. "Only the Gods can shape the Earth and Their fingerprints remain."

"But…" Lilith sputtered to voice her muddled thoughts. "I thought…" Far too many myths had become common beliefs when the land could not be traversed. A show of how deeply Spiro's defiance stunted Augusta's growth.

"The only permanence is damage," he interrupted her thoughts. "Why do you think the Frourío needed reconstruction? A Divine of Thëo's Earth could shift one stone by accident and the whole structure could fall."

"That easily?" Lilith raised a doubtful eyebrow.

"No, but you know what I mean. The result is permanent. Such as the Rift." Wren pointedly refrained from using the title 'Great.'

He smiled, a knowing, warm expression. Perhaps he needed her as much as she needed him. "Now, I want you to try what I just did, but in very small areas. Raise and release."

Nerves frayed from the previous evening, Lilith glanced fleetingly at her Master before striding away. She took sanction where he'd just been a moment before, planting her booted feet and closing her eyes. Lilith grappled for Earth, willing it to obey her silent commandments.

Just like before, the ground beneath her grumbled and quaked. Much to her chagrin, it took a lengthy moment before it began to rise. Opening her eyes, she studied her Master's face. Other than a wry grimace, he displayed no other sign of unease. When no protest was forthcoming, she continued. Rising higher and higher and higher, her stomach flipping.

Wren finally signaled for her to release. She did, then she moved on to the next. She hopped down from the mound she'd just made—humbled by how small it truly was—and, deciding on another patch of land, began the same procedure.

Again.

And again.

And again.

Lilith slumped to the ground, resting her back against the lump she'd just risen. Her breath came in rasps as she gulped down the air. With Wren's sudden appearance, she had thought there would be nothing in her way, nothing to impede upon her progress.

Well, nothing except for her new Master.

Wren was adamant that she begin as all noviciates do. Unfortunately, the way all noviciates begin is draining.

A shadow crept over her, and she opened her eyes. Her Master's silhouette looked over her, his fists set on his hips. Her eyes tapered. "You're aware that the Empire is at war and you're seriously making me sift through *dirt*?"

"Wielding Earth is dangerous, Lilith. As you have witnessed for yourself, might I add. We will start where all novice's do."

The task was akin to the level Zurí was training Aspen. But the little girl wasn't to partake in battle for a decade, or longer. Lilith could be summoned to the fray at any moment, and she was already prepared to wave the white flag.

They needed to move faster.

She wiped her brow as Wren dropped to his knees. No words left her lips, she was beyond speaking at this point, sitting on her ass was signal enough. But when Wren turned to berate her, he merely waved his hand at the eastern horizon.

A horizon that was once austere, flat, and barren, was now jagged. Intricate mounds rose up, awkward peaks of rock and dirt. It was a beautiful sight, if she'd ever seen one, if only because of the satisfaction one experienced to see the fruits of their labor. The sole reason she'd chosen to blacksmith over anything else. A lifetime ago.

"Now release," Wren ordered.

Lilith acquiesced. Slowly the Earth before her sunk, deflating whilst her energy drained away with each second. Her chest heaved as if she'd been sprinting miles, her muscles twitching with exertion.

"How is it possible," she gasped, "to force the Earth to move as quickly as you desire?" She splayed her body out on the grass. "How did Spiro engulf Arduen's feet so quickly? How were you able to raise the ground like you did? So quickly."

"Emotion." He grimaced. "As unorthodox as it sounds... emotion."

What does that even mean?

Wren responded as if she'd spoken her thought out loud. "You have to let go of all pretence. Drop all barriers around your mind, your entity. Let it all go."

"Easier said than done," Lilith grumbled. Arduen had given her a similar instruction before, and she'd yet to master that skill.

Wren shifted through his pack and offered her some jerky and a slice of bread. "Aye, but if it can be done by me, it can be done by you."

"How do you do it?" she asked. "I mean no offence, but you've always come across as impassive, placid…"

Wren smirked. "That's because I reserve it all for wielding. I've learned over the years how to control my emotions, but also how to expel them with influence."

"You use them for fuel."

"Precisely."

Could she open herself up again? Allow all the hurt between her and Julius bubble to the surface and explode? All the pain of losing Larkin, of killing him? The resentment she has harbored toward her mother? Gods knew how much she missed them. How she longed for conversation over a bowl of their mother's fassolatha.

"He was good," Wren whispered, the elegiac note in his voice staying Lilith's tongue. "Gods, he was the best of us all!"

Lilith was silenced by his sudden caprice. He'd never so much as shown more than his arrogance, or his disdain. But here he was, displaying his heart, opening it to her.

"He was good…"

"I know." Lilith moved to place her hand on his shoulder, but hesitated when his hand was inches from contact.

"I wouldn't wish it on either of you," Wren said, contrition writ on his face. "Thëo only knows what Spiro puts his noviciates through. But why did it have to be *him*?"

At least Spiro didn't slit his throat, she wanted to say, but didn't dare. Bringing up Cordova at a moment like this would be like stabbing Wren in the chest with a serrated bread knife.

"You've given me hope, Lilith." He turned to her, eyes glassy.

"I have?"

He nodded. "You've given me purpose."

"Now, if Spiro shows up, Felix at his side, unbound by the Blood Oa—"

"He won't," Wren snapped. "He wouldn't bring Felix to battle without some assurance the boy would remain loyal to him."

Lilith did not challenge his conjecture, especially to spur a debate about such a moot subject. But still, she loathed to give up faith that somehow they could save him. Felix was deserving of so much more. He would have been great.

He could still be great, she thought.

Wren buried his face in his palms, sheltering his glassy eyes from sight. Lilith allowed him a moment to grieve. Gods knew they needed release. The life of the Divine was not for the faint of heart, and it seemed as if they were gifted with organs especially susceptible to fierce devotions.

Lilith trained her eyes on her boots. It was always easier to look away from those suffering. Her mother's ghost was always standing between her and everyone else, a spectral demarcation. Her mother had become a filter that kept others' empathy at bay, much the same way Wren allowed the ghosts of his past to alienate him from his Divine family.

Grief was a narrow path, tenebrous and twisted, best tread in isolation. She knew this better than anyone. Yet she also knew the power of an extended hand, and subsequently, the power of taking that hand.

So she extended hers to him.

Wren started at her touch, expression bemused. But after that brief moment of resistance, he surrendered, wrapping his fingers around her own.

With one last glance up at the sky, Lilith regarded her new Master. "We'll do this together," she said firmly, giving his hand a gentle squeeze. "I have experience on the matter," she deadpanned. "Together, we will avenge Felix."

LATER THAT AFTERNOON, LILITH FOLLOWED EVERY ORDER GIVEN TO her, regardless of how small and trite the commandments were. Playing the obedient noviciate seemed to vindicate her of her former sins.

Together, she and Wren traipsed through the field, looking for areas of land they hadn't yet upturned. It turned out, wielding Earth did leave a semi-permanent mark upon the land; the ground was torn up, grass mutilated.

Eventually, Wren had Lilith locate rocks far beneath them and she'd lift them. Slowly, ever so slowly, they'd break free of the surface, dirt dripping from them like water.

Gods, this would have been helpful back at the mine.

Lilith recalled memories of her and Arduen, of her family, of Julius, and experimented with how the different emotions impacted her gift, how they carved the land before her. She paid special attention to speed. Would anger speed up the process more than lust?

Diffidently, she prevailed, taking on new exercises until she couldn't anymore.

"All right!" Wren clapped his hands. "You've done excellent. No doubt a result of your experience thus far."

Lilith took the compliment with a slight nod.

"What do you say we end here for the day? Have something to eat?"

Wiping the sweat from her brow, she agreed. "When are we to leave here?"

"Hmm?" He glanced over his shoulder askance.

"You said we can't tarry here long, that my place was in Kenora with Arduen and Zurí. So, when will we leave?" She was reluctant to leave Julius behind but eager to see Arduen again.

Wren didn't answer straight away, much to her irritation. "We will take our leave at first light," he said finally. "One day to give you a feel for the gift. That's all you'll need until we return to the capital."

Lilith didn't grouse as they took their seats at camp, settled in, and prepared another meal. Griping would be useless. Wren saw reason and his single-track mind wouldn't allow him to contradict that. So she ate her meal in silence.

When the night became dark and foreboding, Lilith took to her bedroll, pondering just how useful Earth would be in battle when wielded in conjuncture with Water and Aether. Could she use them at the same time? Could she use Earth to hold men in place whilst she struck them with arrows of Aether and siphoned Water from their muscle tissue? It may take years to master, but it would be very useful.

Despite her fatigue, she struggled to fall asleep. The steady rise and fall of Wren's breathing indicated that he'd already reached his dreamscape. Even Mountainslide snored occasionally, as horses do.

She was alone now.

Staring up at the stars, she opened her consciousness to the surrounding world, feeling for predators and interesting forest dwellers of the night. She couldn't feel Wren. He'd kept his own consciousness well-guarded to avoid impacting her own emotions and disrupting her instruction.

Moving far beyond the confines of their camp, Lilith's mind quested wider for variety, for telltale signs of unique creatures she'd never glimpsed before.

But she found a whole lot more than she imagined she would.

Lilith jolted upright. "Wren!" She called her Master to attention. "Beasts are near!"

"How many?" he asked, lucid, already reaching for his sword.

"Thousands."

47

A MURDER IN COLD BLOOD

Hestîa followed obediently as the soldiers led her through the halls of the castle proper. Rarely was she permitted up here, where lavish carpets accentuated the stone floors and priceless tapestries bedecked the walls.

It was first light, and not even the most devoted of Walabeän warriors had stirred. Two of the Emperor's Fruits had roused her, dragging her to the throne room.

Of course she had obeyed. What choice did she have? The soldiers stood vigil as she dressed, their expressions stony, feigning ignorance as their eyes bore blessed witness to her gloriously exposed body. If Agónas had been conscious, he would have cut each of their tongues from their mouths and taunted the nubs before their wide eyes.

They didn't touch her as they led her to the Emperor. They didn't even regard her with more than their original request. When she inquired about the grounds by which Obadïa had summoned her, they offered her no more than vague grunts.

So they'd left her all but blindfolded before the Emperor himself.

Maybe they were escorting her to her death. Was it possible to execute a Walabeän? Surely she wasn't under Obadïa's jurisdiction, but he was an emperor, and she was living under his roof, eating his food.

It wasn't possible, she assured herself. Marlowë would never stand for it. The Emperor would lose the Colony's loyalty and would be left alone to defend the land from Spiro and his wicked ghouls.

Agónas had beseeched her to leave. He'd been on edge since Athena's murder. As he should. As they all should. Orìon was treacherous, volatile. Unpredictable and unrestrained. But she wouldn't leave. Hestîa's place was with her warriors, defending those she loved and her Igítís. She'd trained for this opportunity since she was old enough to walk and hold a blade at the same time. This was where she belonged.

The large entrance to the throne room appeared before her like the mouth of some feral beast. Hestîa entered the maw, her spine ramrod straight as she sauntered down the aisle toward the dais upon which Obadïa sat perched on his throne. She maintained her most calculated gait, making the soldiers on either side of her seem ungainly in comparison.

More legionnaires of the Emperor's Fruits had been stationed around the castle. Obadïa's fear of invasion was strident.

Igítís Marlowë stood beside the Emperor, his posture esteemed, shoulders squared. He nodded once in her direction, his pale eyes glistening with pride. So she wasn't being executed. Still, it was wise, prudent even, to remain respectful. Even if she detested the future emperor.

Hestîa halted before the steps, meeting Obadïa's gaze of night, a smug grin spreading across her lips.

She didn't bow.

Several other courtiers were scattered throughout the room, their flinty eyes locked on her, as if they could fetter her to the ground in submission. Their faces gleamed with disapproval, but Hestîa refused to meet their eyes.

Before Obadïa parted his lips to explain why she'd been summoned, the Crown Prince entered the room and took his place at his father's side. Orìon's blond hair had been combed back, but that did little to assuage his haggard appearance. His eyes were shadowed, his cheeks sunken. Blatantly fighting a hangover, reeking of liquor and sex. He set his leer on Hestîa and gave a cavalier smirk.

Her muscles twitched involuntarily, uneasy in Orìon's presence. For the first time in her life, she wished the Emperor would speak over her.

"Hestîa, the *Savior*." Obadïa practically spat the words out. Orìon's grin intensified. "I have called you here today to inform you that the Walabeän women have been ordered to return to the Isles of Nysía."

Hestîa stiffened. What? How could this be? The women made up nearly two hundred of their force. They needed them. They needed all of the bodies they could get, regardless of their reproductive distinction. She tried not to scowl, but her ire fought to obtain the best of her.

"But you will not be returning with them…"

Now, her heart stilled.

Marlowë cut in, "I have offered you up as tribute. You are my most promising female warrior, and I am afraid an upcoming mission for the Agemas requires your assistance."

Her Chief succeeded in easing her consternation, but only slightly. She was sure there must be a trick. If the Crown Prince left the comfort of his bed to witness this meeting, there had to be some sort of conniving catch.

"This is a proposition, Hestîa," said Obadïa. "You have the right to return with your fellow ladies."

Ladies. She didn't bother to hide her scoff.

"Though, bear in mind, if you do choose to deny my request, another of your colleagues will be sent in your place. You wouldn't want to draw shame to the name of the Savior."

"Fair enough," Hestîa intoned. "When do my women leave?" *Her women,* because they answered to her alone. And Marlowë, of course.

Obadïa ignored her question. "I will be sending my most credible regiment to the Gáea Valley. They will be led by General Achilles." He inclined his head to the general.

Hestîa knew who General Achilles was. Lilith's father, whom she'd thought was deceased. Gods only knew what the Emperor had on him to blackmail the general into serving him, faking his own death, subjecting his family to suffer his loss. Only Emperor Obadïa would ever possess such high expectations of his officials.

Emperor Orìon will be much, much worse.

"Very well," said Hestîa. "What is the purpose of this mission?" She could guess exactly why they were leaving, but she got pleasure out of questioning the Emperor.

"As you know," the Emperor droned on, "we have suffered a considerable loss over the past year, barely surviving two battles. Now, I had hoped that by acquiring the assistance of your people that we would prevail, yet we have not seen the resilience we were hoping for."

Hestîa swallowed her indignation. It wasn't intelligent to insult the Walabeäns in the presence of the Igítís. "If my memory serves me correctly," she mused, "we have only suffered one loss since graciously offering our aid to the Empire." Her eyes flicked to Orìon brazenly. "And that was a murder in cold blood."

The temperature in the room dropped suddenly, yet somehow her body burned. There must have been steam shooting from either of her ears.

Obadïa stared her down, but she ignored his shrewd expression. "Convince the Vunosoï to lend us their assistance and I will dismiss your insolence."

Hestîa stood tall. "When do we depart?"

"It will take a fortnight or longer to gather our bearings. But *you* will be ready at a moment's notice," Obadïa crooned. "You, along with my finest cohort, will be traveling south through the plains to the Orösía Mountains."

Hestîa dipped into the slightest, most curt bow, then she turned on her heels. If this was Marlowë's idea of making a fire-side tale of her, she would give him a most atrocious fable.

"Oh, I failed to mention," said the Emperor.

Seething, she turned to see Obadïa's most malicious grin. Now she knew exactly whom Orìon took after. This was what he loved most, what he craved, the greatest sin he ever took pleasure in. He loved possessing unknown power over his subordinates. Playing with their lives like they are little more than pawns. Replaceable. Recyclable. And it was why she hated him so passionately.

Hestîa blanched as the words left his royal lips.

"You must remain on your best behavior," said Obadïa, humor lacing his onyx irises, "for the Crown Prince will be joining you."

Before Hestîa turned away, she caught a flash of Orìon's grin as it widened.

HE DIDN'T KILL ME, HE MADE ME

Julius ground his teeth in determination. He refused to allow this land to become a necropolis of Dalegonian bones. But as the beasts kept surging toward them, one after the other, offering them mere seconds to recover from the last bout, Julius's hope dimmed out.

Xander's Fire hummed in his veins, singing a song he'd become accustomed to. A song of lust, of love, of passion, of rage and delight. The symphony beseeched him to release all the power he had available, but the battle with the Ophïon a week prior had left him drained. Recovery did not come easily to him, especially when he spent most of his days stressing over Lilith and Annika. If Spiro and his cronies showed their faces, if Felix had been dispatched for battle, Julius would be the only warrior capable to take them on. He needed every last flame Xander gave him.

The rampage evolved to war as his men gathered their wits and fought to control the beasts. Having closed himself off from Discernment—for both his and Lilith's sakes—Spiro's army had caught him off guard. With the advent of battle, Julius's legionnaires assembled gear quickly and marched to meet their enemy. Spiro's beasts awaited them in the open plains outside the oaken forest.

In the first hour of battle, Spiro's beasts, in their brutal lack of tactic, completely destroyed the Dalegonians' militaristic structure, their pristine formation disintegrating. Julius fought at the forefront, bellowing cries of encouragement to his soldiers as more and more Dalegonian bodies piled up, each of the lifeless forms like tinder to his wildfire. Most nobles stood behind the chaos of war, their presence merely tawdry. But Julius wouldn't stand behind them and watch them die, he would lead his men into the fray. It was his duty to them, as Crown Prince, as their future king.

Hailing from the desert, Dalegonians fought with sparse armor. Metal gleamed in the moonlight, golden spaulders, greaves and vambraces, chest and abdomen exposed. Helms with mohawks of crimson fur bobbed in a sea of chitinous skin.

"Keep formation, Dalegonians!" Julius hollered, his voice nearly two octaves higher than usual, cracking like a pre-pubescent boy.

If Spiro showed up, they were done. The war would be lost. Claiming another one of the Divine's noviciates was all the Great Divine needed to secure victory. By month's end, they'd all be sipping his blood.

Blessedly, Lilith was not present for the taking.

Julius wouldn't let them take her. Not only because he loved her, but because it would mean devastation for all. He wouldn't let that happen. Not to his family. Not to his people. Every one of them were driven by altruistic intentions, passions, whilst Spiro was sickened with *Philautia*. A self-serving menace.

Monsters tore through his men, ripping limbs from bodies, shearing them with their poisonous talons. Julius sent up a prayer to each of the Gods to grant his men passage to Elysium.

Quickly. For they would suffer otherwise. Already the earth was soiled with man and beast blood alike. Offal and viscera coalesced, settling into runnels carved into the dirt, glistening black and red.

A beast leapt in front of him, its mouth opened several inches wider than what was considered natural. Several rows of razor-sharp teeth on display, laced together by strings of greenish saliva.

With his Divine strength, Julius thrust Orphëus through the beast's maw. As it struggled against its death, the beast swatted him with its talons, slicing his shoulder.

"Gah!" he roared. The beast got him in the same shoulder as at the battle at the Frourío. Julius grimaced as he pulled his sword free, shuffling to the side as the beast toppled to the ground where he'd just been standing.

Prince Odêus fought steadily behind him, keeping close watch on his nephew. His uncle's heavy breathing was a distraction, sending each of his hairs standing on end. How could he tell the man to give him space? His intentions were from the purest realm, but Odêus's circumspection prevented him from letting Julius out of his sight, and so the prince did not turn his uncle away.

"Are you all right?" Odêus eyed his nephew's wound with paternal concern.

"I'm fine," Julius assured him. "I don't think its talons were poisonous."

Odêus nodded, though the prince didn't appear to be convinced, the muscle flickering in his jaw was proof enough.

Light flared in the distance, and Julius's head snapped toward it.

Fire.

Unmistakable. Bright as the flames that burned beneath his own skin.

Julius cast a knowing glance at his uncle and bound off into the night, in the direction of the light's source. Together, the princes cut down beast after beast, leaving their severed forms to be finished off by the others. Julius glanced around, a beacon of smoke rising into the sky, marking his destination.

A Divine was present. He could sense it.

Julius shut himself off, receding into himself, hoping that would help keep his presence concealed from his Divine counterpart. It was unlikely to work, but he needed something to quell the anxiety plaguing him. If he'd been in the right frame of mind, he'd have told his uncle to run the other way, but he couldn't.

Gods, Julius. He was letting fear dictate his actions.

Fire spurted up into the sky again, its golden glow reflected in the stars above. And when Julius arrived at the source of the Fire, he almost dropped to his knees. Prince Odêus grasped him, holding him around his exposed middle.

Plated fighting leathers! Why hadn't he brought them?

His uncle pressed up behind him, nudging his wounded shoulder. Julius winced, but Odêus didn't seem to notice. Supporting his nephew, he narrowed his stare on their enemy.

Felix stood before them, a cocky sneer distorting his usual affable features. That was enough to make Julius's knees tremble. An automaton stood before him. A daemon caged within an innocuous shell.

"Greetings, old friend." His voice was off, wrong, contaminated.

Julius didn't deign to respond, even if he could.

"Hmm… it's rude to ignore your comrade."

"He's not your comrade!" Odêus barked through gritted teeth. Julius could almost feel his uncle's heartbeat against his shoulder blades. He should have sent him running. He should be helping his warriors. If Julius fell, he would need his uncle to lead his legion and take his throne.

Felix chuckled, the sound sending shivers raking down Julius's spine.

Don't be a coward.

"Blessed by Xander, are we?" Julius asserted, his voice distant in his ears, as if he were dislocated from his own body.

Felix chuckled, the sound a deep rumble, overpowering the clang of metal around them. He sounded older, as if Spiro's tutelage had aged him.

"Blessed by Spiro," Felix amended.

Julius froze, ignoring the urge to peer around him for any sign of the Great Divine.

"Oh, don't act so surprised, Brother." Felix took one step in his direction. "You were well aware there was going to be a sixth God."

There will be a sixth God.

Yes, they'd heard it multiple times, but that didn't make it possible. The beasts all shared a common brain, they didn't know the blasphemy they spoke.

"Shall we?" Felix traced a circle in the air with his sword, the blade incandescent with Fire. As he moved, the Earth responded in kind, rising beneath them, creating a form of plateau, a stage for their Divine altercation.

Julius responded by emblazoning Orphëus in the same manner. He pushed off from his uncle, the prince grasping for his nephew in alarm.

"Julius," he intoned, echoing his father's disapproving timbre.

With a rueful expression, Julius dismissed his uncle with the Dalegonian gesture. Odêus appeared stricken, but he stepped back, allowing his nephew the space to fight. He wouldn't leave, of that Julius was sure. His uncle was unflappable, the deserving Right Hand of the King. Whether or not they were trounced, he would stand by Julius's side no matter the risk, a mere token of his troth.

Before he'd even assumed his defensive stance, Felix attacked with a wanton blow, rife with animosity. Julius raised Orphëus just in time to parry, but Felix was stronger than he'd been back at the Frourío.

Julius commenced a string of attacks, any vestige of consternation abandoned, wiped clean in the name of Xander, in the name of Fire.

The flames swelled within him, beseeching their master to let them release, to let them dance. Julius obliged, not out of will but out of necessity. He was desperate to unleash himself into the world again. Too long he'd let his power simmer, boil within him, contained.

Orphëus exploded with flames in response. Julius ignored the singed skin of his palm. The pain erased any remembrance of the wound in his shoulder, still dripping blood down his arm.

Julius displayed his prowess unvarnished before his old friend, now his enemy. He remembered Felix's moves, his tricks and schemes to throw him off guard. If there was anything he excelled at, it was reading his opponents' minds, knowing their next move before they made it. Predicting their next step before they took it.

But this wasn't Felix.

This Divine moved differently, sporadically. He'd been touched. Corrupted. Erased and resurrected. He was unjust, uncouth, unrefined. A mere puppet for a greater evil.

The ground vibrated, shifting slightly, opening a toothless maw to devour his legs. But Julius was faster, his Divine senses picking up on Felix's intentions far before he acted upon them.

Julius danced as he slashed, meeting every assault with a

veritable riposte. His legs burned, the pain muting the sting of his other wounds.

Felix slashed at Julius with formidable force, enough to knock him off his feet. "You can't best me, Brother," he said. "It would be wise to join me. Spiro's vision—"

"I don't give a fuck about Spiro's vision!" Julius shouted. "He's already *killed* you!"

Felix stepped back, brow furrowed, eyes wide. "I don't think I've ever heard you curse!"

Julius snickered. "First time for everything."

"I'm glad I have that effect on you," Felix simpered. "And by the way, Spiro didn't kill me. He made me."

Felix struck again, and Julius raised Orphëus just in time to block his cut. The gash in his shoulder sang a lamentation, a healer's requiem.

Julius pushed forward, the surge of power pulling a roar from his throat. Felix stumbled back, his feet scampering for purchase. As he struggled to regain balance, he slashed forward unexpectedly, slicing Julius's chest open.

The prince jumped back a moment too late. His uncle shouted behind him, but Odêus's orders were muffled by the tinnitus in his ears. Julius glanced down at his exposed chest. Blood seeped from the gash, torn layers of flesh visible for only a second before the rush of blood commenced. Dalegonè will have to make some alterations to their traditional battle attire, especially if their monarchy fell because of it.

"Silly, your armor. It really is," Felix said, posturing elegance and confidence.

Julius glared at him, at the man who wore his friend's face.

"It's a real pity you make this so difficult," Felix drawled. "Spiro could have used a man like you."

Felix lunged then, and Julius knew it was too late. He didn't have Orphëus at the ready. But Prince Odêus moved before him, blocking Felix's path to his nephew. Julius reached out for his uncle, but it was futile. The pointed tip of Felix's blade sliced through Odêus's back, gleaming crimson in the moonlight.

"No," Julius stammered. "No, no, no, no, no!"

The blade receded with a *squelch*, and Prince Odêus slumped to the ground, limbs limp, lifeless, blood trailing from his parted lips. Julius longed to reach down, to close his eyes, but he didn't dare move under Felix's watchful gaze.

"Well, this has been… *dull*." Felix slowly retreated, leaving Julius kneeling in a pool of his own sweat and blood. "I think I'll let the imps feed on you. Your body will prove useful sustenance."

"Where are you going?" Julius demanded.

"Oh, didn't you hear? I've been sent to bring Lilith home!"

Shards of ice stabbed through Julius's chest at the mention of her name. "Felix…don't," *Spiro is not her home!*

Felix flipped his sword from hand to hand. Insouciant and arrogant. "Truth be told, I think our dear Lilith will offer more of a challenge, being blessed by three Gods."

Julius started. "*Three?*"

"Oh, you didn't know? I thought the two of you were close." He chuckled maniacally. "Thëo blessed her. I can't wait to show her the ropes."

It couldn't be… When he thought she'd been taken from him, could she have been Anointed a third time?

With one last self-satisfied smirk, Felix sauntered off, leaving Julius kneeling before his uncle's corpse.

Felix shouted, "Lilith!"

WELCOME TO THE ILÍOS

"Please explain to me why we aren't indulging in Spiro's luxuries?" Irís asked.

Rhéa passed the girl a chalice filled to the brim with crimson wine, hoping it would silence her griping. They were in Rhéa's bedchamber. Spiro and his army of beasts had left almost a week prior. They were running out of entertainment in the labyrinth of tunnels.

"Because," Rhéa intoned, "I don't want a rendition of last time." *And I don't want to be any closer to Thébés.* She could feel the Sorcerer's morose presence like an impending disease. The creature would know they were there, he could likely sense their exact location, hear their conversation.

"Fair enough." Irís wouldn't pursue the argument further, the dark cast settling over her fine features told Rhéa as much. The girl would likely always remember what occurred the last time they were caught unawares in Spiro's conference chamber, and she would never forget what happened after, when Spiro sought his own punishment.

Rhéa sipped her wine, sighing as the liquid trailed down her throat, warmth detonating in her belly.

"Tell me more about the Marsh!" Irís piped up. She sat cross-legged at the head of Rhéa's bed, smothered in cushions. If there was anything Spiro did right, it was rewarding her with sumptuous chambers. She even had her own bath. One call for a servant, and she'd be swimming in clear waters, the scent of lemon verbena permeating her room.

"What would you like to know?"

Irís pondered the question for a moment, slurping her wine, the liquid staining her thin lips.

"I could swear you into a coven right now," Rhéa offered, "if you've made up your mind."

"But what about Xavier?" Irís's eyes widened with genuine concern.

"If Ophelía doesn't know you exist," Rhéa explained, "she won't know you've forsaken the Obsydían Marsh."

Irís's interest piqued, she set down her chalice on the night-stand, scooting closer to Rhéa. "Tell me of your coven," she insisted, wrapping her tiny hands around Rhéa's arm like a fascinated child.

"Well, the Ilíos are the most sanctified, if I am not too biased to voice the opinion. We specialize in the magical craft of healing."

"Are certain covens limited to distinct types of magic?"

Rhéa waved her off. "No, no. Every Enchantress is capable of all spells, limited only by their own strength of power."

"I see…" Irís mused. "So, if I become an Enchantress of the Ilíos, I would be granted escalated abilities to heal ailments?"

Rhéa nodded slowly. "And more, should the Amalthea choose to Bless you."

Irís sipped her wine again, her face set in a pensive pout as she smacked her lips. "Tell me of the holidays," she said.

"The only holidays we celebrate, if they can even be considered holidays—"

"Why do you say that? *If they can even be considered holidays.*"

Rhéa grinned. "Enchantresses don't work, darling."

"You don't *work* for a living?"

"Why work when you can accomplish most mundane tasks with a few simple words?"

The girl stared into space wistfully.

"But we do have special occasions, my favorite being the Labyrinth."

"Like a maze?"

"Mm-hmm," Rhéa said. "Except it's raised by magic, once every decade marking the Deathday of Astoría Glades."

"That doesn't sound very magical. A Deathday?" Irís scowled with disdain.

"It is quite the contrary," Rhéa said. "Together, the four covens raise the Labyrinth, and once the order is given by the High Enchantress, we enter through our respective corners, racing to the center, to the prize therein."

That drew Irís's interest again. "Prize?"

"Usually in the form of men." Rhéa winked.

The girl blushed in response.

"We understand death very differently from humans. Death does not equal an end for us. That is, unless we are buried."

Irís's dark brows knitted together in confusion.

"When an Enchantress passes, she and all her belongings are gathered in one place, and her coven presides over the site, lighting her Blaze. It's a traditional send-off for the deceased. Her body will be reunited with the Guiding Star of her coven. Her light will be added to the Star, guiding future Enchantresses as they traverse the lands below."

Irís looked bemused. "And when an Enchantress is buried?"

"Her soul is denied access to her Star. It is the worst punishment—condemnation—of all."

Irís stood and paced the chamber, her bare feet sinking into the plush rug Spiro had gifted Rhéa before he took leave. As if she would mourn his absence. As long as he didn't drag her along on his escapades, she was quite content. The less fàrmako in her veins, the happier she would become. If only Xavier had given her the spell to open the entrance to the fortress. He didn't, because he'd sworn not to. The Blood Oath forbade it. And try as she might to remember it, the incantation eluded her.

Not that it mattered. She would need to fly out of the Rift to enjoy the Starlight, and she wasn't brazen enough to attempt a flight spell just yet.

But the thought of remaining beneath the earth's surface with a Sorcerer…

"I'm in," Irís said, turning to Rhéa with her free hand fisted against her chest.

"What's that?" Rhéa broke from her reverie, confused and startled.

"I want to embrace my nature. I want to be an Enchantress of the Ilíos."

"Are you sure?" Rhéa stood now, setting her chalice down on the nightstand.

Irís nodded eagerly. "I've been considering it for weeks."

"You'll be bound for all your days."

"Yes, but I will no longer be powerless."

Rhéa sighed. She knew what it felt like to be powerless, and she didn't have the heart to tell the girl that becoming a sworn Enchantress didn't guarantee her safety. If anything, swearing Irís into a coven would only strengthen her powers, which in turn would coerce Spiro into serving Irís her own dose of fàrmako.

But if the girl wanted this, her eyes could be modified. There was a chance, given that he barely acknowledges the girl now, that he would not notice the subtle change.

"On your knees," she ordered Irís, though not unkindly.

Irís obeyed, the light of the sconces refracting off her wide eyes; those innocuous, guileless eyes. Soon to change to Amalthea's gold.

Would this really protect her? Or would she just be throwing the girl to the wolves? But the power Amalthea would bestow upon her was a greater weapon than any of the blades in this terrestrial fortress. Rhéa resolved to abide by the girl's wishes.

"You must repeat after me," Rhéa said. "Don't worry too much about pronunciation. I'll be the voice calling the magic to us, the presence of the Guiding Stars and Astoría. They will know the words that tumble from your mouth despite whatever accent construes them."

Irís knelt before the Enchantress, eyes wide with anticipation. Rhéa gazed back into them, noting the golden flecks that in only a short moment's time would devour her entire iris. Warmth spread through her belly, and she was sure it had nothing to do with the Krasì wine within.

"Though the ceremonious spell is succinct," Rhéa said, "it is not lacking in power. You will be bound when it is through. Your life will be to serve the Guiding Stars and the Obsydían Marsh beneath them … and your years will be ceaseless."

Irís settled herself comfortably, awaiting the commencement of the ceremony. Her hand rested on her stomach, as if she were holding herself together.

Rhéa stood over the girl, her bones silently called to attention by Amalthea Herself. "Repeat after me." She cleared her wine-slick throat and began, "I, Irís, swear by the Guiding Stars that I devote my life and soul as property of the Obsydían

Marsh. I swear that I shall serve as a Sister of the Sun, a disciple of Amalthea, and a servant of Magic."

Irís repeated line for line, her voice steady, unfaltering.

"Now repeat after me in Elder Tongue."

Irís dipped her chin slightly, conveying her comprehension.

Rhéa clearly voiced the oath, "*Von, Irís, svidrà se qu Gwindr Tristè vat Von quelva Va lyffe teq vuíll sec possïvq un qu Obsydían Marsh. Von svidrà vat Von tèes safí sec sâ tostènn un qu Duín, sâ discílne un Amalthea, teq sâ safíkê un Vâstés.*"

Irís echoed her, and her eyes altered immediately. Rhéa was captivated. She'd only bore witness to an Initiation once before. Rarely did a stray Enchantress seek out the Marsh for sanctuary.

"Welcome to the Ilíos, Irís."

The girl stared up at her, golden eyes framed by lustrous sable waves. Irís stood, and to Rhéa's surprise, embraced her. The Enchantress staggered, but held the girl back, wrapping her arms around her svelte frame.

"Thank you." Irís's breath tickled her neck. "You've helped me so much more than you know."

Rhéa rested her chin atop the girl's head. "And you me…"

A presence shifted. The hairs on Rhéa's skin stood on end.

Sensing this, Irís pulled away and asked, "What is it?" Concern stole over her features. "Rhéa…"

"Get inside the wardrobe!"

Irís stepped away, mouth agape. "What?"

"Get inside *now*!" Rhéa opened the oaken doors and shoved the girl inside. Though Irís resisted, Rhéa was still far stronger, bigger. Finally, Irís relented and mumbled her acquiescence, settling herself at the base of the chest. Rhéa's clothes would offer some shelter, though it would provide little recourse in this situation.

Think, Rhéa. Think!

"Hyssé vaust possé, Hyssé vaust disst, Côstos fostré poiré eures, Fostré töver, essâ, eures, teq quissr." *Hide thou precious, Hide thou scent, Conceal from prying eyes, From nose, ears, eyes, and touch.*

There was a chance this wouldn't work. A chance that the Sorcerer's senses would nullify any magical spell, but she had to try. He wasn't after Irís anyway, but Rhéa wouldn't put it past him to use the girl against her.

Thébés was coming for her. His entity screamed his ire, the emotion pulsing through the walls, intensifying as he approached.

Rhéa sprinted from the room, forgoing her sandals. There wasn't time. He was stronger. If she didn't run now, he'd catch her. She needed to get as far away from Irís as she could, if she wanted to ensure the girl's safety.

The halls seemed to close in around her as if to constrict, to hold her in place whilst Thébés devoured her. Her heart throbbed so painfully, she thought she might choke on it. Her feet slapped against the silt-dusted stone, the hallway an endless expanse before her.

His presence drew nearer, though not close enough to see. Thébés never lingered, she was sure that he hadn't noticed Irís, and if he had, he wasn't interested.

Thank Amalthea!

Perhaps now that Irís had been Initiated, the Southern Star would watch over her. The thought provided Rhéa a sliver of comfort.

Doors passed by on either side of her but to open one would be futile. If she stopped now, he'd catch her. If she hid, he'd find her. If Thébés wished her body rotting beneath the earth's surface, then that's what would become of her.

Stop it, Rhéa, she reprimanded. She was only catalyzing the beat of her heart, the drumming luring Thébés down her path.

Running was useless when being chased by a surly Sorcerer. She was sure he could sense her every breath, every thumping beat of her pulse, in this labyrinthine void.

The Enchantresses of the Marsh would be too far out, they'd never make it in time to save her, if they came at all.

Rhéa had felt a vocation to care for the well-being of Irís since she'd met her in Kenora, the same sense of duty her husband had felt toward the girl. As long as Irís survived, Rhéa would be fine. Even if the Sorcerer's intentions were of a sordid nature, she'd be fine so long as Irís lived.

Rhéa didn't slow her pace. But neither did Thébés. He was closer now, converging on his prey. Her flight had been wearying, but she'd maintained her sprint.

As she drew near the cavernous arena, Rhéa remembered her poniard. She always kept it at her desk inside the infirmary. If she could get to it, hide it under her skirt, she'd at least have some form of defense, some element of surprise.

The dim light of the cavern illuminated the hallway before her. The archway opened to the top floor of the arena. If she could nimbly descend the stairs of the stands, she'd be able to get to the healing chamber. Though her plan was laudable, it was not to be.

Rhéa entered the arena and paled as Thébés met her stare from across the stands.

50

A HURRICANE

"Lilith!"

Felix's voice boomed from atop his self-made plateau, his stride emitting all the braggadocio Spiro obviously bestowed upon him.

Felix raised a long platform of Earth just for Lilith's arrival, the bout intended as a source of entertainment for the beasts surrounding them. Julius would be damned if Felix made a mockery of Lilith's capture.

The prince remained kneeling, blasting spears of Xander's Fire at any beasts who dared to approach. He'd die before he let them feast upon his uncle's corpse.

"Lilith!" Felix called again. He'd forsaken Julius to a slow death in the muck in his ploy to lure Lilith to the battlefield. Julius beseeched the Gods to carry her far away.

Take her back to Arduen. Take her anywhere but here.

The prince kept his chin high. It was all he could do to remain alert, shooting off any beasts that dared near him.

Felix stopped his pacing to observe the northern horizon. The sky was darker there, no stars to be seen in the firmament.

A storm was coming their way. Sheets of lightning flashed, illuminating the bloodbath below, a devastatingly beautiful sight for the ill of heart.

"Lilith!" Felix called again, and Julius thought he'd never become sick of hearing her name.

The storm drew closer. Spiro's beasts separated from the Dalegonian soldiers, loping across the blood-sodden earth to take up formation.

To view the show.

Please, Lilith, don't come!

Julius attempted to open his mind, to sense for Lilith with Discernment; but the skill took far too much of his already drained reserve.

Felix was only jesting, buying time for his Master to arrive and whisk away his newest recruit. Though Julius was a Master, he'd be harder to contain and control. Felix would leave him to die of his injuries, but Spiro would slay him. The Great Divine adored making examples of those who dare oppose him. But if Julius could get inside Spiro's lair, he may be able to take down the Great Divine from within. Somehow, he would have to convince Spiro to capture, not kill him.

Thunder grumbled and forks of lightning shot from the clouds. Beasts screeched, wailing laments of anguish. As the scent of burnt flesh permeated the air, rain began to fall, slapping against bare skin, washing away the ichor and blood.

Julius craned his neck, groaning as the rain cleansed his wounds of beastly toxicity. The water rushed over him, plastering his hair to his brow, to his neck. He reached for Orphëus, held his legendary sword at the ready. His senses prickled, shooting to awareness.

Felix stood upon the plateau, his gaze locked on the horizon. Julius couldn't see what was so alluring about the storm, but it kept his nemesis distracted. For now.

The distraction supplied him with an opportunity to strike. If only he could summon just one lick of Fire. Calling upon Xander, Julius groaned, every muscle seizing up and cramping. Depletion at its worst. Why hadn't he thought to arm himself with a bow? He cursed his impotence.

Felix stood stoic, a hand shielding his eyes from the rain, his mousy hair drenched to look black. A petulant expression clouded his features, so unlike the real Felix. Who was Spiro to change someone so thoroughly?

The sound of cold rain on metal was percussive, almost deafening. The nebulous drew nearer, blocking out the light of the stars.

A nefarious grin stole over Felix's face. Julius's hopes plummeted. Whatever were Felix's preconceived machinations, they were undoubtedly hatching before him, unimpeded.

The ground shuddered, and Julius fell forward onto his uncle's corpse.

What in the Gods' names?

Cheers ensued as the quake intensified. Julius hoisted himself up to stand, just in time to see…

Lilith.

Constance drawn at her side, Obsidian Steel gleaming in the starlight, slicing through the night. She was glorious. Julius's heart leapt to witness her march into battle.

But his excitement quickly drained, replaced by foreboding.

Her attire wasn't palatable, at least from safety's standpoint. She wore no armor, her hair braided back to expose her neck— not that hair offered much protection from a blade. She was dressed in the same plated leather suit he'd last seen her in, the same suit he tore off her sinuous frame. Sickness clenched his abdomen at the memory. *That will not be the last time*, he assured himself.

The Earth beneath Lilith rose like a mountain, escalating her higher and higher until she stood atop the peak, glaring down at Felix. How she'd managed to excel in such a short period of time, Julius would have to wait to find out. She moved with lithe grace, brandishing Constance like the most formidable warrior on the field.

"Hello, Felix," she crooned.

Felix's jauntiness faltered at the sight of her. "Shall we dance?" he asked, head cocked.

Offering no response, Lilith jumped from her mountain to land the first blow.

51

SHALL WE DANCE?

"Lilith!" Felix's voice rang out, overpowering the din of war and drowning out the cries of agony. Wren stilled as the voice of his lost noviciate met his ears.

"I'll handle him," Lilith assured.

Wren's hackles rose, the exact response she'd predicted. "Absolutely *not!*" He grasped her by the shoulders. "You can't, Lilith. You've been blessed thrice. You shouldn't even be here."

"If we didn't come, they'd kill Julius," she said bitterly.

Relenting, he sighed. "Arduen is going to kill me."

The others were too far away to reach them in time. Spiro must have known they'd come to Augusta with a legion of Dalegonian warriors. Perhaps the Gods had warned the Oracle. Perhaps Arduen and the others were nearby, but not close enough to be sensed.

"Let me deal with Felix," Lilith said. "I think I can best him in a little swordplay."

Wren hesitated, but he seemed to be following the same train of thought as she was.

"I'm going to call a storm," she said to him. "Can you raise me up?"

He nodded. "I'll keep watch over you," he said.

"Go find Julius." Lilith prayed he was alive. There was so much she needed to tell him. So much hurt still to unravel between them.

Wren nodded and held his hands out to her. Together, they sang:

"MAY WE FIGHT WITH VALIANT STEEL,
  Forged courage and might.
  May the Gods watch our paths,
  And quell our bleeding and strife.
  When all is done, and we are beyond our power,
  May They carry us into Elysium forever."

"LILITH!" THE DISTANT VOICE OF HER FRIEND RANG OUT TO HER. Calling her. If a grand confrontation was what he desired— what Spiro desired—that's exactly what they would get.

Lilith straightened, the beasts and soldiers parting at the sight of her, Spiro's beasts retreating to the east. The stars hung bright in the clear night sky, a perfect canvas for the gale she now beckoned. The tempest lingered behind her like a magnificent shadow. She'd called upon the storm unwillingly at first, her gifts from Constantine reacting to her emotions. Magnificent forks of lightning arced across the firmament in her wake, promises of the destruction to come.

Arduen would have been proud.

Each olive-skinned beast struck fear into her heart, anger flared inside her at the sight of them. As a result, lightning crashed toward the ground, erupting as the forks met with the beasts. Scalded flesh suffused the inside of her nose, but despite the foul atmosphere, she pressed on.

Today she would avenge another loved one.

As Felix came into view, Lilith sent a prayer up to Thëo and willed the Earth to rise. It answered.

Thank you, Wren.

Flexing every muscle in her body, strutting in Felix's direction, the Earth rose up beneath her, the squalid ground crunching with every step. Lighting struck on either side of Lilith's ascending plateau, until she came to a stop several feet before her adversary. Her heart thundered, the beats amplified by the gale above her. "Hello, Felix," she purred.

"Shall we dance?" He canted his head in mock derision.

Lilith let a smile bring her face to life. If a duel was what he wanted, that's what he'd get.

She jumped.

The ground rose to meet her feet, trampled grass softening her landing. Constance tore through the air in front of her, slamming into Felix's armor, but not enough to inflict damage. The Divine was prepared, he saw this coming, yet he was still stunned.

Was part of the real Felix still in there? Was he hesitating?

Felix retreated, prancing backward on light feet. "Enough!"

Lilith halted, checking her rear before receding. She'd calmed the rain slightly. It wouldn't be useful to her if she slipped and met her demise.

Her gaze narrowed on Felix. He wasn't short of breath, so why weren't they fighting?

Julius's weary soul called to her, just to her right, mere feet away. Every fibre of her being beseeched her to run to him, but Wren was there.

He is alive. He is safe.

Finally, Felix broke his meditative state, clapping his hands together slowly. "Wow. I commend your entrance. Spiro will be thrilled to witness how you've grown!" His expression was ecstatic. "Though you must take me for a fool to think you can best me in appearance alone."

There was no denying this was not Felix speaking to her. It was his body, sure, but the mouthpiece was of the Great Divine. It was happening again. And like the last time, she was the one who would end it.

"The Gods have sent me, Felix." She lifted her chin indignantly. "It is Their call that I have answered, not yours."

Felix snorted, the beasts' derisive snickers echoing.

"But I am here to help you," Lilith continued, "and I am sure you are aware of what I must do." Her grip tightened around Constance's hilt out of instinct.

Felix stepped toward her, inciting a tremor to rake through her body. "You see, dear Lilith, when it came time for me to take the Oath, I knelt willingly. I drank willingly."

She doubted that very much.

"When Spiro brought me to my new home, I felt at ease. When he told me of his vision, well, I knew I was where I was always meant to be." Felix smiled peacefully. "Thëo had taken care of me."

Lilith cast a prompt glance at Julius and Wren. Her Master had his arm wrapped around the prince's middle, his eyes pinned to his former noviciate. But Julius, his hazel eyes burned into Lilith, blazing with distress.

Felix's voice cut through her focus. "And now I've been selected to bring you home, too."

Every muscle in Lilith's body went rigid. "I'm not going anywhere."

Felix's chuckle rumbled, growing louder as the surrounding beasts lent their mirth to his. Lilith echoed it with thunder.

"You don't have an option, sweet Lilith," Felix said, stepping closer. "You see, if I am unsuccessful, Spiro will come for you, and you're no match for the Great Divine."

Lilith raised Constance in defiance.

"Spiro is infatuated with you, Lilith. He will be a good Master. Better than Arduen ever was."

"That's impossible," she snapped.

This wasn't news. She'd known Spiro was after her for some time. She was doubly blessed—now thrice blessed. Of course he wanted her on his side. She was the perfect vessel.

"It's your choice," Felix said. "Come willingly, or I take you." He squared his shoulders, adjusting his feet, preparing to be challenged.

If not for the Blood Oath, she might have considered obliging. Spiro could teach her how to use her gifts simultaneously. Then she would get stronger, more competent, and she'd find a way to take him down from right under his nose.

But this wasn't a legendary tale. If Felix took her, it was over.

For all of them.

And with this duel, she'd buy time. More minutes for Aether to gestate, to roil within her, bubbling over until it forced its way free.

And with Constantine's abyss unleashed, she'd take Spiro.

"You know, Felix?" she said, her voice overly kind, accentuated with a wistful note.

He rolled his eyes, gesturing for her to hurry up and speak.

"You should have slit your own throat!" And Lilith dove for him.

52

DEADLIER THAN NECROMANCY

Rhéa stared across the cavern for one drawn-out moment, her eyes pinned to the Sorcerer's gleaming hair, a beacon of death and decay.

Certain death. It hung like a phantom presence in the stale air swirling between them.

One moment, he was standing a hundred feet across from her, the next he was in the center of the arena floor far below, beckoning.

"Come, Rhéa. Join me," he said, his tone betrayed belligerence.

Rhéa resisted the pull. He was playing with her. He the cat, and she the mouse. She wouldn't be reduced to prey, but there was little choice. Consent did not exist in a Sorcerer's world. And nature had predetermined which one of them was superior.

Her legs moved gradually against her will, the phantom's hands coaxing her limbs to obey. She whimpered, her lips trembling.

Thébés's sibilant voice soothed her. "Don't be afraid, little Enchantress. I don't bite."

No, you're capable of so much worse.

As Rhéa descended the stands down to the rings, she contemplated her options. She didn't have many. She'd never encountered a Sorcerer, she knew not what he could do to her, or what her magic could do to him.

"Now, now, Rhéa. Don't do anythi—"

"Ether!"

The abyss shot toward him. Not as powerful as a Divine, but strong enough to maim. The streams erupted from her fingertips, braiding together as they barreled into the Sorcerer. Thébés deflected her assault, his laugh echoing through the cavern.

"Come now, darling," he said. "You wouldn't want to offend me, would you?"

"Vhazt!"

A torrent of fire burst from her palm, swift enough that any other adversary would have been caught off guard, but the flames were engulfed by an invisible barrier. When the flames faded, the Sorcerer stood unharmed, his scowl deepening, his pale skin flushed.

Thébés lifted his hand, and Rhéa was thrust backward, skirts flailing about her legs. The air was sucked from her lungs as she hit the ground, the back of her head hitting the stone floor with an audible *crack*. She slid across the ground until the wall stopped her, jarring her, only exacerbating her addled mind.

Fighting for air, Rhéa shook as she coughed. This would be an easier way to go, she thought. *But Irís...* Reluctantly, she pried her eyes open, but sight failed her. Her vision blurred and eddied. Stars flickered in her vision, dancing to the tinnitus.

"Rise," Thébés barked.

She couldn't if she tried.

"Get up!"

Ever so slowly, Rhéa struggled to rise, her body aching in places she didn't know it could. Her eyes focused on the ground before her, at the path her body had drawn in the silt.

"Look at me, Rhéa."

She stifled a sob.

"LOOK AT ME!" His roar tugged her eyes up to meet his, or maybe it was the phantom. When Rhéa looked into his depthless eyes, she crumbled to the ground again.

"Please, no! Please!"

The Sorcerer stood upon the ring closest to her, and beside him upon the platform was Miles, strapped to a chair, gagged, blade at his throat. Thébés's hand was wrapped around the hilt, his eyes set firmly on her.

"Now that I have your attention, dearest Enchantress," he snarled, "you must heed my message. It is of the utmost import."

"Please, no." Not Miles. Take her. *Please.*

"Shush, now. I'm only playing."

Rhéa whimpered, down on her knees before the platform. Miles wasn't looking at her. He kept those beautiful emerald eyes locked on the ceiling, baring his throat to the Sorcerer. Every breath Miles took drew blood.

"Tell me what information you gave the High Enchantress."

"N-nothing!" she stammered.

"LIAR!" the Sorcerer bellowed, jerking the knife.

Rhéa screamed. Blood trickled down her husband's throat. Not enough to kill, but enough to terrify her. Miles was unflappable, unwavering, unflinching. His chest remained still as stone.

She had expected magic, not this morbid display of superiority. How was she to defend against this? What was this?

This isn't real, she told herself. She had to believe it, and yet sussing for the truth was more difficult than it should have been. Convincing herself that this was all illusory was futile.

"Rhéa …" Thébés crooned. "Time is of the essence."

"I notified the High Enchantress about your existence!"

The Sorcerer sighed audibly, dramatically, and sliced his blade across Miles's throat. Blood sprayed from the wound, and her husband's eyes rolled back into his head, his body slumping in the chair.

"No!" Rhéa wailed, squirming across the ground to reach her husband. Her knees scraped on the stone, leaving bloody trails in her wake, her need to save him exigent.

As she reached the platform, she pulled herself up. But as her eyes cleared the edge, her husband was gone.

"Over here!" the Sorcerer called to her. "Keep up, Rhéa darling."

Rhéa stepped away from the platform, her head jumbled.

"Time is of the essence!" Thébés lilted.

The Enchantress's eyes followed the sound of his voice, her heart pounding irregularly in her chest, as if it, too, had been thrown off by the strange events.

Where was Miles?

But it wasn't her husband on her mind when her eyes reunited with the Sorcerer's.

Larkin!

"My boy!" Rhéa cried. He'd been tied up, his hands bound before him, a noose tied around his neck, hanging from an invisible beam. His body was supported by a chair that could be easily removed. Thébés stood beside him, a proprietary hand on Larkin's arm.

Reason whispered to her—or was it the phantom?—a soft sound trailing on the nonexistent breeze, *Larkin is dead*. Yet here he was, standing before her, very much alive and frightened.

My boy!

"Now," Thébés said, "tell me exactly what you told the High Enchantress."

Rhéa fought to organize her thoughts, but to no avail. "My son," she breathed, dread turning her insides to liquid.

"Yes, I am aware of who he is." The Sorcerer's eyes flicked to Larkin. "I want to know what you told Ophelía."

"I told her of your existence!"

"WRONG ANSWER!"

Thébés kicked the chair out from under Larkin's feet, and he dropped, his legs dancing in the air sporadically. His face flushed deep crimson, and the more he struggled against death, the deeper that color became, until his eyes shifted to the unseeing cast of death.

"No!" Rhéa screamed, her eyes refusing to leave her son's limp body, swinging like a pendulum. "Please, save him. Please, Amalthea!"

The Sorcerer tutted. "The Guiding Stars can't help you, Rhéa DaSylvà. Not down here."

He was behind her now, Larkin's body disappearing like smoke on the horizon, the phantom washing him away.

"Last chance!" Thébés trilled across the cavern.

Rhéa followed the voice, nous urging her to flee. But she was only in control of her words, for her body was captive to the Sorcerer.

As her gaze settled upon him, she dropped to her raw knees, the pain incomparable to the burn inside her chest. This nature of suffering was insufferable, but nothing scared her more than what she saw in front of her.

Lilith.

Her daughter was clutched in the Sorcerer's arms. Mahogany hair strewn across a blood-drenched face, emerald eyes wide and pleading.

"Mah…" she whimpered.

"Lilith!" Rhéa jolted to her feet, her muscles thrumming with adrenaline only a mother's fierce love could produce.

She's not here, Rhéa! The Enchantress shook her head, tugging at the roots of her hair. *Miles is in Kenora. Larkin is dead. Lilith is not here!*

But the Sorcerer held her mind in his clutch.

"Uh, uh, uh." Thébés held out a hand. "You cannot have her until you answer my questions. You've failed to answer just one of them."

"What do you want?" Rhéa's lips quivered, but her voice was steady. Every word that left her lips thus far had only proved to be a provocation.

"What did you tell Ophelía?" The Sorcerer spoke the High Enchantress's name with anything but reverence.

Rhéa steeled herself, sucking in a sharp breath, reinforcing her lungs. "I told her of your existence. I told her to gather forces. And I gave her the location of Spiro's lair."

The Sorcerer grinned. "Good, little Enchantress." He didn't put his blade to Lilith's throat. Instead, he brushed her long waves away from her bloodied face.

What had he done to her?

Thébés pressed his lips to Lilith's cheek, then licked her from jaw to temple, clearing the blood from her skin. "Delectable."

Rhéa cringed, never taking her eyes off her daughter. Lilith. The only child that could walk the earth with her for eternity. The only one capable of getting her through the sorrow of Miles's death, the eventual loss of her own immortal mother.

No, this was not her daughter. This was all a trick of the mind. A vision conjured by the Sorcerer's strange power.

His power is something deadlier than necromancy, Rhéa thought, *it's subliminal! And what's most terrifying is that Thébés doesn't seem aware of the true extent of his power! For if he did, the entire world would be kneeling beside me. At his feet. Begging for his mercy.* As the realization dawned, Rhéa knew she must play along if she wanted to survive till morn.

"Let her go, Thébés!" she yelled. "I have given you what you've asked for."

The Sorcerer looked down at her, his expression stony. "But I'm not done yet." As he lifted his hand to Lilith's face, his grin faded to a frown, his eyelids drooped, and he fell to the floor.

The only person left standing was Irís.

"Rhéa!" the girl gasped, running toward the Enchantress and throwing her arms around her. "Are you all right? You look as if you've seen a revenant!"

Rhéa couldn't summon words. It was all a mind game. Her family had never been here. She was always alone. Will always be alone.

"How?" she asked the girl.

Irís glanced over her shoulder at the Sorcerer's prostrate form. "I'm not sure…" she clutched her chest. "I felt an instinctual pull, and it just happened."

Rhéa inhaled deeply, gratitude sluicing through her.

"Will he rise?" Irís asked, lacing her fingers with Rhéa's, supporting her weight.

"I don't know."

Irís gulped. "I didn't speak Elder Tongue."

"I know…" Rhéa said, giving the girl's hand a gentle squeeze, as much to comfort herself as Irís. "You've received the Blessing."

5 3

A CATALYST

Streams of liquid ruby cascaded by as their feet danced in the muck; Lilith couldn't fathom how she'd noticed such a morbid detail. Her long, water-logged tresses slapped against her cheeks, blinding her momentarily. Her feet slid through the mud, her own arrogant entrance working against her. Aether sang to her, careening with her emotions. She fought to control it, for it was the only element Spiro was susceptible to, and she needed to reserve it solely for him.

But it would be all too easy to take Felix down now with an arrow of Aether through the heart. A quick death, too, in case any vestige of the genial boy she once knew was still in there. She prayed Spiro would feel his noviciate's death as palpable as if it were his own.

Lilith struck, the impact of their clashing swords jarring her arm. She slashed with surprisingly perfunctory ease, each blow blocked by her adversary, fueled by the knowledge of her growth.

This new corrupted version of her friend was enigmatic, fighting as if in a foreign language. She fought to retain control, fought to conceal her intentions behind a false, impassive mask. Furious, she threw herself at Felix, taking him by surprise. She had the advantage, she reminded herself, he did not want her dead. She could not say the same of her own motive. Her body collided with his and they rolled through the sludge, swords held safely away from their bodies. She could read the muddled surprise on his face. Lilith used the distraction to siphon the Water from his limbs, but as her mind searched for him, there was a disconnect.

The damned boy had learned a lot in his period under Spiro's thrall.

Forgoing Kyril's element, Lilith felt for the Earth beneath them. Felix had much more time under Wren's tutelage, he would likely sense her before the ground even had time to shift. However inane the attempt, it was all she had left.

Felix thrust her from him, Constance torn from her grip. He slashed down at her, his teeth bared and clenched in his rage. Lilith blocked each blow with a sheet of Aether, watched in amazement as the void broke down his sword. Steel disintegrated until all that remained was the cross guard and hilt clasped in Felix's palm. His eyes darted down to the remaining fragment of metal, and Lilith seized the distraction and darted for Constance.

Lightning cracked again as she regained her senses, and she became acutely aware of the burning flesh coating her nostrils. Howls and shrieks ensued. The battlefield erupted into chaotic turmoil. The beasts scampered away, tails between their legs, if they had any to begin with. Lilith smirked as the Dalegonian legionnaires burst into a cacophony of triumphant cheers.

A small victory, but the battle wasn't over yet.

Not for the Divine.

Sloughing his frivolous façade, Felix wasted no time. Bolts of Fire speared her way. At first, she'd thought Julius was assisting her, that he'd been missing his mark. But Julius was a sure-shot, more so than she, and she'd never witnessed him miss a target.

No, she'd been mistaken. The Fire was emanating from Felix's outstretched palm.

He's been Anointed by Xander!

Lilith dodged each flaming arrow as they soared overhead, singeing her skin as she leapt from side to side. It burned through her leather suit, agony erupted over her skin. But she ignored the heat. She had to get closer to Felix, she had to strike him. One good slash and it would all be over.

But she couldn't. Felix held her at bay, obviously well trained.

There was no other option. She had no defense. She'd have to fight back with Aether. But to summon the element to use as a shield would drain too much of her reserve—she'd already used it—and she needed as much of Constantine's element as possible to take on Spiro, should he show himself.

Bloody Hades! I should have shot him the moment I saw him!

Lilith blasted Aether at Felix. The surge within her reveled in its newfound freedom. Her enemy proved to be a formidable match, dodging every assault with lithe dexterity. She'd never witnessed Felix fight like this, and though a part of her wanted to cheer him on, she had to bury that part down deep.

This is not Felix.

Keeping her consciousness open to the fray, Lilith felt Julius's presence, drifting, swaying on the wind in his effort to sustain life. How injured was he?

Abandoning her consternation, she forced herself to focus. But it was too late.

Fire wrapped around her leg, right at the knee. Lilith cried out, her voice arid, crackling like embers. The Fire laced her leg like a ribbon, searing her skin, melting the fabric of her suit away, then her flesh beneath. The pain was near maddening, but she would not beg. Felix released her, and Lilith fell to her knees, the ground rising to capture her in its embrace.

"No," she whimpered, the pain stymieing all of her senses. Her vision flickered, the darkness beckoning, tempting her with relief. But if she gave in, the world would be over when next she opened her eyes. If such a moment ever came.

Fire flared before her, rising like a swell, and as it crested, it plunged down toward Felix. He stepped back warily, turning his insidious gaze on his assailant.

Julius emerged, tattered and beaten, a deep gash tearing open his skin, right above his heart. His beautiful face was covered in dirt and gore, but through it all she could see the determination shaping his features. Lilith cried out for him, but he refused to acknowledge her, his features painted by the brush of fury. She cast her attention to her legs, still encased in the ground. The Earth had hardened around her, a tether. She focused on it, felt it, willed it to move. It gave way just enough to break free of its grasp, but she knew it was not her doing.

Wren rushed to her, scooping his noviciate up into his arms. He scraped against her wounded flesh and she gasped, attempting to stifle her cries but failed. She'd need an Enchantress to make her leg right again. The blackened flesh seemed to peel away to reveal bone, tattered muscle, ripped tendons.

Bile rose in her throat.

Felix didn't notice her escape, engaged in a bout with his former friend. Julius slashed at him without mercy, his intent clearly to kill, not maim.

"You'll be all right," Wren soothed, with his low timbre so much like—

Arduen.

A different kind of pain swelled within her, a far worse

nature of torment. She may never see Arduen again. He had been her confidant when her life had fallen apart again and again. The man who had healed her broken heart and bolstered her weary soul.

"We must get you out of here," Wren said. He turned to leave, but Lilith held up her hand in protest.

"Not without Julius," she said.

Wren nodded. Obliging, he turned back to the match, his face set in a stern scowl, obviously aiding Julius in any way he could.

Then Felix prevailed, the Earth swallowing Julius's legs. The prince roared as he toppled to the ground, both his legs bent at unnatural angles. Wren dropped her, as gently as he could, in his haste to aid their fellow comrade.

Lilith's eyes refused to budge as she beheld Felix standing over Julius, the prince's face contorted in pain until she barely recognized him.

"Hello, my little Goddess," said a cool voice.

Lilith's skin prickled. She turned to face the voice, that sibilant yet smooth resonance she'd heard only once before… and in her dreams. She strained to stand but a giant maw opened beneath her, its jaw closing around her, then clamping in restraint.

No.

Her strength waned, her muscles trembled, her mind adopting a feverish haze.

It was over, but she'd resist until the end.

Spiro stood before her, his broad shoulders stretched under an eloquent black ensemble of glistening metal. Armor fit for a king.

An emperor.

Watching her from a short distance, Spiro's keen eyes

narrowed into slits, his lips spread in a contented smile. Vicious. Malevolent. Gluttonous. "Hello, Lilith."

Fear rendered her mute, save for the rasping of her breath. A fool she'd been to ever assume she could best the Great Divine. But she would accept an untimely death trying. Raising her palm, she shot what remained of her arsenal at Spiro. At the man responsible for Larkin's death. For her mother's death. For her father's absence.

Lilith's spine gave out, but her outstretched hand persisted to send streams of Aether jetting at her enemy. Then her element faltered, and she lost the ability to guide its trajectory.

It was over.

There was one thing that remained: her physicality. If she could get herself close enough to wound him, then maybe he would retreat. Maybe he would give up his assault and return to the blasted fortress he'd hailed from.

Silently, she willed Thëo's Earth to release her, and to her surprise, it obeyed. With a roar, Lilith tore Constance from its scabbard and lunged. Ignoring the pain in her knee, she took small steps, an erratic route, her body screaming for merciful rest.

Spiro didn't move as she approached. That smug smile only twisted, that glint of amusement transformed into one of triumph.

Where Wren had the strength to bring down a castle, Spiro could level an entire civilization. It was the Great Divine's rage that had birthed the Great Rift of Dodöna, and Lilith was wise to remember that as she stared him down.

Realization overcame her like a shroud. He'd let her move the Earth, just to spite her, just as a cruel jest to entertain himself.

What a fool she was.

With a flick of his finger, the ground sucked down Lilith's

foot before she could react. She fell to the ground, Constance falling out of her grasp. A loud snap sounded in her ears, followed by a piercing, excruciating pain. It ricocheted up her leg, wrenching an agonized scream from her throat. Her sight was washed out by tears, but she could see the distinguishable shadow before her.

Spiro.

Aether was a torrent within her now, answering each prayer, awaiting her order, her stores refilled by the God who had first chosen her.

Lilith's body shook violently, threatening to give out—in a matter of two heartbeats, in fact. Each laborious movement bespoke exhaustion, but still she did not relent.

She screamed at first release. Constantine's void shot at Spiro, escaping her so fast, it was as if the element had been siphoned from her body. The Gods were using her, Their force pulled the element from her. She was Their vassal, and she would serve Them until her last breath.

And she would watch Spiro burn first.

A gleeful smile spread across her lips, only to fade when the blast of Aether forked around the Great Divine, bifurcating into two dwindling streams by his Wind. He smiled menacingly, the expression a promise of the horrors to come.

Yes, she could control the one element he lacked, but he still overpowered her. He had centuries on her training. She didn't stand a chance.

Lilith groaned, her body struggling against the outflow of power, but she didn't staunch it. If this killed her, all the better than being forced to serve Spiro, handed a chalice of his blood. Her muscles tensed, seizing up just like they did when an episode—"No," she mumbled. "No, no, no, no, no."

Her reserve had been spent.

Spiro approached her, and she reached toward Constance

desperately. But as her fingertips inched toward her fallen sword, her leg spasmed in protest, and the pain spawned another wail from her lips.

Everything was transpiring in slow motion, as if she'd been semidetached from her body, watching from above as her greatest enemy closed in.

The Great Divine came to a halt before her, his eyes devouring the sight of her suffering. How he must have delighted in it. That would-be beautiful face contorted into a parody of a charming smile.

Felix emerged at Spiro's side, his gentle features sharper somehow, as if he'd aged a decade in just a few months. "Submit, Lilith."

"Lilith!" Wren's voice thundered from behind her.

The boy raised his hand, it flared, incendiary and effulgent. A spear shot forth. She didn't have to look to know Wren was dead. The strangled noise and the thud of his body told her everything.

"My dear Lilith," Spiro crooned. "I would like to formally invite you into my little family."

Lilith's entire body shook, the tremors inciting gooseflesh. She ground her teeth and said, "Delight in my formal rejection."

The Great Divine bellowed a laugh and snapped his fingers. His first crony, the one who'd accompanied Larkin to both battles, emerged at Julius's side.

"Xavier," Spiro said, "impale the prince on a pike if Lilith deigns to refuse me again."

Her lips wouldn't work, her tongue swelling until nothing could slip past, in our out. No air. No words. Nothing. Her eyes fixated on Julius's limp form, helpless at Xavier's feet.

This wasn't happening.

This couldn't be happening.

"Julius…" she groaned.

"You have been given a choice, Lilith." Spiro's reminder achieved little in the realm of persuasion.

Lilith observed in mute petrifaction, slack-jawed and paralyzed. Her heart ruptured, the painful beat silencing her physical injuries. She quivered under Spiro's gaze, forcing herself to look anywhere but on those pale unnerving eyes.

With every rasping breath she drew, hope dwindled.

Julius.

"Xavier…"

"No!" Lilith shouted, the force of it shooting spears of pain through every limb. Her injuries were too severe to consider retaliation. Spiro offering her a choice was a mockery, nothing more.

Julius was likely to die from his injuries without Olga or an Enchantress to heal him. He couldn't save her. They'd run out of time to reconcile, to make things right between them. If she still possessed half her wits and the strength to grasp her sword, she'd slit her own throat with it.

But fear prevailed.

It always did.

When she looked up into the pale eyes of Spiro, she prayed he'd end her too, send her to Elysium with the man who carried her heart in his scarred hands. Those hands now stretched across the cracked earth toward her, her limbs losing vitality at the sight.

It became burned in her mind indelibly.

Thrice blessed and she still failed.

You are my entire universe.

Rage and pain and sorrow coalesced within her. A wondrous concoction, writhing to break free of her skin, to lay to waste the man who was the cause of all her ailments. Lilith wailed until the once searing pain was no more than a distant sting, pale in comparison to the agony trapped inside her flayed chest. Her body was so attuned to suffering now, she hardly even noticed it.

Gods, even her incapacitating fear of losing Julius couldn't perform as a catalyst to strengthen her.

Agony erupted from within her like a great tide, swathing the world around her in darkness. She'd only just learned how to stop keeping the people she cared about at arm's length, and now they were dying, one by one.

Larkin, gone.

Wren, gone.

Felix, gone.

Julius, gone.

Hope… gone.

It was over now. Spiro would take her, and everything they'd worked so hard to secure would begin to unravel. Arduen, Olga, Zurí, Quin, Ambrose, and little Aspen; they were all in grave danger. Julius's and Wren's deaths would be for not; wasted, in vain.

"Lilith."

A shadow crept over her as desolation dawned. What remained of the abyss within her rippled, coiling like a snake in its last effort to defend.

Spiro looked down upon her, expression blank as the sky at dawn. And then he smiled a disconcerting smile. Every intuition flickered out like a flame on the wind. Every instinct floundered in confusion.

Lilith grappled for her bearings, fingers sinking into silicate. But no matter how tenacious her grip, she couldn't fight the powerful undertow. All she was left with was dread. Long sloughed was the stoic façade she'd donned as she marched into battle, storm clouds raging overhead. Now they raged within, beating against the cage that was her body, desperate for release, to wreak the havoc her soul longed for.

Spiro knelt before her, leveling his head with hers. "You must relinquish your freedom for power, or your power for freedom."

Lilith understood now. She must go with him, for only at his side would she grow strongest. And then she would use all he taught her to upend his vision and exact revenge. She would feign subservience, and in exchange gain a vast wealth of knowledge. Of course, such a plight would require abdicating every sense of self, everything that constituted her being. Forgetting all but one thing: the destruction of the Great Divine.

Despite her resolve, her entire body shook, the pain debilitating. She gave Spiro a single nod of acquiescence.

With a voice rich as wine, Spiro crooned, "Sleep deep, dear Lilith."

And she closed her eyes, letting the darkness console her.

MAY WE FIGHT WITH VALIANT STEEL,
> *Forged courage and might.*
> *May the Gods watch our paths,*
> *And quell our bleeding and strife.*
> *When all is done, and we are beyond our power,*
> *May They carry us into Elysium forever.*

EPILOGUE

A voice dulcet as honey yet bitter as vinegar roused her senses. "Rise, my precious one."

Groggily, Lilith opened her eyes, the rhythmic pounding in her temples convincing her that someone had substituted her head for an anvil. Her eyes adjusted. Slick stone surrounded her, darkness before, behind, and within. Memories of the battle's events flooded her. She started at once, but the crude yet gentle touch soothed her anxiety.

"Shhh, you're all right now." He held her close to his hard body.

Spiro.

The dark tunnels did little to alleviate her discomfort. There was no light to speak of, save for the dim circles from the sconces lining the walls at too few, equidistant intervals.

She was alone now, about to suffer a death greater than any she'd suffered before. The Gods wouldn't take her into Elysium now, would They? Elysium was the only place she could be with…

Julius.

You are my entire universe.

Lilith whimpered involuntarily.

If this man thought she'd fight by his side, swear herself to him, mind, body, and soul… he was *sorely* mistaken. She would defy him until he wrung the life from her, until the only remaining option was death. For the Blood Oath must be taken willingly, and she would not drink.

Her nails bit into the meat of her palms. Not even the Blood Oath could temper the rage that boiled within. No Oath could diminish her love for Julius, nor would she forget the image of his prostrate form. Splayed out, arms stretching in her direction as if he'd died trying to crawl to her aid.

No Blood Oath could turn her against her Divine family. No Blood Oath could make her a stranger to Arduen.

Daring to glance up at her captor, Lilith was awed to see the Great Divine so close. His long white hair hung loose, framing stark features hewn from granite, cold as ice. Pale-blue eyes, almost white in the dark, seemed to smolder, lighting their path.

"A little longer," he said softly, his eyes drifting down to meet hers with such tender affection, she blanched.

Lilith averted her gaze, perturbed. *Keep your eyes closed. It's just Arduen.* But the thought of her Master only summoned a sob.

Spiro cradled her head against his chest like the victorious prize she was, his accursed hands accomplishing little in the realm of succor.

All hope was lost. She was as dead as Larkin. Not even her Dâs Thymó could save her now, not if everyone who loved her was dead, too.

I, Lilith Oak, desire above all else that the ones whom I give my heart, and those who have a place in their heart for me, will be spared from bearing witness to my demise.

She repeated it to herself endlessly. But no matter how many times she whispered it, her heart knew the truth that her mind refused to admit: it was over.

"We are here."

Slowly, Lilith pried her swollen eyes open. A large chamber was before her, austere yet lavish, like a sovereign's study. Spiro lowered her into a chair, and she gasped at the shock of pain that lanced up her leg upon impact. Her body shook uncontrollably.

"Xavier," Spiro called.

The minion that had accompanied her brother strode forth from the shadows. His face was stern, no mocking smile this time. He didn't look at her, his eyes were for his Master only.

Spiro placed a proprietary hand on her shoulder. "Summon Rhéa. Her expertise is needed."

Xavier nodded curtly, disappearing. The space before her was then replaced by Spiro and Felix. She glared at her former friend, seething.

"Oh, come now, Lilith." He reached for her cheek but she managed enough strength to swat his hand away, the rage drowning out the pain of her injuries.

Felix's smile faltered, his normally amiable features morphing into a new mask.

"The Blood Oath—"

"I didn't take any oaths," Felix snapped. "I was born loyal."

Lilith shivered, sweat beading her brow. A barrage of questions tousled her mind, but she didn't deign to give voice to them. Fatigue was heavier than the need for enlightenment.

"Do not worry, dear Lilith," Spiro said. "My Enchantress will take care of you. I have a hunch the two of you will get along just fine."

What did Felix mean by being *born* loyal?

As if sensing her confusion, Spiro said, "Felix is my son."

She flinched back away from them both and Felix's eyes lit up with mirth.

"How could you?" She glared at Felix. "How could you be so close to your mother and yet, she didn't even know?"

A momentary shadow passed over Spiro's face, but it lasted only a second, too short a time to decipher what it meant.

"Zurí is not my mother," Felix answered. "My mother was a lowly maid taken in by my father. She died shortly after giving birth to me."

"Bless her soul," Spiro breathed, his face neutral.

Felix repeated his father's sentiments, keeping his eyes locked on Lilith the entire time.

She didn't let her gaze waver. "So, your intention this entire time was to kidnap me?"

"Don't flatter yourself," Felix drawled. "That was only part of my mission."

"And what was—"

"Allow me to expand," he said, cutting her off. "Do me a favor and shut your maw. If you want answers, listen."

Lilith did just that, her jaw clamping shut so hard it hurt.

"I was young when Isidore Anointed me. Too young. Young enough not to speak. Young enough that merely walking was beyond my abilities."

"So you died with your mother?"

"Shut up!" Felix barked. "It was just last year that I was blessed a second time. It came as a shock to both me and my father, but we took advantage of the blessing and concocted a plan." His eyes drifted to meet Spiro's for a brief moment before returning to her. Lilith blanched under his scrutiny. She'd never thought Felix capable of such an icy glare. "I took the opportunity granted me by Thëo, and, since I was staying in

Argolïs, concocted a convincing story. With help from my accomplice, I was even able to convince some witnesses to praise my swift recovery."

Her mind threw her back to Felix's first evening at the Frourío. He'd walked with her and Julius on the beach, telling them his grand tale of woe and how he came to survive a mine sundering. No one had questioned it.

"My accomplice succeeded in a small implosion of the mine," Felix elaborated, obviously pleased with himself for staging such a show. How he must have delighted in fooling them all, the ancient and the young.

"Anyways, Wren was none-the-wiser when he brought me back. Took me for a sixteen-year-old idiot."

Their eyes pierced her, but Lilith kept her head down, eyes affixed on the gleaming stone floor stretching before her. The pain was almost unbearable, but she remained conscious. Her new Master held out a chalice filled to the brim with crimson liquid, not opaque enough to be blood, but the resemblance was unsettling. She refused.

"Now, now…" Spiro tutted, dropping himself into the seat beside hers and wrapping freezing fingers around her wrist. "In a few moments, you will be restored." His voice was gentle, belying his iron grip. "Xavier!" he called impatiently.

There were sounds of shuffling feet behind her, but it was all she could do to keep her eyes open, darkness calling to her, promising a safe place to hide. Every passing second brought her closer to the precipice. If she fell, who knew what he'd do to her in that state? Would she wake up herself? Would she ever wake?

Felix stood over her, his gaze penetrating. It was too difficult to look at him, knowing all that she did now. Betrayal stung.

"Now, Lilith." Felix stroked her sweaty hair away from her brow. "We are still friends, you and I."

"No."

"Yes," he insisted, his fingers wrapping around her jaw. "We are, and will remain to be." She looked up and watched as his smug smile widened.

"Why are you so proud of yourself?" She huffed a laugh. "You failed." She jerked her chin toward Spiro. "After all your planning, your father had to capture me."

The blow cracked, the pain a delayed spark.

"Don't test me!" Felix cried.

"Now, now, Felix," Spiro crowed. "There will be no need for that. The girl has suffered enough. I can't have her training to the best of her ability with bruises and welts."

"That's how I trained," Felix protested.

"And Lilith will serve her time in the rings," Spiro said. "I swear it."

"The rings?" Lilith asked, her voice embarrassingly feeble.

Felix's menacing chuckle was dismantling the last bit of her pride.

"Where is that woman?" Spiro drifted out of Lilith's line of sight. She didn't have the energy to trail him, her fatigue shrouding her curiosity.

But the shadow hovering above her drifted closer.

"I almost had you at the raid," Felix whispered. "I almost had you when we traveled home from Kenora."

"Those soldiers…"

"Were my father's spies, seeded in the capital, at my disposal."

At my disposal.

"You didn't care if we killed them," she said, her tone accusatory. "How'd you convince them to forfeit their lives?"

Felix released a melodramatic sigh. As if explaining his motives was a complete waste of his time. "I hadn't planned for them to die. You see, I didn't surmise Julius would be as reckless as he was, using Xander's Fire in such close proximity to us. But the fool did, and now my comrades are dead."

"A shame," Lilith said, "blaming their deaths on Julius."

The boy—if she could call him that—sucked in a sharp breath. "The prince looked good brooding. It got him into your panties, didn't it?"

She lifted up to strike him, but her strength was waning.

Felix didn't even flinch. "Should have listened to him boast about your little—"

"He didn't!" Lilith bit down on her bottom lip to keep it from trembling. The thought of Julius begging for his life… "He wouldn't do that to me."

"No, perhaps not." Felix finally drew away. "Not when he died for you. And still, you're here with us. Better not disappoint him then."

Light flooded her eyes as Felix left her, and Lilith glanced about the room. At the crystalline chandelier above the table. At the ornate iron sconces upon the walls. At the silver chalice of wine before her. Her mouth watered. It was a play of power, a sick reminder of what was to come.

"Ah, Rhéa. Thank you for joining us," she heard Spiro say. "My newest noviciate is in need of your majestic touch."

A familiar presence dropped into the seat beside her. Lilith's eyes halted their wandering, nonplussed at the sight of the woman sitting at her side.

The carnage changes a warrior. It makes us harder; strangers to mercy and kindness. These ghosts make up the walls that separate us from our kin, from those who can help us heal.

Ride fast so they do not catch you.

The ghosts had caught her.

Lilith started from her seat, mouth agape, muscles tensed, ignorant of the pain.

The svelte figure, the long mahogany tresses—like her own —and the face just like…
"Mother?"

ACKNOWLEDGMENTS

Another one down.

I want to first thank my family, Tyler, and Aslan. Without you, this wouldn't be possible.

Secondly, I want to thank my cover artist, Salome Totladze. Every piece of your creation is marvellous, and I am honored three of them belong to me.

Third, Iveta, my editor. I appreciate your patience more than you know. We went back and forth with this one, disproving my belief that middle books are easy. Get ready for book three!

Lastly, my readers! Thank you for coming with me on this journey. I've learned so much about myself, my characters, and the asinine art of wordsmithing! Without your honest reviews, I wouldn't know where to begin and where to end.

If you don't mind giving LOL and Elysium an honest review on either Goodreads or Amazon, (or BOTH, if you're feeling especially munificent), I would appreciate it more than you know. Every review helps me to reach more readers like you!

Thank you all from the bottom of my heart!

Hillary Oliver

ABOUT THE AUTHOR

Portrait by Mik & Josh Photography @mikandjoshphoto

Hillary Oliver hails from Kawartha Lakes, Ontario. With a degree in English Literature and History from Trent University, she has dreams of delivering rich fantasy with a historical twist. When not writing, she is a telecommunications lineman, fiber splicer, a dedicated crocheter, a loving partner and canine mother.